GIRL IN PIECES

"Equal parts keen-eyed empathy, stark candor, and terrible beauty. This book is why we read stories: to experience what it's like to survive the unsurvivable; to find light in the darkest night."

—Jeff Zentner, author of *The Serpent King*

"Raw, visceral, and starkly beautiful, with writing that is at times transcendent in its brilliance, *Girl in Pieces* is a deeply affecting portrait of a young girl's determination to survive in a world that has abandoned her and a mind that seeks the release of emotional suffering through physical pain. An unforgettable story of trauma and resilience."

—Kerry Kletter, author of *The First Time She Drowned*

"A breathtakingly written book about pain and hard-won healing . . . I want every girl to read *Girl in Pieces*. Reading it is like removing your heart and leaving it in Glasgow's very skilled hands."

—Kara Thomas, author of *The Darkest Corners*

"*Girl in Pieces* has the breath of life; every character in it is fully alive. Charlie Davis's complexities are drawn with great understanding and subtlety."

—Charles Baxter, author of National Book Award
finalist *The Feast of Love*

"Charlie Davis has been damaged and abused after several years of living on the streets, but she is fiercely resilient. Though it will appeal to readers of Ellen Foster, *Speak,* and *Girl, Interrupted, Girl in Pieces* is an entirely original work, compulsively readable and deeply human."

—Julie Schumacher, author of the *New York Times*
bestseller *Dear Committee Members*

"Kathleen Glasgow illuminates not only the anxiety of youth but the vulnerability and terror of life in general. *Girl in Pieces* hurts my heart in the best way possible."

—Amanda Coplin, author of the *New York Times* bestseller *The Orchardist*

"Charlie Davis's voice is diamond-beautiful and diamond-sharp, which, when strung together by a delicious story and memorable characters, creates a rare and powerful read. Kathleen Glasgow's *Girl in Pieces* is a treasure of a novel."

—Swati Avasthi, author of *Split* and *Chasing Shadows*

"An extraordinary coming-of-age story. An unsentimental and affecting tale of a girl who almost doesn't make it to adulthood."

—Summer Wood, author of *Arroyo* and *Raising Wrecker*

"Glasgow has written a *Girl, Interrupted* for a new generation. Her assured debut is a mad-girl story with new edges of intelligence, lyricism, and grit. From institutions to the streets to the secret razors we all keep, whether in our cupboards or our minds, the story of the mad girl is ultimately a story about being a girl in a mad world, how it breaks us into pieces and how we glue ourselves back together."

—Melissa Febos, author of *Whip Smart* and *Abandon Me*

"Dark, frank, and tender, *Girl in Pieces* keeps the reader electrified for its entire journey. You're so uncertain whether Charlie will heal, so fully immersed in hoping she does."

—Michelle Wildgen, author of *Bread and Butter* and *You're Not You*

GIRL
IN
PIECES

GIRL IN PIECES

KATHLEEN GLASGOW

A Rock the Boat Book

First published in the United Kingdom and the Commonwealth
by Rock the Boat, an imprint of Oneworld Publications, 2016
Reprinted, 2016

ISBN 978-1-78074-945-7
ISBN 978-1-78607-139-2 (ebook)
Interior design by Stephanie Moss
Printed and bound in Great Britain by Clays Ltd, St Ives plc

Oneworld Publications
10 Bloomsbury Street
London WC1B 3SR
England

For my mother, M.E.,

and my sister, Weasie

ONE

What's your story, morning glory?

LIKE A BABY HARP SEAL, I'M ALL WHITE. MY FOREARMS ARE thickly bandaged, heavy as clubs. My thighs are wrapped tightly, too; white gauze peeks out from the shorts Nurse Ava pulled from the lost and found box behind the nurses' station.

Like an orphan, I came here with no clothes. Like an orphan, I was wrapped in a bedsheet and left on the lawn of Regions Hospital in the freezing sleet and snow, blood seeping through the flowered sheet.

The security guard who found me was bathed in menthol cigarettes and the flat stink of machine coffee. There was a curly forest of white hair inside his nostrils.

He said, "Holy Mother of God, girl, what's been done to you?"

My mother didn't come to claim me.

But: I remember the stars that night. They were like salt against the sky, like someone spilled the shaker against very dark cloth.

That mattered to me, their accidental beauty. The last thing I thought I might see before I died on the cold, wet grass.

THE GIRLS HERE, THEY TRY TO GET ME TO TALK. THEY WANT to know *What's your story, morning glory? Tell me your tale, snail.* I hear their stories every day in Group, at lunch, in Crafts, at breakfast, at dinner, on and on. These words that spill from them, black memories, they can't stop. Their stories are eating them alive, turning them inside out. They cannot stop talking.

I cut all my words out. My heart was too full of them.

I ROOM WITH LOUISA. LOUISA IS OLDER AND HER HAIR IS LIKE a red-and-gold noisy ocean down her back. There's so much of it, she can't even keep it in with braids or buns or scrunchies. Her hair smells like strawberries; she smells better than any girl I've ever known. I could breathe her in forever.

My first night here, when she lifted her blouse to change for bed, in the moment before that crazy hair fell over her body like a protective cape, I saw them, all of them, and I sucked my breath in hard.

She said, "Don't be scared, little one."

I wasn't scared. I'd just never seen a girl with skin like mine.

EVERY MOMENT IS SPOKEN FOR. WE ARE UP AT SIX O'CLOCK. WE are drinking lukewarm coffee or watered-down juice by six forty-five. We have thirty minutes to scrape cream cheese on cardboardy bagels, or shove pale eggs in our mouths, or swallow lumpy oatmeal. At seven fifteen we can shower in our rooms. There are no doors on our showers and I don't know what the bathroom mirrors are, but they're not glass, and your face looks cloudy and lost when you brush your teeth or comb your hair. If you want to shave your legs, a nurse or an orderly has to be present, but no one wants that, and so our legs are like hairy-boy legs. By eight-thirty we're in Group and that's when the stories spill, and the tears spill, and some girls yell and some girls groan, but I just sit, sit, and that awful older girl, Blue, with the bad teeth, every day, she says, *Will you talk today, Silent Sue? I'd like to hear from Silent Sue today, wouldn't you, Casper?*

Casper tells her to knock it off. Casper tells us to breathe, to make accordions by spreading our arms way, way out, and then pushing in, in, in, and then pulling out, out, out, and don't we feel better when we just breathe? Meds come after Group, then Quiet, then lunch, then Crafts, then Individual, which is when you sit with your doctor and cry some more, and then at five o'clock there's dinner, which is more not-hot food, and more Blue: *Do you like macaroni and cheese, Silent Sue? When you getting those bandages off, Sue?* And then Entertainment. After Entertainment, there is Phone Call, and more crying. And then it's nine p.m. and more meds and then it's bed. The girls piss and hiss about the schedule, the food, Group, the meds, everything, but I don't care. There's food, and a bed, and it's warm, and I am inside, and I am safe.

My name is not Sue.

JEN S. IS A NICKER: SHORT, TWIGLIKE SCARS RUN UP AND DOWN her arms and legs. She wears shiny athletic shorts; she's taller than anyone, except Doc Dooley. She dribbles an invisible basketball up and down the beige hallway. She shoots at an invisible hoop. Francie is a human pincushion. She pokes her skin with knitting needles, sticks, pins, whatever she can find. She has angry eyes and she spits on the floor. Sasha is a fat girl full of water: she cries in Group, she cries at meals, she cries in her room. She'll never be drained. She's a plain cutter: faint red lines crosshatch her arms. She doesn't go deep. Isis is a burner. Scabby, circular mounds dot her arms. There was something in Group about rope and boy cousins and a basement but I shut myself off for that; I turned up my inside music. Blue is a fancy bird with her pain; she has a little bit of everything: bad daddy, meth teeth, cigarette burns, razor slashes. Linda/Katie/Cuddles wears grandma housedresses. Her slippers are stinky. There are too many of her to keep track of; her scars are all on the inside, along with her people. I don't know why she's with us, but she is. She smears mashed potato on her face at dinner. Sometimes she vomits for no reason. Even when she is completely still, you know there is a *lot* happening inside her body, and that it's not good.

I knew people like her on the outside; I stay away from her.

SOMETIMES I CAN'T BREATHE IN THIS GODDAMN PLACE; MY chest feels like sand. I don't understand what's happening. I was too cold and too long outside. I can't understand the clean sheets, the sweet-smelling bedspread, the food that sits before me in the cafeteria, magical and warm. I start to panic, shake, choke, and Louisa, she comes up very close to me in our room, where I'm wedged into the corner. Her breath on my face is tea-minty. She cups my cheek and even that makes me flinch. She says, "Little one, you're with your people."

THE ROOM IS TOO QUIET, SO I WALK THE HALLS AT NIGHT. MY lungs hurt. I move slowly.

Everything is too quiet. I trace a finger along the walls. I do this for hours. I know they're thinking about putting me on sleep meds after my wounds heal and I can be taken off antibiotics, but I don't want them to. I need to be awake and aware.

He could be anywhere. He could be here.

LOUISA IS LIKE THE QUEEN. SHE'S BEEN HERE, THIS TIME, FOR-
ever. She tells me, "I was the very first fucking girl here, back
when they opened, for God's sake." She's always writing in a
black-and-white composition book; she never comes to Group.
Most of the girls wear yoga pants and T-shirts, sloppy things,
but Louisa dresses up every day: black tights and shiny flats,
glamorous thrift-store dresses from the forties, her hair always
done up in some dramatic way or another. She has suitcases
stuffed with scarves, filmy nightgowns, creamy makeup, blood-
red tubes of lipstick. Louisa is like a visitor who has no plans
to leave.

She tells me she sings in a band. "But my nervousness," she
says softly. "My *problem*, it gets in the way."

Louisa has burns in concentric circles on her belly. She has
rootlike threads on the insides of her arms. Her legs are burned
and carved in careful, clean patterns. Tattoos cover her back.

Louisa is running out of room.

CASPER STARTS EVERY GROUP THE SAME WAY. THE ACCORDION exercise, the breathing, stretching your neck, reaching to your toes. Casper is tiny and soft. She wears clogs with elfish, muted heels. All the other doctors here have clangy, sharp shoes that make a lot of noise, even on carpet. She is pale. Her eyes are enormous, round, and very blue. There are no jagged edges to Casper.

She looks around at us, her face settling into a gentle smile. She says, "Your job here is *you*. We are all here to get better, aren't we?"

Which means: we are all presently shit.

But we knew that already.

HER NAME ISN'T REALLY CASPER. THEY CALL HER THAT because of those big blue eyes, and the fact that she's so quiet. Like a ghost, she appears at our bedsides some mornings to take Chart, her warm fingers sliding just an inch or so down the hem of my bandages to reach my pulse. Her chin doubles adorably as she looks down at me in bed. Like a ghost, she appears suddenly behind me in the hallway, smiling as I turn in surprise: *How* are *you?*

She has an enormous tank in her office with a fat, slow turtle that paddles and paddles, paddles and paddles, barely making any headway. I watch that poor fucker all the time, I could watch him for hours and days, I find him so incredibly patient at a task that ultimately means nothing, because it's not like he's getting out of the fucking tank anytime soon, right?

And Casper just watches me watch him.

CASPER SMELLS NICE. SHE'S ALWAYS CLEAN, HER CLOTHES RUS-
tle softly. She never raises her voice. She rubs Sasha's back
when she sobs so hard she chokes. She positions her arms
around Linda/Katie/Cuddles like a goalie or something when
one of the bad people breaks free. I've seen her in Blue's room,
even, on the days Blue gets an enormous box of books from her
mother, pawing through the paperbacks and smiling at Blue.
I've seen Blue melt a little, just a little, at this smile.

Casper should be someone's mother. She should be *my*
mother.

WE'RE NEVER IN DARKNESS. EVERY ROOM HAS LIGHTS IN THE walls that *ping* on at four p.m. and *ping* off at six a.m. They're small, but bright. Louisa doesn't like light. Scratchy curtains cover the windows and she makes sure to pull them shut, tightly, every night before bed, to block out the squares of yellow from the office building next door. Then she drapes the bedsheet over her head for good measure.

Tonight, as soon as she's asleep, I kick the sheets off and pull the curtains apart. Maybe I'm looking for the salt stars. I don't know.

I pee in the metal toilet, watching the silent lump of Louisa beneath her pile of covers. In the weird mirror, my hair looks like snakes. I squeeze the mats and dreads in my fingers. My hair still smells like dirt and concrete, attic and dust, and makes me feel sick.

How long have I been here? I am waking from something. From somewhere. A dark place.

The bulbs in the hallway ceiling are like bright, long rivers. I peek into the rooms as I walk. Only Blue is awake, holding her paperback all the way up to the *ping*-light to see.

No doors, no lamps, no glass, no razors, only soft, spoonable food, and barely warm coffee. There's no way to hurt yourself here.

I feel jangly and loose inside, waiting at the nurses' station, drumming my fingers on the countertop. I ding the little bell. It sounds horrible and loud in the quiet hall.

Barbero rounds the corner, his mouth full of something

crunchy. He frowns when he sees me. Barbero is a thick-necked former wrestler from Menominee. He still has a whiff of ointment and adhesive. He only likes pretty girls. I can tell, because Jen S. is very pretty, with her long legs and freckled nose, and he's always smiling at her. She's the only one he ever smiles at.

He puts his feet up on the desk and pops some potato chips into his mouth. "You," he says, salty bits fluttering from his lips to his blue scrubs. "What the fuck do you want at this time of night?"

I take the pad of sticky notes and a pen from the countertop and write quickly. I hold up the sticky note. *HOW LONG HAVE I BEEN HERE?*

He looks at the sticky note. He shakes his head. "Uh-uh. *Ask.*"

I write, *NO. TELL ME.*

"No can do, Silent Sue." Barbero crumples the chip bag and stuffs it into the trash. "You're gonna have to open that fucked-up little mouth of yours and use your big-girl voice."

Barbero thinks I'm afraid of him, but I'm not. There's only one person I'm afraid of, and he's far away, on the whole other side of the river, and he can't get to me here.

I don't *think* he can get to me, anyway.

Another sticky note. *JUST TELL ME, YOU OAF.* My hands are shaking a little, though, as I hold it up.

Barbero laughs. Chips clot the spaces between his teeth.

Sparks go off behind my eyes and my inside music gets very loud. My skin numbs as I walk away from the nurses' station. I'd like to breathe, like Casper says, but I can't, that won't work, not for me, not once I get angry and the music starts. Now my skin isn't numb but positively itches as I roam, roam, look-

16

ing, looking, and when I find it and turn around, Barbero's not laughing anymore. He's *Oh, shit*-ing and ducking.

The plastic chair bounces off the nurses' station. The container holding the pens with plastic flowers taped to them falls to the floor, the pens fanning out across the endless beige carpet. The endless, everywhere beige carpet. I start to kick the station, which is bad, because I have no shoes, but the pain feels good, so I keep doing it. Barbero is up now, but I grab the chair again and he holds out his hands, all *Calm down, you crazy fucker*. But he says it really soft. Like, maybe he's a little afraid of me now. And I don't know why, but this makes me even angrier.

I'm raising the chair again when Doc Dooley shows up.

IF CASPER IS DISAPPOINTED IN ME, SHE DOESN'T SHOW IT. SHE just watches me watch the turtle, and the turtle does his thing. I'd like to be that turtle, underwater, quiet, no one around. What a fucking peaceful life that turtle has.

Casper says, "To answer the question that you asked Bruce last night: you have been at Creeley Center for six days. You were treated in the hospital and kept for observation for seven days before they transferred you here. Did you know you had walking pneumonia? Well, you still have it, but the antibiotics should help."

She picks up something chunky from her desk and slides it to me. It's one of those desk calendars. I'm not sure what I'm looking for, but then I see it, at the top of the page.

April. It's the middle of April.

Casper says, "You just missed Easter at Creeley. You were a little out of it. You didn't miss much. We can't really have a giant bunny hopping around a psych ward, can we?" She smiles. "Sorry. That's a little therapist humor. We did have an egg hunt, though. Thanksgiving is a lot more fun around here: dry turkey, lumpy gravy. Good times."

I know she's trying to cheer me up, get me to talk. I slide my face to her but as soon as I meet her eyes, I feel the fucking sting of tears and so I look back at the stupid turtle. I feel like I'm waking up and going back into my darkness, all at once.

Casper leans forward. "Do you remember being in Regions Hospital at all?"

I remember the security guard and the forest of hair inside

his nose. I remember lights above me, bright as suns, the sound of beeping that never seemed to stop. I remember wanting to kick out when hands were on me, when they were cutting away my clothes and boots. I remember how heavy my lungs felt, as though they were filled with mud.

I remember being so scared that Fucking Frank was going to appear in the doorway and take me away, back to Seed House, to the room where the girls cried.

I remember crying. I remember the splatter of my vomit on a nurse's shoes, and the way her face never changed, not once, like it happened to her all the time, and I wished my eyes to tell her *sorry*, because I had no words, and how her face didn't change then, either.

Then nothing. Nothing. Until Louisa.

Casper says, "It's all right if you can't remember. Our subconscious is spectacularly agile. Sometimes it knows when to take us away, as a kind of protection. I hope that makes sense."

I wish I knew how to tell her that my subconscious is broken, because it never took me away when Fucking Frank was threatening me, or when that man tried to hurt me in the underpass.

My broken big toe throbs beneath its splint and the weird foot-bootie Doc Dooley put me in. Now, when I walk, I really am a crazy freak, with my nesty hair and my clubby arms and trussed-up legs and limp.

What's going to happen to me?

Casper says, "I think you need a project."

IT ISN'T TRUE THAT I WANT TO BE LIKE THE TURTLE AND BE alone. What's true is that I want Ellis back, but she can never come back, ever, ever. Not the way she was, anyway. And it's true that I miss Mikey and DannyBoy, and I even miss Evan and Dump, and sometimes I miss my mother, even though missing her feels more like anger than sadness, like I feel when I think about Ellis, and even that, really, isn't true, because while I say *sadness* what I really mean is *black hole inside me filled with nails and rocks and broken glass and the words I don't have anymore.*

Ellis, Ellis.

AND WHILE IT'S TRUE THAT MY CLOTHES ARE FROM THE LOST and found, it isn't entirely true that I have nothing, because I *do* have something, they just keep it from me. I saw it once, when Doc Dooley told me to stop watching the movie during Entertainment and come to the nurses' station. When I got there, he pulled a backpack, *my* backpack, from beneath the desk. Doc Dooley is super tall, and handsome, the kind of handsome where you know he knows how handsome he is, and that his life is that much easier for it, and so he tends to be kind of easygoing with the rest of us, the unhandsome. So when he said, "Two boys dropped this off. Does this look familiar to you?" I was momentarily blinded by the whiteness of his teeth, and fascinated by the velvety quality of his stubble.

I grabbed my pack and sank to my knees, unzipping it, shoving my hands inside. It was there. I cradled it, sighing in relief, because Doc Dooley said, "Don't get excited. We emptied it."

I took out my tender kit, the army medical kit that I'd found when I was fourteen and trolling the St. Vincent de Paul thrift store on West Seventh with Ellis. The metal box was dented, the large red cross on the front was scratched and losing its paint.

My tender kit used to hold everything: my ointment, my gauze, my pieces of broken mason jar in a blue velvet pouch, my cigarettes, my matches and lighter, buttons, bracelets, money, my photos wrapped in linen.

The box made no sound when I shook it. I dug deeper in the green backpack, but it, too, was dark and empty. No extra socks and underwear, no rolls of toilet paper, no film canister filled with panhandled cash, no pills in a baggie, no rolled-up-tight wool blanket. My sketchpad was missing. My bag of pens and charcoals was gone. My Land Camera, gone. I looked up at Doc Dooley.

"We had to take everything out, for your safety." He offered his hand to me, and even his hand was handsome, with slender fingers and buffed nails. I ignored it, standing up by myself, clutching my tender kit and the backpack tightly. "You have to give the bag and the box back. We'll keep them for you until you're discharged."

He reached out and tugged the backpack away, slipped my tender kit from my hand. He put them behind the desk. "But you can have these."

Doc Dooley pressed the square of linen into my hands. Inside, protected by the soft fabric, are photographs of us: me and Ellis, Mikey and DannyBoy, perfect and together, before everything blew to hell.

As I walked away, pressing the photographs to my chest, Doc Dooley called out, "Those boys, they said they were sorry."

I kept walking, but inside, I felt myself pause, just for a second.

MY PHOTOGRAPHS ARE WHAT I'M DOING WHEN JEN S. COMES
to find me the night after the toe incident: thumbing through
them, greedy like I always am when I let myself think of Ellis,
poring over the black-and-white images of the four of us in
the graveyard, posing stupid like rock stars, cigarettes in the
corners of our mouths, DannyBoy's harelip almost invisible,
Ellis's acne hardly noticeable. DannyBoy always said people
looked better in black-and-white and he was right. The photos
are small and square; the Land Camera was old, something
from the sixties, the first kind of Polaroid. My grandmother
gave it to me. It had bellows and made me feel cool. We found
some film at the camera store by Macalester College. It was a
cartridge, and you slipped it into the camera, took the picture,
ripped the film strip from the side, and set the little round
timer. When it buzzed, you peeled back the film and there we
were, old-timey and neat-looking in black-and-white, Ellis so
beautiful with her black hair. And there was me, dumb little
me, arms folded across my chest in my holey sweater and my
hair all ratty, dyed red and blue in the real, color world, but
muddy-looking in black-and-white. Who could look anything
but gross next to Ellis?

"Cool." Jen S. reaches down, but I wrap the photos back up
in the linen and slide them under my pillow.

"Dude," she sighs. "Okay, whatever. Come on, then, Barbero's waiting in Rec. We've got a surprise for you."

In Rec, the smell of popcorn clings to the room from the
movie we watched earlier; the empty bowl rests on a circular

table. Jen licks her finger and swipes the bowl, sucking off salt and bits of congealed butter. She makes oinking sounds. Barbero's floppy lips curl. "Schumacher," he says. "You kill me." She shrugs, flicking her wet finger against the hem of her baggy green T-shirt.

She digs in one of the several "everything" bins, looking for her favorite deck of cards. The colorful bins are stacked on top of each other against the ivory walls of Rec. They hold playing cards, frayed boxes of crayons, markers, games.

A bank of three computers is tucked against one wall. Barbero fires one up and shoos his fingers at me while he enters the password.

"Here's the deal, crazy." Barbero flings a booklet at me. I have to bend to pick it up. He starts typing. *ALTERNA-LEARN. THE RIGHT PLACE FOR YOU* pops up on the page. "The good doctor thinks you need something to do to curb your anger issues, of which there are apparently many, and also your weird habit of not sleeping. So, looks like it's back to school for you, dumbass."

I look over at Jen S., who grins wildly while shuffling the cards. "I get to be your *teacher*," she giggles.

Barbero snaps his fingers in my face. "FO-CUS. I'm over here! Here."

I glare at him.

Barbero ticks off his fingers. "Here's the deal: don't look at anything but the school site. Don't look at your Facebook, your Twitter, your email, anything at all but the school pages. Your friend Schumacher here has volunteered to be your teacher and she'll check your quizzes and all that shit when you finish a lesson."

He looks at me. I stare back. "You don't wanna do it," he

says, "the good doctor says you have to start taking meds at night to sleep and I have a feeling you don't wanna do that. She'd rather have you in here than creeping down the halls like you do. Because that's fucking *weird*."

I don't want drugs, especially at night, when I'm most scared and need to be alert. Doctors filled me up from the time I was eight until I was thirteen. Ritalin didn't work. I bounced off walls and stabbed a pencil in the cloudlike flab of Alison Jablonsky's belly. Adderall made me shit my pants in eighth grade; my mother kept me home the rest of the year. She left lunch for me under plastic wrap in the refrigerator: spongy meat loaf sandwiches, smelly egg salad on soggy toast. Zoloft was like swallowing very heavy air and not being able to exhale for days. Most of the girls here are doped to the gills, accepting their pill cups with pissy resignation.

I sit in the chair and type my name in the YOUR NAME HERE box.

"Good choice, freak."

"Jesus, Bruce," Jen says, exasperated. "Did you skip that day in nursing school when they explained bedside manner?"

"I got bedside manner, baby. Let me know when you wanna try it." He flops on the creaky brown Rec couch and pulls his iPod from his pocket.

One whole wall of Rec is a long window. The curtains have been opened. It's dark outside, after ten o'clock. Our wing is four stories up; I can hear the *whoosh* of cars in the rain down on Riverside Avenue. If I do school, it will make Casper happy with me. The last time I was in school, I was kicked out the middle of junior year. That feels like a lifetime ago.

I peer at the screen and try to read a paragraph, but all I can see are the words *fucker* and *pussy bitch* scrawled on my locker door. I can taste the tang of toilet water in my mouth, feel myself struggling to get free, hands on my neck and laughter. My fingers tingle and my chest feels tight. After I got kicked out of school, everything went haywire. Even more than before.

I look around Rec. Like a fussy little mouse, thoughts of who's paying for this nibble at my brain, but I push them away. My mother cooked meat loaf with onions and ketchup and hills of mash on the side, in a diner for years, before even that went away. We aren't people with money; we're people who dig for change at the bottoms of purses and backpacks and eat plain noodles with butter four nights a week. Thinking about how I'm able to stay here makes me anxious and afraid.

I think, *I'm inside and warm and I can do this if it means I get to stay.* That's what matters right now. Following the rules so I can stay inside.

Jen's fingers shuffle and flutter the cards. It sounds like birds rushing to empty a tree.

CASPER ASKS, "HOW DO YOU FEEL?"

Every day, she asks me this. One day a week, someone else asks me—Doc Dooley, maybe, if he's pulling a day shift, or the raspy-voiced, stiff-haired doctor with too-thick mascara. I think her name is Helen. I don't like her; she makes me feel cold inside. One day a week, on Sundays, no one asks us how we're feeling and that makes some of us feel lost. Jen S. will say, mockingly, "I am having too many feelings! I need someone to hear my feelings!"

Casper waits. I can *feel* her waiting. I make a decision.

I write down what it feels like and push the paper across Casper's desk. *My body is on fire all the time, burning me away day and night. I have to cut the black heat out. When I clean myself, wash and mend, I feel better. Cooler inside and calm. Like moss feels, when you get far back in the woods.*

What I don't write is: I'm so lonely in the world I want to peel all of my flesh off and walk, just bone and gristle, straight into the river, to be swallowed, just like my father.

Before he got sicker, my father used to take me on long drives to the north. We would park the car and walk the trails deep into the fragrant firs and lush spruces, so far that sometimes it seemed like night because there were so many trees, you couldn't see the sky. I was small then and I stumbled a lot on stones, landing on mounds of moss. My fingers on the cold, comforting moss always stayed inside me. My father could walk for hours. He said, "I just want it to be quiet." And we

27

walked and walked, looking for that quiet place. The forest is not as quiet as everyone thinks.

After he died, my mother was like a crab: she tucked everything inside and left only her shell.

Casper finishes reading and folds the paper neatly, sliding it into a binder on her desk. "Cool moss." She smiles. "That isn't a bad way to feel. If only we could get you there without hurting yourself. How can we do that?"

Casper always has blank sheets of paper on her desk for me. I write, then push it to her. She frowns. She pulls a folder from her drawer and runs her fingers down a page.

"No, I don't see a sketchbook on the list of items from your backpack." She looks at me.

I make a little sound. My sketchbook had everything, my own little world. Drawings of Ellis, of Mikey, the little comics I would make about the street, about me and Evan and Dump.

I can feel my fingers tingling. I just need to draw. I *need* to bury myself. I make another little sound.

Casper closes the folder. "Let me talk to Miss Joni. Let's see what she can do."

MY FATHER WAS CIGARETTES AND RED-AND-WHITE CANS OF beer. He was dirty white T-shirts and a brown rocking chair and blue eyes and scratchy cheek stubble and *"Oh, Misty,"* when my mother would frown at him. He was days of not getting out of that chair, of me on the floor by his feet, filling paper with suns, houses, cats' faces, in crayon and pencil and pen. He was days of not changing those T-shirts, of sometimes silence and sometimes too much laughter, a strange laughter that seemed to crack him from the inside until there wasn't laughter, but crying, and tears that bled along my face as I climbed up and rocked with him, back and forth, back and forth, heartbeat heartbeat heartbeat as the light changed outside, as the world grew darker around us.

LOUISA SAYS, "YOU'RE SO QUIET. I'M SO GLAD THEY PUT SOME-body quiet with me. You've no idea how tedious it is, listening to somebody talk out loud all the time."

She'd been silent for so long, I thought she was sleeping.

Louisa says, "I mean, I'm talking to you, do you know that? In my head, I mean. I'm telling you all sorts of things in my head, because you seem like you're a good listener. But I don't want to take up your thinking space. If that makes sense."

She makes a sleepy sound. *Mmmmm.* Then, "I'm going to tell you my whole story. You're a good egg, a keeper."

A good egg, a keeper, a good egg, a keeper—a cutter's nurs-ery song.

IN GROUP, CASPER DOESN'T LIKE US TO SAY *CUT* OR *CUTTING* OR *burn* or *stab*. She says it doesn't matter *what* you do or *how* you do it: it's all the same. You could drink, slice, do meth, snort coke, burn, cut, stab, slash, rip out your eyelashes, or fuck till you bleed and it's all the same thing: *self-harm*. She says: whether someone has *hurt* you or made you feel *bad* or *unworthy* or *unclean*, rather than taking the *rational* step of *realizing* that person is an *asshole* or a *psycho* and should be *shot* or *strung up* and you should *stay the fuck away from them*, instead we *internalize* our abuse and begin to *blame* and *punish* ourselves and *weirdly*, once you start *cutting* or *burning* or *fucking* because you feel so *shitty* and *unworthy*, your body starts to release this neat-feeling shit called *endorphins* and you feel so *fucking high* the world is like cotton candy at the best and most colorful state fair in the world, only *bloody* and *stuffed with infection*. But the fucked-up part is once you start *self-harming*, you can never *not* be a *creepy freak*, because your whole body is now a *scarred* and *charred* battlefield and nobody likes *that* on a girl, *nobody* will love *that*, and so all of us, every one, is *screwed*, inside and out. Wash, rinse, fucking *repeat*.

I'M TRYING TO FOLLOW THE RULES. I'M TRYING TO GO WHERE I'm supposed to go when I'm supposed to go there and sit like a good girl even though I don't say anything because my throat is filled with nails. I'm trying to follow the rules because to not follow the rules means to risk OUTSIDE.

WHEN DOC DOOLEY TOLD ME TWO BOYS DROPPED OFF MY backpack? Those boys, once, twice, I guess, saved me. And when he said they said to tell me they were sorry? I've been thinking about that.

Evan and Dump. Were they sorry they saved me from the man in the underpass who was trying to mess with me? Were they sorry when the winter turned so fucking cold here in Minnie-Soh-Tah that they couldn't NOT take all three of us to live with Fucking Frank? I was sick. We couldn't live outside in the van any longer. Evan needed his drugs. Dump went where Evan went. Were they sorry I wouldn't do what Fucking Frank asked? (What he wanted all the girls in Seed House to do, if they wanted to stay.) Were they sorry they didn't let me die in the attic of Seed House?

Sorrysorrysorrysorrysorrysorrysorrysorry.

I cut that word out, too, but it keeps growing back, tougher and meaner.

LOUISA DOESN'T COME TO GROUP. LOUISA MEETS WITH CASPER in the evenings. Louisa has phone calls at night; she presses herself against the wall in Rec, twirls the cord between her fingers, the toe of her glittery ballet flat petting the carpet delicately. Louisa can come and go as she pleases, she doesn't need a Day Pass. Louisa whispers in the dark, "I need to tell you, you aren't the same as us, you know? Look around. These sheets, this bed, our meds, the doctors. Everything here speaks money. Are you listening?"

Her bed creaks as she shifts, leans on her elbow to face me. In the half-light, her eyes are egg-shaped, shadowed underneath.

"You need to prepare yourself, is all I'm saying."

But I let her words glide over me, smooth and warm. She turns away. Money, money. I don't want to think about where it's coming from or where it isn't.

I just want her to go back to sleep, so I can eat the turkey sandwich I've hidden beneath my bed.

—■—

THE DOOR TO GROUP *WHOOSHES* OPEN. CASPER SIDLES IN, takes the seat next to Sasha, who wriggles and smiles at her like a puppy. Casper's wearing brown pants and her elf clogs. There's a red bandanna like a headband in her yellowy hair. Moon earrings, pink cheeks, she's a goddamn rainbow.

I wonder what she was like in high school. She must have been a good girl, the kind that holds her books over her tits, always has nice combed hair, bites her lips when she takes a test. Probably on yearbook, or math team, maybe debate.

But there must be something else, something under Casper's scrubbed surface that we can't see, like a hidden hurt, a tender secret or something, because why the fuck would she make being with *us* her goddamn life?

She passes out paper and markers and we tense up. When we have to write, we know Group will be rough. She makes us put the pens and paper on the floor, do our accordion breathing. I can't concentrate. I'm watching the clock on the wall; I get to leave early. Today I get my bandages off. The thought of it makes my stomach flutter.

Casper says, "I'd like you to write down what you say to yourself before you harm."

Blue groans out loud, runs her tongue across her mouth, flexes her naked feet. She never wears shoes. Silver rings glisten on three of her toes. From across the circle, she looks as young as any of us, but up close, in dining hall, or Rec, you can see the hard grooves at the corners of her eyes. I haven't drawn in such a long time, I hardly ever go to Crafts, and looking at Blue is hard because she makes me ache for my pencils and charcoals. There's a *something* in her that I want to put on paper.

I don't write anything at first, I just make little lines with my red marker and then I sneak looks at Blue, to sketch her, lightly, faintly. It feels good, my fingers holding the marker, feeling my way around her cattish eyes, the fullness of her mouth. It's a little awkward, pressing the paper against my thighs, but it's like my fingers never forgot what to do. Like they've been waiting for me to come back.

Blue's mouth is so full. My own lips are kind of thin. Ellis would say, *You have to accentuate.* Take my chin in her fingers, press the cool lipstick to my mouth. But it never worked. It never looked right on me. I didn't see someone with a beautiful mouth. I saw someone who had lipstick on the skin of her face.

My brain starts to circle, circle, even as I keep drawing Blue. There are things happening that I don't want to think about, not right now. Words happening, like *sorry* and *attic* and *underpass* and *hurting me.*

Sasha sniffles. Francie clears her throat.

My pen writes *OUT. GET IT OUT. CUT IT ALL OUT.* I put a big red X over the drawing of Blue's face, crumple up the paper, shove it under my thigh.

"Isis." Casper folds her hands, waits for Isis to read from her paper.

Isis picks at her nostrils, her face reddening. "Okay," she says finally. She says, so softly it's almost a whisper, "Why can't you ever just fucking learn? This will teach you." She squeezes her eyes shut.

Francie says, "Nobody. Blank. Who cares." Rips her paper in half.

Sasha's body is so warm from crying a weird heat shimmers off her and I shift my chair a little away. I can feel Blue's eyes on me.

Sasha looks down at her paper and chokes out, "You. Fat. Ass. Fuck."

Bird-quick, Blue is up and across the circle, yanking the paper from beneath my thigh. She glares at me from the middle of the circle.

Casper looks at her evenly. "Blue." A warning.

Blue uncrumples the paper, smooths it flat. As she scrutinizes it, a smile spreads across her face, slowly. "Is this me? This is pretty good, Silent Sue. I like that you Xed me out."

She shows the paper to the group. "She erased me." She crumples the paper back up and tosses it in my lap. I let it fall to the floor. On her way back to her seat, she tells Casper, "She said it better than I could. That's pretty much what goes through my head when I *self-harm*. Erase me."

Casper turns to Sasha, but before she can start, Blue interrupts her. "You know, Doctor, it's very unfair."

"What's unfair?" Casper regards Blue. My face starts to heat up. I look at the clock. Just a few minutes to go before I can get up and leave, get these clubs off.

"She never has to say anything. We all have to talk, spill our fucking guts out, and she doesn't have to say shit. Maybe we're like a little comedy show for her."

"Group is voluntary, Blue. If a member doesn't want to speak, she doesn't have to. In Char—"

"Tell everybody what you wrote on your paper, there, Silent Sue," Blue says. "No? Okay, I will. She wrote, *Out. Out, cut it all out.* Cut what out, Sue? Pony up. It's time to pay the piper."

Fucking Frank wore heavy silver rings, malevolent-looking skulls he was forever buffing across his shirt until they gleamed with perfection. His fingers were stained and singed from lighters and they dug into my neck, lifting me off the attic floor. Evan and Dump made kitten sounds behind him, but they were just boys who needed drugs. It was freezing outside. April had dropped a surprise snow that turned into freezing sleet. That was the worst kind of weather to be outside in: icy water that froze your bare face and turned your fingers to stiff husks of bone.

I should've known when Fucking Frank greeted us at the door that he wouldn't let me stay for free. I should've looked closer at the faces of the girls on the ripped couch as Evan and Dump carried me in. In my stupor, my lungs like cement, my eyes blurry, I thought they were just stoned, their eyes gone hazy. I know, now, that their eyes were dead.

Just do it, Fucking Frank said that night, my breath disappearing in the tightness of his fingers. *Do it, like the other girls. Or I'll do you myself.*

If you were a girl, and you were at Seed House, and you wanted to stay at Seed House, there was a room downstairs with only mattresses. Frank put girls in the room. Men came to the house and paid Frank, and then went into the room.

OUT. CUT IT ALL OUT. Cut out my father. Cut out my mother. Cut out missing Ellis. Cut out the man in the underpass, cut out Fucking Frank, the men downstairs, the people on the street with too many people inside them, cut out hungry, and sad and tired, and being nobody and unpretty and unloved, just cut it all out, get smaller and smaller until I was nothing.

That's what was in my head in the attic when I took broken glass from my tender kit and began to cut myself into tiny pieces. I'd done it forever, for years, but now would be the last time. I'd go farther than Ellis had. Wouldn't fuck it up like Ellis had: I would die, not end up in some half-life.

That time, I tried so hard to fucking die.

But here I am.

The music in my head makes my eyes cloud over. I can barely see Blue with her smarmy face and her fucked-up teeth but as I walk toward her, I can practically taste what it will feel like to grind that face into Group floor. My body is weirdly heavy and light at the same time and a little bit of me is leaving, floating away—Casper calls this *dissociation*—but I keep lurching in Blue's direction, even as she kind of nervously laughs and says, "Fuck *me*," and gets up, alert.

Jen S. stands up. She says, "Please, don't."

On the street, where I used to live, I called it my street feeling. It's like electrical wire is strung tight through my whole body. It meant I could ball my fists and fight for the forgotten sleeping bag by the river against two older women. It meant I could do a lot of things just to make it through the night to another endless day of walking, walking, walking.

Casper's voice is even and clear. "Charlie. Another altercation and I cannot help you."

I stop short. Charlie. Charlie Davis. *Charlotte*, Evan said, his eyes shiny, drunk, smears of my blood on his cheek, that night in the attic. *What a beautiful name.* He kissed my head, over and over. *Please don't leave us, Charlotte.*

My father taught me to tell time by telling me how much time was left. "The long hand is here, and the short hand is here. When the short hand is *here*, and the long hand *here*, then it is time for Mama to come home." He lit a cigarette, pleased with himself, and rocked in his chair.

The hands on the wall clock in Group tell me it's time to get my bandages off.

I lurch, the stupid bootie catching on the rug, until I reach the door. I let it slam shut behind me.

IT'S ONE OF THE DAY NURSES, VINNIE, WHO DOES IT, HIS BIG hands chapped and methodical. It's chilly in the Care room and very neat. Paper crinkles beneath me as I settle on the table. I look at the glass jars filled with tall Q-tips, the bottles of alcohol, the neatly labeled drawers. Vinnie has a silver tray all ready with scissors, tweezers, clips, and creams.

He pauses before he begins unpeeling the pads on my arms. "You want someone here? Doc Stinson's done with Group in fifteen minutes." He means Casper.

He gives me his special smile, the one where he opens his mouth and bares all his teeth. Each tooth is framed, like a painting or a photograph, in gold. I have a sudden urge to touch one of those shining teeth.

Vinnie laughs. "You like my sweet teeth? It cost a lot to get this smile, but it cost a lot to *get* this smile, if you know what I mean. You want the doctor or not?"

I shake my head, *No*.

"Yeah, that's right. You a tough girl, Davis."

Carefully, he unwinds the gauze from each arm. He strips the long pads from my left arm. He strips the long pads from my right arm. They make a wet, soft *thwack* as he tosses them in the metal trash bin. My heart beats a little faster. I don't look down yet.

Vinnie leans close as he tweezes and clips the stitches. He smells silky and brittle all at once, like hair oil and coffee. I stare at the ceiling lights so hard dark clouds form over my eyes. There is a kidney-shaped stain on one of the panels, the color of butter heated too long in a pan.

"Am I hurting you?" he asks. "I'm doing the best I can, girl-friend."

There's the sound of trickling water. Vinnie is washing his hands. I lift my arms up.

They're pale and puckered from being wrapped up for so long. Turning them over, I look at the red, ropy scars rivering from my wrists to my elbows. I touch them gingerly. Vinnie hums. It's an upbeat tune, with a lilt.

I'm only another day to him, another hideous girl.

"Okay?" He rubs cream between his palms and holds them up.

Underneath these new scars, I can see the old ones. My scars are like a dam or something. The beaver just keeps pushing new branches and sticks over the old ones.

I nod at Vinnie. The cream has warmed in his hands and feels good against my skin.

The first time I ever cut myself, the best part was after: swabbing the wound with a cotton ball, carefully drying it, inspecting it, this way and that, cradling my arm protectively against my stomach. *There, there.*

I cut because I can't deal. It's as simple as that. The world becomes an ocean, the ocean washes over me, the sound of water is deafening, the water drowns my heart, my panic becomes as large as planets. I need release, I need to hurt myself more than the world can hurt me, and then I can comfort myself.

There, there.

Casper told us, "It's counterintuitive, yes? That hurting yourself makes you feel better. That somehow you can rid yourself of pain by causing yourself pain."

42

The problem is: *after.*

Like now, what is happening now. More scars, more damage. A vicious circle: more scars = more shame = more pain.

The sound of Vinnie washing his hands in the sink brings me back.

Looking at my skin makes my stomach flip.

He turns. "Round two. You sure you don't want someone else here?"

I shake my head and he throws me a sheet, tells me to scoot back on the examining table, motions for me to pull down my shorts. I do it quick under the sheet, without breathing, keeping the sheet tight over my plain underwear. My thighs prickle up, goose-pimply from the chilly room.

I don't think I'm afraid of Vinnie, but I track the movements of his hands carefully, bring my street feeling to the surface, just in case. When I was little and couldn't sleep, I used to rub the bedsheet between my forefinger and thumb. I do this now with the underwear, the soft pink underwear, brand-new, left on my narrow bed with a little card. There were seven pairs, one for each day of the week. They had no holes, no stains, and they smelled like the plastic wrap they came in, not like funk and piss or period blood. Thinking of the underwear, feeling the clean cotton in my fingers, makes something shift inside me, like the loosening of stones after one is plucked from the pile, a groan, a settling, an exhalation of air—

"Nurse. Ava. Bought. Me. This. Underwear."

I don't know why I whisper it. I don't know where it came from. I don't know why words have formed now, I don't know why *these* words. My voice is scratchy from not being used. I sound like a croaky frog. It's a long sentence, my first in I don't know how many days, and I know that he will dutifully log

43

this: *C. Davis spoke in a complete sentence while bandages being removed. C. Davis spoke about not having underwear. Patient does not usually volunteer to speak; Selective Mutism.*

"That was mighty nice of her. Did you say thank you?"

I shake my head.

When I cut myself in the attic, I was wearing a T-shirt, underwear, and socks and boots. There was so much blood, Evan and Dump didn't know what to do. They wrapped me in a bedsheet.

"You should thank her."

I came to Creeley in hospital scrubs and slippers. Nurse Ava found clothes for me. Nurse Ava bought me brand-new underwear.

I should thank her.

The gauze and pads from my thighs look like stained streamers as Vinnie holds them up and lobs them into the bin. He pulls and clips with the tweezers.

It's the same as my arms: it doesn't hurt as he removes the stitches, but my skin twinges, prickles, as he pulls the tweezers up and out.

In a rush, it happens again, only this time it's remembering what it's like to cut, and cut *hard*. The way you have to dig the glass in, deeply, right away, to break the skin and then drag, and drag fiercely, to make a river worth drowning in.

Oh, it hurts to make that river. The pain is sharp and bleary all at once; curtains part and shut over your eyes; bull breath from your nostrils.

It fucking hurts, hurts, hurts. But when the blood comes, everything is warmer, and calmer.

Vinnie catches my eye. I'm breathing too fast. He knows what's happening.

"Done." He watches me carefully as I sit up. The delicate paper beneath me tears.

Ladders. The scars on my thighs look like the rungs of ladders. Bump, bump, bump as I run my fingers from my knees to the top of my thighs. Vinnie's creamy hands are very dark against my paleness. It feels nice. When he's done with my thighs, he motions for me to pull up my shorts and hands me the blue-and-white tub of cream. "You apply this twice a day. That shit's gonna itch real bad now that it's out in the air. Gonna feel tight and kinda prickly."

I hug the tub to my chest. I can still feel his hands on my legs, the gentleness of his fingers on the ugliness of me. I kind of want his hands back, maybe curving around me this time. Maybe just being so light on me that my head could kind of fall against him, and I could stay there awhile, breathing him in, no big deal, heartbeat heartbeat heartbeat, like with my dad. Pressure builds behind my eyes.

I wipe my face, ignoring my trembling hands. Hot. My body is starting to heat up. I feel afraid. Vinnie clears his throat.

"Everybody's in Crafts, girl. You want me to walk you there?"

"Room." I hug the warm tub to my chest. "Room."

Vinnie looks sad. "Okay, baby. Okay."

Louisa is not in our room. They're all at Crafts, bent over gluey Popsicle sticks, bags of buttons and yarn, reams of glittery star stickers.

My eyes are fierce with water and I bury my head in my pillow so no one hears me. My body is so, so sore from my wounds. I want Ellis, the Ellis who would dab my cuts and steal wine from her dad so we could cry together in her room, sipping from the bottle and listening to our music, watching the solar system night-light rotate and glow on her ceiling. Because when you're hurt, and someone loves you, they're supposed to help you, right? When you're hurt, and someone loves you, they kiss you tenderly, they hold the bottle to your mouth, they stroke your hair with their fingers, right? Casper would be proud of me for my rational thinking.

I'm in a place filled with girls who are filled with longing and I want none of them. I want the one I can't have, the one who is never coming back.

Where do I put them, these dead ones, these live ones, these people who hover about me like ghosts? Ellis once said, "You were too young to lose a dad."

A little over a year ago, Mikey cried on the phone to me, "She never cut, that wasn't her thing. Why did she cut? You were *right there*." But he was miles and states away at college and didn't know what had happened between Ellis and me. It was the last time we talked; after that, I was on the street, becoming a ghost myself.

My mother is alive, but she's a ghost, too, her sunken eyes watching me from a distance, her body very still.

There are so many people who are never coming back.

WHEN I'M DONE, WHEN MY BODY GETS THAT WORN, WASHED-out feeling from crying too much, I get up and stumble back down the too-bright hall to the nurses' station. Vinnie was right, my scars itch horribly.

The outside of me is on fire and the inside of me is empty, empty. I can't cut, but I need something taken away from me, I need relief.

Vinnie gives me the gold smile from behind the nurses' station. All of the nurses have photographs pinned to the cubicle wall behind the desk. Kids, tons of them, chubby ones, skinny ones, unsmiling teenagers, and dogs, lots of dog pictures. Vinnie's girls, they must be the ones in the frilly white dresses, with the dark, dark hair, just like his.

I point to my own hair, that awful nest. Just smelling it makes me feel sick, all of a sudden. I want it all gone, that last bit of being *outside.*

"Off," I say hoarsely.

Vinnie holds up his hands. "Nah, nah. You wait till you earn your Day Pass, girl. Then you go out with the others, go to Supercuts or something. I'm not touching no girl's hair."

I pound my fist on the counter, lean in. "Now. Has to be *now.*"

"Puta madre," he says under his breath.

He jerks his fingers to the Care room. "Come, come. And don't cry, neither. There's only one way with hair like that."

IN THE CAFETERIA, IT'S ISIS WHO SPEAKS FIRST, HER LITTLE mouth opening, macaroni and cheese sliding back onto her plate. "Holy fucking Christ, Chuck, check you out."

Blue begins to laugh, a deep, infectious sound that startles Francie, who sits next to her and never eats. Francie smiles, too. Blue says, "I hate you, Silent Sue, but you look a shit-ton better. Almost human."

Even Vinnie whistled as he ran the electric shaver across my scalp, my hair falling in heavy clumps to the floor. "A face! The girl has a face," he said.

I peered at myself in the Care room mirror, a real mirror, a long one on the back of the door. I kept my eyes above my shoulders, just looking at my face, but not for too long, because I started to feel sad again, seeing me.

The girls get quiet as I start eating. You wouldn't think it would feel strange to show your scars to a group of girls who are nothing but scars, but it is. I keep my eyes on my plate.

I'm going to rifle the lost and found for a long-sleeved shirt after dinner. I feel exposed and cold. I miss my ratty mustard-yellow cardigan that I used to wear before I left home. It kept me hidden and safe. I miss all my clothes. Not my street clothes, but my long-ago clothes, my band T-shirts and check-ered pants and wool caps.

Isis swallows. "Christ, Chuck, what'd you use? You really went to fuckin' town."

Isis has a terrier's thin, nervous face. She twists the shaggy

48

loops of her braids through her fingers. The others wait. From the end of the table, Louisa gives me a faint smile.

I loved the breaking of the mason jar. You had to strike it hard, because it was thick. Unlike other glass, mason jars broke in hunks of curved, gleaming sharpness. They left wide, deep cuts. The thick pieces of glass were easily washable, savable, slipped into the velvet pouch and hidden in my tender kit for the next time.

Thinking about it fills me with anticipatory shivers, like how I felt in the Care room, which is *unacceptable,* Casper says, a *trigger,* and I can see some of the others now, like pale Sasha with her sea-blue eyes, beginning to frown. Blue and Jen S. wait, faces blank, sporks in the air.

I think I want to tell them, I think I want to talk. I feel a humming in my chest and I think I might have some words, maybe, though I'm not sure how to order them, or what they would mean, but I open my mouth—

From down the table, Louisa speaks. Her voice is throaty and lush; the band she sang for was called Loveless.

"Glass." Louisa gathers her dinner things. She is a peckish eater; just a little bit of this and that, and she never stays for long. "She used glass. Breakfast of desperate champions." She shrugs at us, wafting to the trash can with her cardboard cup and plastic plate and spork.

The air around the table stiffens at first, as each girl thinks, and remembers her favorite implements. And then the air loosens.

Isis resumes eating. "Hard-core, Chuck."

I fix my eyes on my glistening mound of macaroni, the single row of green beans, the brownish pool of applesauce.

"It's not Chuck, Isis. It's Charlie. *Charlie Davis*." My voice isn't hoarse now. It's clear as a bell.

Jen S. says, "Whoa. *Somebody's* got a voice."

Blue nods, gazing at me. "Things," she says, sipping her coffee thoughtfully, "are about to get interesting around here."

CASPER SMILES AT ME. "BIG CHANGES," SHE SAYS. "TALKING. Cutting your hair. Bandages off. How do you feel?"

I reach for the sheets of paper on her desk, the blue ballpoint, but she says, "No."

The turtle has paused in the tank, like he's waiting for me, too. His tiny body bobs in the water. Does he like the little ship at the bottom, the one with the hole big enough for him to swim through? Does he like the large rock he can hoist himself up on and rest? Does he ever want to come out?

I pull the hoodie I found in the lost and found box tighter around me, close the hood tight around my face.

Ugly, I tell her, my voice muffled and my face hidden by the hood. *Ugly. It still feels ugly.*

IT ISN'T THAT I NEVER NOTICED EXACTLY, THAT JEN S. DIS-appeared every night as soon as Barbero fell asleep on the Rec couch. I mean, she would tell me. "I'm going to the bathroom," she'd say, her long ponytail falling across her shoulder as she leaned in, looking at what I was doing on the computer. "My stomach is really acting up. I might be a while." Or, "I'm just gonna go jog the halls. I feel a little pent up. Be good." And then she'd go.

I was, weirdly, getting a little caught up in this class thing. I had finished twelve units so far, putting me near the middle of a mythical senior year. It was kind of satisfying to click SUBMIT and then wait for Jen S. to come back and do the grading with the secret password. School, it turns out, is super easy once you remove all the other kids, asshole teachers, and disgusting shit that goes on.

So I'm waiting for her, and waiting, and sort of watching Barbero snore on the couch, when it occurs to me she might not be doing exactly what she says she's doing. But before I can even think about what she might be doing, I think about what *I* could be doing, while she's gone and Barbero is comatose.

It only takes a few minutes. I open another window, set up a Gmail account, wrack my brain for his last known email address, enter it, hope for the best, and open the chat box. I haven't talked to him in over a year. Maybe he's there, maybe he's not.

Hey, I type.

I wait, picking at my chin. My head feels a little cold now, with all my hair gone. I pull my hoodie up. He has to be there, though, because it doesn't say *Michael is offline* or anything.

And then there he is.

OMFG is that rlly u

Yes

R u ok

No. Yes. No. I'm in the loony bin

I know my mom told me Your mom told her

I'm wearing clothes from the lost and fucking found

Im at a show

Who?

Firemouth Club called Flycatcher U know Firemouth? U wd lk them

My fingers hover above the keys. *I miss you*

Nothing. My stomach starts to squeeze a little. A little bit of the old feeling is coming back to me: how much I like-liked Mikey, how confused I was that it was Ellis he wanted, even though she didn't like him like that. But Ellis isn't here anymore. I bite my lip.

I look back at Barbero. One of his legs has drifted to the floor.

Michael is typing . . . then: *Ill have mom bring u some of T's clothes*

His sister, Tanya. She must be out of college by now. Mikey's house was always warm. In the winter, his mother made fat, soft loaves of bread and big pots of steaming soup.

Chat says, *Michael is typing.* He didn't say he missed me or anything. I take a deep breath, try to stifle the growling little voice in my head that tells me, *You're dirty and disgusting, idiot. Why would anyone want you?*

Im coming up in May for a show at 7th Street Entry with this band I work with. Be there for two days. Can u put me on some visitor list or something?

Yes! I start grinning crazily. My whole body has turned to feathers, I feel so light at the thought of seeing Mikey. Mikey!

Michael is typing: *I hv to go, show ending have class tmrow I cant blv its u u have a phone # too?* and I am up and running to the phone on the Rec wall, where the number is written in black Sharpie ink, along with no phone calls after 9 p.m. no phone calls before 6 p.m. I'm running back, repeating the number in my head, when my bootie gets caught on a plastic chair and I go sprawling. Barbero's up in a flash, quicker than I've seen him move, ripping the buds from his ears. He whirls around. "Where's Schumacher? Where the fuck is Schumacher?" As I try to scramble up, he's busy, reading what's on the computer.

He presses his fat finger on a key and the computer screen fades to black. Mikey disappears.

"Back to your hutch, rabbit. I've got to go hunt down your friend."

BARBERO AND NURSE AVA FOUND JEN S. IN THE EMERGENCY stairwell. Her stomach wasn't bothering her, and she wasn't doing laps. She was, Louisa informs me later that night, doing Doc Dooley.

I'm under my sheet. When I blink, my eyelashes brush against the fabric. I grunt at Louisa.

"They've been fucking for a loooong time," Louisa whispers. "I'm surprised they didn't get caught sooner."

Down the hall, there's a flurry of activity: phone calls being made, Jen S. crying at the nurses' station. Louisa says, "Too bad, really. They'll kick her out now and fire him. Or maybe he won't get fired, just reprimanded. He's only a resident. They fuck up all the time." She pauses. "I hope Jen doesn't think they'll get together on the outside, because that is not going to happen."

She peels the sheet from my face. "You're young, so you don't really understand." She hasn't taken off her makeup yet. Her mascara is smudged beneath her eyes.

"He chose her because she's easy. We're so easy, aren't we? Hell, I thought I found the one, too, once."

Tentatively, I say, "Maybe . . . he really liked her, though." He could, couldn't he? Doc Dooley is a dreamboat, he doesn't need to troll on damaged girls. He could get anyone he wanted.

Louisa's eyes flicker. "Guys are weird, little one. You never know what floats their boat." She places the sheet back over my face and climbs into her bed. Her voice is muffled now, like she's under her own sheet. "I let this guy—I thought he was so beautiful, and kind—I let him take pictures of me. Then he turned around and sold them to some freak site on the Web."

Is she crying? I hesitate. Jen S. is really sobbing out there now and I can hear Sasha starting up in her room, a low, mewing sound.

This whole place is a world of sobbing girls.

Louisa is crying. The whole fucking hallway is crying, except me, because I am all cried out. I kick off my sheet and climb out of bed. Mikey was so *close* and I lost him. I lost him.

Louisa mumbles, "They should tell you, right when you get here, that that part of wishing is over. What we've done, no one will love us. Not in a normal way."

Her hand snakes from beneath the sheet, groping in the air. I step into the cradle of her fingers. Her nails are painted a glossy blue, with tiny flecks of red. A sob catches in her throat.

"You need to understand, little one. Do you understand what it's going to be like?"

I do what people say you should do, when someone is hurt and needs help, so they know they are loved. I sit on the edge of Louisa's bed, on top of her Hello Kitty bedspread. She's the only one of us who has her own bedspread and pillowcases and a selection of fuzzy slippers peeking from beneath the bed. I peel the pink-and-white sheet off her face slowly, just enough so that I can pet that hair, that wonderful riot of hair.

I THINK OF JEN S. LATER, AFTER THE HALL IS QUIET, AFTER she's been taken back to her room to pack, to wait. She'd been screwing Doc Dooley this whole time. Where did they go? Did they use the Care room, did they spread the crinkly paper on the floor? Did they do it on the table or always in the stairwell? Was it cold? What did they talk about? They're both so tall and good-looking, clean-faced and sexy. I picture them pushing at each other and the insides of my thighs get warm. And then Mikey is in my head, his blond dreads soft and never gross-smelling, smiling at me and Ellis from the old lounger in his room, letting us get wild and play music as loud as we wanted. I was never with Mikey, but I would have tried, I mean, I wanted to, so much, but he loved Ellis. The boys I found smelled like burned glass and anger. Dirt streaked their skin, and tattoos, and acne. They lived in garages or cars. I knew those boys would never stick. They were oily; they would slither away after what we did in a dirty back room at a show or in the bathroom of someone's basement at a party.

. Ellis had a boy. He had wolf teeth and a long black coat and he fucked her in her parents' basement on the spongy pink carpet while I listened from across the room, cocooned in a sleeping bag. He left her things: silver bracelets, filmy stockings, Russian nesting dolls filled with round blue pills. When he didn't call, she cried until her throat was raw. When she mentioned his name, Mikey would look away, and you could see his jaw get tight, his face darken.

Thinking about bodies fitting together makes me sad and hungry for something. I roll over and press my face into the pillow, try to make my mind go blank, ignore the itching of my scars. Louisa sighs restlessly in her sleep.

I don't want to believe she's right.

JEN'S MOTHER IS DOUGH-PLUMP, WITH ROUND CHEEKS AND pinched lips. Her dad is a fatty, the zipper of his coach's jacket straining across his belly. Her parents stand in the hallway, watching us apprehensively. In a little while, Nurse Vinnie herds us into Rec and locks the door. We won't be allowed to say goodbye to Jen. The girls flit about the room, pulling cards and games from the bin, setting up with Vinnie at the round table. Blue stands at the window. Her dirty-blond hair is tied in a messy knot today; the tattoo of a swallow gleams faintly on the back of her neck. After a little while, she murmurs, "There she goes."

We rush to the window. In the parking lot, Jen's father heaves two green suitcases into the trunk of a black Subaru. The day is gray and cold-looking. He tucks himself in the driver's seat, the whole car sinking down with the weight of him. Jen towers over her mother like a bendable straw. Her mother pats her once on the arm and opens the rear door, leaving Jen to fold herself into the front, next to her father.

She never once looks up at us.

The car melts into traffic, disappearing down the long block of cafés and bars, Middle Eastern trinket shops, and the place where they sell twenty-two kinds of hot dogs. Mikey worked there one summer; his skin radiated relish and sauerkraut.

The sky is pulpy with dark clouds. There have been a lot of storms lately, unusual for April. The sound of Blue's voice brings me back. "Poor Bruce," she says softly, pointing out the window.

Barbero is standing in a corner of the parking lot. He's not wearing scrubs today: he's wearing a light blue hoodie and collared shirt, jeans and white sneakers, just like any other guy on the street.

"Oh," I say. Then, *"Oh."*

He liked Jen. His name is *Bruce.*

He's got little wire-frame glasses on that make him look not so ... *oafish* ... but kind of ... nice. Blue and I watch as he wipes his eyes, climbs into his own car, a rusty little orange hatchback, and drives away,

"Poor, poor Bruce," Blue murmurs.

Bodies fit together. And sometimes they don't.

ISIS FINGERS THE SCRABBLE TILES. HER NAILS ARE BITTEN down even farther than mine. Her tongue works at the corner of her mouth.

"Almost ready, Chuck." She yanks a tile from the board. "Almost."

I fiddle with my tie-dyed T-shirt and flowery hippie skirt. Mikey's mom did come by with a box of Tanya's old clothes, left over from her Deadhead phase: tie-dyed shirts and flimsy, whispery skirts, hemp sandals and grandma shawls. There were some old sweaters, though, too, and I'm wearing the best one: blue argyle cardigan with silver buttons in the shape of acorns. I didn't get to talk to Mikey's mom. If you aren't on a visitor list, you can't get in, and I don't have a visitor list, since I broke the rules. I don't know who would come, anyway, except for Mikey, but that's weeks away. Casper promised she'd put him on my list. Otherwise I know there's just one name on it: my mother. But I don't expect her to come, and Casper doesn't mention it.

When the phone in Rec rings, everyone looks around for Barbero. The phone only rings up here after a caller has been approved downstairs against a master list. Callers have to be checked against a list approved by your doctor, and only at the doctor's discretion.

Still, we aren't supposed to answer the phone by ourselves. "He must have gone to the shitter," Blue says, shrugging.

The phone keeps ringing. Francie nudges Sasha. "Get it."

"*You* get it." Sasha resumes Connect 4. No one likes to play with her; she cheats.

Blue heaves herself up from the couch. "Wimpy Bloody Cupcakes," she says to us. That's what she calls us, every once in a while: Bloody Cupcakes. *We could all be so cute, don't you think,* she said one day in Group. *If we didn't look like fucking zombies!* She raised her arms. Her scars made her look like a rag doll horribly resewn.

"Crazy Hut. Who is calling, please?" She twists the phone cord in her fingers.

She drops the phone so that it hits the wall, *ka-thunk,* and dangles, helpless, on its white cord. "It's your mother, Silent Sue." She returns to her paperback, wedging herself into the stiff green couch.

I stop breathing. Isis is pushing tiles and muttering under her breath. Francie is busy watching a movie.

My mother. Why would she call? She hasn't even come to see me.

Slowly, I walk to the phone. I press the receiver to my ear and turn away from the girls, to the wall, my heart beating like fucking crazy in my chest. "Mom?" I whisper, hopeful.

The breathing is thick, raspy. "Noooo, Charlie. Guess!" The voice threads through my body.

Evan.

"I pretended to be your mom! Her name was in some stuff in your backpack." He pauses, giggling, and suddenly switches to a honeyed, high-pitched voice. "Hello, I need to speak with my daughter, please, Miss Charlotte Davis."

I don't say anything. I don't know if I'm relieved or disappointed.

"We had to take your money, Charlie." He coughs, a splatter of mucus. "You know how it is."

The empty film canisters in my backpack, the one he and Dump dropped off. The canisters I kept what little money I could scrounge in.

Evan is asthmatic and the drugs and the street do nothing for him. I've watched him curl up into a ball, wheezing until his face is purple, pissing his pants from the effort to not pass out. The free clinic only gives inhalers with medical exams and they won't look at you if you're high and Evan's life is about being high. He's from Atlanta. I don't know how he got all the way up here.

I keep close to the wall so the girls can't hear me. Hearing Evan's voice is taking me back to a dark place. I try to breathe evenly to keep in the moment, like Casper says.

Carefully, I say, "I know."

I say, "It's okay."

I say, "Thanks for bringing my backpack."

He coughs again. "You were pretty messed up in the attic, you know? I thought me and Dump was gonna shit our pants. All that, like, blood."

I say, "Yeah."

He's so quiet that I almost don't hear him. "Was it Fucking Frank? Did he . . . did he finally come after you? Is that why you did it?"

I scrape the wall with what little nails I have left. Fucking Frank and his black eyes and those rings. Seed House and the red door where girls disappeared. He had boxes of sugary cereal on the shelves, and beer and soda in the fridge, and drugs in special locked boxes. He had filthy skin but teeth that gleamed like pearls.

The men who came to Seed House for the room with the red door, they had hungry eyes, eyes with teeth that moved over you, testing, tasting. That's why I hid in the attic for so long. Like a mouse, trying not to breathe so no one would notice me.

I say, "No. No, he didn't get me."

Evan sighs, relieved. "Yeah, okay, that's good, yeah."

"Evan," I say.

"Yeah?"

"But he's part of *why* I did it. You know? Like, the straw and the camel. Everything. Do you understand?"

Evan is quiet. Then he says, "Yeah."

I wonder where he's calling from—skinny Evan with his bad lungs and ripped pants, the funny houndstooth sport coat.

I ask him how he found me.

He tells me this is the place they send all the nutty girls. He tells me, "Dump and me found a ride to Portland."

The night they saved me in the underpass, Dump broke a bottle over the man's head. It happened lightning quick. I saw a boy's terrified eyes appear over the man's shoulder and then the bottle in the air, gleaming against the yellowy lights. I picked slivers of glass out of my hair for days afterward.

Dump was mesmerized by the glass that glittered in the palms of his hands. He looked at me and his smile was a deep, curling cut. Bloody splinters of glass sparkled on the tips of his black boots.

The man who messed with me was at the bottom of the underpass, a lump of motionless, dark clothing. Evan wrapped me in his coat.

Evan tells me, "I just wanted to make sure you were okay and shit, you know?"

They said, *Holy fucking shit.* They said, *We've got to get the fuck out of here.* They said, *You crazy fucking bitch, you can't be out here by yourself.*

"You were cool and all, for a wacko." Laughter and coughing.

They walk-dragged me to a van and hauled me into the back. The seats had been taken out; the flooring was damp and there were patches of dirty carpet thrown over rust holes. Evan and Dump were keyed up, eyes popping, hands shaking. *Did we fucking kill that dude?*

I stayed with them for seven months.

Evan will die on the street, somewhere, someday. I have seen what he will do for a high. I have seen the sadness on his face when he thinks no one is looking.

"So, yeah, also, I wanted to tell you, and, like, I'm sorry and all, but I took your drawings." Evan clears his throat. "You know, that comic book you made. I don't know, I just like it. It's cool, you know, like, seeing *me* in there. Like I'm famous or something. I read a little every day."

My sketchbook, *he* has my sketchbook. Dump would say, *Make sure you give me a cool superpower, like X-ray vision or something, okay? I wanna see through chicks' clothes.*

My heartbeat picks up. "Evan, I need that back. Evan, please?"

He coughs and gets quiet. "I'll try, you know, see if we can get over there, but I don't know, we're leaving kinda soon. It's like, I just really like that book. I don't know. Makes me feel like I *exist,* seeing me in there."

Evan, I say, but only in my head.

"You get out, you come up to Portland, okay? Like, head to the waterfront and ask around for me. We do good together."

I say, "Sure thing, Evan."

"Later, gator." The phone goes dead.

Isis is nibbling at a new tile. I fold my hands in my lap. These are my hands. They have taken food from Dumpsters. They have fought over sleeping spaces and dirty blankets. They have had a whole other life than this one here, playing games in a warm room, as the night keeps moving far from me, outside the window.

Isis says, "How's your ma? That musta been weird, huh?"

She has spelled *ball*. It took her ten minutes to spell *ball*.

I tuck my hands under my thighs and bear down on them. The pressure against my bones feels good. He has my book, but I have food, and a bed.

"She's excellent." My voice is mild and uncomplicated. "Going on vacation. To Portland."

WHEN I TOLD CASPER IT FELT UGLY, DO YOU KNOW WHAT SHE said? She said, *Does IT feel ugly or do YOU feel ugly, Charlie? Because there is a difference, and I want you to think about what that difference might be. It will be integral to your healing.*

They really fucking ask a lot of you in this place.

IN GROUP, CASPER ASKS US, WHO ARE OUR FRIENDS? DO WE have a community? Is there someone we can talk to, who makes us feel safe, on the outside?

She asks, *Who keeps your secrets?*

YOU KNOW, I KNOW WHO I AM. I MEAN, I DON'T *KNOW* KNOW, because I'm only seventeen, but I know, like, who I *am* when I'm with people, or when they're looking at me, and putting me into a slot in their mind. If you have one of your class photographs, I bet you can find me. It won't be hard. Who's the girl who's not smiling? Who, even if she's between two other kids, kind of still looks like she's standing alone, because they're standing a little apart from her? Are her clothes kind of ... plain? Dirty? Loose? Kind of *nothing*. Do you even remember her name? You can spot the girls who will have it easy. I don't even have to describe them for you. You can spot the girls who will get by on smarts. You can spot the girls who will get by because they're tough, or athletic. And then there's me, that one, that disheveled kid (say it, *poor*) who never gets anything right, and sits alone in the cafeteria, and draws all the time, or gets shoved in the hallway, and called names, because that's her slot, and sometimes she gets mad, and punches, because what else is there? So when Casper says, *Who keeps your secrets?* I think, *Nobody*. Nobody until Ellis. She was my one and only chance and she chose *me*. You don't know what that feels like, probably, because you're used to having friends. You probably have a mom and a dad, or at least one who's not dead, and they don't hit you. Nobody moves away from *you* in the class picture. So you don't know what it feels like to every day, every fucking day, be so lonely that this black hole inside is going to swallow you down, until the one day this person, this really beautiful person? comes to your school and she just seems to not *care* that everyone is staring at her in her black velvet dress, her fishnets, her big black boots, wild purple hair, and red, red mouth. She comes to the door of the cafeteria on the first day and she doesn't even get in line for a tray, she just looks around the whole fucking zoo of second lunch period and suddenly she's walking toward you, that big red mouth smiling, her enormous black backpack swinging down on the table, and she's digging out Pixy Stix and Candy Buttons and sliding them to you, *you* (your pencil frozen in the air over your sketchbook because this could be a joke, some elaborate plan by the jocks, but *no*), and she's saying, "Christ on a crutch, you are the only fucking normal person *in* this hellhole. I'm dying to get high. Wanna come over after school and get high? God, I like your hair. And your T-shirt. Did you get that here or online? *What* are you drawing, that's fucking *angelic*." That's what she called things she loved: angelic. *This pot is positively angelic. Charlie, this band is angelic.* And it was like the world was coated in gold from that moment on. It sparkled. I mean it was shit, still, but it was better shit, do you understand? And I learned secrets. I learned that underneath her heavy white makeup was a quilt of acne, and she cried about it. She showed me the bags of junk food in her closet and she showed me how she'd throw up after eating too much. She told me her father had had an affair with her aunt and that's why they moved and that her parents were *working on it.* And her name wasn't really Ellis, it was Eleanor, but she decided to try something new when she moved, but oh God, don't say it in front of her mother, because her grandmother's name was Eleanor and she had recently died, and her mother would have a *fit,* an absolute *fit,* and Oh, wow, Charlie, your arms. Did you do that? It's kind of beautiful. It makes me a little scared, but it's kind of beautiful. I met this guy named

Mikey yesterday at Hymie's. The record store. You ever been there? Of *course* you have, look at you. He invited us over. You wanna go? He's got, like, these *angelic* blue eyes.

And in her room, with the wild blue walls and so many posters and solar system ceiling, I could tell her anything, and I did. *Charlie, Charlie, you're so beautiful, so fucking angelic.* Her hand in mine. She wore white flannel pajamas with black skulls on them.

And that was that. My secret keeper.

I DID HAVE THIS TEACHER ONCE, IN THE FOURTH GRADE. SHE was totally nice, even to the bullies in class. She never yelled. She just let me be, really, she never made me go out to recess if I didn't want to go, or to gym. She'd let me stay in the classroom and draw while she worked on grading or looked out the big square windows. Once, she said, "Charlotte, I know things are so hard right now, but they'll get better. Sometimes it takes a while to find that special friend, but you will. Oh, gosh, I don't think I had a really good-good friend until I was in high school." She fingered the little gold heart on a chain around her neck.

She was right. I did find my special friend. But nobody told me she was going to fucking kill herself.

EVERY NIGHT, LOUISA SCRIBBLES AWAY IN ONE OF HER BLACK-and-white composition books. When she's done, she caps the pen, closes the book, and bends over the side of the bed so that her hair tumbles over like a waterfall and I can see her neck, unscarred and pale, faintly dusted with down. She slides the book underneath the bed, says good night, and pulls the bed-spread across her face. Tonight I wait until I hear her breathing flatten into sleep before I creep out of my bed and sink to my knees on the floor.

I peek under the edge of her bedspread. Underneath her bed are dozens and dozens of those composition books, all her secrets piled neatly into black-and-white rows.

I SHOULD MAKE A *CORRECTION.* I DON'T WANT TO BE *MIS*-leading. I say that Ellis killed herself, but she did not *die* die. She isn't in the ground, I can't visit a graveyard and drop daisies over well-tended grass or mark an anniversary on a calendar. There were *drugs,* there was the *wolf boy,* and she slid very far from me, the wolf taking up all of her heart, he was that greedy. And when the wolf was done, he licked his paws, he left her *gaunt,* my Ellis, my *plump* and *glowing* friend, he took all her light. And then, I guess, she tried to be like me. She tried to drain herself, make herself smaller, only she *messed up.* Like Mikey said, cutting wasn't her *thing.* I imagine her room *soaked* in blood, *rivers* of it, her parents fighting *upstream* to get to her. But there was *too much,* do you *understand*? A *person* can only *lose* so much *blood,* you can only *starve* the brain of *oxygen* for so long, or you can suffer *anoxic brain injury after hemorrhagic shock,* which emptied out my *friend* and left only her *body.* Her parents *sent her* somewhere, a place like where I am, but far, far away, across whole states, and *tucked* her into her new home full of *soft sheets* and *plodding, daily walks* and *drooling.* No more hair dye, no more fucking, no more drugs, no more iPod, no more clompy boots, no more fishnets, no more purging, no more heartbreak, no more *me,* for Ellis. Only *days* of *nothing-ness,* of Velcroed pants and *diapers.* And so I *can't can't can't* do what I am supposed to do: *touch* her, make it *better,* brush the wild hair from her face, whisper *sorrysorrysorrysorrysorrysorry.*

I HAVE TO DO SOMETHING OR I WILL EXPLODE.

Talking to Evan, finding Mikey, waiting for him to come visit me, thinking of Ellis, I miss miss miss so *much.*

I find them all in Crafts, bent over the long plastic tables, Miss Joni walking around, murmuring in her deep, warm voice. Miss Joni wears purple turbans and lumberjack shirts. When I came to Crafts the first time and just sat, doing nothing, she only said, "Sitting's all right, too, girlfriend. You just sit as long as you want."

I didn't just sit because I didn't want to paste sparkly stars on colored paper or blend watery paints, I sat because my arms hurt. My arms hurt all the way to my fingertips and they were so heavy in their bandages.

They still hurt. But today when Miss Joni says, "Dr. Stinson and I had a little chat," and slides me a beautiful, blank pad of all-purpose newsprint paper and a brand-new stick of charcoal, I greedily clutch the stick in my fingers. Little sparks of pain shoot up and down my forearm. My scars are still tender and tight and will be for a long, long time, but I don't care. I breathe hard. I work hard. My fingers take care of me. It's been so long, but they know what to do.

I draw her. I draw them. I fill my paper with Ellis and Mikey, Evan and Dump, even DannyBoy. I fill every last piece of paper until I have a whole world of *missing.*

When I look up, everyone is gone except Miss Joni and she's turned the lights on. It's dark outside the window. She's sipping from a Styrofoam cup of coffee and scrolling on her pink phone.

She looks up and smiles. She says, "Better?"

I nod. "Better."

TODAY I'M EXCITED TO MEET WITH CASPER. I WANT TO TELL her about Crafts, and what I drew and what drawing means to me. I think that will make her happy. But when I push open the door, she's not alone. Dr. Helen is with her.

The turtle is hiding inside the sunken ship.

Dr. Helen turns around when I enter the room and says, "Oh, Charlotte, please sit down, here." And she pats the brown chair I always sit in. I look at Casper, but her smile isn't as nice as it usually is. It looks . . . smaller.

Dr. Helen is a lot older than Casper, with lines at the edges of her eyes and rouge that's too dark for her skin.

"Dr. Stinson and I have been reviewing your progress, Charlotte. I'm happy to see you've made some strong strides in such a short time."

I don't know if I'm supposed to answer her, or smile, or what, so I don't say anything. I kind of start pinching my thighs through the flowery skirt, but Casper notices and frowns, so I stop.

"You've been through so much, and at such a young age, I just . . ." And here, weirdly, she stops, and kind of sets her jaw and says, very sharp, to Casper, "Are you not going to help at all with this, Bethany?"

And I'm still absorbing Casper's name, *Bethany Bethany Bethany,* so it takes a while for me to understand what she's telling me.

I say, "What?"

Casper repeats, "You're being discharged."

Dr. Helen talks then, about a special sort of psychiatric hold that allowed me to be treated at the hospital, and about my mother having to meet with a judge and sign papers, because "you were a danger to yourself and others," and insurance, and my Grammy, who I haven't thought of in a very long time. All the words kind of bang around my brain as my heart squeezes into a tinier and tinier thing and I ask about my mom, but it comes out in a stutter. I bite down on my tongue until I get a faint, metallic taste of blood.

Casper says, "Your mother's not working right now, so there isn't any possibility of coverage. As I understand it, some of your stay has been covered by your grandmother, but she's unable to continue due to her own health and financial care issues."

"Did something happen to my grandmother?"

"I don't know," answers Casper.

"You talked to my mother?"

Casper nods.

"Did she . . . did she say anything about me?"

Casper looks at Dr. Helen, who says, "We're working as hard as possible to locate resources for you. In fact, Bethany, how are we doing on the bed at the house on Palace?"

When Casper doesn't answer, Dr. Helen flips through the pile of papers on her lap. "There's a halfway house that may have room for you, possibly as early as next month. They specialize in substance addiction, but that is one of your subsets. You'll need to stay with your mother before then, of course, since you can't stay here. No one wants you back in your previous situation, no one."

Previous situation: meaning, homeless. Meaning, Dumpster diving. Meaning, cold and sick and Fucking Frank and the men who fuck girls.

I look at the turtle. His legs twitch, like he's shrugging at me: *What do you expect me to do? I'm a goddamn turtle trapped in a tank.*

Outside the window, the sky is turning hard and gray. Fucking Frank. A halfway house. I'm being sent back outside.

When I say it, I sound like a little baby, and that makes me even madder. "It's still *cold* outside."

Dr. Helen says, "We'll do everything we can, but is there absolutely no possibility of long-term reconciliation with your mother, even with counseling? She's agreed to house you until a bed opens at the halfway house. That says something to me, that she's trying."

I look at Casper in desperation. I think her eyes are the saddest things I've seen in a long, long time.

Very, very slowly, she shakes her head from side to side. "I don't see any other option, Charlotte. I'm very sorry."

Once my mother hit my ear so hard I heard the howling of trains for a week. I get up and walk to the door.

Casper says, "We're not abandoning you, Charlotte. We've investigated every possible option, there just isn't—"

"No." I open the door. "Thank you. I'm going to my room now."

Casper calls after me, but I don't stop. My ears are a sea of bees. Our rooms are on the fourth floor, Dinnaken Wing. I pass by Louisa and go into the bathroom and stand there for a while. Louisa says my name.

Then I step into our shower and pound my forehead into the wall until the bees die.

When Casper comes running in, she grabs me around the waist and pulls at me to get me to stop. I take her beautiful yellowy baby bird hair in my hands and I yank so hard that she cries out and pushes away. I slide to the floor, warm blood trickling down to my mouth.

I say *sorrysorrysorrysorrysorrysorry.*

Feathery strands of her hair flutter in my hands. I'll never be beautiful or normal like Casper, and just like that, just realizing that, out everything comes, all she ever asked of me.

I tell her: After my father died, my mother curled up into something tight and awful and there was no more music in the house, there was no more touching, she was only a ghost that moved and smoked. If I got in her way, if the school called, if I took money from her purse, if I was just *me*, the yelling started. She yelled for years. When she got tired of yelling, she started hitting.

Casper blots my face with a cloth as I talk. Louisa wrings her hands in the doorway. Girls pile up behind her, pushing, trying to get a look.

I say: She's been hitting me for a long time. I say: I started hitting back.

I say: Please don't make me go back outside. I tell her about the man in the underpass, he broke my tooth and broke me, and it hurts swelling out of me, but I give it to her, all the horrible words in my heart—about Ellis, about Fucking Frank.

I stop. Her eyes are watery. I've given her too much. Two orderlies muscle through the crowd of girls. There are little pinpricks of blood at the roots of Casper's hair, little blips of red amid the yellow. They help her up and she doesn't say anything to me, just limps away.

A TIMELINE

A girl is born.

Her father loves her. Her mother loves her father.

Her father is sad.

Her father drinks and smokes, rocks and cries.

Into the river he goes.

The mother becomes a fist.

The girl is alone.

The girl is not good in the world.

No one likes the girl.

She tries.

But her mouth is mush.

Stupid girl. Angry girl.

Doctors: Give her drugs.

Lazy girl. Girl is mush on drugs.

Mother hits girl. Girl shrinks.

Girl goes quiet. Quiet at home. Quiet at school. Quiet mush
mouse.

Girl listens to radio. Girl finds music. Girl has whole other
    world.

Girl slips on headphones. World gone.

Girl draws and draws and draws. World gone.

Girl finds knife. Girl makes herself small, small, smaller.
    World gone.

Girl must be bad, so girl cuts. Bad girl. World gone.

Girl meets girl. Beautiful Girl! They watch planets move on
    the ceiling.

They save money for Paris. Or London. Or Iceland.
    Wherever.

Girl like-likes a boy, but he loves Beautiful Girl.

Beautiful Girl meets wolf boy. He fills her up, but makes her
    small.

Beautiful Girl is busy all the time.

Girl hits mother back. They are windmills with their hands.
    Girl on street.

Girl stays with Beautiful Girl, but wolf boy leaves drugs.

Beautiful Parents are angry. Beautiful Girl lies and blames
    Girl for the drugs.

Girl on street. Girl goes home.

Beautiful Girl texts and texts *Something wrong Hurts*

Girl slips headphones on. Girl slides phone under pillow.

Beautiful Girl bleeds too much.

Girl gets messed up, too messed up, broken heart, guilt.

Girl breaks mother's nose.

Girl on street.

World gone.

I'M STAYING HERE, BUT I DON'T KNOW FOR HOW LONG. I'VE been released from individual sessions with Casper. My paperwork and discharge dates are being sorted out. They have another emergency stay from a judge while they work out an arrangement with my mother and with the halfway house.

Casper is still kind to me, but there is something else there now, between us, a distance that makes my heart ache. My *sorry*s start up again, but Casper just shakes her head sadly.

Vinnie checks the stitches on my forehead every morning, clucking his tongue. Blue calls me Frankenstein in a horror-movie whisper. I go where I'm supposed to go. At night, I just pretend to do my online classes. I've tried to message Mikey when Barbero is busy or napping, but the only response is an empty white chat box. I watch the Somali office cleaners at night, drifting across the windows in the building next door, pulling their carts of solutions and mops and cloths.

The sky is postcard dreamy now, the clouds less full of rain, the sun a little stronger every day. If I look farther out the window, between the towering, silvery buildings, I can see the endless terrain of the university and, beyond that, the snake-like wind of the river that leads to St. Paul, to Seed House and being hungry and dirty and hurt and used up, again, because I have nowhere else to go.

Sasha is making popcorn. Vinnie has brought in tiny canisters of powdered flavoring: butter, cayenne, Parmesan. He cooked a pan of brownies at home and Francie is helping frost them. The room phone rings. I'm blazing through the channels, one by one, until I hear my name. Vinnie wiggles the phone at me.

I listen to the breathing on the other end before I tentatively say hello.

"Charlie, you didn't put me on the list!" *Mikey.*

I almost drop the phone. I grip the receiver in both hands to keep it from shaking.

"I told you I was coming! You were supposed to put me on a visitors' list or something. I'm only here for one more day. I'm here for the show later tonight and then we go in the morning."

"I did put you on the list!" My mind races frantically. Did Casper forget? Or did they just take him off since I'm going to be leaving? "Where are you? I need you. They—"

"Hang up, Charlie. Is there a window? I'm in the parking lot out front!"

I hang up and run to the window and press my face to the glass. A shock of orange catches my eye. He's standing in the parking lot, waving an orange traffic cone in the air. When he sees me, he lets the cone fall.

Mikey looks the same somehow. He looks open and worried. And safe.

There's a light rain, droplets glistening on his dreadlocks. He looks bulkier, though he's still small. He holds out his hands, as if to say, *What happened?*

The glass is cold on my forehead. Vinnie is playing Go Fish with Sasha and Francie in the corner. Blue is on the couch, humming to herself.

My face is swimming with tears as I watch him in the falling rain, his mouth open, his cheeks red.

Vinnie says pointedly, *"Charlie."* Blue stirs on the couch. She joins me at the window.

"A boy." Blue's breath makes a foggy circle on the glass. "A real live boy."

Sasha and Francie throw down their cards.

The first time Ellis brought me back to her house in the fall of ninth grade, after we'd known each for about a week, she didn't blink an eye to find an older boy already there, in the basement, reading comics with one hand and stuffing the other in a bag of salty pretzels. There were anarchy symbols Magic Markered on his sneakers. He looked up at Ellis, his mouth full of pretzels, and smiled. "Your mom let me in. Who's this?"

He was wearing a Black Flag T-shirt. Before I could stop myself, I said, "Are you having a nervous breakdown."

He put the comic book down. "My head *does* really hurt." He waited, his eyes gleaming.

Surprising myself, I started yelling the lyrics to him, startling Ellis at the bar. She glared at me.

Mikey and I sang the rest of the song while Ellis rifled through her parents' mini-fridge. She was a little miffed, you could tell. She didn't like that sort of music. She liked goth and mopey stuff, like Bauhaus and Velvet Underground. Nobody else at our school could recite the lyrics to "Nervous Breakdown," I was sure of that.

But she shouldn't have worried. Mikey always loved her more.

"Oh," Sasha and Francie say in unison as they gather at the window.

I push up the sleeves of my sweater and press my arms to the window. Can he see my scars, all the way down there?

Mikey covers his face with his hands. I remember that gesture. He used to do that, a lot, when Ellis and I did things that overwhelmed him. "You *guys*," he would say tiredly, "stop, already."

Vinnie stands next to Blue and groans deeply. "Shit."

"Girls," he grunts. "Goddamn girls and boys." He raps on the glass roughly, making Sasha jump back.

"Go!" He shouts to Mikey through the glass. To himself, he mutters, "Don't make me call anyone, son."

He turns to me. "You! Put down your damn arms."

"It's like that movie!" Francie exclaims. I'm waiting for Mikey to take his hands away from his face. His T-shirt is soaked from the rain.

Sasha starts to cry. "No one's ever come to see me," she wails. Vinnie mutters "Shit" again as he punches the buttons of his pager. Blue's fingers are on my shoulder.

"Shut the fuck up." Francie is getting agitated. "Nobody ever comes to freaking see *me*, either." She picks at her chin with her fingernails, drawing tiny specks of blood.

Blue says, quietly, "Look."

Mikey has opened his messenger bag and is furiously scrawling with marker back and forth on a notebook pressed against his knees. He holds it up. I squint through the glass, through the rain.

DON'T.

He drops the paper. It flutters and flattens on the wet ground, settling near his sneaker. He rips another page from the notebook.

YOU.

Nurse Vinnie raps his pager against the window as Sasha's wailing grows.

Francie tells her, "Shut *up*." Gives her a pinch that only increases the wailing.

"I have a situation here." Vinnie is at the phone.

Mikey struggles with the next piece of paper; it's stuck in the notebook's rings. Two hospital orderlies amble across the parking lot. They shout to Mikey; his head shoots up at the same time the paper rips free and is caught in a pocket of wind. Running after it, he slips in a puddle and crashes down. Blue sucks in her breath. We look at each other. Her eyes are glittering.

"Outstanding," she whispers. "Absolutely outstanding." She twines her fingers through mine against the glass.

Blue says, "That's *utter* devotion, Silent Sue. You know that, don't you?"

The men, college boys, really, weekend workers with well-sculpted arms and clipped hair, slip their hands under Mikey's armpits and haul him up. He struggles with them, the soles of his sneakers slipping in the puddle. He's crying messy, ashamed boy tears. They set him down, faces changing from annoyance to curiosity. It's odd to see him, smallish with his crazy dreads and thrift store clothes, next to the two orderlies fairly bursting from their blinding white uniforms. They're all almost the same age; they're all light-years apart.

"You pieces of shit!" Nurse Vinnie yells. "You fucking pieces of shit. Don't you do it, don't you let him goddamn do it!"

The orderlies shrug at Vinnie, furious behind our fourth-floor window.

Mikey holds up the soggy paper.

DIE.

Don't you die. The ink bleeds in the rain.

Sasha bangs her head dully on the glass. Vinnie pulls her

away, patting her arms tenderly, as close as he dares to get. Nurse Ava, who will hold anyone, who isn't careful about rules, has come into the room and lets Francie lean into her, her sobs muffled against Ava's white shirt. Blue and I watch as the college boys brush rain from their bare arms, jerk their chins at Mikey. Next to them, he looks seventeen again. But he is twenty-one now, and he's come all this way to see me. I want to crash through the window, fly down to the parking lot, and let him hold me. *Utter devotion*, Blue said. Maybe Mikey could love me now, if it could be just us.

My body surges with hope.

He wipes his face, slides the wet notebook back into the messenger bag. He raises his hand to me.

Bye.

The boys give him a shove to get him on his way. He scuffles down the wet sidewalk and disappears.

EVERYTHING IS HAPPENING FAST.

I stare at the computer. I'm on the page for my online class, though I have no intention of doing any work. I'm leaving in the morning, going home with my mother. There won't be a bed at the halfway house for weeks.

Ellis pursed her mouth at Mikey and me after we sang the Black Flag song. She turned away from us and dropped a record on the turntable. Like me, she had a record player and actual records, lots of them, not the usual jumble of CDs or an overloaded iPod or phone like other kids. There were blues albums framed on the walls and big posters of the Velvet Underground and the Doors. A ratty, stained suede couch slumped against the wood paneling; the bar was a fake-brick wall with three tall stools and humming refrigerator. The basement ceiling was low, the air damp and musty. I liked it, this cramped and comfortable space. It had an air of easiness to it, unlike my mother's apartment, which she kept dark, magazines and full ashtrays everywhere. Ellis set three cans of beer on the bar top.

I wondered why she'd picked me to be her friend: me with my haphazardly cut red-and-black hair, my holey cardigans and ripped jeans hiding the stuff Ellis didn't know about yet. I was used to walking the edges of school, ignoring the nasty words scrawled on my locker, gritting my teeth at shoves in the bathroom, but she found me, somehow, this creature of velvet dresses and striped tights and Frankenstein boots, white-powdered face and deep purple lipstick. I watched the older boy watch Ellis. There was an intensity to his face that both interested and disappointed me.

Ellis took a bearlike gulp of her beer, wiped her mouth, and shook her head, her newly jet-black hair bobbing against her powdery cheeks. "Mikey lives down the street but he goes to some loopy liberal charter school."

The insistent bounce of the Smiths, the clever, driving sound of Johnny Marr's guitar that I could not resist, despite preferring music that throttled my brain and stormed through my heart, and heaved itself into my body. The older boy, Mikey, got up, tossing his comic to the side, grabbing Ellis's hand. They pogoed up and down, singing to "Is It Really So Strange?" in unison.

They held out their hands to me, Ellis's face flushed and giddy.

On the way to her house that afternoon, she'd said, "The only way I get through the stupid day is knowing I can go home and get trashed at the end of it."

The beer was cartwheeling hotly in my stomach; the poppy music burrowed in my skin. The basement smelled of old wood paneling and stale popcorn and dirty pink shag rug. For years no one had wanted me. For years I'd been pushed around, yelled at, made fun of, and now, now I had two beautiful people who'd picked me. *Me.*

I let them pull me in.

At the computer, I shake my head to clear my thoughts. Fuck this. What could they possibly do to me now, at this point? I look back at Barbero, who shrugs and looks down at his iPod. He hasn't been the same since Jen S. left. I log into the email and open the chat box, my heart beating fast. *Please be there, please.*

A little blip and *Michael is typing*, and then:

Sorry I lost it at the hospital. Don't want you to end up like E. Leaving tomorrow morning for a three week run of shows. I'll try to call u again at the hospital.

My mother's dank apartment on Edgcumbe, the second floor of a leaning house with broken siding and a can on the balcony filled with butts and tabs. I don't have any other choice. I have to take a chance.

Mikey, I type. *Please save me.*

I DREAM OF FLIES, SWARMS OF THEM LIGHTING ON ME, BITING at my clothes. Flies are the demons of people who live on the outside. They peck at you, crawl over your stink, feed on you, make you sick. I wake up, swatting blindly, and hear, "Stop."

It's Blue, kneeling next to my bed, pushing my swinging hands out of the way. Her hair falls against her face. "Listen. I need to tell you something."

She tells me, "I did get away from my dad, once. Made it all the way to Indiana, of all places. Fucking Indiana."

She tells me she was flipped on crack and working at an A&P. She says, *My whole body was electric, like all I could think about was getting out of there, going back to my shit apartment and cutting and how much better I would feel, how I'd be able to forget this piece of shit job.*

She worked faster and faster, trying to get all the cereal boxes on the shelves, organized and price-stamped. She was sweating, using her purple smock to wipe her face, when she started to hear laughter.

"Like, the store itself was laughing at me. The cereal boxes, the price-stamper, the fucking loading cart, the lights. The things *in* the grocery store were laughing at my stupid ass. Like, now even *inanimate* objects knew what a fucked-up asshole I was." Her face is splotchy and her eyes are wet. "And I knew then, right then, that I was going to go home and kill myself. And. Here. I. Am."

From the other bed, I can hear Louisa breathing. She's awake, listening.

Blue pins those wet eyes on me and takes a deep breath. "The moral of the story, Charlie, is this: Don't let the cereal eat you. It's only a fucking box of cereal, but it will eat you alive if you let it."

CASPER SAYS, "IT MAKES ME VERY UNCOMFORTABLE, YOU LEAV-
ing with your kit. Even if it's empty."

I'm sitting on the edge of the bed. My backpack, with the
empty tender kit inside, rests at my feet. Louisa gave me her
suitcase, a square, tough old-fashioned thing she's covered with
stenciled skulls and roses. She shrugged. "This is my last stop
for a while, anyway."

Her smile was thin, and worried me, but she just stroked the
tips of her hair. She stepped forward and gave me a feathery
kiss on the cheek. She whispered, "I wish you'd stayed longer.
I had so much to tell you. I just know you would have understood."

They returned everything to me. It's all tucked in the suitcase: my Land Camera, my socks, my bag of charcoals and
pencils. Miss Joni gave me a brand-new sketchbook, too, a
super-nice one, which she must have bought with her own
money, and which made me feel a little guilty.

Casper is perched across from me on a folding chair borrowed from Rec. Doctors are not allowed to sit on the beds of
patients.

Her enormous blue eyes are kind. I still feel so bad about
what I did to her.

She raises her hands and traces the shape of my body in the
air. When her fingers reach my boots, she says:

"You own all of yourself, Charlie. Every last bit." She pauses.
"You understand what's going to happen, yes?"

I swallow hard. "I'm going back to live with my mother."

Casper has given me a piece of paper with the numbers for the halfway house, a support group, a hotline number, her email address. This paper is tucked at the bottom of my backpack.

"No drugs, no drinking, no silence. You have to work hard, Charlotte, to stay ahead of your old habits. Old things, old habits are comfortable, even when we know they'll cause us pain. You are going out into the unknown."

I pull the backpack up on my lap and hug it close. I can't look at Casper. I concentrate on the slippery quality of the backpack's fabric. *Mamamamamama.*

Casper says, "Cool moss," and smiles at me. I don't say anything.

She tries again. "You look like a farmer, Charlotte. A very disturbed, balding farmer."

I look down at Mikey's sister's overalls, the Dead T-shirt, the ratty peacoat his mother put in the box. I wiggle my feet in my boots. I missed my boots, the heavy, definite feel of them. When Vinnie brought them to me, I held them close for a long time.

We don't say anything in the hallway as we pass the closed Rec door. I can hear them murmuring inside. Like with Jen, they're not allowed to say goodbye to me. As the elevator descends, the heat in my stomach builds into an enormous ball. My words start slipping away again. The doors slide open.

She's at the desk, holding a sheaf of papers and an envelope. She's all gray: gray zippered jacket, gray jeans with a hole in one knee, gray sneakers, gray knit hat.

The only color on my mother is her hair.

It's still like fire, a deep red that she's wrangled into a slippery ponytail.

My own hair is dark blond tucked under Mikey's sister's red wool cap, just the slimmest bit of it since I cut my dyed black nest of street hair off.

My mother doesn't smile, but I didn't really expect her to. Just for a minute, though, I see something, some wave of *some thing*, flit across her eyes.

Then it's gone.

Inside my pockets, my hands tremble. I close them into fists, tight as I can make them. I haven't seen her in almost a year.

Casper is all business, striding to my mother. "Thank you for coming, Misty." She looks back and motions me forward. "Charlie, it's time."

The closer I get, the less I feel myself. I am slipping away— there it is again, what Casper says is *dissociation*. If only my mother would smile, or touch me, or something.

She looks at me for only a minute, before she turns to Casper. "It's good to finally meet you. Thanks for everything. With Charlotte, and all."

"You're welcome. Charlie, take care."

Casper doesn't smile, she doesn't frown, she just touches my arm, and then gives me the smallest push before turning back to the elevators.

My mother begins walking to the bay doors of the hospital, ponytail limp against her jacket. Without looking back, she says, "You coming?"

Outside, the sky is a quilt of puffy clouds. My mother's cheap sneakers squeak on the sidewalk. "I don't have a car right now," she says into her chest, lighting a cigarette as she walks. I wonder how she got to the hospital, if someone dropped her off. She's always hated the bus.

It's warm out; the tip of her nose is shiny. I can tell already that the peacoat is going to be too hot. As we come to the corner, I look back, and there they are behind the window of the fourth floor, assembled like dolls, watching me, Blue's hands against the glass.

My mother rounds the corner.

I have to run to catch up with her. I start to say what Casper and I rehearsed. I try to make it sound believable, because I know what the alternative is. "I'm going to follow rules, Ma. Whatever you want. Get a job and stuff, okay?"

She stops so abruptly I crash into her shoulder. I'm almost as tall as she is now, which isn't saying much. We're both small.

She holds out the envelope. "Here, this is your stuff, bus ticket, birth certificate, all that shit."

I don't understand. "What?"

I don't take the envelope, so she grabs my hand and curls my fingers around the edges. "This is as far as I go, Charlotte. You've got everything you need in there, okay?"

"I thought . . . I thought I was going home. With you."

As she smokes, I see how dry her hands are, how chapped. She takes a last pull from her cigarette, crushes it under her sneakers.

I sneak a look at her, at the slight bump on the bridge of her nose. The nose I broke with a pan. Her mouth wobbles as she watches the cars slip past in the street. She won't look at me and I can't look at her for too long.

There is so much broken between us. My eyes blur.

"Your friend Mike came by late last night. We all know it's not gonna work out, you with me, or you in some freaking teen halfway house. That's not you, Charlotte. I don't know what *is* you, but *I'm* not it, and I'm pretty sure some curfewed house isn't it. Mike's mom bought you a bus ticket to Arizona. You'll stay in his apartment down there. He says he'll help you."

She roots for another cigarette in her pocket. "He left a letter for you. You'll be alone for a little bit, until he gets back from his trip. I guess he roadies for some band? Mike's the good kind, Charlotte. Try not to fuck anything up."

So Mikey did do something after he got my message. I'm not going to live with my mother. I'm getting on a goddamn bus. To the goddamn desert. Far, far away from Fucking Frank, from the goddamn river, from all of this.

I'm so happy and so scared and so confused I don't know what to do.

Slowly, my hands trembling, I open the envelope and rifle through the bus ticket, my old ID, my birth certificate. There's a folded-up letter—that must be from Mikey—and something that makes my heart jump.

A rubber-banded stack of cash wrapped in Saran wrap. I stare at the cash, gradually realizing what it is. "How . . . how did you get this?"

My mother inhales deeply on her cigarette. "Eleanor's mother found it a while ago. They're selling the house and moving out west. To be closer to her. She's in Idaho, you know."

Paris, London, Iceland. Just, anywhere. Ellis and I mowed people's lawns, we helped Mrs. Hampl over on Sherburne clean out her garage. That was hard and took a long time. She was some sort of writer and had all kinds of files with news clippings and old magazines. We tried anything to earn money.

"Judy thought you should have it."

I slide it into the pocket of the peacoat and quickly swipe at my eyes. I don't want her to see me cry.

Something catches in my throat—*sorrysorrysorrysorryImiss*

you—but it stays there, tucked and quiet. My mother says, "I have to go now, Charlotte. I have to be somewhere."

She starts to walk away but turns suddenly, wrapping her arms around me so tight I can't breathe and so tight I see red rings around the puffy clouds, and then she presses her mouth against my ear.

She whispers, "Don't you think this isn't freaking breaking my heart."

Then she's gone, and my body grows cold, cold, as I stand there, on the corner of Riverside and Twenty-Second, the emptiness of the world so large, and so small, all at once. The Greyhound station is a long walk. I don't even know what time it is.

I stare down at the ticket. Departure: Minneapolis, Minnesota, Arrival: Tucson, Arizona. I flip through the rest of it, the names of the cities we'll stop in blurring in front of my eyes. The desert. When I asked Mikey to save me, he didn't say anything for a while, then he finally typed, *On it,* and logged off.

I'm going to the desert. I'm going to ride a bus alone across God-knows-how-many-states to be with Mikey when I've never been anywhere my entire life. And how am I supposed to get to the bus station? What time is it? I look back at the hospital and wonder if I should go back in, but then realize I can't. They think I left with my mother. And what am I going to do when I get there? How long will Mikey be gone? How long will I be alone down there?

Things are moving too quickly and I can't breathe. I'm too hot in the peacoat.

"Need a ride, tough girl?"

I turn, the white van with the hospital logo idling next to me. Vinnie throws his cigarette out the window. "Get in."

In the van, he says, "All I know is, right now I'm on my way to pick up some anorexics on Day Pass at Mall of America, got it? I am not transporting a minor, away from her legal guardian, to an undisclosed location." He guns the van. "Buckle up! I don't need any dead girls in this piece of crap. Where we headed?"

I tell him. We don't say anything until we get to the Greyhound station. There are a few people inside, surrounded by suitcases and boxes, paper bags and plastic sacks. He fishes in the pocket of his black coat and pushes some bills into my hand.

"I don't ever wanna see you here again, Charlie-girl."

I nod, my eyes blurring with tears.

"Everything and everybody that's busted can be fixed. That's what I think." He glances at the bus station. "Now, you go in there, girlfriend, and when you get on that bus, you sit in the goddamn front, not the back. The back is badsville. Stay away. Don't take nobody's cigarettes if they offer, don't take a drink unless it's from a machine. You stay like this. Tight." He hugs himself. "And when you get to where you going, it's gonna be sunshine and sunny days forever, yeah? Don't ask me how I know, but I do. I got my ways of knowing things about you girls. Now, go." He reaches across me and nudges the door open.

He smells like strawberry Swisher Sweets and warmed milk, like the streets and like a home.

I breathe him in deeply, in case he is the last kind thing I will know for days, and then I get out of the van, dragging Louisa's suitcase and my backpack behind me.

TWO

I could be a girl, a real girl

THE BUS IS A GIANT, LUMBERING MONSTER FILLED WITH SAD-ness and stale air. In each town, it shits us out for twenty min-utes, two hours, three, it doesn't matter, it's all the same: a diner, a convenience store, trash in the restrooms, trash in the gutters. I hide the money Vinnie gave me deep in my pockets and use it only for chocolate bars and sodas and salty chips and once an egg salad sandwich with the expiration date blacked out. The taste of chocolate in my mouth is like an explosion of bliss.

I don't talk to the people who sit next to me. They drift in, smelling like smoke or dirt, and then drift off at the next stop. In Kansas the bus breaks down in the middle of the night in a town where Christmas is still happening in mid-May: faded wreaths on darkened storefronts, fat lights twinkling in the window of a gas station. The woman next to me drops her chin inside the thick shell of her fake fur coat and mumbles *Blessed be* as we lurch off the bus and stand awkwardly in the lot of a boarded-up diner. The men in the back of the bus simply move their shell game outside to an alley while the driver paces and waits for help. I sit on a curb away from everyone else, still too warm in the peacoat. My ticket says we'll drive through six states before we reach Arizona and that it will take one day, twenty-one hours, and forty-five minutes. The driver says he doesn't know how long until a new bus comes.

I cry in toilet stalls, warm tears spilling into the neck of the peacoat, staring at the money Ellis and I earned. I'm finally going someplace, maybe someplace better, but she isn't with me, and it hurts. *Everything* hurts me again, sharp and scary against my scary skin. I just keep trying to think of Mikey, and how good it will be to be with him, and maybe, this time, a little more than just friends.

It's the middle of the night when we arrive. The driver's sudden, cheerful shout of *Toooooo—suuuun* fills the bus and jolts several people awake. I join the sleepy line of people stumbling off the bus and into the warm, murky air.

A couple of passengers have people waiting for them and I watch them hug and kiss. I've got no one, so I pull out the envelope from Mikey, to keep myself from feeling lonely.

I read the letter over and over on the bus, just to remind myself that this was really happening, that I was really getting out.

Charlie! Everything is going to be okay, I promise. I'm sorry, I won't be back for a little while, so you'll be on your own. Don't worry, my landlady's cool, she's an artist, she knows you're coming. Her name is Ariel and if you need anything, ask her. Your mom said she had some money to give you, so you should be okay to get food. Here's directions to my place and a map so you know where to buy groceries and stuff. CHARLIE: I can't wait to see you.—Mike

I actually hold the notebook paper up to my face, just in case there's a scent of Mikey that I can inhale to stop the stuttering of my heart, but there isn't. I take some deep breaths, trying to calm myself.

I look at the map, struggling to make sense of where I am, where I'm supposed to go, and what Mikey's arrows mean. The streets are empty, but I keep my head up.

Evan always used to say that it wasn't what you couldn't see that you should be afraid of, but what was right in front of you, in plain sight.

I grit my teeth as I walk through an underpass, willing myself not to think of *that night*. The handle of Louisa's suitcase digs into the palm of my hand. The peacoat is way too heavy for this weather. I'm sweating, but I don't want to stop and take it off. I pass a lot of little bars and shops. The sky here is like dense, dark cloth, stitched with faint white stars, something I want to put a finger to.

Mikey's note is three pages long. *You'll see a house with a bunch of HUGE silver birds in the yard. 604 E. 9th Street. She lives in the Pie Allen neighborhood. Mine is the purple guest house in the back. Use the yellow bicycle and lock. Ariel left them for you. Key for door is under yellow pot.*

They don't look like birds to me, but they are luminous, glinting in the night air, their fierce wings open. The guest house is in back. I find the key under the pot. A yellow bicycle with a new-looking willow basket is locked to a laundry-line pole. I unlock the door and grope for the switch along the wall, blinking at the sudden glare of light. The walls inside are painted purple, too.

I have no idea what to do. Is the landlady home? Did she hear me?

There are no *ping*-lights here. No endless everywhere beige carpet. No crying girls. No secret room.

I am alone. For the first time in months and months, I am utterly alone. No Evan, no Dump, no Casper, not even irritating Isis. For a minute, pinpricks of panic shoot through my body: if something happens to me between now and when Mikey gets here, who will know? Who will *care*? For a moment, I'm back *there*: those terrifying days of street before Evan and Dump found me, when every day was heightened heartbeat and the nights lasted years, waiting for the dark to end, jumping at every sound, trying to find a safe place to hide.

There is being alone, and then there is being *alone*. They are not the same thing at all.

Breathe, Charlie. Breathe, just like Casper said. I slide my fingers underneath the peacoat and pinch my thighs, too, hoping the pain will snap me back in place. Bit by bit, my panic subsides.

My stomach growls loudly. Grateful to have something else to focus on, I scout the mini-fridge tucked into a corner. There are some bottles of water and mushy bananas. I eat a banana, suck back a bottle of water super quick. There are also two pieces of pizza in a small cardboard box. They're so stiff and stale that they snap when I shove them in my mouth, but I don't care. I'm ravenous. Slowly, my panic ebbs away, exhaustion bubbling up to take its place.

The neighborhood is still. What time is it? There's a big trunk in the corner and I push it in front of the door, just in case. My whole body is sore from the bus trip and my legs are weak. I turn off the light. Even though my body is slicked with sweat, I don't take off the peacoat. Taking it off would make me feel even more exposed right now. I need a little protective armor, just in case.

I arrange myself on the futon, *Mikey's* futon, on the floor. I can feel things lifting from me, disappearing into the silence around me. I'm not listening to the sadness of several girls living along one hallway. Fucking Frank is far, far away, his hands cannot find me here. I have a little money in my backpack. My body is becoming lighter and lighter.

I can feel it, finally, after months and months of fighting

it, and it's pulling me deeper into the peacoat, into the futon: sleep. I bury my face in the pillow and it's here that I finally find Mikey's smell, something cinnamon-tinged. I breathe it in as deep as I can, letting it slip into all the crevices of me and rock me to sleep.

When I wake up, sunlight is pouring through the sole window in the guest house. I look around groggily, sliding the damp peacoat off. After almost two days on the bus, I can smell myself.

It takes me a minute, but I realize the guest house is just a crappy little converted garage: the two doors on the back wall against the alley have been soldered awkwardly together, their square windows covered with small blue curtains. The kitchen is just a sink set into a countertop on top of an old metal cabinet.

There's a ceiling fan and an air conditioner set into one of the walls. The floor is cement and the bathroom is an old closet with a toilet and plastic insert shower.

I crawl out of bed and make my way to the bathroom. Pee and then turn on the shower. It spurts and then a thin trickle eeks out. I turn it off. I'm not ready to shower yet. Not ready to look down at myself and touch my new damage. Touching it will make it all the more real. And my scars, they still hurt. They will be tender for a long, long time.

At Creeley, most of us made do with just washcloth-soaping our pits, shits, and splits, as Isis referred to it, because if you wanted to take an actual shower, you had to do it with a female attendant present, just in case you tried to, you know, drown yourself with shower spray or something. And nobody wanted an audience while they were naked, so most of us preferred the other option.

Back in my overalls and out of the bathroom, I run my hands over the kitchen counter. It's plywood overlaid with Mod Podge, postcards of foreign cities sealed underneath. Some of the postcards are turned over, with scrawled messages: *A: Meet me at the fountain, love, four o'clock, like last year.* A must be Mikey's landlord, Ariel. I look at the postcards, the images, the messy handwriting. A little story unfolding beneath my fingers.

I spread out the money Ellis and I made. *Fly over the ocean,* Ellis said, arms out, spinning around her room. *Touch down in London, Paris, Iceland, wherever.* All the romantic-seeming places she wanted to live. *Sipping espresso on the Seine will be fucking angelic, Charlie. You'll see.*

Nine hundred and thirty-three dollars and only one of us got out alive. Semi-alive.

I stare at it for a long time before tucking it far back under the sink, behind the dinky one-cup coffeemaker.

I have to find food.

The sun is so bright when I step into the yard that spots cloud my eyes, so I unlock the door again and root around a desk drawer until I find sunglasses that are painted gold and flecked with black, something a girl would wear and carelessly leave behind; did Mikey have a girlfriend? *Does* Mikey have a girlfriend? I don't want to think about that right now.

Mikey's hand-drawn map is filled with arrows and notes: *Circle K, three blocks →; Fourth Avenue (thrift, coffee, bar, eat, book) six blocks* ↑*; the U seven blocks* ←. My face and arms begin to heat up as I trudge along the sidewalk to the Circle K. It's weird to think that only a few days ago, I was in sleety weather with gray skies, and now, here I am, sun everywhere, no jacket.

Inside the Circle K, the air is cool; it's like being underwater in a clear, deep pool. The guy behind the counter has huge black plugs embedded in his earlobes. He looks up from his thick book as I stumble down the aisles, grasping at bottles, boxes of gauze, sunblock, tape, tubes of cream. In the air-conditioning, the sweat dries quickly on my face. It feels gritty and sticky. I grab a glass bottle of iced tea from the cooler.

I have to restock my tender kit, just in case. I don't want to hurt myself; I want to follow Casper's rules, but I need these.

Just in case.

I pay, stuffing everything in my backpack.

Outside on the sidewalk, I unfold Mikey's map. There's a grocery called the Food Conspiracy, up the street, so I start walking.

It's a co-op, earthy and expensive-seeming, with whispery music drifting down from the ceiling. I'm not sure what to get. I never looked at what Mikey had to cook with, if anything. I sweep a box of crackers, a block of pepper jack cheese into the wire basket.

The store hums with activity. Two hippieish ladies squeeze pears. A tall guy ladles curry from the salad bar into a Tupperware. I was shoving my bare hands in Dumpsters, and then I was shoving cardboardy mac and cheese in my face with a spork, and now I'm *shopping.*

At the checkout, I'm suddenly afraid I don't have enough money. I'm using Vinnie's money. Did I even count it? Did I even check the prices on the shit in my basket? I've forgotten how much food can cost. Blue comes back to me. *Don't let the cereal eat you.*

The cereal is eating me. The cereal is eating me alive.

Is everyone looking as me as I fumble for the bills in my pocket? They are. Aren't they? My fingers tremble. I jam the food in my backpack, don't wait for the change.

Outside, the sounds of cars and people are chain saws in my ears. I squeeze my eyes closed. "Don't float," Casper would tell us when we got stressed, when the pressure in our brains began to fight with the pressure inside our bodies and we'd start to disassociate. "Don't you dare float. Stay with me."

I walk too far in the wrong direction and end up inside the underpass, cars whirring by.

The concrete reeks of piss. My boots crunch broken glass. He comes back to me.

Passing cars make grimy shadows on the graffitied walls. I was tucked all the way at the top, trying to sleep, my throat choked with gunk and my body steaming with fever. I was sick on and off my whole time outside. Now I know I had pneumonia.

The first thing I felt was his hand on my leg.

I try to remember: what did Casper say, what did Casper say. *Stop. Assess. Breathe.*

In the dark and clammy underpass I clamp my hands over my ears and close my eyes, holding my breath and letting it out in slow waves. The cars blow warm, musty air against my legs; I concentrate on that. Gradually, the fire leaves, the saws drift away, the memory disappears..

Hands lowered, I turn and walk straight for blocks up Fourth, passing everything on Mikey's map: Dairy Queen, a coffeehouse where men are playing a game with white pieces on a table on the sidewalk, bars, restaurants, vintage stores, feminist bookstore. I go too far again and have to double back, finally reaching Ninth Street and practically running, so desperate am I to reach the purple guest house.

I lug Mikey's trunk in front of the door to keep the world out.

I have to find a way to quiet the black inside me. First, I take out the glass bottle of iced tea and drink it down all at once. I find a faded hand towel in Mikey's tiny bathroom and wrap it around my hand. I close my eyes.

And then I smash the bottle on the cement floor.

It's like a thousand birds of possibility, all beautiful, spread over the cement, glinting. I choose the longest, thickest shards and carefully wrap them in the linen that held my photographs. I slide my photos into a baggie. Mikey's got a dustpan and hand broom under the sink. I sweep the rest up of the glass up and throw it in the trash.

I take out my tender kit and prep it: nestling all the rolls of gauze, the creams, the tape, the glass in the linen, side by side until everything fits perfectly.

It's all I need for now. I just need to know it exists and is ready. Just in case. I don't want to cut. I really don't. This time, I want so much to be better.

But I just need it. It makes me feel safer, somehow, even though I know that's all messed up. Casper can tell me to breathe, she can tell me to buy rubber bands to snap on my wrists every time I panic or get an urge to cut and I will, I will try all of it, but she never said, or we never got around to talking about what will, *or would,* happen if those things ... didn't work.

I tuck it under some T-shirts in Mikey's trunk.

I crawl across the floor and pop the locks on Louisa's suit-case.

Looking at the inside of the suitcase calms me. It was never filled with clothes. Mikey's sister's clothes fit well enough in my backpack. The suitcase is for everything else: the sketch-book, pens, and pads of paper Miss Joni gave me; the baggies of charcoal, wrapped so carefully in paper towels. My Land Camera.

I open the sketchbook, unpeel a charcoal from the paper towel, and take a real look around at Mikey's apartment.

Purple-painted walls covered with band flyers and set lists. Mikey's single futon with the one black pillow and a worn blue-and-white serape blanket. A rickety desk with a wooden chair. An old record player, tall speakers, the shelves of LPs and CDs that surround them. Stacked red milk crates leaking T-shirts, boxer shorts, and frayed blue work pants. A white toothbrush resting in a tin cup on the kitchen counter. The casual accumulation of Mikey's *being*.

I start there. I draw where I am. I put myself at this new beginning, surrounded by the comfort of someone else's eas-ier life.

FOR TWO DAYS, I SLEEP AND DRAW, NIBBLING THE CRACKERS and cheese, drinking all the bottles of water until they're gone and I have to refill them from the tap.

On the third day, I've got a pair of Mikey's headphones on while I draw. Morrissey's singing sweetly at me when I hear a dull pounding. I slip the headphones off, my heart thumping wildly, as the door swings open. Mikey? Is he back already? I scramble to my feet.

The woman at the door is tall, her lean hands grasping each side of the doorframe. Her hair is white and straight, just past her ears. I'm wearing overalls, but my arms are bare in my short-sleeved T-shirt, so I tuck them behind my back. I'm disappointed it's not Mikey—my heart slows back down.

She squints down at me. "Blind as a fucking bat. Forgot my glasses in the house. Michael texted me. He wants to know if you're okay. In case you haven't figured it out, I'm the lady who owns this place."

There is a rough edge to her voice, some type of accent I can't place. She has the kind of lined face that people call etched. The kind that looks beautiful and intimidating and slightly creepy. I always wonder what these women looked like as children.

I nod cautiously. I'm always careful around new people, especially adults. You never know what they're going to be like.

"Michael didn't say you were mute. You mute?" Turquoise rings on her fingers clack against the doorframe. "So you okay, or not okay?"

I nod again, swallow.

"Bullshit."

She moves quickly, reaching around me to grab my wrists. She flips my arms so the raised lines are visible. Instinctively, I stiffen and try to pull my hands back, but she tightens her grip. Her fingertips are tough with calluses.

She makes a growling sound. "You girls today. You make me so fucking sad. The world hurts enough. Why fucking chase it down?"

The breath through my nostrils is bullish, panicky. *Fucking let go* careens inside my head like a pinball and shoots from my mouth. I'm surprised by the sound of my own voice and she must be, too, because she opens her hands and lets my arms fall away.

I rub my wrists and consider spitting at her.

"A girl with teeth." Her voice is weirdly satisfied. "That's in your favor."

The edge of the door brushes my shoulder; in my head I slam it in her face. I step away from her so that I don't make that happen in real life. Who is this bitch?

"I'm Ariel. Here." She presses a piece of paper to my chest. "I have a friend down on the Avenue. She's got a shop. She needs some help. Tell her I'll take her for appletinis on Friday."

Halfway across the scrubby yard, she turns, shading her eyes. "You get a job, Michael's friend. You find a place for yourself. You don't stay here longer than two weeks."

IT TAKES ME TWO HOURS TO GET UP THE NERVE TO LEAVE THE house. I spend those two hours walking the perimeter of the small guest house, talking to myself, rubbing my arms, doing my breath balloons. Going out to the shop to ask about a job means *talking*. It means opening my mouth and hoping the right words come out. It means letting people look me over, cast their eyes up and down me and my weird overalls and long shirt, funny hair, all of it. Right? Isn't that how job things go? You have to tell people where you're from, where you worked, what you like to do, all that shit.

My answers: nowhere, nowhere, get messed up, and cutting.

That's not going to go over well.

But the alternative is telling that fierce woman in the front house that I never went to find her friend, and maybe getting kicked out before Mikey gets back. The alternative is ending up right back where I was.

And I promised myself I would do better.

I finally get myself out of the fucking guest house by running out the front door and locking it before I give myself a chance to make another lap around the walls inside.

I find the shop easier than I thought I would. It's called Swoon. It's already late afternoon, and very hot. Through the glass window, I watch two girls in silver minidresses flit among the clothes racks, straightening hangers and laughing. Silver glitter sparkles on their eyelids; they have matching white bobs. This is a store where pretty, cool girls work, not scarred girls in overalls. I will *not* be getting a job here.

I look up and down the street. An Italian restaurant, a thrift store, a bookstore, the co-op, a fancy-looking café.

I don't have a phone. How will someone call me if I fill out an application? And what about short sleeves? Waitresses are always wearing short sleeves. Who's going to hire me with my arms the way they are? The hole in my stomach starts to grow. I'm in the middle of the breathing exercises when I hear a soft voice say, "Can I help you?"

Except for Ariel, I haven't talked to anyone in four days. One of the glittery Swoon girls is standing at the door, peeking out.

"I was just ... my friend ... somebody told me you were hiring, but ..." Gah, my voice. I sound so ... *timid.*

She looks me up and down. "No offense, but we're more vintage-y. You're more ... grunge-y. You know?"

I give her a look like, Yeah, I *know*, because we don't have to pretend. These girls and me? We're fucking miles apart in terms of our exterior maintenance. I move on.

"Do you ... I mean, do you know of anything else around? Like, better suited to me, or something? I really need a job."

She purses her mouth. "Mmm. Most everything cool is sealed up on the Avenue right now, I think. Hold on." She shouts back into the store. "Darla! Kid out here's looking for a job. You know anything?"

The other girl pokes her head out. I feel disoriented just looking at them, with their blinding white hair and lips and matching dresses.

Darla smiles. "Hey there." Like her friend, she looks me up and down, but not in a bad way. They work in a cute vintage clothing store. I get it. They're used to placing people by what they wear.

"Oh, yeah, you know what? Try Grit. It's a coffeehouse up the street, next to the DQ. I think somebody quit yesterday. You look like total True Grit material. Ask for Riley."

The other girl elbows Darla. "Riley. Oh, *yeah*. Riley *West*." She draws it out like it tastes delicious in her mouth: *Weessssst*.

"Keep your panties on, Molly."

Molly rolls her eyes at me. "Riley's kind of hot," she explains.

Darla says, "Kind of. On a good day. There aren't many of those. Anyway, just tell him we sent you, okay? And buy a hat or something, girl. Your face is starting to get real pink."

They laugh and retreat inside the store before I can ask about Riley, his hotness, or falling panties. I hope he's having one of his good days, whatever that means.

I'm nervous walking up the street, psyching myself up to have to talk again. What if this doesn't work out? I touch my face. Darla said I was getting pink. That's just brilliant: a sunburn.

I get distracted, though, by the bright colors everywhere. The sides of buildings are blazing with murals: dancing skeletons in black top hats drink wine from jugs, their white bones loose and floppy. Jimi Hendrix and Jim Morrison look out over the street, the Beatles walk barefoot down a wall. Everywhere I look, I see something unusual and cool.

A bunch of boy punks in heavy leather gear are sprawled on the wooden benches in front of the Dairy Queen, nibbling sprinkled cones. There's just one girl with them and she's not eating, only smoking and picking her black nails. The boy punks eye me as I walk by.

Next door, several older men sit at wrought iron tables, staring down at square boards with perfectly round white and black stones. They chew their fingers and take slow sips from chipped white mugs. Behind the players, against a cloudy glass window, a blinking, slightly crooked neon sign spells out true grit. Coffee urns and potted ferns on the inside window ledge peek through the lettering. The sad strains of music drifting from a speaker mounted above the window outside come to me gently: Van Morrison singing about stars and young lovers.

The screen door to the coffeehouse clatters shut behind a thinnish guy wearing an apron smeared with red sauce and grease. He lights a cigarette, his eyes moving over the game boards. Plumes of smoke billow in front of his face.

The music keeps me rooted to my spot on the sidewalk. My dad played this album over and over when I was little, sitting in the back room of the house on Hague Avenue the rocking chair creaking back and forth. It was a creamy clapboard house with a small, square backyard and a crumbling chimney. Listening to the music, I have a rush of longing for him that's so strong I almost cry.

"Lost in the reveries, eh, love?" The voice is accented, light, and shakes me out of myself.

The men at the tables chuckle. The guy in the apron cocks his head at me. His face is crackly with stubble. Lines spider his eyes.

His attention takes me by surprise. His eyes are very dark, resting with curiosity on my face.

Something shifts inside me. It's electrical, and golden. He sees this happening, or senses it, and his face breaks into a gigantic, shit-eating grin. My cheeks flood with red.

One of the boy punks yells, "He's not really British!"

"Nah," says a narrow-faced man at one of the tables, leaning his head in his palm. "He's an all-American asshole, that's for sure."

"Aw." The man in the apron grinds his cigarette out on the sidewalk. He speaks without the accent now, his voice lazy and pleased. He's still got the grin. "Care for a coffee? Espresso? Bagel? Enchilada?" He sweeps an arm to the coffeehouse. He pronounces it *en-hee-lada*.

Checked shirt with silver buttons, bulge of the lighter in his pocket. He is a person entirely comfortable in his body. Why is he paying any attention to *me*?

"Cat's got her tongue, Riley." The girl punk's got a crooked, glazed smile. I like her pink hair.

They are all terribly high. "She never met nobody famous before."

Riley. Riley *Wessssssst.* The one who makes Molly-from-Swoon's panties fall down. I can see why, kind of, now. This must be one of his "good days."

"*Semi*famous," another punk corrects, spitting on the ground.

"Semifamous *locally*," one of the game players asserts, wagging a finger.

The girl punk cackles. "Semifamous locally in his *head* on this *street*." The punks bark with laughter. The guy in the apron glowers at them good-naturedly.

A super-skinny boy punk says, "Riley, man, you look like shit, dude. You look *old*."

I sneak a look at him. Riley. Maybe he hasn't noticed how red my face is? It's true; his face looks worn out, a little too pale. He glances at the punks dismissively. "I'm a good and goddamn twenty-seven, children, and nowheres near heaven, so don't you worry none about me." He lights another cigarette, twirling the gold lighter. When I raise my eyes to his, his face splits back into that wild grin.

And for some reason, I smile back, that electrical feeling fluttering inside me.

And now we're smiling stupidly at each other. Or, Riley's smiling at me like he might smile at anything with breasts, and I'm the one smiling stupidly because I'm a stupid jackass.

Because if he really knew me, if he could really *see* me, what would he think? Once when we went to the Grand Old Day Parade, hoping to scoop up fallen wallets and half-drunk beers, Dump made us stop to watch the dance team girls go by in their purple hot pants and spangly gold tops. Evan noticed me watching them, too. After a while, he said, "You're kind of excellent-looking, Charlie, you know?" He grinned. "Under all that dirt and shit."

I just looked at him, not knowing what to say. Before, Ellis was always the one who got noticed, for obvious reasons. And the boys I'd been with? There hadn't been any need for sweet talk or flowers there. But what Evan said . . . made me feel kind of nice inside.

Dump glanced over at us. He scanned my face intently. "Yeah. You got good eyes. Really blue, like the ocean or some-thing. You got nothing to worry about."

Now Riley tilts his head at me. "Well, Strange Girl? You got something to say?"

That's right. A job. I'm here to ask about a job.

I blurt it out. "Darla sent me. From Swoon. She said you might need somebody."

"Darla knows me so well." He smiles, blowing a smoke ring. "I need somebody, all right. I think you'll do."

The men at the tables snicker. I feel my face heat up again. "For a *job*. I need a damn job."

"Oh, right, right, right. That. Now, see, I'm just a lackey here.

My sister owns the joint, and she's not back until day after to-morrow. I just don't—"

"Gil quit," says one of the players at the table. "Remember? The incident?"

Riley scoffs, "She doesn't want to wash dishes."

"Yes, I do," I say quickly. "I do."

Riley shakes his head. "You'd make more waiting tables somewhere."

"No, I don't like people. I don't want to give them food."

The men laugh and Riley smiles, stubbing out his cigarette. From inside, I hear "Riley! *Riley!* Order *up!* Where the fuck are you?"

"Looks like my time here is done. Gentlemen." He salutes the players, then turns to me. "All right, Strange Girl. Come back tomorrow morning. Six a.m. No promises."

He winks at me. "That's how hearts get broken, you know. When you believe in promises."

The green door slams behind him. I stand there, thinking (hoping?) the players, or the punks, or anyone, might talk to me, but no one does. They just go back to what they were doing before I showed up. I wonder if everyone at Creeley has forgotten me. I start walking home.

A job. Washing dishes. I breathe deeply. It's something.

When I get back to Mikey's, Ariel's house is dark, so I decide to sit in the backyard for a little while. I find an extension cord and plug it into Mikey's lone lamp, dragging it outside and setting it up on the dirt. I arrange my sketchbook and char-coals around me. I take off my boots and socks and wrinkle my nose at the smell. I'm now going on about a week without washing. No wonder everyone in the co-op was staring at me: I stink. I sniff my armpits. I'm going to have to take a shower. But not right now. I've lived for longer without washing.

From somewhere, not far away, comes the sound of guitars and drums, the noisy lurch and sudden silence of a band practicing.

I listen with my eyes closed, toes pushing into the sandy ground. The bass player frets and shifts, unsure of his fingers; the drummer is playing out of time. The singer is frustrated with everyone's awkwardness. His voice cracks as he tries to hit notes, match the bridge. The band stops abruptly, the bass slyly petering out; the singer barks *one two three* and they leap in again, scrabbling to find each other in the noise. It makes me miss Mikey even more; he was always taking me and Ellis to see his band friends rehearse in garages and basements. It felt electric and real, watching a guy try to figure out a chord over and over, or a girl pounding away at the drums. Ellis always got bored pretty quickly and would take out her phone, but watching and listening as something was created could feed me for days.

In time, fingers and voices come together, the music happens; the song inside the music awakens.

> Oh I don't want to be
> *your charity case*
> *I just want you to see*
> *my for-real face*
> *Can you do that for me?*
> *It'll take a minute or three*
> Oh, can you do that for me?

The faces of the day run through my brain, setting themselves up like dominos: the game-playing men, the punks with liquid eyes and chapped lips on the Dairy Queen benches, Riley at the coffeehouse, with his smeary apron and who-cares attitude.

At Creeley, we would be gathered in Rec at this time of night, a rustling scrum of girls with iPods and approved novels. I miss Louisa. Who is she talking to tonight, in the dark, in our room? Have I already been replaced?

The sound of my charcoal on the paper is like a dog quietly working at a door, its nails methodic and insistent.

My father's face comes slowly as I draw. The shape of his large, dark eyes, his sand-colored hair. The shoulder bones I could feel through his T-shirt when I climbed on his lap. I wish I could remember the sound of his voice, but I can't.

Sometimes he wouldn't let me in the room where he rocked in the chair and so I sat outside with our rust-colored dog, burying my face in his fur, listening to Van Morrison through the door.

I wish I could remember what happened to our dog. One day he was there and then one day he wasn't. Just like my father.

Where his teeth should be, I give him tiny, tiny pill bottles. I regret it instantly. It looks awkward and wrong.

He was smoke and despair. He had dark almond eyes that were kind. But when I looked closer, I saw something else, something quivering in the background.

Riley at the coffeehouse has those eyes, too. Just the thought of him makes my body flood with scary warmth.

When I sleep that night, though, I push thoughts of Riley away: it's Mikey's smell on the pillow and blanket that comforts me, like a promise, a tangible good thing that will happen soon. I fit myself against his blanket like it's his body, filling my lungs with the scent of his sweat, the oils from his skin. I hold him to me as closely as I can. I can't let him go.

I STAND ACROSS THE STREET FROM THE COFFEEHOUSE FOR A good ten minutes. I've been up since four a.m., even though I found a little travel alarm clock in Mikey's trunk and set it for five, drawing and working up my nerve to come here. It's almost six a.m. and Fourth Avenue is starting to liven up, stores rolling up gates, people lugging tables out onto the sidewalk.

The neon true grit sign is lopsided, the u blinking on and off.

I cross the street, taking deep breaths. Just as I'm about to knock on the heavy front door to the coffeehouse, the green screen door a few feet down pops open, the one Riley emerged from yesterday.

And there he is, already smoking. And smiling.

"Strange Girl," he says amiably. "This is the first day of the rest of your life. Welcome. Come in."

A woman with pink fox-tipped hair rides up on a blue bicycle. She looks at us curiously. She's older, blocky, in a torn sweatshirt and long tasseled skirt.

"What's up, R? What's going on?" She smiles at me nicely as she locks her bike to the rack.

"Temporary disher, Linus. Hey," he says, looking down at me. "I don't believe I actually know your name, Strange Girl."

"It's Charlie," I say quietly. "Charlie Davis."

He holds out his hand. "Well, it's excellent to meet you, Charlie Charlie Davis. I'm Riley Riley West."

I hesitate, but then I take his hand. It's warm. I haven't

touched anyone nicely since I petted Louisa's hair. My body floods with a sudden warmth and I pull my hand away.

"Right," he says cheerily. "Back to the matter at hand, yes? Dirty dishes, coffee, ungrateful peons, and the long slow march to death."

Linus laughs.

We walk through the green door, which Riley says is the employee entrance. There is a gray, industrial-looking punch clock on the wall and slots jammed with time cards. Linus heads to the front and in a few minutes, I hear the grinding of coffee beans and the air begins to smell thick, almost sweet, from the smell of fresh coffee brewing.

Riley shows me how to load the dishwasher, what buttons to press, where the dish trays are stacked, where to rinse and store the bus tubs. The dish and kitchen area is steamy and hot, the floor mats slick with soapy water and slimy food scraps. The sink is filled with pots, pans, crusted dishes. Riley frowns. "Those girls didn't do a great job of cleaning up last night, I guess."

Linus slips past us to get something from the grill area. "Welcome to the madhouse, kid," she says, smiling, and lopes back to the front counter. She starts fussing with CDs.

Riley tosses me a grimy apron and begins slicing bell peppers and onions, flinging them into a stainless steel bin. I pull the apron over my head and try to tie it in back. It's too big, so I have to loop the strings around and tie it in front.

From the corner of my eye, I see Riley pause as he waits for whatever Linus is going to put on. She presses a button and there it is, *Astral Weeks*, plaintive and sad. He nods to himself, as though he approves, and starts dropping bread on the grill.

I turn back to the sink, staring at the piles of dishes and pots. I turn on the water. *This is what you came here* for, I tell myself. *Here you are. Work.*

In an hour or so, Linus unlocks the front door. We don't have long to wait before people begin to show up, a hive of voices and cigarette smoke. Some of them nod at me, but mostly they just talk to Riley and Linus. I don't mind. I've never minded listening. I'm better at that than talking, anyway.

I spend the morning loading dishes into the washer, waiting, yanking the rack and restacking in the cook and wait areas. To restack in the cook area, I have to walk behind Riley and reach up to the shelves. The cook station is small and opens onto the dish area. There's a grill, fry pit, oven, two-door stainless steel refrigerator, the cutting board counter, and a small island.

From listening to Riley talk to the waitpeople, I learn what meager food True Grit serves and who works there. A lot of them seem to be in bands or in school. The sturdy, crackling whir of the espresso machine is always in the background. I'm getting thirsty, but I'm afraid to ask for anything. Do you have to pay for drinks here? I didn't bring any money. Everything Ellis and I made has to be spent on a place to live. When I think no one's looking, I take a glass and drink from the sink tap. Pretty soon, though, my stomach starts rumbling, and having to scrape leftover food into the garbage gets pretty painful. I think about snagging some uneaten halves of sandwiches and mentally make a note to figure out where to hide them.

Once, when I return with more dishes and silverware, Riley's not cooking. He's looking at me intently, which makes my skin prickle with embarrassment.

"Where you from, Strange Girl?"

"Minnesota," I answer warily. I scooch by him to put some dishes on the rack above his shoulder. He doesn't make room for me, so my back brushes against the front of his body.

"Oh. Interesting. Minnie-So-Tah. You betcha. I played the Seventh Street Entry once. You ever go there?"

I shake my head. The punks had called him semifamous. The 7th Street Entry is a club where cool bands play in downtown Minneapolis. Is . . . *was* . . . Riley in a band?

"You moved out here for a boy, I bet, huh?" He smiles wickedly.

"I did not," I say, my voice flaring with anger. *Not really,* I think. *Maybe. Yes?* "What's it to you?"

"You're kind of a strange one, you know that?"

I'm quiet. His attention is freaking me out. I can't tell if he's being nice in a real way, or trying to bait me. You can't tell with people sometimes. Finally, I sputter, "Whatever."

"You can feel free to talk me up, Strange Girl. I don't bite, you know."

Linus sticks an order slip on the pulley. "Not right *now*, you don't."

Riley tosses a crust of bread at her and she ducks.

At four-thirty Riley says I can go. I take off my apron and run it through the dishwasher, just like he showed me. I'm sweaty in my long-sleeved T-shirt and push up my sleeves to cool off.

Riley is about to hand me some cash when he says, "Whoa, whoa, now, hey. What's up with that?" I look down, horrified, and quickly yank my sleeves down over my arms.

"Nothing," I mumble. "Just cat scratches." I grab the money and stuff it into the pocket of my overalls.

Riley murmurs, "I hope you get rid of that cat. That's a fuck-

130

ing horrible cat, Strange Girl." I can feel his eyes on me, but I don't look at his face. That's it. I'm out. No way he'll let me work here now.

"Absolutely," I answer, flustered. "Today. Right now, as a matter of fact." I walk quickly to the back door.

He shouts, "Come back tomorrow at six a.m. and talk to Julie. I'll put in a good word for you!"

Grateful and surprised, I look back. I can come back another day, which means maybe another day after that. I smile, even though I don't mean to, and he kind of laughs at me before turning back to the grill.

I'm achy and tired. The smell of wet food clings to my clothes and skin, but I have money in my pocket and more work tomorrow. I buy a loaf of bread and a jar of peanut butter at the Food Conspiracy co-op across the street.

Back in Mikey's garage, I lie in bed as the light fades outside, my body filmed over with dried sweat, old food, and soapy water. It feels good to rest after being on my feet all day, lifting heavy bus tubs and dish trays. I slowly eat one peanut butter sandwich, then another. The first day of work wasn't so bad. The people seemed okay. Riley seems nice enough, and plenty cute. It's something, anyway. When I finish the second sandwich, I start the rickety shower and strip. The water is cold on my body and I shiver. I look around. No shampoo or soap. I take care not to look at myself too closely, but it doesn't work, and I see flashes of the damage on my thighs. My stomach sinks.

I'm Frankenstein. I'm the Scarred Girl.

I tilt my face up toward the spray and suddenly the water switches to hot, hot, all at once. I pretend that sudden sting of heat is why I'm crying.

MIKEY'S SCREEN DOOR SLAMMING SHUT WAKES ME. I SIT UP and rub my face slowly.

I dressed in just a T-shirt and underwear after the shower. I must have dozed off, tired from my long day at True Grit. I scramble for my overalls, turning around so Ariel can't see the scars on my thighs. I'm sore from all the lifting I did today. I haven't used my muscles so much in months.

Ariel is bent down, flipping through my sketchbook, making a sound like a hungry bee. She pauses on the sketch of my father. I'm protective of my drawings, and him, so I pull the book away, pressing it to my chest. She shrugs, standing up.

"Prescription bottles. Interesting choice, but too distracting. In portraiture, it's the eyes that explain the person, that give us our window. If you put the whole story in his teeth by making them pill bottles, it's too easy for us. You just gave us the ending to the story. Why would we stick around? We need to move over the whole face, we need time to think. You understand?"

Move over the whole face, time to think. Before I can ask what she means, she says briskly, "Come. Let's have breakfast. I love breakfast for dinner, don't you? I bet you're starving."

I slip a hoodie on and pull on my boots hastily. I'm not going to turn down free dinner. Even though I ate before my shower, I'm hungry again. I guess I have a lot of space to fill inside. My mouth waters as we cross the yard. I look up. The stars are perfect pinpricks of white.

Her house is airy and comfortable. The cement floors are

painted with large blue and black circles. It's like stepping on bruised bubbles, which is kind of cool, and I like it.

I've never been in a house that had so many paintings and it takes my breath away. Ariel's cream-colored living room walls are slathered with large, blackish paintings. Some of them have slanted strips of light cutting through the darkness, like light from beneath closed doors or up through the branches of tall, old trees. Some of them are just different shades of darkness. Some of the paint is so thickly applied, it rises off the canvas like minuscule mountains. My fingers itch to touch them but I'm afraid to ask if I can. Everywhere I look, there is something to see, and I love it.

Ariel stands in the doorway of the kitchen, watching me. "You can touch gently."

I do, very carefully laying a finger on the tiny hill of one particularly dark painting. It feels, strangely enough, cool to the touch, and very firm, almost like a healed, raised scar.

Ariel says, "What are you thinking, Charlie? Speak. I always tell my students that whatever they feel about art, it is true, because it is true to *their* experience, not mine."

"I'm not sure ... I don't know how to say it." The words bubble inside me, but I'm not sure how to arrange them. I don't want to sound dumb. I don't want to *be* dumb.

"Just try. My ears, they are as big as an elephant's."

I step back. The paintings are so large and dark, except for those tiny sprays of light. "They make me ... they make me think of being stuck somewhere? I don't know, like weighted down, but then these little patches ..." I falter. I sound stupid. And looking at so much darkness is kind of pulling at something inside me, because, I think, only a very sad person could have done these paintings and what would have made Ariel so sad?

Ariel is behind me now. "Go on," she says quietly.

"Those little parts that stick off? It seems like the darkness is almost trying to leave the whole thing, because the little light is back there, and it's turning its back on the light. That's stupid, I know."

"No," answers Ariel thoughtfully. "Not stupid, not stupid at all." She walks away, back to the kitchen, and I follow her, relieved that I don't have to say any more about the painting, at least not right now.

Her glossy red kitchen table is laid out with an iridescent platter holding sliced strawberries, chunks of pineapple, scoops of scrambled egg, and red, soft-looking meat. "Chorizo," she says. "You'll like it."

I'm almost ashamed at how ravenous I am for real, cooked food. I calculate how much to put on my plate so it doesn't look like I'm being too greedy all at once.

The chorizo isn't hot so much as spicy; it has a strange, mashed-hot-dog quality that's slightly gross, so I eat some eggs instead. It's been a long time since I've eaten a real meal in someone's house. Maybe the last time was with Ellis and her parents, at their grainy dining room table, the one that leaned a little to the right.

The silverware is cool in my fingers, the plates sturdy and definite. I try to eat slowly, though I really do want to shove everything into my mouth at once.

Ariel takes a large mouthful of chorizo and egg and chews luxuriously.

"Where are your people? Your mama?"

I make a pile of strawberries and top them with a wedge of

pineapple, like a little hat. I fill my mouth with food again so I don't have to answer Ariel.

"Maybe you think she doesn't care, but she does." She turns a strawberry between her fingers. I can feel her watching me.

"Michael says you lost a friend. Your best friend. I'm so sorry." She looks over at me. "How awful."

It's unexpected, what she says, just like the fresh tears that suddenly well up in my eyes. I'm surprised Mikey told her about Ellis, but I don't know why. And I also feel weirdly betrayed that he did. Ellis was . . . is *mine*. "I don't want to talk about that right now," I say quickly, jamming pineapple and strawberry into my mouth. I blink rapidly, hoping the tears stay put.

Ariel licks chorizo grease from her callused fingers and wipes each one with a napkin, dipping the edge of the fabric into her glass of ice water.

"Most girls your age, they're off to school, they fuck boys, they gain weight, they get some good grades, some bad grades. Lie to Mommy and Daddy. Pierce their tummies. Tramp stamps." She smiles at me.

"That's not you, though, right? Michael says you didn't finish high school, so you can't go and study boys and fuck books." She laughs at herself.

"I *did* finish," I answer defensively through a mouthful of food. "Well, almost. Sort of. Soon."

Ariel nibbles her pineapple. She regards me steadily, her eyes slightly enlarged by the lenses of her glasses. Then she makes a crackling, explosive sound low in her throat. "Boom!" She spreads her fingers. "You keep people inside you, that's what happens. Memories and regrets swallow you up, they get fat on the very marrow of your soul and then—"

I look over at her, startled by her strange words. Her face

softens as she says, "And then, boom, you explode. Is that how you got those?" She gestures at my arms, safely hidden underneath the hoodie.

I fix my eyes on my plate. Boom. *Yes.*

She smiles again. "How are you going to live this hard life, Charlotte?"

The sound of my full name makes me look up. Pinkish powder dusts Ariel's tan cheeks, minuscule lines of lipstick swim into the wrinkles above her mouth. I can't imagine ever being her age, how she got here, this airy house, her life. One day from now is hard enough for me to imagine. I don't know what to say.

She reaches across the table and brushes the scar on my forehead. Her fingertips are warm and for a second I relax, sinking into her touch. "You're just a baby," she says quietly. "So young."

I stand up, clumsily knocking into the table. She was getting too close, I was letting her. The food and her kindness made me sleepy and complacent. *Always be alert,* Evan would warn. *The fox has many disguises.*

She sighs, squares her shoulders, and brushes crumbs from the table into her cupped palm. She raises her chin toward the back door: my invitation to leave.

On my way out, my hip bumps against a slim table. Something glittery peeks out from under a jumble of envelopes and circulars. I don't even hesitate before sliding it into the pocket of my overalls. Ariel has taken a little from me tonight and so I am taking a little of her.

I PULL THE OBJECT FROM MY POCKET AND PUT IT ON THE floor of Mikey's garage. It's a red cross, slightly larger than my hand, made of plaster and encrusted with fat white skulls with painted black eye sockets, black nostrils, black-dotted mouths. The sides of it have been dipped in thick red glitter.

The skull-cross is gaudy and cheap and wonderful and showers me with a palpable ache: Ellis would have loved it, would have bought several more to nail to the walls of her blue-painted bedroom, where they would share morose space with posters and cutouts of Morrissey, Elliott Smith, Georgia O'Keeffe, and Edith, the Lonely Doll.

I find an old striped scarf in Mikey's trunk and gingerly wrap the cross in it and push it under the pillow. I get up and look around the smallness of Mikey's place, thinking about what Ariel said, which overwhelms me and makes me long for the safety of my kit in the trunk, so I go into the teeny bathroom and rock back and forth on the toilet for a while. Casper said repetitive motion, like rocking, or even just jumping in place, can help soothe your nerves.

When I get overwhelmed and I can't focus on just one thing, when all of my horrible hits me at once, it's like I'm one of those giant tornados in a cartoon, the furry gray kind that suctions up everything in its path: the unsuspecting mailman, a cow, a dog, a fire hydrant. Tornado Me picks up every bad thing I've ever done, every person I've fucked and fucked over, every cut I've made, everything, everything. Tornado Me whirls and whirls, growing more immense and crowded.

I have to be careful. Being overwhelmed, feeling powerless, getting caught up in the tornado of shame and emptiness is a trigger.

Casper told me, "You can only take one thing at a time. Set a goal. See it through. When you've finished one thing, start another." She told me to start small.

I tell myself: You made it out of Creeley, however it happened. You got on a bus. You came to the desert. You found food. You have not hurt yourself in this new place. You found a *job*.

I repeat the sentences until the tornado stops whirling. When Mikey gets here, everything will be just a little better.

Out loud, I say, "A place to live."

I have money. I can find a place to live. This is what I tell myself, in a kind of mantra, as I arrange myself on Mikey's futon and fall asleep.

LINUS IS WAITING FOR ME OUTSIDE THE COFFEEHOUSE THE next morning, pulling her pink hair into a scrunchie. Her lower lip puffs out. "Did you see Riley, by any chance?"

When I shake my head, she frowns. "Shit. Okay. Onward." She unlocks the door to the coffeehouse, presses some buttons on the security alarm. She hangs her stuff up on a peg.

"Julie got a little delayed in Sedona. She might be late. It's all cool. She runs on kind of a loosey-goosey energy, not clocks, like the rest of us. Meanwhile, you can help me set up. I hear Peter Lee and Tanner closed down the Tap Room last night, so they won't fucking be on time. That's a bar downtown. You look a little young to know that."

She slides aprons from the dishwasher, winces at their dampness, and throws one to me. "I'm guessing Riley didn't give you any kind of new employee lowdown, so here's the basics: you can have regular coffee for free, as much as you want, and mostly any kind of espresso drink you want, within reason, unless it seems like you're taking too much, and then Julie will start charging you. You're supposed to pay for any food, but again, that can get iffy. Like, what if we make the wrong order? You know what I'm saying? Smoke breaks are outside in front, but sometimes you can smoke in the lounge"—she grins, pointing down past the grill and dish area to à dark hallway littered with mops, brooms, and buckets—"but don't let Julie catch you. Her office is down there and she hates the smell of smoke."

She pauses. "And then there's Riley. There are all sorts of

Riley rules and Riley breaks all sorts of rules, but Julie lets him, because he's her brother, and she has fucked-up notions of what love is. So what this means for *you* is . . . sometimes he smokes back there when he's cooking, when she isn't here. And sometimes he drinks back there, too. And since you're back there, and I'm usually up here, it's kind of your job to keep an eye on him, and tell me if things seem to be going to hell. If you know what I mean."

She eyes me carefully. "Deal?"

I nod.

"Okay, moving on. First, we make the mojo."

She leads me to the espresso machine, the urns that hold five different types of coffee, the smudgy pastry case that faces the seating area of the coffeehouse.

"But *first* first," she says, "we put out the tunes." She flicks through the stacks of CDs and tapes on the countertop. More CDs are jammed inside the bottom cabinet amid green order pads, boxes of pencils and pens, extra register tape, and a bottle of Jim Beam, which makes Linus sigh very heavily. She shoves it to the side of the case, out of view.

She looks up at me. "We choose according to our mood. Later, we may choose according to customer, unless we hate them. This morning, we are feeling very . . ."

She pauses. "Sad. So many things left unsaid in my life. I'm sure you're too young to understand, right?" She winks at me.

"Van Morrison it is. Familiar? I'm kind of in a Morrison mood at the moment."

I nod, but I tense up a little, because of my dad. But when *Da da dat dat da da da da* fills the space, I start to relax; the music is familiar, and soothing, and I try to think of it as maybe my dad being here with me, in a weird way.

She runs through the oily-looking beans in the see-through bins: kona, french, guatemalan, ethiopian, blue mountain, kenyan. The teas sit loosely in wooden pull-out shelves. They look like small and fragrant piles of twigs. Out the enormous window that opens onto Fourth Avenue, other places are opening up, too, windows are being washed, sale racks placed on sidewalks, patio tables being lugged out. The whole day is starting for everyone on the Avenue, including, I realize, me. I have a *job*. It's kind of disgusting, but it's *mine*. I'm a part of something. I've hauled myself up at least one rung on a ladder. I wish Casper was here. She'd probably give me one of her goofy high fives or something. I'm so kind of proud of myself that I'd probably let her.

A body appears in front of the True Grit window, blocking the light.

Linus elbows me out of the way, making the watch movement to a dirty-faced man on the sidewalk: tapping her wrist ten times, which must mean he needs to wait ten more minutes. He nods, the brim of his straw hat stiff over his eyes. He leans against the bike rack, tucking a newspaper under his arm. He begins to have an intricate conversation with himself.

Linus resumes grinding, shouting over the sound of beans being mashed. "It's Fifteen-Minute-Shit Guy. He's here every day at open. He brings in a newspaper and a bucket. He takes a fifteen-minute shit in the can and then we let him take the old coffee grounds in the bucket." She points to an empty five-gallon pickle bucket.

I stare at her. I have to yell over the grinder. "For reals? Like, the shitting part? Fifteen minutes?"

She nods. "Reals. And it's going to be your job, as the disher, to go in there after he's done and check it. Make sure everything is clean." She winks. "But you know, he uses the grounds for his garden down on Sixth and damned if that fucker isn't god-damn beautiful. Sunflowers up to my fucking eyeballs and tomatoes the size of my tits."

I laugh without thinking, a big fat guffaw, and quickly cover my mouth. Linus says, "It's okay! You can laugh. I'm fucking *funny*, aren't I?" She nudges me with her elbow. I let my hand drop away from my mouth.

I smile back at her.

"That's more like it. I like that." She fills up an urn with water and hands me the filter of Ethiopian beans, ducking her head so our eyes are level. There's a slight mist of dark hair between her eyebrows.

"Julie's gonna love you, don't worry. She loves the damaged and you reek of it. No offense or anything. It's a good thing, in a weird way, for this place. We are all fifty kinds of messed up here."

She fills two mugs of coffee from the urn and hands me one.

"Now, go let Fifteen-Minute-Shit Guy in."

By eight-thirty, Linus's face has bloomed bright red and she's swearing, running from the front of the coffeehouse to the grill station, slicing bagels and throwing them on the toaster shelf. The waitstaff is late; Riley is still not here. He was supposed to come in at six to get the breakfast items ready: the chili sauces in the pots, the home fries on the grill. She's already asked me to man the potatoes and then sworn at me when I didn't remember to flip them at regular intervals.

"You have to go get him," she says finally, shoving a fork-ful of scrambled tofu into her mouth. My stomach growls as I watch her. I forgot to eat before I left the apartment this morning. "He doesn't have a phone and I can't leave or close the café. Julie would fucking kill me."

She scribbles an address and directions on a piece of paper. She tells me to get one of the moon-faced Go players outside to wait tables while she cooks. "Tell him coffee's free for the rest of the day."

Outside I look at the directions she's given me. It's downtown, not far, through the underpass, I think. I unlock my bike and take off.

He lives around the corner from a plasma bank in a robin's-egg-blue bungalow set back behind a few drooling cottonwoods, on a street of funkily colored houses and old cars with peeling band bumper stickers. On the front porch I walk by a full ashtray and a single, empty bottle of beer next to a green Adirondack chair stacked with dog-eared paperbacks.

No one answers my knock and I can see that the screen door isn't latched. When I push the front door, just a little, it gives. I call out, softly, "Hey, anybody there? You're late for work. . . ."

No answer. I debate for a few seconds, peeking through the crack in the doorway. I don't want to find him naked in a bed with some chick, but I don't want to have to go back to Linus without even trying. And I'm kind of curious, too, about what Riley is doing, exactly. What his life is like, this person who was once in a band and now slings hash.

I push open the door the rest of the way and walk in, nudging aside a pair of faded black Converse. The front room is filled with books—piled on the floor and jammed into a glassed-in oak bookcase that rises from the floor to the ceiling. A sagging burgundy velvet couch is up against the far wall, beneath an open, curtainless window.

I pass into the kitchen and the calendar on the wall catches my eye. Curvy pinup girls from the forties with sun-soaked hair and long legs, breasts pulsating against the fabric of swim clothes. The page is on November.

Today is the last day of May. In the past forty-five days, I've tried to kill myself; been put in a psych ward; been shipped by bus across the country; got a job washing dishes in a dumpy coffeehouse; and now I'm lurking in the house of a weirdo with an apparent drinking problem. A cute weirdo, but still a weirdo.

Not even Ellis could make all that sound angelic.

I walk down a dark hallway and slowly push open a door. Tiny bathroom, painted white. Claw-foot tub with a shower. Dirty mirror on the medicine cabinet. Framed postcard photograph of Bob Dylan in front of a Studebaker. *Woodstock, 1968*, it says across the bottom. I inspect the postcard wistfully. My father loved to listen to *Nashville Skyline*. He told me Bob had a bad motorcycle accident and stopped drinking and smoking and that's why his voice was pure and deep on the album. God was coming back to Dylan. That's what my father told me.

The other door is cracked open just a little. I hesitate before knocking. My heart pounding, I tap softly on the door and then push it carefully, my eyes just barely open, just in case.

He is lying on his back on the bed, still in yesterday's clothes: the food-stained white T-shirt, the loose brown pants. His arms are behind his head and his eyes are closed. He's using a folded quilt for a pillow. Clothes are tossed on a puffy leather chair. On the floor next to the bed there's a loaded ashtray and two crumpled packs of cigarettes. The room smells of old smoke and sweat.

Heart racing, I take a breath, say his name.

No answer.

Is he dead? I walk closer, staring at his chest, trying to see if it's rising and falling, however slightly. *"Riley."* A curious odor lingers about his body. It isn't the same as alcohol, the same as sweat or smoke. It's something else. I bend down and sniff.

Suddenly, his eyes snap open and he sits up.

Before I can jump back, he grabs my wrist, pulling me between his legs and locking me in the grip of his knees. It knocks the breath out of me. Adrenaline shoots through my body.

My brain fuzzes in and out with images of Fuckin Frank's terrible face. Riley's breath is hot against my ear. I'm struggling, but he's holding me too tight, even as I cry, "Let go! Let go!"

His voice is low and slightly hoarse. "Who are you, Strange Girl? Sneaking into my house. You gonna rob me?"

"Fuck off." I work hard not to panic, to stay in the moment, not float. I can't understand why he's doing this. He seemed so nice before. I position my elbow and try to jab him in the gut, but his fingers are so tight on my wrists, my skin is starting to burn and I can't move.

"Fucking let go." Gasping.

His breath swarms against my cheek and neck and now Fucking Frank is gone and it's the man in the underpass who zooms back to me, a dark memory of fear that triggers my street feeling again, something I thought I'd left behind. *No!* I yell it.

I use all my strength to twist my hips, gaining some leverage, and then I stomp on his fucking foot as hard as I can. He cries out, his arms springing open, releasing me. I scramble to the open door, a safe enough distance away. He holds his naked foot, his face scrunched in pain. I rub my stinging wrists, glaring at him.

"Jesus, I was just playing around." He scowls at me. "You think I was gonna do something, or something?"

"Asshole." I'm gulping breath, trying to force the air down hard enough to put out the tornado starting in my body. "You're so horrible. That's not funny. Why would you think that's funny? Get your own fucking ass to work."

I keep gulping air, only now I'm hiccupping, too, and tears are pouring down my face, which is the last thing I want.

"Jesus, honey," Riley says, suddenly serious. "I'm sorry."

I swipe at my face angrily. Fucking *hell*. Fucking *people*. Crying in front of him.

Riley stares at me, the circles under his eyes like black half-moons. Whatever caused those dark stains, it wasn't just alcohol, I'm sure of it.

"I'm sorry. I'm really sorry. I'm an asshole, I am. Don't cry. I didn't mean for you to *cry*." His voice is different now, softer.

We look at each other and I see something pass across his face, very gently, a sadness, some realization of *me* that makes me want to cry even harder, because he *knows*, he knows it now, that something happened to me, and grabbing me like that wasn't okay.

He looks ashamed.

"Linus . . . Linus says get your ass to work." I turn and run out of his room. I'm out of the house, slamming the door behind me, and then peeling away on my bicycle as fast as I can.

On my way back to the coffeehouse, as I pass through the Fourth Avenue Underpass, somewhere in that sudden flash of darkness that replaces the impossibly white sunshine of this city, it occurs to me that he knew Linus wouldn't be able to come herself. He knew I was going to be working at the coffeehouse, that I would have to come instead.

He wasn't sleeping at all. He was waiting for me. I thought he was a nice person and now I remind myself: *People aren't nice, people aren't nice, you should know that by now.*

I stop my bike. I could just turn back, go back to Mikey's, shut the door, push the trunk in front of it, rescue my kit. Not go back to Grit. Not have to see him. Not have to deal.

But then I will lose what little I've gained. I take deep breaths, close my eyes. Blue comes back to me. Was what happened cereal?

A car honks at me, jolting me out of myself. Before I can even process what to think, I'm pedaling to the coffeehouse again.

Outside True Grit, the sidewalk tables are already full, Go players scowling at empty cups of coffee, people fanning themselves with menus. The high drone of customers erupts as I rocket through the employee screen door and rush to get into my apron.

Linus throws down the spatula and swears when she sees me by myself. "Shit. I knew it. Usually, he's just drunk, but if he's late like this, like *this* late? It means he's been using. I knew it."

Before I can ask her about *using,* a guy with neck tattoos bursts through the double doors and calls out "Order!", slamming the green sheet on the counter in front of Linus. He runs to the front to ring people up as Linus hustles around the grill, sliding eggs onto plates and toasting bagels. I turn back to the dishwasher, steam coating my face. What Linus said about Riley using echoes in my head.

Before he face-planted in the craggy stream in Mears Park and almost drowned, DannyBoy had started trolling Rice Street, looking for a lean-faced man in a black vinyl jacket with purple piping. Whatever DannyBoy took, it first made his face gray, his stomach clench; after that, he was like a baby.

But Riley's weird smell, the forceful way he grabbed me. Whatever he was on wasn't what DannyBoy was on. Danny-Boy became all heat and sighs. Whatever Riley did last night turned him mean.

THE RUSH OF BREAKFAST HAS DIED DOWN AND I'M UP TO MY elbows in dishes and coffee mugs when the screen door swings open. I look over to see Riley slouching in just ahead of a wide woman dressed like a kind of female tepee in long, loose brown fabric. She looks around, shaking her head at Linus behind the grill, who promptly finds an apron to cover her dirty shirt. Riley has showered: his hair is less matted, and his clothes, though again a white T-shirt and brown pants, appear to be a *cleaner* white T-shirt and brown pants.

He looks at me, amused, with a glint in his eye. "Well," he says cheerfully. "Looks like you're going to have that job interview now."

He says it like nothing happened at all. There are still faint red marks around my wrists from where he pinned me so tightly.

The woman nods toward the long hallway, and I follow, not taking off my damp apron. Halfway down the hall, I turn around to face Riley, who is loping after me. I hiss, "You suck."

"Not the first time I've heard that, sweetheart."

The woman collapses in a swivel chair behind a desk mountained with papers, receipts, folders, cups full of pens and pencils, and a bowl of luminous blue stones. She puts her forehead down on the desk. "I'm so tired."

On the grayish wall behind her, there is a framed portrait of a girls' softball team, sunburned faces, sun-bleached hair bunched under green caps. I look at the dark road map of freckles on the woman's face. She's easy to locate in the photograph, far on the right-hand side, bat against her shoulder, thighs straining the hems of her shorts.

Her hand feels around the desk for something, pat-pat-patting. She seems confused, but in a kind of funny, nice way.

Riley has stretched out on the couch and closed his eyes. I don't know what to do, so I stand by the door, pressing my back against the wall.

"You didn't bring in any coffee," she tells Riley.

"You didn't tell me to bring in coffee."

"Well, go get me some."

She lifts her head in my direction. "Julie. Julie Baxter. And you are?" She lays her head back on the desk and whimpers.

I wonder why she and Riley don't have the same last name. Maybe she's married?

"Riley? Why are you not getting my coffee?" Julie's voice is muffled on the desktop.

Riley shuffles up from the couch. He pauses next to me. "Would you like a cup of coffee?"

I shake my head. I'm still angry, and weirded out, by what he did. His face seems tired, yet he's kind of jittery, walking out the door in a funny way. I wait until he's through the door before I turn back to Julie.

Softly, I say, "My name is Charlie."

Julie is sitting up now. She seems to not hear me. "Huh," she says mildly. "That's curious."

She gazes at the ceiling, her mouth slightly ajar. Then she says, looking directly at me, "You see, a *normal Riley* never would have asked if you wanted coffee. A *normal Riley* would have just brought back coffee for you, probably something extravagant, like a mochaccino with extra whipped cream and strawberry sprinkles. Because *normal Riley* must flirt with every female person. Young, old, in between, fat, thin, mid-dling. Doesn't matter. He would have brought back his pretty gift for you and you would have fluttered and giggled and he would have assured himself of another ally. Though, to be fair, you don't seem the fluttery type."

She pauses and folds her hands. "Not a conquest, necessar-ily, but certainly an ally. He thrives on mass affection, even as he appears to want to push it away. So this is interesting. Very interesting.

"Something has passed between you two." She rolls a pencil between her hands. "I can tell. I have real intuition."

Her hazel eyes dart across my face, but I keep it blank. I'm not going to tell her what happened. She might not keep me around. I'll just try to steer clear of him.

She opens her mouth to say something else but Riley has come back with two cups of coffee. She gives him the same searching, intent look she gave me.

"What?" he says crossly. "What are you looking at me like that for?"

"Intuition. I'll have to develop my thesis further." She twines her hands greedily around the coffee. "Anyway! So. Charlie! See? I was listening. I bet you thought I wasn't. You have an awfully painful-looking scar on your forehead and you're wear-ing overalls in the desert, two things that strike me as both interesting and sad." She takes a long sip of her coffee. "Why are you here?"

I look at Riley without thinking, but he only shrugs, settling back down on the couch, resting his coffee mug on his chest.

I flex my fingers behind my back. "Money?"

"No, why are you *here*?" Julie closes her eyes briefly, as though very annoyed.

"Like, on the planet type of thing?"

"Just in Arizona. We'll talk about the planet at some later date. That's a much more complex conversation." She crinkles her eyes at me as she sips her coffee.

"I moved here? From Minnesota?" What more am I supposed to say?

"For a boy, probably," Riley laughs.

"Shut *up*," I snap. "Why are you so stuck on that? It isn't even *true*."

Julie says, "Then what *is* true?"

And before I can stop myself, because this whole morning has been a clusterfuck that now includes this weird *job interview*, I blurt out, "I tried to kill myself, okay? I messed up, and here I am. And I'm fucking hungry, and I need money. I need a stupid job." As soon as I say them, I desperately want to gather the words up and shove them back inside my mouth. *Freak*, she's probably thinking. Instinctively, I feel for my shirtsleeves, making sure they're pulled down far enough.

I can feel Riley staring at me, hard. It's all I can do not to look over at him.

Abruptly, he gets up from the couch and leaves the office.

Julie squints a few times, like she's trying to evacuate unexpected dust from her eyes. My stomach flip-flops. She's going to tell me to get out. There's no way she's keeping me now. I start to untie my apron.

Instead, she cocks her head at me. Her eyes are kind and sad. "There's a lot of *stuff* in here, isn't there?" Like a bird, her hand flutters before her chest, near her heart.

She nods to herself, touching the bowl of blue stones on her desk. "*Yes*, this is what I *do*. I like to *talk* to people. It gives me a much better sense of them than wanting to know if they've ever washed dishes or brought out a plate of food or handled a mop or what they studied in school." She looks right at me, her freckled face open, her eyes clear. "Come here," she says.

I step forward and she takes my hands in her own. Her eyes are little ponds of warmth. Julie's hands are sure and smooth, *motherly*. Pat, pat, pat. The scent of lavender oil drifts off her skin.

She closes her eyes. "Right now, I'm really *feeling* you."

When she opens her eyes, she lets go of my hands, reaches into one of the bowls, and presses a stone against my palm, closing her fingers around it. The stone has a curious heat.

"Lapis lazuli," she tells me. "They have such an amazingly strong healing ability, do you know? Their power is to carve a deep path through confusion and emotional turmoil. Really helps me work through shit sometimes. You into stones at all?"

"I don't know anything about them," I say. My voice feels small. How can a little stone have so much power? I close my fingers around it. "Do you, like, pray to it, or something?" Talking to rocks. Blue would have a field day with that one.

"If you want." Julie smiles. "Or you can just hold it, and close your eyes, and let yourself really feel its energy, and trust that the stone's energy will feel *you*."

She starts writing on a pad of paper. "It's some really beautiful knowledge, stones. You should think about it. Tomorrow I'll bring some aloe vera for that scar on your head. Keep the stone. It's yours."

She slides some forms across the table. "Here. You need to fill these out for taxes and payroll. Bring them back tomorrow along with your ID and we'll get you on the books." I take the papers and fold them, putting them in the pocket of my overalls.

She hands me a piece of paper, with days and hours written down. Four days a week, seven a.m. to three p.m. "That's your schedule, Charlie. My brother can be a real prick, but he's my brother. He falls down, I pick him up, he shoves me away, he falls down, I pick him up, et cetera, et cetera."

The phone rings, and she swivels away to answer it.

I stand there for a moment before I realize it's my signal to go. I walk down the hallway slowly, the stone still in my hand. When I see Riley in the dish area, wiping the counter, I look away quickly, slipping the stone into my pocket.

I start unloading coffee mugs from bus tubs, trashing the soggy napkins and bent stirrers. Riley comes over and picks up a mug, tilting it so I can see inside.

"You'll want to soak these, see the coffee stains? Soak them once a week or so, with a couple capfuls of bleach in hot water. Just fill up one of the sinks or an empty pickle bucket. Whenever you notice, really. Julie likes them nice and clean."

I nod without looking at him.

Riley whispers, "I'm a lousy person. But you've learned that already."

When I don't say anything, he presses a finger against my sleeve, just above my wrist. He leans closer to me. "You didn't have to lie to me about a cat. I'm no stranger to fucking up."

"Riley!" the tattooed guy yells from the wait station. "Tell us about the time you threw up on Adam Levine's shoes!"

"Oh, that's a good one." Linus laughs hard, like a cartoon horse. I turn around and she winks at me.

Riley lights a cigarette and inhales deeply, smoke sidling from his nostrils as he walks back to the dish area. "Now, now. Vomiting is not uncommon in rock and roll. It's kind of a staple, actually. I was not the first and I am sure I will not be the last to vomit on Mr. Levine. But I'd like to remind you, it was not just his shoes, it was Mr. Levine himself that was the unsuspecting target of my sudden digestive vulgarity. The story begins like this. ..."

I go back to the dishes, still listening to Riley spin his story, following the lilts and cadences of his cigarette-gravelly voice, but I'm also thinking about what he said: *I'm no stranger to fucking up.*

Even though I don't want it to, what he said kind of touches me. What he said: I should have it printed on a fucking T-shirt, because it's the motto of my life, too. Which means that however horrible he was this morning, and however kind he's being to me right now, and very funny, with this story, he and I are closer than I'd like to admit.

My face flushes. I slip a hand into my pocket and wrap it around the stone, will it to tell me to stop thinking what I'm thinking, but the stone stays silent.

After work, I take some of the cash Riley gave me and buy a bag of chips and an iced tea at the co-op. I'm so hungry that I rip into them right away, stuffing my face while looking at the for rents on the community board outside.

It doesn't look promising. My heart kind of sinks. Most of them ask for first, last, and security. Even for a one-bedroom for six hundred dollars, that's eighteen hundred dollars up front, plus utilities. How do I get utilities? Do I have to pay up front for those, too? I do some math in my head: with what True Grit will pay, I'll hardly have anything left over for rent anywhere, not to mention any extras like food or gas or electric.

I ride around downtown for a while until I find the library. I head to the bathroom first, and wait until a woman leaves before I take one of Mikey's empty water bottles from my backpack and fill it with lemony hand soap from the dispenser. I can use this for the shower, but I'm going to need to find a toothbrush and toothpaste. I bundle toilet paper around my fist and stuff it in the pack. There aren't any more rolls left at Mikey's.

Downstairs, I find out you have to sign in to use the public computers, and that they time you. The young librarian looks at me warily when I write my name on the sign-in sheet, but I figure it must be because of the scar on my forehead, because I know I don't stink, and my arms are covered.

I sit in front of the computer and pull out the sheet of paper Casper gave me. Her email address is typed, but in neat, round handwriting next to it she wrote *Charlie, please don't hesitate to contact me. I* am *thinking of you.* She even signed her real name. *Bethany.* I ignore the information about the halfway house and support group, because that was for Minnesota, and I'm far from there now.

I log in to the email account I set up at Creeley during my ALTERNA-LEARN studies. I don't really know what to say, so I just start typing.

> Hi—I'm not where you think I am and I'm sorry. It wasn't going to work out with my mom and she knew it. My friend Mikey lives in Tucson and I'm down here now. I have a little money and I'm staying at Mikey's place. It's not the greatest, but at least it isn't outside. I found a job, too, washing dishes. I guess that's what I'm good for. I've been drawing in my book a lot. I don't think I'm scared, but maybe I am. It's weird. Everything is just weird. Like, I don't actually know how to live. I mean, I

managed to live on the street and everything, but that was different than normal living—that was kind of just about not getting killed. I don't know anything about utilities, or rent, or "security deposits" or what food to buy. I've hardly talked at all to anyone, but I'm already tired of talking. Tell everyone I say hey and tell Louisa I miss her.—Charlie

When I'm about to log off, I notice another message, buried in alerts from the online education center asking me when I will resume classes and from people in Nigeria asking for money.

The subject line is *Bloody Cupcakes*. My heart drops. I hesitate for a moment, then click on it.

Hey soul sister—Sasha snuck around on Ghost-Doc's desk and found your file. Had some emails from that online school thing you were doing—found your email addy in there. GhostDoc's got a whole FILE on yooooo. Talk about dramarama—you never said anything about some weird sex house. You with your mom now? How's THAT working out? Tsk tsk on GhostDoc for leaving your file out, too, but how the hell are you? Francie's out—she never came back from Pass one day. Louisa is still up to the same old same old, writin writin writin, blah blah blah. So whats it like outside, Charlie? Ive still got so much time ahead of me baby, I have no hope. Give me some hope!

Isis will be sprung in three wks and she is freaking
OUT. C U Cupcake, write back soon. BLUE

The sound of the timer startles the mouse from my grip. A large woman with meaty arms nudges me from the chair, barely giving me time to log out.

I make my way out of the library to the plaza. The sun is starting to go down, the sky turning pretty shades of pink and lilac.

Why did Blue want to find *me*? She didn't even *like* me at Creeley. At least, it didn't seem like it.

I want that world to stay hidden. I want that world to stay sixteen hundred miles away. I want a fresh start.

Three grubby guys on the library lawn catch my eye. They're rolling cigarettes, sitting against their dark backpacks. I grit my teeth. I don't want to talk to them, but I'm going to, because they'll have information I need.

Two of them grunt when I ask where the food bank is, but the third man points down the street and tells me the name of the place. One of the other men says, "Yah, but you won't get in, girl. Got to get in line for dinner practically at the crack of fuckin' dawn and lately, it's all babies and they mamas. Can't take a plate of food might be for a baby, girl."

I say thanks and unlock my bicycle. Riding home, I snag a damp plaid blanket from a fence. Someone must have left it out to dry. Next up on my list of fresh start items is a place to live. The blanket will come in handy.

THE NEXT MORNING, I'M UP BEFORE THE SUN RISES, DRAWING in the half-light, eating a piece of bread with peanut butter. I'm drawing Ellis, what I remember of her. She liked me to talk to her when she took a bath, her skin wet and shiny. I loved her skin, the smoothness of it, rich and unscarred.

At work, Riley is on time, but he looks terrible, his face ashen and his eyes dark. He gets a little color back after he sneaks some beer from the fridge. I pretend like I don't see, but I think he knows I know. Mostly, I just stay quiet and so does he. I get the feeling you have to tiptoe around him a lot.

After work, I ride my bike back downtown. I find the shelter and the kitchen; the men were right. Lines of resigned-looking women and jittery-eyed kids are camped out under tarps hiding from the sun, waiting for the kitchen to open for dinner. Around the back of the building are bins of clothing and household goods under a long gray tent. A shelter worker reads a magazine while I rifle through the bins, taking some plates and coffee-stained cups, utensils, a chipped pink bowl. I find a tub filled with bags of sanitary napkins, boxes of tampons. The shelter worker hands me two rolls of toilet paper, tells me that's the limit. She gives me a Baggie with a toothbrush, floss, two condoms, a tube of toothpaste, a flyer with directions to a food shelf that looks miles and miles away, and a pile of pamphlets about STDs and food stamps. I tell her thanks and she smiles a little. I don't feel weird about coming here. Evan called places like this godsends. It is what it is. I take my meager supplies back to Mikey's and draw until it gets solidly dark.

It's after ten o'clock when I ride over to Fourth Avenue and head down the alley behind the Food Conspiracy. I've been thinking about this ever since I came to the co-op that first time—that this would be the ideal place for vegetables and fruit in the Dumpster. I'm still against using any of the money Ellis and I made. If I spend that, it should be for a place to live, and the money I get from Grit isn't much. My stomach is starting to hurt from all the peanut butter sandwiches. I need something else.

I work quickly, filling my backpack with bruised apples, dented peaches, too-soft celery. Just as I'm zipping it up, I notice a figure at the end of the alley, watching and swaying slightly.

At the shelter, I snagged a fork for protection and wedged it into my pocket. My fingers curl around it now as I stare down the alley at the weaving figure. But then I let my breath out and my fingers loosen.

Riley takes a drag from his cigarette. Before I can stop myself, my words are out, tentative, unfurling down the alley to him.

"Riley," I say. "Hey. Hi."

I want him to talk to me, but he only takes a drag from his cigarette and keeps walking. "Bye," I call out, but he doesn't look back.

I wait for him to mention it the next morning at work, but he doesn't. In fact, he doesn't say much of anything all day.

But when I go to punch out, he appears with a brown bag. There are circles underneath his eyes.

"If you're hungry," he says, "ask. I don't want to see you in dark alleys anymore, Strange Girl. Okay?"

He walks back to the cook station without waiting for my answer.

I'M SITTING OUTSIDE ON MY BREAK, NEXT TO THE GO PLAYERS, when I realize that the kind of place that will rent to me, the kind of place I could probably just barely afford, isn't the kind of place that even advertises in something like the *Tucson Weekly* or on the Food Conspiracy co-op board. Credit checks, first and last, security deposits, and, as one Go player helpfully tells me as he looks over my shoulder at the ads, "If you ain't lived in Tucson before and never had no utilities in your name? You have to pay fucking two hundred and forty dollars just to get your gas turned on. They call it a *deposit*."

Another player says, "Seventy-five dollars to turn on the electric."

They all start grumbling about rents and the economy. I wonder where they live and what they do, because they don't seem to have jobs. They just come here every day, all day, and drink coffee and eat bagels and then go home, leaving their coffee mugs filled with cigarettes. For me to clean out.

Evan.

Evan liked to cruise restaurants and bars that had outside seating, snatching half-spent cigarettes from ashtrays. He would lead us through the narrower parts of St. Paul, where people looked out the windows of high, stuffy-looking apartments with listless eyes, or slumped inside three-season porches. If we could work up the money, sometimes we were able to find a room for all three of us for just a week or so in some crappy house, barricading a shoddy door against the druggies who came looking for late-night handouts. It was nice to be in a room, though, instead of crouching together in an alley, or trying to find a good spot by the river with the others.

The place that will have me won't have fees, or first and last. It won't even be in the paper. I toss the *Weekly* on a chair and go back to work.

After my shift, I ride my bicycle back down to Riley's neighborhood and then a few blocks farther, where the sidewalks become cramped and cracked and the houses squat closer together. Just like in St. Paul, in this neighborhood people are still doing nothing, but doing it on porches of decrepit apartment buildings or while leaning against telephone poles, because it's warmer here. I ride until I find a scrawled sign Scotch-taped to the chain-link fence in front of a peeling white building: room for let, ask inside, 1a. The front door to the building is wide open. Two houses over is a drive-in liquor store.

Inside, an elderly man answers the downstairs door marked 1a, office. The room behind him is dark. He blinks as though the light hurts his eyes.

"You Section Eight? Don't matter if you are. Just want to know up front."

"I don't know what that is," I tell him.

He shrugs, pulling a thick jumble of keys from his pocket. We walk down the matted red carpet in the lobby to some creaky-looking stairs. There are doors all along the first floor, most with peeling paint.

Blue duct tape holds in loose plaster on the stairwell walls. The old man stops to lean on the banister. I hesitate and then touch my fingers to his elbow to help. The skin there is whitish and dry, cracked.

"Sixteen steps," he breathes. "I bet you don't know how old

I am." His crinkled eyes are tinged with pink. His nose sprouts hair and blackheads. My grandmother always took care of herself: she had her hair done every week and she smelled like creams and cinnamon. I wish I had remembered to ask my mother about her, what happened to her that made the insurance for Creeley stop.

This man is crumbly old, and not well taken care of. He laughs, revealing a damp and largely empty mouth. "Me neither!"

On the second floor, he pauses. "You seem a little young for a place like this, but I don't ask questions. A lot of people here have troubles. I just ask they don't bring any extra, you understand?"

I nod as he leads me to a door that has been plastered and painted with a sickly shade of brown over an already strange shade of orange. I lived in some crappy places with my mother, where mice ate through cupboards. I lived outside with rain and icy snow. I lived in Seed House. These shitty, broken walls and crappy paint and this old, old man: it all falls somewhere in between. After what I'm used to, it's not paradise, but it isn't hell, either.

The room isn't much bigger than a large bedroom, with an extra room off to the side. That room, I find out when I peer in, is actually a combination kitchen and bathroom, with a dented pink refrigerator and an old-looking sink on one side and a toilet and tiny claw-foot tub on the other. There's no stove and the tub is the smallest I've ever seen. When I climb in and sit down, my knees press almost to my chest. It's weird, yet I kind of like it.

He shrugs. "The building is old. Nineteen eighteen, maybe? Back in the day, tubs was a real luxury. People laid a board across them to eat supper. That was the dining table! There's a common bathroom down the hall for the men. I try to give the rooms with toilets to the ladies."

He says *across* like *acrost. People laid a board acrost them to eat supper.*

The ceiling is a maze of peeling paper and red and yellow splatters. I look over at the man.

He rubs his chin thoughtfully. "Well, see, that was old Roger. Sometimes he'd get the fits when he was drinking, start the fighting with the mustard and the ketchup. He liked his hot dogs, our Roger.

"Got a ladder you can use to clean it up. Knock twenty bucks off the first month since the room isn't cleaned. There's a fella down on the first floor used to do my handiwork, but he don't wanna do it no more." He pauses. "Call him Schoolteacher, cuz that's what he used to do, I guess. He's always jawing about something. I guess you can't really get rid of what you used to be. It kinda sticks to you."

Outside, sometimes that's what older people became known for: not their name, but what they used to do, before they ended up on the street. *MoneyGuy. BakeryLady. PizzaDude.* If you were a kid, though, that's all you were: Kid. I wonder what I'll be known as here, if I'll just be Kid again.

I wonder how Schoolteacher got from his classroom to this broken-down place.

The old man glances back out at the front room. He seems puzzled for a minute; then he says *Ah.*

"No bed," he tells me. "Took that away when Roger passed. Knock another ten off the monthly rent, then. Was just a mattress really, anyways."

In the front room, there's a lamp with a dubious-looking

shade, a plain card table, and a green easy chair. He sees me looking and smiles. "Partially furnished," he says.

"Three eighty-five a month includes utilities, but if you bring a television in and want the cable, you'll have to set that up and pay yourself, though a couple of gentlemen on floor one seem to have figured something out on the sly. And I don't have any of that wiffy."

He says, "Most of us are just month-to-month, you know, one or two week by week, if that's what they want. I do need a security deposit, though, that's my rule, even if you're short-term and you don't seem like trouble. You never know when someone's gonna do some damage, am I right? That'll run you two hundred dollars, but you get it back if you leave your room in good shape."

He pauses, looking down at me sternly. "Liquor store gets a little noisy if that's a bother to you. I'm not particular, but like I said, just bring the troubles you already got and no more than that."

A television across the hall sends off the sounds of tinny laughter. Someone down the hall sings softly in Spanish.

I don't know how to do any of this. I don't know if this is a good place, or a bad place, or what I should ask about. All I know is that this is the place I have money for right now, and that this man seems nice, and he's not asking for an application fee or a credit check or anything like that. I've been in worse places, and I feel scared, but I look up at him anyway and nod. I can't find my words, and my hands are trembling. I don't want to think about what might happen if this turns out to be a horrible place.

He stoops to brush a fly off his pants leg. His toes are gnarled and dirty in his sandals. "I'm Leonard. Why don't you

tell me your name and we can start this beautiful friendship."
He reaches down to help me up from the tub.

I take his hand. It's surprisingly soft, and I smile in spite of
myself. I relax a little. He seems so nice, and honest. "Charlie,"
I tell him. "Charlie Davis is my name."

WHEN I GET BACK TO MIKEY'S APARTMENT, THERE'S A CD leaning against the screen door, with an envelope taped to the front. *Mike* is written in flowing purple ink, with the *e* drifting off into a series of pert purple flowers. I don't have time to really think about what it means, so I leave it by the door. I write a note to Mikey with my new address.

It doesn't take long to repack my stuff. I wrap the dishes from the shelter in the plaid blanket I snagged from the fence and wedge them into Louisa's suitcase, throw my clothes into my backpack. I find some rope and lug everything outside, strap Louisa's suitcase to the back of the yellow bicycle, and hoist my backpack onto my shoulders.

Opera pours from the windows of the front house. I stop for a second, listening, and wonder if I should say goodbye to Ariel, or thank her, or something, but I don't. I use the garden gate to leave and I don't look back. It's just another thing I've never learned how to do: say goodbye.

It's a slow, hard ride to the white building. The suitcase keeps shifting behind me on the bicycle and I struggle to keep my balance and keep pedaling. I'm a little worried about leaving my bike outside, even locked up, but I do it, hoping for the best.

I drag everything I own up the rickety stairs and stop. Wiping sweat off my face, I stand at the doorway to the room for a solid five minutes, waiting for someone to let me in, when I realize I can let *myself* in. Because I have a *key*. I look down at it, cool and silver, in my hands.

When I flick the light switch in the room, nothing happens. I can see in the shadows that there's no bulb in the light fixture, only an empty, dark hole. I drag my backpack and Louisa's suitcase into the room and shut the door, sliding the chain lock into place.

I pull the cord on the standing lamp; nothing. When I unscrew the bulb, I see the stain of blowout. The kitchen area is only a few steps away from the door. The tiny bulb above the sink there works, though I have to stand on my tiptoes to reach the string, which turns out to be a dirty shoestring.

The sunlight is fading. From the street comes the dull and insistent *whee-hoo, whee-hoo* of cars hitting the driveway bell of the drive-through liquor store.

I've finished my bread and the jar of peanut butter and just have one bruised peach left from the Dumpster at the co-op. My stomach rumbles, but I don't want to go anywhere else tonight. Yellow light streams through the window from the streetlamp outside. I cup my hands and drink musty water from the kitchen tap, thinking about what to do. I decide Leonard is my best bet.

I unlock the door and ease it open. The hallway is empty. I can smell cigarette smoke. There are three doors on my side and three across the hall, with the door to the bathroom at the end of the hall. That door is closed, though I can hear some grunting. I shut my door and head down the stairs quickly, grateful that the hall light works.

At Leonard's, he hands me a hammer and nail. I offer a quarter for a spare lightbulb, and he accepts it, grinning. In the room, I screw in the lightbulb.

I pound the nail into the wall and hang the glittery skull cross from Ariel's house above the tub.

I push the green chair in front of the door, make sure the door is latched, then lie on the floor, my head on my backpack. I count to myself: I had nine hundred and thirty-three dollars of the Ellis-and-me money. I paid Leonard a total of five hundred and ninety-five dollars for rent and security, so I have three hundred and thirty-eight dollars left. It was scary and sad to hand over so much money at once, to have to let go what she and I had dreamed about.

But I do have a room of my own, at last. I'm not in an alley, or an underpass, or a leaky, cold van, or a red room in a horrifying house. I'm here.

I don't feel sad. For just now, I don't feel scared. I feel, for right now, well, kind of triumphant.

I hug myself, listening to all the life outside this grimy room, the shouts from the street, muffled voices from the other rooms, televisions, crackling radios, the blare of a siren several blocks away, thinking, *My room. My room.*

IN THE EARLY MORNING, THE CLATTER OF BOOTS OUTSIDE MY door wakes me up. Over and over, the door down the hallway opens, shuts, then sounds of pissing or sighing, then flushing, then more boots. Groggily, I swipe at my eyes. My hand comes away gritty and salty.

The tub doesn't have a shower spigot. I peel off my clothes as the water runs. I look everywhere but at my body: the hooks on my overalls, the stains on my blue jersey shirt. I don't feel comfortable just standing while the tub fills, so I step in and sit down. I feel a rush of gratefulness for the warm water. I use the lemony hand soap from the library to soap my hair, then I close my eyes and splash water over my thighs, stomach, breasts, face. Finally, when I feel clean, I scrunch way down on my back and submerge my head, enjoying the silence.

When I'm about to step out of the tub, I realize I don't have a towel. Just one more thing to add to the list of things I need.

I brush water off my body, using my hands as best I can. I don't have to worry about my hair, it's still so short. I choose a clean long-sleeved shirt from the pile of Tanya's clothes and then slip on my overalls. I almost forget to lock the door on my way out to work. *My* door.

I'M DOZING ON THE FLOOR THE NEXT AFTERNOON, AFTER work, using my backpack as a pillow, when I hear the soft sounds of tapping coming from the hallway. At first, I think it's from a television in one of the other rooms. When I realize it's not, when I realize someone is knocking at *my* door, I stand up, grabbing the bent fork from the backpack, just in case. Warily, I push the green chair out of the way. I tug open my door just a tiny bit, but keep the latch on, and peek out.

A blond, dreadlocked figure smiles widely at me, pressing his face through the crack. The fork clatters to the ground. My heart starts beating wildly.

"Charlie Davis," Mikey sings softly. "It's you. *Look* at you."

I fling the door open, my face already wet. "Mikey," I whisper, burying myself against him. "Oh, you're here. You're finally here."

He hugs me so hard we fall to the floor, laughing and crying. It's a great relief to be held, to feel arms around my whole body, arms that clasp my stomach, another pair of legs spooning, a face pressed into my neck, absorbing my heat, my tears. Mikey's voice is a soft *Hey now, come on now, it's all right* against my ear, lips dry on my temple. He rubs my back as he rocks against me. He nuzzles my head with his chin, his stubble catching in the bristly tines of my hair. I say, *I missed you,* and he answers, *Me too. My fault,* I say. *No,* he says. *Never.* I say, *I didn't answer her.* Ellis's texts had come slowly, one by one: *Smthing hrts. U never sd hurt like this. 2 much.* Seeing him brings it all back. I hadn't seen her in almost three months. I stared at the bright yellow text and turned the phone facedown on the bed, using all the anger I had at her to steel myself, and when I woke up the next morning, my mother was in the doorway, saying my name in a funny voice, her mouth trembling.

Wrapped in Mikey's body, on the floor on the stolen plaid blanket, I think of those photographs taken inside waves, the ones with surfers in slick suits on boards coasting through the tunnel of water, eyes wide. I think they must feel protected inside that curl of water, inside the sudden silencing of the world, even if only for a few minutes. I feel like that, right now, in my small, gloomy room: everything I've done and pretended to be in the past year, in the weeks past, is washed away and I am being cleaned, transported, polished for the new world.

"So, out with it. Tell me. What did they tell you in there? Is there, like, a name for what you ... have? The cutting thing." Mikey stares at me intently. When did he get so handsome? I look down at my plate. We're at a place called Gentle Ben's and sharing a Black & Blue Burger and peppery fries.

His question makes me nervous—how much should I tell him? What's the squick factor on cutting and psychotic behavior, after all? I swallow a French fry and take a deep breath. "It's called NSSI. Non-Suicidal Self-Injury."

He wipes his mouth and takes a sip of his Coke, his eyes flashing. "What's that supposed to mean, exactly? Did ... does Ellis have that, too?"

"It means I hurt myself, but I don't want to die." I take a bite of the burger. Cooked food tastes so good. I ordered a lemonade, too. I take a drink, savoring the sweetness that floods my mouth before I have to talk again, because Casper said to talk.

I force it out, slowly. "It's hard to explain. I have other stuff, too. Impulse-control disorder. PTSD."

He frowns. "Post-traumatic stress disorder? Isn't that for vets and stuff?"

I chew my burger carefully. I don't mean to, but what I say comes out in a whisper. "It's from a lot of stuff." I never told Mikey about what happened to my dad. I guess he just assumed my parents were divorced because most everybody's parents were divorced. He didn't know about my mother hitting me until just before he went away.

He never knew about the cutting, or about Ellis's eating problems. We held each other's secrets tight.

"Jesus, Charlie. I'm so sorry." He pushes his plate away. "You know when I came back for break once, I tried looking for you. With DannyBoy. But we couldn't find you."

His face is leaner, harder, in a way. *Adult-like.* He pulls his knees up against his body, resting his sneakers against the edge of the plastic chair.

Of *course* he would look for me. Of the four of us, Ellis, Charlie, Mikey, and DannyBoy, Mikey was the most responsible, the most well-spoken. He could talk us out of trouble with police officers in Lowertown. He could smooth over missed curfews and alcohol breath with parents. He could put his small, wiry body between DannyBoy's loose, fleshier one and the hard body of a crusty punk with hands the size of fresh hams.

He clears his throat. "I don't drink anymore, Charlie, or anything. I'm totally straight now. I thought you should know. I just want to set that out right now."

"Okay," I say slowly, kind of grateful. I'm not supposed to do any of that, either, and if Mikey's clean, that will make things easier. "I can't drink, either, or do anything, really. My doctor doesn't want me to. And it was okay in the hospital. It wasn't bad. I was safer, anyway."

Mickey looks relieved. Happy. "That's good," he says, "that's really good you aren't drinking. For me, it was like, after I got here, I was so tired of all that shit. I just wanted to start fresh. I mean, we spent so much time wasted back home, do you realize that? We were fucked up *all* the time."

"I know. Some of it was fun, though." I smile.

"Yeah, but sometimes you have to let stuff go if you want to move forward, you know? Did you know DannyBoy got clean?"

"Are you kidding?" I remember how things got worse and worse for DannyBoy, and he would spend hours walking Rice Street, looking for the man in the black vinyl jacket with purple piping, and after he found him, he'd go soft, like a baby, and loll in the grass in Mears Park by the shallow pond, the sun illuminating his slack face.

"No lie. I talked to his mom when I was back for Christmas. He spent six months at some rehab way up north, by Boundary Waters, way out in the forest, where they had to chop their own wood for heat and raise chickens for eggs and food. Crazy stuff, but he did it. He's been clean for a year. He works with old people now, like taking care of them. Feeding them and stuff. In Duluth."

I try to imagine lumbering DannyBoy spooning oatmeal into an old person's mouth, or changing their diaper, but I can't. I can only see him high, or sad, or pummeling someone in the alley after a show.

"It can be done, Charlie. You see? You can change stuff in your life, if you want to."

I nod carefully, because I'm not sure that's possible, or if it's even something I can do, since I always seem to be fucking up. Mikey smiles, slipping money from his pocket and tucking it under his plate. I'm sorry to see him do it. It was getting easier and easier to talk to him here, our words drifting like water.

"Well," he says slowly. "I don't like where you're living, but first things first, right? We need to get you something to sleep on. I've got no wheels, so this means some legwork. You up for legwork? Looks like you could use some legwork."

"Hey!" I say, my face reddening a little, realizing that he's been looking at my body, which makes me feel scared and kind of hopeful. I shift in my seat. Does he think I'm too chunky now, though?

"They wouldn't let us exercise. And the food was really starchy."

"Just teasing," he says, smiling. "A little weight looks good on you. You were always kinda scrawny."

We stand up. He stretches, his green hoodie inching up. His belly is brown and downy, pierced with a silver ring. I have a sudden urge to place my hand on the sharp bone of his exposed hip, to feel the warm skin there. I feel my face color again. I wish I knew for sure if he was thinking the same thing about me.

Suddenly I want to ask him about the CD on his doorstep, the purple-scripted envelope. I'd forgotten all about that, that Mikey might have a girlfriend. I'm about to ask him when he steps closer to me and says quietly, "Show me."

I know exactly what he's talking about. I flinch, worried about what he might say, but then, slowly, I push up one jersey sleeve, then the other. It's almost dark now; the white lights dangling along the patio's roof are as fuzzy as the snow I left behind in Minnesota. He takes a deep breath; the warm exhalation coats my face. His eyes water as they fix on my damage. I push my sleeves down. "Time's up," I say lightly. I'm very aware of how close we are and the fact that his lips are not far from mine.

What would he say if I told him there are even more scars on my legs?

Mikey rubs the heels of his hands against his eyes.

"Everything got very big," I say.

He doesn't say anything.

Casper said, *You have to talk, Charlotte. You can't be silent.* "It's like I was talking about," I say, forcing the words out. "Like, everything got very heavy, you know? I couldn't hold it anymore."

I missed Ellis so much and I was so mad at her and it was all my fault. And Mikey, there was this house, this really bad house.

But that stuff stays inside.

He shakes his head. We stare at each other. He says, "Okay, then. Let's try to keep it small, all right? One thing at a time."

"Small." I test the word carefully. "Small." I like the sound of it. Nothing more than I can hold in two hands at once. Small.

We borrow a pickup truck from his chubby friend, Rollin, who lives on Euclid Avenue. All around the university, desks and tables and mattresses are lumped in alleys or stacked in teetering piles on sidewalks outside apartment buildings and dorms. Mikey says, "This is a good time. Everybody's moving out since it's summer break. Throwing out perfectly fine stuff."

We find an aluminum Wildcats garbage can, a box fan, a toaster painted with black and white polka dots, a water pitcher, a small end table. Later, driving slowly down an alley, we spot a twin futon wedged between a glass-topped coffee table and a stack of framed Hooters posters. Mikey checks it for cigarette holes. I try to joke with him, saying that doesn't much matter, seeing as how I used to sleep in an underpass, but that just makes him grimace.

He runs down the street to his apartment for rope to tie the futon in a roll. The futon smells like smoke and beer. I'm tired, rubbing my eyes, when I hear the sound of shuffling footsteps.

It's Riley, holding a canvas tote bag in one hand and a cigarette in the other. It's almost midnight, but he's wearing sunglasses. He regards the futon and the other items in the pickup truck.

"Ah." His voice is thick, slightly slurred. "Excellent season for road furniture."

The light of the streetlamp turns his face yellowy, sallow.

He pushes the sunglasses to the top of his head. "What did I tell you about hanging out in alleys?" He tosses his cigarette into the road. He slips a beer out of the tote bag and wrenches the cap off with his belt buckle, tilts it toward me.

He shrugs and takes a drink when I shake my head. Warm light flickers into his eyes. He smiles—and a flare inside me, a tiny *whoosh,* like the flick of a pilot light, heats my face. He moves toward me, so close I can feel his breath on my lips, smell the tang of his beer as he whispers, "I felt that happen, too."

The crunch of gravel knocks us loose: Mikey is slowly jogging back up the alley, rope swinging in his hand. I pinch my thighs through my pockets to stop the thudding of my heart.

Mikey stops short when he reaches us, looking back and forth. "Hey," he pants. "Riley. How's it going?"

"Michael." Riley takes a pull from his beer. "It goes well. How was the Cat Foley tour?"

"Freaking awesome." Mikey grunts heavily as he moves around the futon, tightening the rope. "Got some great crowds out east. DeVito was really on for the Boston show. Hey, this is my friend, Charlie. Charlie, this is Riley."

"We're already old friends, Michael."

Mikey looks from Riley to me and back again, confused. "What are you talking about?"

"I work at True Grit," I say reluctantly. "Washing dishes. I started a week ago."

Riley nods. "She really knows how to bleach a coffee cup, I'll give her that. And you two . . . you know each other . . . how?"

There's a glint in his eye that I don't like. Even though he's drunk, I can see the wheels turning, can see him remembering our conversation about why I moved here. He thinks Mikey is the boy I moved here for.

Mikey says, "We kind of grew up together. Back in Minnesota." He walks around the futon, tightening the rope.

I sigh. Wait for it.

Riley looks over at me. "That's so *interesting*. Charlie didn't mention it." His eyes are bright and the quirk of his smile is catty. "What a nice co— I mean, what nice friends you make."

I glare at him.

Mikey is blissfully unaware of Riley's innuendos, busy jerking the rope into a knot. "Hey, Charlie, Riley was in a band, did you know that? You remember that song 'Charity Case'?"

Riley's expression changes suddenly. "Let's not go there," he says, his voice sharp. "No need to reopen old wounds."

The song title pings around my head until it lands on the night I sat in Mikey's backyard, drawing. The lyrics trickle back to me. "Yeah," I say. "I heard some band playing it the other night, too."

Mikey nods. "Oh, yeah, it's a big cover staple around here, for sure. Riley didn't usually sing lead, but he did on that track." He laughs at the annoyed look on Riley's face.

I do remember. It was a big song for a while, four or five years ago. Vague images flash into view: a video of four guys with tousled hair, black low-tops, crummy T-shirts under short-sleeved checked shirts, singing a song from the bed of a pickup truck as it rambled across the desert. There were close-ups of lizards and girls swing dancing with each other, wearing Daisy Dukes and kicking up dust. All the guys looked similar, but the singer had a thrilling voice, a high, romantic twang that fell into deep ache with sudden swoops.

I look at Riley and it hits me. The singer in the video, laconic in the back of the truck, staring straight into the lens as two perfect model types in halter tops leaned against him, nuzzling his cheeks, singing *I just want you to see my for-real face . . .* A little stoned, lazing on Ellis's bed in the middle of the night, skipping through channels; she stopped at the video, growled, *Hotsy-totsy, that one,* and then flipped to something else.

"You," I say, almost gleefully. "That was *you.*"

Riley holds up a hand. "I'm all done here, kids." He extracts another beer from the tote bag. "I'll be seeing you, Michael. Strange Girl, don't forget to get your beauty sleep. Those dishes won't wash themselves."

We watch him lumber away.

"That guy," Mikey says. "Superior musician, stellar songwriter, but major fuckup. Talk about a waste of talent." He shakes his head and we watch as the alley gradually, gently absorbs Riley's body.

Getting the futon up the sixteen stairs requires the help of one of the drunk guys on the porch, but when we're done, Mikey looks satisfied and happy. He brushes the dirt from his hands onto his pants.

"Charlie," he says softly.

His eyes are kind and I move toward him. It's been so good to be with him after so long, so safe. I've been holding him for more than two weeks, breathing him from his pillow, waiting for him to come back. He already knows me; maybe he wouldn't care about my scars.

I put my hand on his belt, super lightly, and hold my breath. It's not going to be true, I tell myself, what Louisa said. That nobody normal would ever love us. It's *not* going to be true.

He kind of laughs, but he doesn't meet my eyes. Instead, he wraps his arms around me and talks into my hair. "I gotta get a move on, Charlie. It's almost two in the morning and I'm working tomorrow at Magpies. But everything's going to be cool now, all right? I'm gonna help you, you know that, right? I have a lot going on with the band and work and stuff, but I'm here now. I'm here. And it's so cool that you already found a job. That's such a good start."

I listen to the patter of his heart beneath his shirt, disappointment ringing in my chest. "Okay, Mikey." I wish he was staying. I wonder what he means by *stuff,* and if that has anything to do with the envelope and the CD. He gives me a little wave as he leaves.

The door falls shut behind him. I push the easy chair that smells like dried wine and unloved cat in front of it. The junk we found is in piles around the room, the stupid things you're supposed to fill your house with. The people in the building move quietly tonight, running water in sinks, whispering on phones.

The temperature outside has dropped, so I shut the window above the kitchen sink, wrap myself in the plaid blanket, and take out my sketchbook and bag of pencils and charcoals. My fingers find a pattern on the page; the night replays, a loop in my head, in front of my eyes.

Whoosh. That electrical warmth hits me again as bits of Riley's face form under my fingers, the beginnings of a person on paper.

Riley's sway as he disappeared down the alley, I recognized it. It wasn't all booze. It was the thing that happened when a little too much got a little too messed up. That sway, it's what creeps over a person when they've begun to empty out and don't care enough to put anything back, to replace what has been lost.

I feel like I walk like that, too, sometimes.

I look at the drawing. His face is more worn than that face from the video a few years ago. He looks more tired than hotsy-totsy now. Something's disappeared. And there's an edge, too, that I can't quite get a fix on.

Whatever he is, or whatever happened to him, I don't want any part of it, no matter how much my body starts to freak out when he's near me. I turn the page. I start drawing fields of dreadlocks instead, intricate nests of hair, the kind slope and open heart of Mikey's face.

THE NEXT MORNING, RILEY DOESN'T SAY ANYTHING ABOUT meeting me and Mikey in the alley. He must have been so messed up, or gotten so messed up, that he doesn't remember. Or he doesn't care. It's hard to tell with him. He's super talkative with Linus and the waitstaff, but not me, though he does slip me half of a grilled cheese sandwich at lunchtime.

After I get off work, I head to the library. All the computers are taken, so I camp out upstairs, in the art section. Ellis used to think it was weird, that I liked to look at old art and stuff, like Rubens and all his pillowy women with soft hair and flushed cheeks. I like Frida Kahlo, too, she seems so pissed off, and her colors are all angry. There are like a million stories inside her paintings. Even though Evan said my comics made him feel great, and famous, they seem dumb to me, just stupid stuff about loser kids on the streets, high as kites, dancing around in dark capes and pretending they're superheroes.

This art seems important. It's in *books*. It *lasts*. I have to teach myself, I *want* to teach myself, how to make something great. I want my drawings to be great.

Before I go, I'm able to slip onto one of the computers. There's an email from Casper.

Dear Charlie,

Well, I was afraid something like this might happen. I wasn't entirely confident in your mother's ability to help you. I am glad that you seem to be safe, and will have a friend looking out for you. I hope you're

182

following the rules I set out for you, and I hope you're looking for some help. There might be some free counseling available to you, or a group that you could join. Perhaps your friend could help you look for something? I want you to be safe, Charlie. Sometimes we can get overconfident when things seem to go well, and we might not recognize the danger signs that could derail our progress. Take everything slow, Charlie, and one thing at a time, yes? Your first priority is YOU.

I think it's wonderful you've found a job. A job can lead to important gains in confidence. Well done!

You asked about Louisa. I wish I could tell you about Louisa, Charlie, but I can't. Patient confidentiality and all that "blah blah fuck-all," as Blue likes to put it. Be well, and I hope to hear from you soon.

P.S. I know all the nicknames, like "Casper" and "GhostDoc," by the way. Just FYI, as you girls like to say.

I'm just starting to reply when the timer goes off. I promise myself I'll come back tomorrow after work and write her an email. I should probably write Blue, too. I know how lonely it can get at Creeley. I feel bad that I didn't reply to her email the last time I was at the library.

When I get home, there's a note from Mikey shoved under my door. *Meet me at Magpies at 9. I got suckered into a double shift today. I'll take you to a party after, okay? See you.*

I fold the note tenderly, my heart thrumming at the thought of seeing Mikey again. A party. Like a date? Something? I'm not sure. I use a lot of soap in the bathtub, pick a clean shirt. I slip into the bathroom down the hall, wincing at the smell of piss in the toilet and the overflowing wastebasket. I inspect my face in the dirty, cracked mirror.

"Excellent-looking underneath all that dirt and shit," Evan had said at the parade.

I don't have any dirt and shit on my face now. It's pink from the sun and clean, with a wave of freckles across my nose. It's still a shock seeing my real hair after years of dye. Who is this person? What's she becoming?

I blink at myself. I could be a girl, a real girl. I could be a possibility, with Mikey.

Couldn't I?

WE CAN HEAR THE PARTY A BLOCK AWAY, THE HEAVY THROB of drums and bass and laughter. Throngs of people spill onto the sidewalk, mill in the street. Outside the house there's a blue velvet cowboy hat on top of a squat cactus.

Before we go into the backyard, Mikey stops suddenly, his face dropping. "Oh, man," he says, looking down at me. "I completely forgot. The drinking thing. I'm cool with it, but how about you? I want to make sure you're comfortable."

I take a deep breath. "It's okay," I say. "It's fine. I want to go. I'll be okay." I smile. "Swear."

Inside, though, there's a little part of me that wonders if I really am ready.

"Shit." He stares ahead of me at the yard, where tons of people are dancing and milling around. "I really want to hear this band. Are you sure?"

"Yeah. It's cool."

"Okay." He bites his lip and his face flushes. "There's something else, too, and I probably should have told you, but—"

He's interrupted by a heavily sweating guy who runs up and yells something unintelligible in Mikey's ear. Mikey gives me the "one minute" sign with his finger and follows the guy to where the band is playing. He leans down behind some amps. I lose sight of him as I get swept along in a crowd of people decked out in various combinations of sneakers, combat boots, vintage dresses, piercings, T-shirts, and porkpie hats. Everyone here seems much older than me.

The band is a tangle of wires and amps, holey jeans,

horn-rimmed glasses and sweat-soaked checked shirts. The music is loose and fiery with lots of raspy vocals and high-pitched howls. The singer splashes his face with a cup of beer, lights a cigarette, throws it into the crowd, and hunches back over the microphone, singing about coyotes and girls and beer and being a garbageman. People are dancing along, red cups held over their heads.

I close my eyes for a moment, letting the music fold over me, feeling the gentle crush of people pushing my body. This is something I missed, being at a party or a show, being a *part* of people, of something.

I miss the warehouses and basements. I miss the screaming singers, the shredded, bloody fingers of the bassists. I miss the pit at hard-core shows. Ellis didn't like it, but she came with me anyway, standing at the edge of the crowd while I hurled myself, and got hurled, around in the pit. No one cared for you in the pit. No one asked your name. You fell in and moved and swung and circled and bashed and when you stumbled out, your bruises and cuts felt beautiful.

I feel a brief surge of glimmering possibility: if I could just move forward, one foot, two, I could join the undulating bodies, could lose myself to skin on skin, bone against bone.

But when I open my eyes, I have not moved and Mikey isn't behind the amp anymore.

"Hello, Strange Girl."

The voice in my ear sends chills down my neck. Riley. I turn and he grins and moves closer to me. I hadn't noticed before that there's a thin scar under his jawbone by his ear. It's pearl-white, perfect and flat.

Usually he's behind me, in the cook station, tossing out his little quips to the waitstaff, and I'm only really near him when I have to take dishes into the station, and I try not to look at him when I do that, because my skin starts to heat up.

But out here, up close under the white lights strung across the trees, I can see that his skin is ruddy, traces of pockmarks under the stubble on his cheeks. His brown T-shirt fits loosely over his body, as though he was heavier once but never replaced his old clothes.

And I notice, too, that if I leaned against him, my head would fit right under his chin.

That's a bad thought, so I step away from him and wrap my arms around my body. However kind of cute he is, he's a mess, and I don't need a mess right now.

"So. Strange Girl. How are you liking our fine, hot, and dry state? Our . . . creative and energetic citizens?" He motions with his beer to the throngs of partyers.

Riley fixes his eyes on me and they aren't unkind, they seem almost nice, in a little bit of a sad way, and the weird thing is, he seems almost . . . interested in what my answer might actually be, which is not something I'm used to. And it's confusing, because of my feelings for Mikey.

Suddenly, I wonder if the mess thinks I'm a mess, too, but it doesn't bother him in the least.

Which makes me blush, so I duck my head, in case he can tell what I'm thinking by the look on my face. I'm about to try to answer, though, when Mikey shows up, clutching two plastic cups of water, a tall blonde by his side. She's one of those girls Ellis would call, in a jealous way, *willowy*: smooth and lean in her tank top and long, flowery hippie skirt, two shiny braids nestled against her chest. She's wearing not one, but two ankle bracelets.

The blood drains from my face.

She's exactly the type of person to write in purple pen.

Riley chuckles. The blonde is now kneeling, wiping spilled water from Mikey's sneakers with the hem of her skirt. Riley whispers in my ear, "*That* looks like a problem. Did you know Michael had a friend? Watch out for Bunny there. We boys are suckers for ankle bracelets."

Before he drifts away, Riley says, louder, "Enjoy your evening, Strange Girl. Looks like it's going to be an interesting one. Can't wait to hear all about it at Grit on Monday."

The girl named Bunny stands up, practically towering over me. She's taller than Mikey. Her skin is flawless, with naturally flushed pink cheeks that look exuberant instead of, say, blotchy and sad, like mine.

She smiles prettily. "Charlie! I'm Bunny! Oh my God, were you talking to Riley West? Isn't he the best? He's so funny and my God, *such* an awesome musician!"

She says, "It's just so great to finally meet you. How are you feeling? Mike said you had a kind of rough time? You doing okay?" Her face is pursed with concern, but then brightens. "Oh, I bet you can tell me all sorts of stories about Mike's old girlfriends!" She pinches his arm playfully.

A furious blush creeps up Mikey's cheeks. When Bunny turns toward the band, Mikey says softly, so low I can barely hear, "I was trying to tell you, before."

I was breathing Mikey in for two weeks, I was thinking about him saving me, and what it might mean, I had this hope, a tiny hope, some flickering thing—

Stupid. Just fucking stupid. I bite my lips and watch as Bunny turns and leans into him, her back pressed against his chest, her head resting against his.

Mikey says, "Charlie."

I bolt. There are so many people here, I can get lost. I can always get lost. I know how. I squeeze my way to the back of the crowd, where the kegs are set up. I think about Casper, and her rules, and—

It's so easy, isn't it, to grab a cup and pull the spigot and drink it down. To tamp down the fire stoking itself inside me.

I'm just a shit girl in overalls and a dirty jersey shirt. Frankenstein face and Frankenstein body, so who really cares, or notices, what I do? If I drink just one or two? Or three or four? Casper didn't give me directions for what to do if somebody I used to really like-like, somebody who would be somebody good to love, somebody *right*, somebody *understood* about me, turned out to not have the same ideas about me.

Who forgot me when he moved away, and moved on.

The night is peeling itself back, opening up, the beer flooding through my veins. Through cracks in the crowd, I watch him kiss her, softly, one hand gently stroking a lock of her hair, twining it through his fingers. I drink one, then another, and one more, like water, water, water.

A fissure begins inside me and it's an ugly thing. For all the people here, I am utterly alone. I let the plastic cup drop from my fingers and run.

I can hear Mikey shouting for me, but I don't stop. The bars downtown are just starting to close; dismayed, disheveled people are being popped back out onto the street, lurching into me, bouncing away as I push through them.

He shouts my name again and then his hand is pulling on my arm. "Stop! Charlie, just *stop*."

"Go back," I sputter. "To your *girlfriend*." I'm weaving a little from the beer. I haven't drunk anything in so long, my eyes are already starting to blur. I wonder if he can tell that I drank.

He sighs heavily, clenching his jaw. "Bunny and I have been going out for a while now and yeah, I should have told you right away, but honestly, what's the big deal here?"

I start walking away quickly, but he follows me, muttering, "I'm not going to let you walk home alone, Charlie." I don't look back, but I can hear him following me, the slight squeak of his sneakers on the pavement.

Three men are slumped on the steps of my building, bare chests shining in the heat. They pass a paper bag back and forth. They squint up at us, nod politely.

I stumble going up the sixteen steps to the second floor and almost knock out a tooth. Swearing, I push myself back up. Mikey says, "Jesus, you okay, Charlie?" But I don't stop. The stairwell light is out and I jam the key around the lock in my door, finally hitting the slot. I try to shut the door on Mikey, but he pushes at it gently and steps inside.

"Charlie, come on," he says finally. I ignore him. I'm afraid if I say anything, I'll cry. After unlacing my boots, I put them as neatly as possible in the corner of the room. I turn on the standing lamp. I make a practice, just like I used to when my mother was in one of her rages, of making things as orderly as possible. I straighten my sketchbooks on the card table. I put my pens and pencils in the glass jar. The plaid blanket flares out before me as I settle it softly on the futon. It was bad, really bad, to drink that beer, because now I've loosened something inside. I've chinked away at a wall I didn't know would be so important and now I want my tender kit. I want him to leave. I need my tender kit.

Roar of ocean, swirl of tornado. I'm being swallowed.

Mikey sighs. "Is this going to be like it was with Ellis and that guy all over again? Come on, Charlie. You're older than that now."

I whirl around, blood in my ears.

When Ellis took up with that boy, he stepped into my place beside her, easy as a chess move, and I was nudged to the edge. I was so angry, and hurt.

I didn't think I'd be on Mikey's edge.

"What's the problem here, Charlie?" His voice is tired and blurry. "Talk to me. You're acting all weird, all jeal—"

He stops suddenly, his mouth dropping open. He's still standing in front of the door. I turn my head away, flushes of shame threading my skin.

"Just get out," I whisper. I can feel waves of tears behind my eyes.

"Oh my God. Did you ... you thought we ... that I ..." He lets out an enormous breath all at once and covers his face. Behind his hands comes a muffled "Shit, shit, shit."

"Just get out, please. It's fine. It's nothing. I'm cool, just go." Blathering, staring at the wall, anywhere but at him. Gritting my teeth so hard my jaw hurts. I'm mortified.

But he doesn't. What he does is even worse, because he's *Mikey*, because he's *nice*.

He comes over to me and *puts his arms around me.* "I'm sorry, Charlie. If I did anything to lead you on, I didn't mean to. The last thing I'd want is to hurt you."

But it makes it even worse, being held by him, being warm inside the cocoon of his arms, because when he angles his head to look down at me, and his breath is warm on my face, and his eyes are so sad and he is just so near to me, I kiss him.

And for a second, just a blip of a white-hot second, he kisses me back.

And then he pushes me away.

And wipes his mouth.

Because of *course* he would wipe his mouth.

"No, Charlie," he says. "No, I can't do that. I don't want to do that."

I shut my eyes so hard I see red clouds pulsing inside my eyelids.

"Please just get the fuck out, okay?"

When I open them, he's gone, and the door's closed. I turn off the lamp, because I need the dark right now.

I can still feel the press of his mouth on mine, the nano-second of warmth it gave me. But it doesn't stop the flood of shame I feel: how stupid am *I*, echoing through my whole body. Like Louisa said, "Nobody normal will love us."

I've already broken one of Casper's rules: I drank. And I want to break another, but I *don't* want to, *Idon'tIdon'tIdon'tIdon't*, and so I get my tender kit from under a pile of clothes, and cover it with the plaid blanket, and then cover it with a bunch of shirts, and then my boots, and then I shove it into Louisa's suitcase and wedge the whole thing way back under the claw-foot tub, where I can't see it.

I practice those fucking stupid breath balloons for as long as I can, until I'm practically wheezing, and then I find my sketchbook, because drawing is my *words*, it's the things I can't *say*, and I let loose in the pages with a story about a girl who thought a boy liked her, and maybe could save her from herself, but in the end she was just stupid, stupid, because she's a fuck-ing freak, but if she could just make it through the night, there was going to be another chance, another day.

Maybe, maybe, maybe.

MY FINGERS START TO HURT JUST AS THE SUN STARTS TO RISE. I finally put down the charcoal when the first colors come in the window, soft and golden. I drink a cup of water and listen to people using the toilet down the hall, the sounds of Leonard shuffling to the porch to drink coffee out of his pink mug.

My head is bursting from the beer. My eyes hurt and my mouth tastes terrible. I'm grateful that I don't have to be back at True Grit for two more days. I peel off my clothes and sink to the futon and fall into a deep sleep.

When I wake up, it's the afternoon, and my room is sweltering hot. I made it through the night, but I'm still jittery and tense. I want to talk to someone, but the only person I know is Mikey, and now I've probably ruined that. I decide to go to the library and email Casper. Like, maybe I should tell her I've failed, now, by drinking, by throwing myself at Mikey.

Outside, the heat is stifling already, but I don't want to *not* wear my overalls because I feel more comfortable, protected, somehow, with them on. I go back into the apartment building and knock on Leonard's door. He lends me a pair of scissors without a word. Upstairs, I cut a couple of pairs of overalls off at the knee. That way, I might be cooler, but my thighs are still hidden.

I'm sweating profusely by the time I get to the library. Everyone else seems so cool, even in this heat. Maybe I'll get used to it after a while. There's a thermometer outside the library. Ninety-seven degrees and not a cloud in sight.

I log on. I reply to Blue first, because I know she'll know how I feel, exactly.

> Dear Blue,
>   I am my own worst disaster. I did something stupid to someone. I just wanted to feel better. My own body is my deepest enemy. It wants, it wants, it wants, and when it does not get, it cries and cries and I punish it. How can you live in fear of your very self? What is going to happen to us, Blue?

I wait, stupidly, like she's going to respond right away. Of course she can't—she'll have to wait to sneak a turn at the computer and who knows when that will happen. But just writing it eases something in me.

And then I write to Casper, because I should tell her what I did. I tell her I drank three beers, that I tried to kiss Mikey, that I *did* kiss Mikey, and that he didn't like it. But I also tell her I didn't cut, even though not cutting made me exhausted.

I press Send. I just sit at the terminal for a little while, watching the people in the library. The longer I sit and watch them as they pick books, whisper on their phones, fall asleep in chairs, the more lonely I feel, the more weighted down inside. Everyone seems to have a grip on life but me. When is anything going to get better?

Mikey is waiting on the front steps of the building when I get back, a grocery sack next to him on the top step. I panic a little and start to walk past him, but he pulls the buds from his ears and grabs my hand.

He says, "Hey. Charlie. Don't do this shit, okay? Sit down."

I drop down heavily, avoiding his eyes, trying to block out the scent of him, the nearness.

Down the block, the line outside the plasma bank moves like a slow snake. I wipe sweat from my forehead self-consciously. I bet Bunny never sweats.

"Hey, look what I brought for you." Mikey parts the top of the grocery sack so I can see what's inside: a loaf of bread, a jar of peanut butter, an apple, and an orange. I sigh. I'm so sick of peanut butter.

I pull out the apple, rub my thumbs over its shininess. "Thank you," I say softly.

He clears his throat. "What happened, that can't happen again. That was . . . not good. Kissing."

A stinging, a tightening in my chest. Angrily, I say, "You kissed back, you know, before you . . . didn't."

"And you drank. I tasted the beer. You promised."

"I'm sorry." It's a whisper, spoken to the sidewalk.

"Is that the only thing you've had to drink since you've been here?"

"Yes."

"Are you sure?"

"*Yes*. Yes!"

He sighs. "Charlie, do you know why I decided to go to college all the way out here? You and Ellis were exhausting. Your little games with each other, with *me*, that shit tired me out. Did you ever realize that? Probably not. You two were so wrapped up in yourselves."

"You came to the hospital. You said you didn't want me to die. I just thought . . ." My voice cracks. I press my head against my knees to block him out. I want to cry all over again.

I thought, I thought? What did I think? That Mikey would like *me,* dumb little me?

"Of course I don't want you to die! I *never* want you to die. You're my *friend.* But I didn't mean that I . . . that we . . ."

Mikey goes silent. After a while he says, "This is what it is, Charlie. I'm here, but I'm with somebody. I've moved *forward.* Coming out here really changed something for me. I've moved *on.* I made goals for myself. I want to help you get better, and I will, but I can only help you if you want to be helped."

I lift up my head, blinking in the daylight. Mikey looks at me head-on.

"Okay?" he asks. He takes my hand. "Are we okay?"

What else am I supposed to say? "Okay," I answer. "Okay."

He stands up, all business, pulling me with him. The apple tumbles off my lap. Like the good person he is, he jogs down to the sidewalk to get it.

I'VE AGREED TO MEET MIKEY AT A GALLERY DOWNTOWN after he gets off work. He's drawn a map to a place not far from my building. At first, I consider not going. I'll just feel awkward, and Bunny will probably be there, too, but then I decide to go. I only have one friend here, and he's it, and maybe sometime I won't feel like such a jerk around him. Casper would probably be proud of me for that. I change into another pair of overalls and a long-sleeved jersey shirt and slide my key and the lapis stone into my pocket.

The gallery is in the middle of the smallish downtown, not far from where I got off the Greyhound, on the third floor of a pink building wedged between a bar and a diner called the Grill. The gallery is narrow, crowded and deep with creaky floorboards and an aroma of dark wine and exotic cheese. There are a lot of older people dressed in black with silver jewelry and clean, styled hair. I'm glad I wore my hoodie over my overalls; I feel a little awkward and out of place here. It feels better to burrow in it, to know I can pull the hood up if I need to. I notice Mikey talking to Ariel in the corner. I breathe a sigh of relief: Bunny doesn't seem to be anywhere around. They wave me over.

I look down at the bright jewels on Ariel's sleek, flat sandals, so shiny next to my grubby boots. Did Ariel ever wear clunky clothes and hide her body? She seems eons away from anything like that. She was probably born sexy.

Ariel takes a sip of her wine. "Charlie! You're here!"

Mikey says, "Hey, Charlie, glad you made it." He socks me

lightly on the shoulder. I give him a small smile. "This stuff is a trip, don't you think?" He wanders away to look at the paintings.

Ariel leans down close to me, conspiratorially, like we're best girlfriends or something. "What do you think, Charlie? My friend Antonio worked very hard on these."

I look around carefully. They just seem like triangles and squares to me, painted in primary colors. I shrug. "They're really bright." I try to imagine what it would be like to have my drawings in a place like this, or any place, really. But who would come see a bunch of drawings and comics about loser kids? Or even the sketches I've been doing at night, alone in my room, of Mikey, of Riley? My dad?

"Boat paint." Ariel takes another glass of wine from the buffet table. There are little pieces of bread in the shapes of hands. I nibble one. "It really shines, doesn't it? I'm so glad he doesn't burn his paintings anymore. So bad for his lungs, but he thought it necessary. He used to do that, you know, years ago, when we were both just frisky pups in the desert, smoking our brains out with hash and laying anybody who cracked a smile at us."

I choke a little on the bread-hand.

"But," she continues, examining the rings on her fingers, "he was in a Kiefer stage then. We all have our Kiefer stages, when we want to destroy ourselves in order to create. To see if that's beautiful, too."

She gestures across the room at a very handsome man with slick, blackish hair wound into a ponytail. He's barefoot, wearing a gleaming gray suit and what looks like an immensely heavy turquoise necklace. "That's him. Tony Padilla. He's going to sell the shit out of these paintings. What about you? How is your drawing coming along? Sometimes I catch myself thinking of your drawing. That one, the man with the pills for teeth."

"My dad." It comes out before I can stop myself. I pinch my thigh. Stupid.

Ariel looks at me, her face softening a little. I wonder what she's thinking.

"I see," she says. She sips her wine. "Well, it was very good. All wrong, of course, but good. You're not confident in that type of line work—I can tell. You need some classes. I'm teaching a workshop this July in my studio. Drawing and portraiture. Weekend warriors sort of thing for the retired set. It pays the bills, and I do love them. Unlike most of the students in my U classes, they *try*. They *want*. They don't just *assume* that art belongs to them."

"I don't . . . I mean, I have a job now, but it's just washing dishes. I don't have any money. Sorry."

"I know you have no money. I was once a starving artist, too. You can come and sit in. You can help me clean the studio after. How about that?" She swirls wine in her mouth, surveying the crowd of people. Her eyes move rapidly, lighting on one person, resting, then searching for another, like a bird looking for the perfect branch.

"I think, Charlie, you have talent. I do. But I don't think you'll get far until you examine yourself and study. Until you let yourself be your subject. That's the exquisiteness of youth: you are allowed the luxury of vanity, of self-examination. Take it! Don't be ashamed of yourself."

I don't understand half of what she just said and I know I should probably say thank you, but instead, what comes out in a rush is "Why are you being so nice to me? You don't even *know* me."

"Because when everything is said and done, Charlotte, the world runs on kindness. It simply *has* to, or we'd never be able to bear ourselves. It might not seem so to you now, but it will when you're older." Her voice is very fierce. She takes a large sip of her wine and looks straight at me.

She says, "And I do know you. I *know* you, Charlie."

And for just that moment, I think I see a terrible cloud of sadness pass over her eyes.

But Mikey comes tumbling back, excited and out of breath, and Ariel's face returns to being smooth and cool.

"I wish I had tons of money," Mikey chatters. "I'd buy one of these. These are fucking cool."

"Maybe that band you are always driving around will finally hit it big, Michael, and you can buy all the paintings you want." Ariel laughs. "Charlie doesn't like these paintings."

"It's not that!" I say quickly, feeling a little embarrassed. "It's just . . . I like a story, I guess. I like faces, or people doing things. These seem kind of like just painting colors . . . to paint colors?" Talking like this makes me nervous. Nobody has ever really talked to me about art before, and I wonder if I'm saying all the wrong things.

Ariel gazes at me. "Colors by themselves can be a story, too, Charlie. Just a different kind. Come to my class. I'll give Mikey the info. It was good, Charlie, to see you. Mikey, your rent is due, sweetheart." She lays a hand on my arm and waves to someone across the room, drifting away.

Mikey raises his eyebrows. "Wow, Charlie, that's cool. Ariel wants to teach you? That's totally positive. Ariel Levertoff's kind of a big deal, you know." He beams at me and I let myself smile back, grateful to be caught in a good moment with him, even if it hurts a little to be so close to him. I make a mental note to look up *Kiefer* and *Ariel Levertoff* the next time I'm at the library.

He holds up two tiny bread-hands and we pretend to do battle. I don't even care that some of the people in the gallery are staring at us like we're just dumb kids, or that when he leaves tonight, it will be to go back to Bunny, probably, and stay the night with her. Ariel likes my drawings, she likes *me*, I think, and Mikey is with me. And after he walks me home, when I read the note taped to my apartment door, my heart feels even lighter, in a weird way: *Come and wake me up. Five-thirty tomorrow. I promise I won't bite this time. R*

I hold the note in my hands, my skin tingling with warmth.

I left Mikey's travel clock at his guesthouse when I moved. I've been relying on the sound of the other people to wake me up in time for work every morning, but suddenly, I don't want to take a chance on being late or not having enough time. To talk to Riley tomorrow, when it's just us.

Riley came and *found me.*

As I bound down the stairs to see if Leonard has a spare clock, I'm in a little bubble of warmth, just like I had with Ellis, a place I never thought I'd be again.

WHEN RILEY DOESN'T ANSWER HIS DOOR THE NEXT MORNING, I don't even hesitate before going in. In the front room, I find a battered acoustic guitar and a four-track cassette recorder in the middle of the floor, surrounded by sheaves of notebook paper. They weren't there the other day.

He's in the same position in his bed as last time: hands behind his head, legs crossed at the ankles. A couple of empty bottles rest on the floor by the bed. He opens his eyes slowly. It takes him a few minutes to register me standing in the door-way to his bedroom, but then his face breaks into a smile. It's so sudden and surprising that I can't help but grin, too.

"Hey," he says drowsily. He looks at me in a weirdly com-fortable way that makes my stomach jump. A look that says it's perfectly natural for me to be in the doorway to his bedroom at five-thirty in the morning. I hope he can't see the warmth that's spreading across my cheeks.

"It didn't take me long to find out where you lived. Just asked around for the girl on the yellow bicycle and poof, there you were. Or *weren't*, I should say. I enjoyed meeting your neighbors. Fine lot of men, they are."

"You should get up. You look wrecked," I say. "Are those ashes in your hair?" Jesus Christ, this guy.

He rolls over on his side and looks up at me sleepily, but grinning. "Hey, speaking of fine men. How'd that work out the other night? With your friend Michael? And his friend . . . Bunny?"

I purse my lips, but I'm not really pissed off. That comfortable look he gave me earlier is still working its magic. He looks delighted. "It didn't, if you must know. Now get up. We can't be late. I don't want to be late."

"Well," he says, groaning as he sits up. "Michael's loss, then." He moans, like something hurts.

"Do you need help?" I ask warily. I don't want to get too close yet, not after last time. "You look like total shit."

"There you go with that sweet talk, Strange Girl. No, no help. I'll be good as new after a quick dip in a scalding shower." I step out of the doorway to let him pass. He heads to the bathroom. As soon as I hear the water running, I slip into the kitchen and cruise the refrigerator, my stomach churning, looking for something to eat, and also to distract myself, because as much of jerk as he is, he's still a kind of used-to-be-better-looking jerk, and he's also, at this very moment, very naked.

A carton of eggs, a packet of tortillas, a jar of green salsa. A block of yellow cheese, a block of white cheese. I find a knife in a drawer and hastily cut a hunk of yellow cheese and cram it into my mouth. I'm careful to wrap the rest of it back up and replace it, just so, in the refrigerator. A half-drunk bottle of Chardonnay in the side pocket, next to a crusty jar of jam. Three oranges. I peel one open quickly, eat a few sweet slices, and shove the rest into my backpack. It's an open, square kitchen, plain and weirdly clean and empty. Maybe he does most of his eating at True Grit. There's a teakettle on the stove, which I wouldn't have expected.

Under the sink is where I find his stash of bottles. I wonder where he keeps his other stash, the one Linus was talking about. Through the back-door window, I can see a sturdy wooden building in the yard, surrounded by fat cactuses.

Bare feet slap on the hardwood floor. Riley stands beside me at the window, droplets flaring off him as he rubs a towel against his head. "It's my recording studio. I built it with some of the money from the second, and last, Long Home record that I was on. Kinda ramshackle, nothing fancy inside or anything, but it works. At least, it used to." He runs his fingers through his hair.

"How come you're not in a band anymore?" I ask. "I mean, you guys were kind of famous, right?"

He shrugs. "It's the same old rock and roll story. Boy joins band, band gets big, or almost big. *Nearly* big. Big *enough*, anyway, so that egos grew, money floated from the sky, excess occurred, demons were created, or, in my case, simply crawled to the surface after remaining carefully cloaked. And what once rose high and mighty thus fell really, really fucking hard back to earth. The end."

"Are you ... do you still play?" He's gazing at the studio with a faraway look in his eye.

"Sure. Sometimes." He clears his throat, gives his hair a final scrub with the towel. "But you know what I'm really good at? Being a disappointment. You've gotta work with the talent you're born with, I guess."

He throws the towel on the kitchen counter. "Let's hit the road, Strange Girl. Don't want to make Linus mad."

We're quiet as we walk, me pushing my bicycle.

Being a disappointment, he said. I was always disappointing people, too, like my mother, my teachers. After a while, why bother trying? I can see what Riley's talking about.

It's just before six a.m. and the air is already warming up. I tie my hoodie around my waist. "Is it ever *not* hot here?" I ask. Riley laughs.

"Oh, shit. You ain't seen nothing, girl. Wait until July. It's like a hundred and twenty fucking degrees outside."

We cross through the darkness of the underpass, silent, and after a while, it seems kind of comfortable, this not talking. I mean, I want to ask him more about the music thing, and what happened, but it's okay not to talk, too. And a little part of me is still nervous; I don't want to make him angry.

Half a block from True Grit, he stops and lights a cigarette. His hands are trembling fiercely, but I don't say anything. "You go in first, okay? I'll come in a few minutes." Smoke drifts from his nostrils. "We shouldn't go in together."

I want to ask why, but I don't. I just keep going and lock my bicycle to a pole. Linus shouts out a hearty "Hello!" when I get inside. Riley comes in a few minutes later and heads straight to the coffee. When he comes back to the dish area, he has two cups and hands me one.

I help Linus with the coffee urns and the espresso machine and then start on the dish area. Whoever worked dishes last night left plates of dried food stacked in the sink, topped with stained mugs, tea strainers, and the tiny, delicate spoons for the espresso cups. I lose myself in the task of scraping food into the trash, soaking plates and cups in the sink.

Linus walks back from the front, her face pale. "R, Bianca's at the counter. She wants her money." She lowers her voice. "Do we . . . *have* her money? Where the hell is Julie?"

Riley gets very still. "Uh, yeah. Let me just go cut her a check. I'll be back."

Linus bites her lip as Riley rushes down the hallway to the office. The doors to the kitchen swing open. A curvy woman in a loose purple dress looks around, her eyes suspicious. Linus says, "Riley went to get a check."

The woman looks me over kind of grumpily and then huffs to Linus, "I don't want to have to beg every time for my money, Linus. You guys want my goods, you pay and you pay on time. Julie needs to get her head together."

"I know, Bianca. Things are a little wonky right now. Business is off some days and then roaring the next. We're working on it." Linus twists a dish towel in her hands.

Riley jogs back down the hall. When he sees Bianca, he slaps a hand to his forehead. "Lady B! I swear, it's all my fault. My sister asked me to run some cash by the bakery yesterday and I forgot. My apologies."

Bianca takes the check and inspects it. "A check, Riley? Is this one good? If this one tanks, I'm out. You people need to get your shit together."

"It's all good, Lady B."

She grimaces and takes off through the kitchen doors. Linus glares at Riley. "Again, R? *Again?*"

"It's not what you think, Linus, so why don't you go back to work?"

Linus stalks back to the front. Riley walks past me without saying anything.

I listen to the murky burble of the fryer, to the drone of the grill, the dishes as they sway back and forth in the washer; I wonder what's going on. What happened to the cash Riley had for that lady? What did Linus mean by *again*?

Then I find myself listening to the unmistakable sound of choking, and the rush-jumble of vomit. I whirl around.

Riley holds a hand to his mouth. He's bent over the trash bin by the grill, liquid dripping from his chin.

I quickly hand him a towel and then cover my nose. The smell is awful.

He wipes his chin and neck, throws the towel into the bin, and opens the refrigerator door, blocking his face. When it closes, he's drinking deeply from a can of beer. He sets it back inside, his chest heaving. The color's returning to his face, spreading up his cheeks like a pink river.

There were older people, men and women, on the streets who acted like this. Who drank and drank and drank so much their bodies were slick with the stench of old wine, beer, vomit. The only thing, the next morning, that made their hands stop trembling, that made them stop heaving up bile or chunks of soup kitchen food? was more alcohol. The DTs, Evan called it. *That's some fucking nasty shit,* he'd say, shaking his head.

The finger Riley presses to his lips has tiny red nicks from his chef's knife. Because his hands were trembling so badly, I realize.

Shhhh, he mouths. He nudges the trash bin in my direction. I look over at Linus, who's ringing someone up at the register. She told me to tell her if stuff like this happened.

Riley's eyes plead with me. I'm not sure what to do.

And then Ellis's texts flash in my brain. *Smthing hurts. U never sd hurt like this. 2 much.* My stomach churns with shame. I didn't help her and I lost her.

Quickly, I pull the bag from the trash bin, tie it, and take it out back to the Dumpster. He did get me a job, after all.

Later, when my shift is over and I'm almost out the screen door, Riley appears with a brown paper bag.

"Messed up an order. *Bon appétit.*"

I hesitate before taking the bag, because by taking it, I know I'm agreeing to keep some sort of secret, and I'm still not sure I want to do that.

But the hunger knocking around in my stomach wins out.

I'm so sick of stale bread and peanut butter. And as soon as I get home, I tear into that food: a green chili bagel with scrambled tofu and Swiss cheese, with a broken oatmeal raisin cookie wrapped in wax paper.

THE LIBRARY IS NEARLY EMPTY, SO I HAVE PLENTY OF TIME ON the computer. Casper has finally sent a message.

> Dear Charlie, I'm sorry it's taken me so long to respond to your last message and I'm sorry you're feeling anxious. I should be clear, here, though: I'm not your doctor, anymore, legally, so I have to be very careful with what advice or thoughts I give you. And I am helping others, too, so sometimes I may not be able to respond to you as quickly as you'd like. I hope you can understand that. I've looked up some resources for you in Tucson, they may be of help. You'll find them at the end of this message.
>
> The most important thing, Charlie, is to keep yourself active and keep yourself aware at all times. Such as: no drinking, which you haven't followed. Have you had anything to drink since the email to me? Is there anyone you can talk to, like your friend? It's very, very important that you follow steps every day to keep yourself sober and safe. It's going to be a hard road, Charlie, and the hard work is largely up to you. You were given very few emotional resources as a child and your life, until now, has been one of hiding your feelings until they become simply so powerful you can't control them

anymore. Practice your breathing, take walks, do your art. Be kind to yourself.— Dr. Stinson

I may not be able to respond to you as quickly as you'd like. I look at her list of resources: Alateen, a therapy group for survivors of suicide, a women's shelter. Alateen? I think about sitting in a group of kids talking about drinking. About what happens if you drink.

And then I think: *I'm* probably what happens if you lose control. A kid will end up on the street, no home, etc. I don't want to sit in a group where I'm the whole thing they're trying to not *be*. I look at the survivors' group on the Web: a lot of pictures of sad people sitting in a circle on the grass. I don't even look up the shelter, because I do have a place to live now, even if it isn't the greatest.

I start to write back, but then I delete the message. What could I tell her? Whine more about messing up with Mikey? She'd say *Make another friend,* probably. She'd tell me to go to one of these groups. Frustrated, I click on another message, from Blue. It's a week old.

> SILENT SUE WHR R U? I miss you, my good girl. Re: your last email: yeah, we are our worst enemies. But it doesn't have to be all that. I've been kind of really paying attention in Group lately, and some of what GHOSTDOC says, it's not all bad, especially not that::::!!! Im getting sprung!!!! Don't know when. Been following rulez, eating up meds, thinking about hooking up with Isis in KANZ ASS. Maybe we will cum on out and check u out

!! Have u been a good girl? PLZ talk 2 me. Everyone you knew here is gone but me and Louisa and I tell you, that girl is NOT doing well. Something's going on. BLUE

I stare at the message. She wouldn't come out; that's just Blue being a poker again. Right? I look at the list of Blue's messages on my email. For someone who started out being so mean to me at Creeley, she sure does seem to like me. And she might, I think suddenly, and kind of sadly, be really lonely, too. I'm not sure what to do with feeling sympathy for Blue.

Make a friend. What would be the harm in answering Blue? She's the only one I have right now who could possibly understand what it's like to live this way.

Blue—Good on you for listening to Casper. What else are you gonna do, right? The desert is a hot mess—if you come down bring your halter tops and sunglasses and lots of sunscreen because every day is like fire on your skin. I'm not sure what I'm really doing here, but here I am, so here I am, I guess. I have a job washing dishes and it isn't so bad. What is going on with Louisa? Tell her I miss her before you go, okay? Maybe you could give her my email or something. I'm not a good girl, I'm bad all the way through.—Charlie

A FEW DAYS LATER, OVER THE RUMBLING SOUND OF THE DISH-washer, Riley calls out, "I hear the boyfriend's going to roadie for that band on a big West Coast roll. Won't you be lonely for the next few months!"

I yank the lever down on the machine. "What?" I blow steam away from my face. The swamp cooler in the kitchen is broken and it's apocalyptically hot outside, which means it's even hotter by the dishwasher and fryer and the grill. Riley says this heat is unusual for June. There are box fans set up and Riley's got a fan jerry-rigged to the wall, but his face is slicked with sweat and pocked with red blotches by his nose and hair-line. He's hiding a sweating can of beer under the counter and smoking a cigarette, the ashes sinking to the floor. He sweeps them away with his boot.

He pretends to choke on a sip of the beer. "Oops. Did I spill beans that weren't ready to be spilled yet? Looks like Michael's in the doghouse."

I blink. "Mikey?"

"*Michael.* He's a man, call him by his man's name, girl."

I wonder if he's taking Bunny on the trip. I wonder if he's *told* Bunny.

I practically just got here, I think, morosely dunking plastic water glasses in the soapy sludge of water. *And he's leaving al-ready.*

But then I remember what Mikey said: *It's not going to be like it was,* and I think, *It doesn't matter anyway.* My one friend: gone, already.

Riley scrapes a block of hash browns across the grill, twirling the spatula in his hand. His cigarette rests on the lip of his beer can. Julie is away for the next week. "In Ouray," Linus said this morning. "Learning about her *doshas*." It seems like Riley is being even more careless than usual about drinking at work since she's gone.

Riley finishes his cigarette and drops it in the can. He stands up, lobbing the can over my head and into the trash bin. "And stop wearing those long-sleeved shirts, Charlie Girl. You make me hotter just looking at you in those things. Buy some goddamn T-shirts or something."

I don't answer him. Instead, I dump some food on top of his beer can in the trash.

I FINGER THE BUNDLE OF CASH IN THE POCKET OF MY OVER-
alls as I walk the aisles of the art store near the coffeehouse.
Willow charcoal sticks, the airy, soft bristles of watercolor
brushes. I press my fingers against the stacks of bound drawing
paper, feel the raised teeth under the plastic-wrapped covers.
Elegant Winsor & Newton paints in pristine bottles, lined up
in perfect rows: scarlet lake, purple madder, lemon yellow. They
have pads with comic panel templates already in place; no more
using a ruler and a finely sharpened pencil, like I did with mine.
I see a lot of canvas messenger bags, low-slung army pants, and
filmy scarves on the necks of the girls in the store. The boys
all look like car mechanics in sandals, light scruffs of hair on
their chins. I wonder if some of them are in Ariel's classes in
the program at the university. Her workshop is starting next
month. I still haven't decided if I will go. *Art School Tools,* that's
what Linus called a tableful of kids in paint-spattered pants
and horn-rimmed glasses. They had full messenger bags and
black portfolios duct-taped together. They drank cup after cup
of tea and coffee. They left tips of stacked pennies and hand-
rolled cigarettes, sometimes a napkin sketch of one of the waitpeople. I check the prices on sticks and graphite and paper. I
have to buy some soap and toilet paper, tampons, and underwear. The soles of my boots are thinning; I can feel the bumps
in the pavement on my feet as I walk and it's so hot outside,
maybe I should just get some sneakers or something instead,
a lighter, cooler shoe. I have to pay Leonard rent, but I'm not
sure when I'll get a check from Julie. And then I think: *Where*

am I going to cash this check? I don't have a bank account. I try to add some figures in my head, but the numbers get complicated and I lose track of them, and myself. Everyone here seems to know exactly what they need, but I leave without a thing.

MIKEY LOWERS HIS EYES TO HIS PLATE OF SWEET POTATO fries and vinegary green beans. "Yeah," he says, "I'll be gone about three months. It's summer, so I won't miss out on any school. It's a really big chance for the band. And I'm the manager, right? Manager slash van driver, I should say. I mean, I don't get paid or anything, but maybe this will turn into something. Maybe a record. This is all super positive."

He pushes the plate toward me. "You'll be cool, right?" He looks at me with a look that really says *I need you to be cool.*

The fries I've stacked look like a tiny orange log cabin. There's a buzzing in the air; some of the hanging lights on the restaurant deck are fritzing, going dim.

I count in my head: three months. June, July, August.

"It's a long time." He plucks a fry from the cabin and it falls apart. Salt glints on his lips. "A friend is subletting my place."

I can't stop thinking that when he goes, I will be alone again.

"Are you going to do Ariel's class? That would be really good for you. You might meet some people, too."

I move food around my plate. "She said they'd all be older."

"She was just joking. I helped her last summer. They weren't *all* old. And I think if she wants to help you, you should let her, you know? It might help her, too."

I put down my fork, suddenly pissed. "Help *her*? How could I help *her*? Hello, *look* at me."

Mikey frowns. "Don't be like that. I just mean . . ." He takes a breath. "Her son died. A couple of years ago, before I moved into the guest house. Drug overdose. I think . . . I don't know

216

all the circumstances, really, but she hadn't heard from him for a long time before it happened. She's always talking about you to me. I think her wanting to help you . . . maybe makes her feel more hopeful? She really was in a bad place for a long time."

I suck in my breath. Ariel's son died. An overdose. Here I thought she had such a perfect, pretty life, filled with art and interesting things, all the time.

Now I know what she meant in the gallery. Why she said, "I *know* you." Why that cloud passed over her eyes.

The thought fills me with a weird heaviness. Is that why she was so pushy with me about finding a place to live, finding a job, taking her class? To make sure I didn't . . . become like her son? Disappear, too?

I think of the paintings in her house. So, so dark, with just a little light, but the light is turning away from the dark.

"Her paintings," I say slowly. "Those really dark ones in her house. When I saw those, all I could think of was that only a really sad person could have made them."

He nods. "She hasn't painted since then. She did all of those in a rush, right after he died, then she just stopped. Zilch. Nothing."

He says cautiously, "Bunny's around, too, if you need anything. It wouldn't kill you to get to know her."

The mention of *Bunny* knifes me. I shred my napkin, gather the stained bits in a mound on the table, blow them away like snow. Mikey smiles. *Michael* smiles.

"Serious. She's really cool. I mean, you don't have to be such a cold fish, okay?"

My face colors. "Cold fish? What the fuck?"

"You know, Charlie, it's just . . . well, you *know*. I mean, you're not the most outgoing person, are you? You were always kind of . . . remote, right, back in the day? Now you're more or less, I don't know . . ." Mikey stutters, sighs. "I mean, plenty of people would like you, but you don't even give them a chance. This is your chance, right here, now, to change some things. Make the right friends."

"Make the right friends? What are you even talking about, *Michael*?" Make the right friends? I feel like our conversation has taken a weird turn.

"Charlie." His voice has cooled. "Listen. Bunny says she's seen you walking with Riley West. You know she works at Caruso's, right? Across from Grit? She's seen you two walking to Grit together in the morning."

I twist a fry between my lips with my tongue and waggle it at him. I'm mad, and scared, that he's going, and I want to be mean to him.

"What's going on there, Charlie?"

"Why do *you* care?"

He grabs the French fry from my mouth and pushes it against my plate, an angry little mash of pale potato guts.

"Riley West was tremendously talented. But now he's a tremendous waste. Don't go there. He has a . . . history. You shouldn't get messed up with him when you should be working on your own recovery. *That's* what I mean by making the right friends."

"He gave me a job. A fucking job washing dishes." I push the plate away angrily. "He can't fucking get up in the morning, so I go over and get him. Don't worry, *Michael*, I'm just his alarm clock. I mean, who's going to want to fuck me when I'm all scarred and crap? Not *you*, right? You wiped your mouth after we kissed."

Mikey's face flushes. "You tasted like beer, that's why I

wiped my mouth. I don't drink, and you tasted like beer and I have a *girlfriend*."

I can't stop it, it all comes tumbling out in a hot rush. "And what kind of conversation should I have with my potential suitor, *Michael*, when he asks me how I spent the last year? Shall I tell him that I spent it eating rancid food? Or helping my friends rob men in the park? Did you know that, *Michael*? You left and I lost Ellis. I was *alone* and I did what I had to do. And now I look like a freak. And I feel like a freak. I don't think you need to worry about my dating life."

His face is blazing red. "I'm sorry, Charlie. That's not . . . just keep your shit together, okay? The object is to move forward, not back, right? I don't want you to get hurt. *More* hurt."

He reaches out and takes my hand. I try to pull it away, but he grips it tight. "There's nothing wrong with you, Charlie. Not one thing. Can't you see that?"

But that's a lie, isn't it? Because there are so many things wrong with me, obviously and actually. What I want Mikey to say is: There are so many things wrong with you and it doesn't *matter*.

I have one hand on the stone in my pocket and the other one trapped in Mikey's grasp. What I want to tell him is: You left once, and look what happened, and now you're leaving again, and I'm scared, because I don't know how to be with people, but I don't know how to be alone, either, and I thought I wasn't going to be alone again here.

And how is it even possible to be more hurt than I've been in the past year?

But all I say is "I'll miss you, Mikey. I'll be okay. I promise."

* * *

When I get home, I wait until it's dark and then I ride my bicycle over to Ariel's house. I don't lock my bike, just lean it against a pole, since I'm not staying. There are no lights on in her house, though I can see a stream of whitish light from the backyard, where she has some strands hanging. I walk quickly up her steps and put the little brown bag up against the screen door. Inside is the red, glittery cross, and a little note that says *I'm sorry.*

THE SHIFT IS SLOW. LINUS AND TANNER, THE WAITPERSON with the neck tattoos, are discussing cover songs. Tanner is a stocky guy with short purple hair and a barky laugh.

Strands of damp hair stick to my forehead. *Cold fish.* That's what Mikey said. Every day when I come here to wash dishes I listen to all of them as they banter and nudge and tease and yell and talk about stupid shit and smoke. I've caught them giving me sidelong glances, curious looks. Ellis always took the lead when we met people at a party or on the street; I was her silent accomplice. *You're so fucking still,* a boy grunted at me in Dunkin' Donuts once, the morning after a long, confusing party. Ellis had dragged us all there, bought a dozen jelly doughnuts and burning cups of coffee. The boy's face was pimply and pale. *What are you—you're like made of fucking stone or something.* He and his friend laughed. Sweet-tasting jelly sat on my tongue like a blob. I reached out and took another doughnut, crushing the gritty dough against his stunned face. His friend just kept laughing as the other boy sputtered and grabbed at his sugary face. Ellis glanced over from the counter where she was flirting with the cashier and sighed. *Time to go!* she called out to me, and we ran.

I've watched Mikey. I watched people in school. I watched everyone at Creeley. I've been watching the people here, and it seems like for some people, making friends is like finding a shirt or a hat: you just figure out what color you want, see if it fits, and then take it home and hope everyone likes it and you. But it's never been like that for me. I've been on the outside

221

ever since I was little, getting angry in school and picked on. Once all that happened, I was damaged goods. There wasn't going to be any way back in, not until Ellis, and we kept to ourselves. I say the wrong thing, if I can bring myself to say anything at all. I've always felt like an intrusion, a giant blob of *wrong*. My mother was always telling me to keep quiet, not be a bother. "Nobody's *interested*, Charlotte," she'd say.

Ellis was interested. And she brought me Mikey, and DannyBoy.

I take a breath. *Cold fish.* I'm not a cold fish. I just don't think I matter.

I want to make myself matter. And even if Ellis isn't here with me, maybe she can still help me find a way in.

"Hey," I say, perhaps a little too loudly. My voice is slightly hoarse and I have to clear my throat. "My friend once had this great idea for, like, a country cover of 'You're the One That I Want.'"

Linus and Tanner-with-the-neck-tattoos blink at me. The only person I really talk to is Riley, and even then, not much, and mostly on our walks to work. He's been very careful with me since the vomiting incident.

They look at each other and then back at me. "You mean that song from *Grease*?" Tanner folds forks and knives into paper napkins, wraps them tight as sausages.

"Yeah." I stammer slightly, twisting the hem of my apron. "J-just think about it for a minute. Add some, like, slow strumming, just the guitar and singer, and then at that point in the chorus where they all sing 'Ooh, ooh, ooh . . .'" My face flushes, I lose sight of what I was trying to say, why it was even important. *You have the shittiest singing voice*, Ellis would laugh. *No wonder you like all the music where people just scream.* I turn on the hot water, run a hand under it quickly to force myself back to the present.

"Oh my God." Linus nods, squints. "Yeah, I see it. I mean, I can hear it."

Nobody laughed at me. I release my breath. That wasn't so bad. It worked.

"You could do some wicked acoustic licks with that." Tanner considers and then sings softly, making the *Ooh ooh ooh* sound like *Owh owh owh,* a slow, catlike growl.

Riley shakes his head. "No, no. There is no way to erase the cheese from that song. None." He slurs a bit and Linus frowns.

She says, "Riley, that's your fourth one this morning."

"Fifth, pet. *Maybe.*" He lowers his beer can, out of her sight. "Our secret."

He bumps up next to me, running knives under the hot water, taking longer than is necessary. Linus watches Riley's back like she's willing him to turn around. When he doesn't, she walks off, the screen door clacking behind her as she leaves the café.

Water drips from the wet knives in Riley's hands to the sloppy, dirty floor mats. He stumbles on the mats as he turns back to the grill.

I hesitate when I hear him open a fresh beer. I should go outside and tell Linus this has gone too far, but my feet are rooted to the spot as I listen to him take a large gulp. I mean, what will it matter? She'll send him home, but he'll be back tomorrow. Like Julie said, she'll protect him forever. And what if I do tell Linus? What if I'm the one who gets in trouble and loses my job?

Instead, I help him. When his hands start getting too loose and slices of bread start slipping to the floor, I just pick them up and throw them away, and he starts over. When the orders come faster and he gets overwhelmed, I help him do plates, flip home fries on the grill, dish out scrambled tofu, and toast bagels. Be nice, right? He did give me this job. Not a *cold fish*.

And that afternoon, I get a brown paper bag filled with a turkey and Swiss sandwich on an onion bagel, with mustard and mayonnaise, and a slice of stale lemon cake carefully wrapped in foil. There are tiny flakes of ash in the sweet yellow icing, but I just flick them away with a finger before I take a bite.

IT'S SO HOT OUTSIDE, THE SWEAT IS POURING FROM MY FACE when I get inside the library. I spend some time mopping up in the bathroom. My room was too hot, the building too noisy with people running fans and coolers and playing music too loud.

At the computer, I type in *Ariel Levertoff + artist*. A bunch of articles come up and some galleries that sell her work. I scroll through, not sure what I'm looking for, until I see one article titled "Death and the Disappearance of Ariel Levertoff." It's a long article, in some fancy art magazine, with tons of huge words and a black-and-white photograph of Ariel and a little boy with dark, dark hair falling in his eyes. They are surrounded by paintings. He holds his hands up, happy. They drip with paint. Ariel is laughing.

Her son died of a combination of pills and alcohol. His body was found in an alley in Brooklyn. *Alexander.* He'd flunked out of school, he was bipolar, she'd lost touch with him and even hired a detective, but she couldn't trace him. She'd canceled shows, stopped painting.

He disappeared on her. They found him on the street. A little hole starts to burn inside me.

I wonder suddenly about her paintings, the tiny, tiny shafts of light in all the stormy dark. She said in the gallery that sometimes a painting of just color can tell a story, too, just a different one. Is her son the dark or the light in the paintings? Which one is Ariel? I'm struggling to understand, but it's hard, so I click off the article. I miss Ellis so much it's like a huge dark cavern inside my heart. That must be magnified a million times for Ariel when she thinks about her son.

Is my mother at all frantic, wondering about me? Or is it just another day for her, every day, one where I'm gone and not her problem anymore? Was she relieved to hear from the hospital, even if she didn't come right away? Does she ever think about the times she hit me?

She would get even madder after she hit me, holding her hand up like it burned, staring down at me. Because I tried to hide, especially when I was small. It's how I first learned to be small, scrabbling away under a table, or finding the corner of a closet.

Was she worried I would tell, in the hospital? I look away from the computer, down at my lap, at my fingers busily pinching my thighs to keep me from floating.

Before I can stop myself, I'm opening up my email and I'm typing in her address, or at least the last one I know she had. I write: *I'm okay.*

My finger hovers over Send. She would want to know, right? That I'm at least alive out here?

She knows Mikey's number. They talked in Minnesota. But she hasn't called him, or anything, to see how I am.

Sometimes when Fucking Frank was very high, he would tell us, all of us in the house, "Where are Mommy and Daddy now, huh? Are they at the front door, begging you to come home?" Smoke would drift across his face, his eyes burning like coal in the white plumes. "I'm what you have now. I'm your fucking family and don't you forget it."

My mother hasn't called Mikey. Or Casper. Or done anything. Mikey's leaving. Ellis is a ghost. Evan is all the way up in Portland. I delete the email to my mother.

I'm utterly alone.

MIKEY LEAVES IN THE MIDDLE OF THE NIGHT A WEEK LATER, the end of June, parking the band van outside my building at two a.m.

He knocks softly on my door, calling my name. When I open the door, he says, "We have to leave early. It's crazy, we're on a weird schedule to make the first show tomorrow." He's jittery, excited. I can feel the nervous energy coming off him.

He puts a piece of paper on top of the card table. It's got his cell phone number, Bunny's and Ariel's numbers, and his tour schedule. "I know you don't have a phone, but maybe you can use Leonard's or the phone at work if you have an emergency, okay? And you can email me from the library."

Mikey bends his head close to me, so that I can almost feel his cheek against mine.

"This is really going to be something, I think," he chatters. "I think we've got a line on doing a record at a studio up in Northern California, too. I mean, that would be fucking awesome, right, C?"

I duck my face, but he catches me in his arms. I count to twenty, very slowly, in my head. He kisses my forehead.

Keep your shit together and stay strong, he whispers in my ear.

I RUB MY FACE WITH A FRESH DISH TOWEL, TRYING TO ERASE the steam and heat of the kitchen. Little drops of sweat fall from my chin into the hot water pooling in the sink. Riley is walking down the corridor from the office, holding a folder of papers. He catches sight of me and frowns. He seems better today. It's almost eleven o'clock and he hasn't cracked a beer yet.

"Oh, for fuck's sake," he says. "What did I tell you about the shirts? It's hot back here, sweetheart. I don't need you dying of heatstroke."

"I don't have any." I busy myself by sliding plates into the tray.

"Well, get down to Goodwill and buy some after shift today." He sets the invoice folder on the cutting board. "At least roll up your fucking sleeves, though. Just for me."

I insert the tray in the machine, clang down the door, take up a load of wet silverware from the sink so I don't have to look at him.

Riley's voice becomes firm. "Roll up your sleeves, Strange Girl."

He's very close to me now. I can smell him through the dish steam, a mixture of sweat and spice, coffee and smoke. I stay very still.

Riley looks over at the front counter, where Linus is absorbed in cleaning the pastry case. He loosens my fingers so that the silverware drifts back into the sink water. Slowly, he pushes up one sleeve of my jersey shirt, just a little at first and then all the way to my elbow. He turns my forearm over.

I sense rather than see his chest suck in, and then out, deeply. I concentrate on the dirty food that floats in the sink, soggy chunks of meat and bread, tendrils of scrambled egg, but my heart is stuttering.

Something is happening as he's touching me, though, something confusing: an electricity, a wire being strung through my skin.

He pulls that sleeve down. He checks my other arm. His fingers are warm and gentle.

"You've been dark places, Strange Girl." He tucks the folder under his arm, slides the cigarette pack from his shirt pocket. He likes to sit and smoke with the men playing Go. "I remember you saying you tried to kill yourself, but that's just goddamn annihilation."

I look right at him. His eyes are dark and tired. He knows something about annihilation, too, which makes me a little less ashamed of my arms, I think.

He fits the cigarette into the corner of his mouth. "But you've got to own your travels. You're a big girl now. There's no going back from that shit, you know? Buy some goddamn short sleeves and fuck the world, you know?"

Halfway to the screen door, he turns back and hands me an envelope. "Almost forgot. Your first check. You're finally officially on payroll, no more swanky cash in pocket for you. Sorry it took Jules so long to process it. Don't spend it all in one place, y'all." The screen door bangs shut behind him.

After the lunch rush, I open the envelope and my heart sinks almost immediately. The amount is smaller than I counted on, because I didn't think of the taxes. I stare at the amount taken and the amount left over, which will just barely cover my rent. And then how will I buy anything I need until the next check? It was almost better when he paid me in cash. Tanner sees me looking at the check and he nods grimly.

"Fucking sucks, doesn't it? I'm up to my ass in loans for school, but I can't get a second job or I wouldn't be able to study." He dips his head in the direction of Linus, ringing somebody up at the front counter. "She works doubles here all the time and still has to sell plasma and shit to send money to her kids. Maybe ask your parents for some help?" He expertly rolls silverware in napkins.

I fold up the paycheck without answering him. Tanner swipes at his nose. "Most everybody here is in school and gets by on loans or money from parents, except for Temple. You haven't met her. She works nights. She's got four jobs. This one, driving an old lady to get groceries, working a booth at a sex shop, and tutoring some kid in Spanish."

"I was lucky enough to find *this* job," I say softly.

Tanner shrugs. "Gotta do what you gotta do to get by, I guess. Roommates help, even though that can suck, too. At least I make tips." He gathers the napkined silverware in his arms and kicks open the door to the front of the café.

In a minute, he sticks his head back in. "Go check with Linus. She can probably cash that pitiful thing for you. I'm guessing you don't have a bank account? If you try a check cashing place, they'll just take a slice for themselves."

I TAKE A LONG TIME BIKING HOME, TRYING TO QUELL THE panic building in me about money and rent and buying regular things and what to do. Linus did cash my check. I'll have to pay Leonard tonight. To make myself feel better, I decide to visit a house I like where they've used bedsprings as trellises in a garden. The curvy bodies of green beans lace through the tendrils and coils. Beyond the bedspring trellis, the giant heads of sunflowers droop over cosmos and cactuses. Brightly painted paving stones have been looped throughout the yard, a path between the dazzling flowers, the cactuses, the glinting hubcaps suspended from cottonwoods like oversized chimes. Orange fish bob on the hazy surface of a round pond. The whole outside of the small house has been muraled with swirling clouds of color, thunderbolts, baying coyotes, lazy turtles. Sometimes when I walk by, I see a woman touching up the paint, her thick gray hair gathered at her neck. She works carefully, moving her brushes just so, a cigarette dangling in an ashtray at her feet. Once, she turned and smiled at me, a flash of white in the white-hot day, the mural a bright explosion behind her, but I hurried past her, shy. I like this house, and I like thinking about it, and that strange woman, the tidy wildness of her garden, and I want to know how to get there, to get a tiny spot on the earth, a little house to paint inside and out, a backyard to fill up and shape, how to feel comfortable in the very air around me.

IT'S A BAD DAY IN THE KITCHEN: RILEY HAS ASKED ME SOME-
thing, and that something is floating in the air between us,
becoming heavier and heavier by the second.

Riley is staring at me, waiting for me to answer his question.

Riley's fingers are the color of watery coffee. How many
cigarettes has it been today? Orders have been sent back: bagels are black on one side, the scrambled tofu is missing chives,
home fries are brick-hard. Two plates broken, their jagged
white edges kicked beneath a stainless steel prep table.

He says he needs this to get through the shift. He says
the house has a black door and a blue pickup out front. The
espresso machine is whining, puffs of steam clouding Linus's
face. Tanner is cleaning the tables out front. Julie's in her office.

"You have a break." He takes a drag on his cigarette. His
eyes are tinged with red. This morning when I came to get
him, he was already up, sitting on the couch, smoking, staring
at nothing, a peculiar, plasticky smell tacked to his skin. "I'm
not allowed to leave during work hours. House rules." He tries
to wink, but it looks more like something's caught in his eye.

"Please." A hoarse echo in his throat, just like Evan when he
got needy. "Your shift's almost over anyway. I'll pay you."

I remember Ellis, tugging on my arm, her face frantic with
need. *Please,* she begged. *Just tell my mom I'm in the bathroom if
she calls. I told her I'm staying over. Please, Charlie. I just need to be
with him. Help me, Charlie, please?*

He reminds me of Evan, too, when he needed a fix, just
something, he'd say, to stop the *motherfucking abyss threatening*

to eat my fucking soul, and I would steel myself, and wash up in a bathroom somewhere, enough so my face wasn't too dirty, and stand on a corner a few blocks from Mears Park in St. Paul just after dark, waiting for a man to show up, and to lead him to the park, where Evan and Dump would be waiting.

But Ellis needed that boy, and I needed her. And Evan had helped me, saved me, so I helped him. And now Riley is asking for help. And he said he'd pay me. I need that extra money.

Casper said it would be easy to fall back into old habits, old patterns. But Casper is busy now, a million miles away. The comforting beigeness of Creeley Center is a million miles away. I feel a million miles away.

A familiar numbness comes over me as I take off my apron and lay it over the dish rack. I don't say anything to Riley. I hold out my hand for the money and close my fingers around it. It isn't until I've slid the money into my pocket that I realize I've forgotten my lapis lazuli stone today. My fingers fish about for it for a minute, then give up.

Outside the café, the heat sizzles the dish steam from my skin. Riley didn't notice me hiding the knife in my pocket.

The man who answers the door looks me up and down and then past me, to the street, like he wants to make sure I'm alone. He's chewing on the cap of a pen. His teeth are yellow. The house stinks of canned cat food.

Evan and Dump taught me silence is the best weapon. People will trick you with words. They'll twist what you say. They'll make you think you need things you do not need. They'll get you talking, which will relax you, and then they will attack.

The man falls back on the couch. I stay close to the door.

Cats are everywhere: black-and-white, gray, tabby, milling around and mewling throatily. The coffee table in front of the man is littered with papers and cups, wrinkled magazines. "You Riley's girl?" The pen in his mouth rolls wetly against his teeth.

"Cat got your tongue?" He points to the sea of fur moving on the raggedy carpet and laughs. "Huh, huh." His smile dies when I stay silent.

He asks me what I've got.

I put the money on the table. *Assess,* Evan would say. Always assess before you *progress.* From the corner of my eye, I see a baseball bat leaning against the wall. I see dirty plates with dirty forks and knives balanced on top of the television. The television is an arm's length away. My pocket is closer.

The man counts the money, reaches back, and raps against the wall six times.

"That's a big-ass scar on your forehead." He tosses the lighter back on the table, leans back into the couch as he exhales. The cigarette bobbles above his knee.

I keep my face blank. Talking is what gets you in trouble. It's the way you get trapped.

A door opens down the hallway. A woman appears, sleepy-eyed, barefoot, her tank top sagging across her stomach. Her hair's messy; long strands of dyed red and yellow hang in her face.

She, too, looks behind me, at the door, disappointed. The man on the couch appraises her. "Wendy, looks like your guitar guy sent a little friend instead. Should we trust her?"

Wendy drops a brown bag on the coffee table. She looks me up and down, a smile playing at her lips. "She looks harmless enough. I'm a friend of Riley's, too," she says to me coolly. "A very good friend."

The man tells her to go, and I watch her swish back down the hall. The ash on his cigarette has grown. Slowly, he pushes the bag across the table with his bare toes, until it plops on the carpet. I pick it up, feeling the knife against my thigh as I bend.

"You want anything for yourself, you know where I am."

I don't answer, just turn and leave. I don't stop or look back until I'm pushing through the screen door of True Grit.

Riley pulls me into the grill station, holds out his hands. He tucks the bag under his shirt. He whispers for me to cover the grill for him.

On his way to the bathroom, he motions to the refrigerator. When I open it, I see my thank-you: another bulky bag of food. I take it like a robot, no feeling, no expression, and wedge it all the way into the bottom of my backpack. Riley comes back more alert, licking his lips. He gives me a wink and goes right back to flipping potatoes on the grill.

I don't know what to think of what I just did or why. I've blanked myself out, erased myself. I spend the rest of the shift in a haze.

In my room, I push my green chair against the door. I put the bag of food on the table. I slide the knife from my pocket. I don't know how I forgot I had it.

And then just like that, all the numbness I had drops away and my heart starts beating like a crazy caged bird. Doing that for Riley, it felt *good*. It was wrong, but I did it, and it made feel like I sometimes felt with Evan and Dump and what we would do: like, yes, it was *bad*, yes, it was *wrong*, but there was also an element of danger that was appealing. Like: how far could you take something before it snapped? Would you recognize the moment that something was about to go terribly, terribly wrong?

But I also realize that I'm getting really far down the ladder of Casper's rules and all of a sudden I'm flooded with despair. I get up and pace around the room. I try the breathing exercises, but I just gasp, I can't slow down. I'm too keyed up. Mikey said move *forward* and I went *backward* big-time and oh, fuck, here comes the tornado.

My tender kit is still wedged far back under the claw-foot tub, hidden inside Louisa's suitcase. I don't want that, I don't. I run the blade of the knife lightly across my forearm, testing. My skin prickles and longing fills me up; my eyes grow wet.

I'm so close to feeling better, feeling release, right here, with this stubby little blade. But I turn my arms over, force myself to look at the rough red lines ridging my soft skin.

Anything but that.

I let the knife clatter into the sink. Now I'm kind of coming down. Now I don't feel very good at all. Too close today, with Riley and that man. Too close to what I used to do, and part of me wanted to see what it would feel like again, but I also wanted to make Riley's eyes stop blinking, wanted him to stop shaking, wanted to be a good egg, a keeper, just like with Louisa. Just like I'd do for Ellis.

And that one time, that one time when I didn't help her, when she needed help the very most she'd ever needed it, I did not help her and I lost her.

The room is closing in on me. I yank open the door. I could go downstairs, have one of the men on the porch take my money to the liquor store. I'm just about to leave when the door across the hall opens and a small, dirty-faced woman comes out. I don't know her name, she's only been here a few days, but we've passed in the hall, with her pressing herself against the wall if I get too close. She talks to herself a lot in her room at night, a lot of muttering.

"Hey," I say, before I chicken out. "You got anything to drink in there? I'll pay you." I pull out a five-dollar bill from my pocket.

Her little eyes are like raisins. She's wearing a stained tank top. Faded tattoos stretch across her chest. Names, mostly, but I can't make them out. She looks down at the money. My hand is shaking. When she reaches out to snatch the bill, I see her hand is shaking, too. She goes back into her room and slams the door.

When she comes out, she shoves a cheap bottle of wine, a screw-top, at me and then takes off down the hall. Her flip-flops thwack down the sixteen steps to the first floor.

I don't even wait to eat something. I unscrew the cap and take long pulls until I start to gag a little, then I pour the rest down the sink before I drink any more. It hits me quickly, the dizziness, the warmth followed by the little feeling of elation in my stomach. It's enough to tamp down my anxiety. I feel bad, but I made a choice. Cutting or drinking, and I chose drinking.

In the bag Riley gave me, I find a small burrito wrapped in foil. It's stuffed with chicken, shredded cheese, chilies, and sour cream. A tiny mountain of crisp hash browns borders the burrito. They're still warm, lovely and greasy on my tongue. I finish everything, even the wet bits that fall on my lap. I pull the white napkin out of the bag to wipe my face and a twenty-dollar bill falls out. I can only guess that it's an extra thank-you from Riley.

I pick up the book I checked out of the library earlier in the week. *Drawing is a state of being,* I read. *An interaction between eye, hand, model, memory, and perception. The representational method . . .*

I sigh, closing the book and pushing it to the edge of the table. I think of the woman with the muraled house, her garden like a castle. Soon, Lacey in 3C will begin to cry in her room, like she does every night, a snuffling, hiccupping sound. Schoolteacher downstairs will watch reruns of *The Price Is Right* all night, the bells and whistles and audience chatter trickling up through the floorboards. The men on my floor will stagger down the hall to the shared bathroom, groan and piss.

I draw like a demon, but this time on the wall next to my bed, filling up all the emptiness that surrounds me, some kind of mural of my own to wrap me up and keep me safe, until the wine pushes me into sleep.

THE NEXT TIME, THE MAN ON THE COUCH ISN'T SO TALKATIVE. This time, the red-and-yellow-haired woman lingers a little longer as I gather the sack and stuff it into my pocket and as I leave, she says, "You tell Riley Wendy says hey. You tell Riley, Wendy sure does miss him." That makes me wince. Were they together once? I try not to think about that.

At the café, I hand him the bag, watch as he rushes to the bathroom. Tanner is paging through a book of glossy, odd-looking photographs. He lifts it up for me to see. "Eye out of orbit," he says. "I'm gonna be an EMT."

The photograph shows the profile of a stunned-looking man, his eyeball sprung from the socket, connected by a cartoonish zigzag of artery. It's gross and I make a face. "Shit happens," Tanner murmurs. "The human body is a wonderful thing in all its fucked-upness."

Linus walks through the double doors, wiping her hands on her apron. She gags at the photo and Tanner laughs. I look up, catch her smiling at me, but I look back down at the white plates, the squares of wheat bread and hot cheese that I'm flipping while Riley's in the bathroom.

Linus says, "It's okay to talk to us, you know. We don't bite."

Tanner says, "Sometimes *I* do," and they laugh, but not *at* me, I can tell, so I kind of laugh, too. I'm getting better at being around them, talking a little more.

Riley returns. I can tell he's deliberately avoiding looking at Linus because he gets busy right away with prep work.

His skin gives off the cold scent of water. The color's

returned to his cheeks, his eyes are liquid light. Whistling, he slips the spatula from my fingers and quick, quick, he flips the hills of hash browns, preps a plate, oils a dry spot on the grill. He's quiet until Linus and Tanner have walked to the front to check the coffee urns. When they do, he leans down, his breath warm on my cheek, and whispers, "You're a real good girl."

THE RAIN HAPPENS VERY EARLY, WHILE I'M RIDING MY BICY-cle to Riley's to wake him up for work. It was humid all night and I slept with the fan right against my body, but it didn't do any good. I rinsed off in cold water in the tub, but my clothes stuck to me the instant I got outside.

About halfway to his house, it's as though someone drew a dark curtain across the sky and suddenly, the fattest rain I've ever seen or felt starts pouring down. It's like a thousand faucets have gone off in the sky at once. The street fills up instantly and cars driving by skitter and splash even more water all over me. I almost crash when someone hits a puddle and the water slashes across my face. The rain is warm and powerful.

I'm soaking when I get to his house. I run up on the porch, kick off my boots. I call out through the door, but there's no answer. I don't want to get his floor wet, but then I think, *What's he going to care, anyway?* So I run through his house straight to the bathroom. The only towels are on the floor. I start mopping myself off, shaking water from my hair.

Riley appears in the doorway, his hair tousled. He's shirtless, which makes me blush. "Well, look what the cat dragged in. This your first monsoon?"

"What?" Now I'm shivering, my overalls heavy with water and my shirt sticking to my body.

"It's practically the best thing about Tucson. Monsoons. Absolutely epic rainstorms. They can shut down parts of the city in minutes, flood the roads. Let me go take a look."

He comes back, whistling. "That's a pretty bad one. We can't head out in this. We'll have to wait it out. You better take off those wet clothes."

I look at him. "Excuse me?" His eyes are gleaming.

"You're a real wet cat, Charlie. You can't stay in those clothes. I don't have a washer and a dryer. I do that stuff at Julie's apartment. You'll just have to be naked." He laughs.

I wrap the towel around myself.

"I'm just joking. Hold on."

My teeth are chattering. I can hear the rain beating against the roof, the sides of the house.

Riley comes back with a T-shirt and a pair of jeans. "Here," he says, handing them to me. "Left over from a houseguest."

Houseguest. When? Who? I look down at the clothes. Riley closes the door. I peel off my wet clothes and hang them carefully on the shower curtain. It feels weird to be in different clothes. The jeans are a little big around the waist. I have to roll them down at the top and then roll up the legs. He didn't bring me any socks, so I have to walk barefoot.

I feel bare in the short-sleeved T-shirt. And cold. I grab another towel and wrap it around myself.

The front door is open. Riley is sitting on the porch cross-legged, smoking. I sit next to him.

"I love this weather," he murmurs. "I love rain."

I look out at the blustery sheets of water. Everything seems to have a gray-brown, shimmery gauze over it. "I don't," I say. "I don't like it at all. I don't like snow that much, either."

"You and Mother Nature don't get along, huh?"

I think of the times Evan and Dump and I got stuck out in the rain, when we couldn't find a place to go. How when you're standing in the rain, pressed together, getting wetter and wetter, knowing that the wetness will grow a fungus in your dirty, wet socks, that you'll probably get sick for days, it feels like you'll never be dry again.

"I lived outside for a while," I say, surprising myself. "Before I came here. It isn't fun when it rains and you have nowhere to go to get dry."

I can feel Riley's eyes on me. He's quiet for a while and then he says, "I'm sorry to hear that, Charlie. That's no good. That's no good at all."

"It wasn't." I can feel a ball rising in my throat. I pinch my thigh so I don't start crying. I feel kind of good for telling someone, for telling *him*. Out of everyone I've met so far here, I feel like he'd understand fucking up and being lost.

He puts out his cigarette in the ashtray and reaches over, touching my hand. "You're still cold." He rubs my skin with his fingers and then stands up, holding out his hand.

"Let's get you back inside. That blanket on the couch? It's the best, trust me. You go wrap up in that and I'll make some tea."

He smiles. "Okay?"

I look at his hand for a moment before I take it. "Okay."

AT FIRST, I THINK THE KNOCKING MUST BE HAPPENING TO someone else's door, like Manny down the hall, whose mother, Karen, often staggers in at strange hours, bearing cans of Coors Light and *Lost* DVDs, which they proceed to watch back to back while drinking beer and eating microwaved popcorn. Karen has a loud, insistent knock, because Manny is usually on the verge of passing out by the time she gets off her shift at Village Inn and arrives by cab in front of the building. She's the most common last customer at the liquor store next door, showing up just as they're locking the door and tugging down the grate. Through my window I can hear her wheedle and whine and offer them extra money, money she's spent all night earning, pulling moist bills from malt cups and from under the leftovers of grilled cheese. I know this part because sometimes Karen cries about it to Manny, that she has to work such a late shift, that she has to deal with mean college kids and drunk clubbers. Manny comforts his mother, heating up a cup of coffee in the microwave to get himself ready to drink again. Manny and his mother are possibly the loudest people in the building.

I frown, looking up from my sketchbook. Only Mikey and Leonard, once, to unplug the sink, have come to my room. I've been sitting in just a T-shirt and underwear because the room is so hot, even with the fan I bought at the Goodwill. I pull on my overalls.

My heart quickens when I open the door and see it's Riley, leaning against the doorframe, the darkness of the hallway spreading out behind him. He's swinging a plastic bag in one hand.

"That's so cute," he says, "the way your face gets all pink around me."

"What are you doing here?" I don't even try to hide the pissed in my voice, though I'm not sure if I'm pissed at him for noticing and saying something rude or pissed at myself for getting all blushy around him.

"I see you wear short sleeves at home," he continues, like I've said nothing. "You going to invite me in?" He's been quiet at work the past few days, strangely calm.

I sniff the air around him, to stall. "Are you drunk?"

"I brought you a present." He dangles the bag from a finger.

My mouth's gone dry. His eyes are shining and he looks happy. I think, *Everything will be easier if you don't come into the room.* Because now I'm sinking into his happy eyes, and remembering how kind he was the other day when it rained, and how nice it felt to talk to him on the porch, the warmth of his hand in mine.

But gently, he eases past me, tossing the plastic bag on the rumpled easy chair.

"You always hang out in the dark, Strange Girl?" He tries the lamp, but it just says *click, click.*

"I ran out of lightbulbs and my job doesn't pay me enough to buy more," I say grumpily. "The streetlight, and the light from the store over there, that works."

He flops on the futon, kicking off his boots, and links his hands behind his head.

"Open your presents." He points to the easy chair, his eyes glinting. "Right there." Instead, I throw the bag at him. He laughs, rummaging inside. He holds up a faded green T-shirt with m*a*s*h on the front. "I know how you kids like the irony, and all." He lays the shirt on the bed and puts the bag aside.

"Anyway, I was drinking at the Tap Room and I dropped my keys on the way home, I think. I'm locked out of my house. Can't break a window, they're fucking expensive." He pauses. "I looked everywhere on the damn street, but it's just so fucking dark out. Can't see so well in the dark."

He shifts onto his side.

I kneel down, spread out the T-shirt. "It's too small," I lie.

"Bullshit," he says. "You love it and it'll fit perfectly. I've had a lot of time to ponder your size, staring at your back four days a week for weeks on end."

He pauses. "We aren't so different, you know. I got you something else."

There are other shirts in the bag and beneath them, I feel the flat edges of a card. In the half-light, I hold the postcard close to my face. A redheaded woman with patches of pink clouding her cheeks. Her face is half hidden in shadow, one enormous dark eye looking directly at me. *Wife of the Artist, 1634.*

"I saw you looking at all those books in the library. A while ago. I found this card in a junk shop way up on Twenty-Second. Thought you two had the same eyes. Kind of stormy. Sad."

There is a stream of streetlight crossing his cheek. He saw me at the library? My stomach tightens. "What . . . what were you doing at the library? Why didn't you say hi?"

"I read, you know. And there you were, looking at some big old art books, like nothing else mattered. You looked happy."

He places a finger on my leg, making little circles on the denim. Circle, circle, traveling up, up, until his finger reaches the shoulder of my overalls. I stop breathing.

I bite the inside of my cheek, glad for the grayish dark, the streetlight that allows just enough for me to see him.

Louisa said no one would love us in a normal way, but I'm still a person, and I'm aching to be touched.

"You must have a million stories inside you," he says softly.

He sits up. Fine lines spackle the corners of his eyes. I can smell the remnants of hard alcohol—bourbon?—something sharp and deep coating his breath. The electrical wire is coursing through my legs, through my stomach.

He says, "I'm a walking cliché," and unhooks the shoulders of my overalls, the straps falling with a soft *clank*. He takes up my arms, turns them over and over, his fingers running up and down the rivers and gulleys of my skin. I'm sinking, and I'm not trying to stay afloat, because I do, I do want to go all the way under.

"I'm not going to hurt you," he says, grazing my neck with his lips. "We get each other, don't we?"

He pushes me back on the futon, pulling my overalls off easily, moving his hands down my thighs, exposing the ladderlike lines there. He rubs his thumbs across them like he's testing guitar strings, easily and without apprehension.

This is happening, and I'm letting it. It's one more thing that's falling away, one more thing on Casper's list, and soon, everything about Casper will disappear. I cover my face with my hands and listen to my breath ricochet against my palms.

And then he moves his hands higher, lighting on my stomach outside my T-shirt for a brief second, then slipping under so suddenly my breath sharpens. His thumbs brush my chest.

I pull his face down with force, greedy for the feel of his mouth on mine. I don't mind the taste of his mouth, the smell and lingering heat from cigarettes in his hair, on his skin. I see *blue* and *tangerine* on the insides of my eyelids. His hands knead my waist, travel down my legs, the insides of my thighs. I barely feel his weight, he feels light, he fits somehow with the makeup of my bones. I let my hands wander over his pants, a few fingers tucking experimentally between the waistband and his skin. But he pushes my hand away, nuzzles his face against my neck, slides his fingers down my boxers, between my legs, and inside me.

I say *No, no,* and Riley pulls back, saying, *You want me to stop,* and I say *No, no,* taking big gulping breaths, because I *don't* want him to stop but I do, and everything gets all tangled up inside me then. When I try to unbutton his pants, he stops me, *No, just this, let me do this,* and I understand then that he's way drunk, too drunk, but the insides of my eyelids are on fire, bursting into black and red, and I can't stop what's happening to me. He laughs softly into my neck as I shudder. Far down the hall, we both hear Kate shout, "Jack! Jack!"

In the morning, I wake to him tracing the faces of the people in my sketchbook. He doesn't say anything about them, though, just smiles at me, a smile that shoots through my blood and makes me ache. He rolls on top of me, says, "I was drunk last night, but I'm not now," and I'm shy at first because we are in the full light, no more dark, all of me is open and exposed, but that falls away in time.

We rise and dress without speaking. My body feels a blur, still, my brain is fuzzy from confusion. Like a couple, we buy coffee at a bustling, tidy, fern-filled café on Congress Street, so unlike True Grit with its grubby walls and fingerprint-laced pastry case. Like a boyfriend, he buys me a chocolate coffee concoction with whipped cream and sprinkles.

I have never had a boyfriend. I had those boys in garages, but that wasn't anything. I'm almost eighteen, and a boy has never bought me anything chocolaty until now.

We trace the sidewalks from his house to Hotel Congress, where the Tap Room Bar is, looking for his keys. The hotel lobby is a gleaming, sunlit place with leathery couches and a Western, punkish feel. An enormous painting of a beautiful, creamy blonde in denim shorts, flicking a whip, adorns a whole wall. He shows me the main room of Club Congress off the lobby, the small, squat black stage with loamy red curtains, the long, old-fashioned bar at the back of the room. He stares at the stage for a minute and murmurs, "We opened for John Doe here once," but I don't know who that is. He seems in his own world and I have to remind him that we have to be at work soon.

Off the club is the door to the Tap Room and through the window I see a plain, empty bar with high stools, a jukebox, homey cowboy art high on the old-timey papered walls, and simple, worn red booths.

We find his keys glinting in the early-morning sun, in the simplest of places: at the base of a stop sign. He has a keychain that says iceland.

"The band, we stopped there, once, on a layover. It was the prettiest place I've seen," he says. "You ever travel?"

Iceland. He's been to Iceland. I wonder what Ellis would say to him about that. *Paris, London, Iceland,* wherever.

"Here," I answer. "I've traveled here."

That makes him smile.

On the way to work, he smokes and offers me drags, which I take without even thinking. We separate, as usual, a block away, me heading in first, smiling cautiously at Linus. I empty the urns from last night and give them a quick rinse in the washer, returning them to the front counter. The screen door bangs, followed by Riley's easy "Hello" as he shuffles to the telephone and listens to messages from last night, writing things down for Julie. He fires up the grill, dumps a vat of home fries on it, squirts butter and oil over them, and messes them around with the spatula. He makes himself an espresso, brings me a cup of coffee, asks Linus something about a loom.

I tie an apron around myself, listening to the bell clang as the first customers straggle through the door. Steam seeps out of the dish machine, but I'm not as hot as I usually am, not nearly, because I'm dressed in the faded green short-sleeved T-shirt with m*a*s*h on the front.

When I turn with a stack of saucers, Riley is sipping his espresso, looking at me. A current shoots through me again at the sight of him, electrical and sharp. Flashes of last night, his mouth and hands; I can still feel his breath on my neck.

I catch the saucers before they escape my fingers. He grins.

I sense, throughout the day, sneaked looks at my arms, whispered talk among the waitstaff, but I am also aware of Riley watching over it all, issuing silent, stern looks, raising his eyebrows. He makes a point of conversing with me, making light jokes, including me in his conversations with the staff. It is as though he is spreading a veil of protectiveness over me, and I am greedy for it.

IN MY DARK ROOM I WAIT FOR HIM, CLEANED OFF, SKIN STILL hot from the bath, but he doesn't come. I listen to the men drinking on the porch, to the far-off, hazy sound of a band finishing a set at Club Congress down the street, but there's no knock at my door. I wait until it feels like my insides will explode, until I feel like a mass of fire, heat trickling from my pores, and then I get dressed, get on my lemon-yellow bicycle and ride to his house.

When he opens the door and sees me, he tucks the crook of his elbow in his hand, the smoke from his cigarette lifting dreamily into the air. "Where have you been?" he asks. Throaty voice, amused eyes. Then he takes my hand, leads me inside.

OF *course* IT STARTS AGAIN. IT STOPPED FOR A LITTLE BIT AND I thought, now that we are *together*, I won't have to do this anymore, because he wouldn't ask me *now*, would he? All of it is *wrong*. I *see* it. I *understand* it. I've seen *movies*. I know boys should come to your house in a *car*, and take you to *dinner*, and buy you *flowers*, or some shit like that, and *not* make you wait, wait, wait, in your dingy apartment until your body can't stand it anymore, and you get on your bicycle and ride to his house, instead, so *grateful* that he even opens the door and *smiles*. "I lost track of time." "Hey, you, I was just thinking about you." But he does ask. "Would you, could you, think you could go on a little run for candy for me? Then we can watch TV, or *you know*." He calls me "my nighttime visitor." He's like the desert itself: it's so *beautiful*, it's so *warm*, but there are *sharp edges* everywhere that you have to watch out for. You just have to know where they are. SO: I know this is all wrong. But maybe, me being me, this is as good as it's going to get. It's too late, anyway, you see: I've already fallen in.

I LEAN BACK ON MY BIKE SEAT, LISTENING, THE BAG FROM Wendy in my hand. Every night I've stopped at the same cross street, the same stop sign with the dented pole, and listened to the sound of Riley's guitar drifting down the street. I know that later, when he opens the door for me, I'll find the four-deck on the floor with a loose-leaf notebook open, Riley's messy, scrawled notes all over the pages, an ashtray mounded with crushed butts. On some nights, it's just the tender, warm sound of the Gibson Hummingbird hanging in the close air; Riley doesn't sing all the time. Once, at the library, I looked up Long Home on the computer. Tiger Dean still maintained the band's website. I clicked on songs like "Stitcher" and "Charity Case," Riley's big solo number. It was Tiger's voice that was initially captivating, a powerful blend of personality and tone, but it was the lyrics that kept everything together, that kept me listening closer, instinctively seeking out certain phrases and words. There was one other song that Riley sang solo, a ballad called "Cannon," about a man so heartbroken his heart tears from his chest and rolls away and he follows it (*And my heart burst from me / like a cannon / And it rolled to the bottom of the canyon / And here I will stay / Emptied in these empty days / Until you come back / And marry me, baby*), and I think it worked precisely because he wasn't a natural singer. It made the song all the more sad that his voice broke in some parts, wavered in others, and disappeared altogether at the end.

On Riley's street, people sit on porches, beer or wine in hand, listening to him, too, their faces open to the sound of him. When he gets it right, when there aren't any mistakes, when he can sail through a song completely from start to finish, it's thrilling, it pierces right through me. The faces of his neighbors light up. When he's done, they mime applause, because nobody wants him to know they're listening, nobody wants him to stop playing. Everyone is careful around him, like he's an egg they have to cradle.

But he does stop playing when he hears me clatter up onto the porch. He settles the Gibson on the couch, rustles his papers, takes a long drink of his beer, lights a new cigarette, takes the bag from me, and disappears into the bathroom.

When we're in his house, together, with all the signs of Riley-ness, his well-thumbed old books in the sturdy bookshelf, his records alphabetized on shelves all around the room, the comfortable, elegant, and crumpled velvet couch, the carelessly full ashtrays, I think it's somewhere I could stay: inside a life already lived and firmly in place.

AT FIRST, THEY LAUGH A LITTLE TOO MUCH, NERVOUS, AND I
have to wait until they calm down, let them drink a bit more,
before I start.

The sunlight is fading, but I have enough light on the porch
to draw them. It's Hector, who lives in 1D, and Manny and his
mother, Karen. I think they're used to people staring at them,
not *looking* at them. She shifts in the rusty metal chair, playing with her fingernails. Manny is on the steps, leaning back
against the railing. "Yeah," he finally says. "You can do it, right,
Ma?"

On the porch, I study the folds and lines in their faces and
work quickly, smudging, blowing away the gray dust of charcoal. "Your big romance," Karen says to me. "I need to know."

I just say, "Mmmm. Not much to tell."

Karen shakes her head, says, "The mens can be so *difficult*."
Manny is edgy, his dark brown eyes steady on my face. He
squirts beer through his gritted teeth and tells me that his job
consists mainly of other people not showing up for their jobs.

Each day he and Hector and some others from the building wait on a sweltering street corner downtown with dozens
of men as trucks crawl by looking for day laborers to water the
gardens of those who live high in the hills on the North side,
clip their hedges, help gouge the dirt for new pools, for elaborately tiled Jacuzzis. "This one place," Hector says, slurring,
leaning forward, out of the pose he held so well just a moment
ago. "The pool tile was like his woman's face, you know? Like
her picture, under the water. She's going to have to swim on

her own *face*." He spits on the porch, glancing at Karen, who frowns.

Manny says, "We make this fucking city run and they want to run us out. Build some stupid wall."

When I'm done, they hold my pad reverently in their hands. They're pleased they can finally see themselves, just like Evan was when he saw himself in my comic. Their happiness fills me up.

AT THE CAFÉ, I'M WIPING DOWN TABLES WHEN A MAN AT THE counter snaps his fingers at me. "A little help, please?" He taps the counter insistently.

Everyone is gone, so I make him his cappuccino, pouring the silky froth carefully over the espresso into a to-go cup. I usually don't do this, but I've watched Linus enough, and it feels kind of thrilling to try it out. The man hands me his money and I ring him up, which is a first for me here, too. I did work that little bit at my mom's friend's deli, so I remember the basics of the cash register. The bell on the door tinkles as he leaves.

"What are you doing, Charlie?"

Julie has appeared, her face furrowed.

I look down at the still-open cash drawer, the slots of bills and change. "Nothing. That guy, he bought a coffee." I point, but the man's already left. The café is empty.

Julie reaches around me and bangs the drawer shut, narrowly missing my fingers. I flinch, surprised at her anger. "Where is everybody? You're not supposed to run counter."

Riley appears, shoving his cup under the urn, a big smile on his face. "What's up, Jules?"

Julie's voice is strained and high. "Riley. Am I paying you to drink coffee and get drunk on shift? No. You can do that shit when you punch out. I'm sick of all of you taking advantage of me. I *need* you to supervise. She's not supposed to be on the register. We've been low on end counts for days."

Panicked, I blurt, "I didn't take any money. I wouldn't take money." I don't like that I can feel my face heat up as I say it.

It makes me look guilty, but I wouldn't do that to Riley. Or to Julie. "I'm sorry. No one was around, I thought it would be okay."

"Nobody's saying you took money, Charlie. That's not what she's saying, right, Jules?" Riley sips his coffee calmly, watching his sister's face carefully. He doesn't look over at me.

Julie shakes her head. "Why do you do that? Why do you always undermine—"

She stops suddenly, a troubled look crossing her face. She steps closer to me, looking down. "What is that? What did you . . . I didn't know it was so ba— Jesus, you can't be out here like that."

She waves her hands over the scars on my bare arms, staring at my skin. I step back, instinctively sliding my arms around my back. I bump up against the pastry case.

"Charlie, we've got people here trying to heal. *The Sisters,* Charlie." Julie's voice sounds desperate. I haven't ever seen her like this; it can't just be about me and my arms. Can it?

The Sisters come in every Tuesday and Thursday and push the tables together, open their journals and free-write. They cry softly, rubbing each other's backs. They drink fruity teas and wear loose, hand-sewn clothes. Their hair is plain and flat and they eat too many carob brownies and lemon poppy seed muffins. Linus says they used to belong to a cult on the border of Arizona and New Mexico.

"Jesus, Jules, are you listening to yourself?" Riley says, his voice suddenly hard. He shoves the bus tub at me and tells me to go finish up. I don't move. I'm frozen against the pastry case.

Julie whirls back around to me. "I don't want you wearing short sleeves, okay, Charlie? I know it's hot in here, we'll get that cooler fixed, but seeing that's a trigger, you know? I have to keep the customers we've got, do you understand?" Her voice breaks. "There's not a goddamn customer in the whole fucking place, Riley. Where is our lunch rush?" She buries her head in her hands.

I step around them, Riley patting her shoulder, and go back to the dishwasher. I hear them whispering, but I can't make out the words. When Riley comes back, he won't meet my eyes. "I told her nobody's going to look at anything but your pretty face, but she's in a weird spot right now, okay, so maybe, tomorrow, just do the long sleeves. Just for a little while, okay?" My heart drops with disappointment. I thought maybe he would stick up for me a little more. I look up at him. He averts his eyes.

I get a queasy feeling in my stomach.

"Riley," I whisper. "What money is missing? What's she talking about, Riley?"

He winces, his fingers trembling as he positions an onion on the cutting board. "Just don't worry about it, okay?"

"I didn't take any money. I don't want her thinking I took any money."

"Everything's going to be cool, all right? I'll take care of it." He turns to the grill and starts scraping grease into long, caramel-colored hills.

He sold you out, baby. Evan's voice, wheedling, in my ears. But I push it away, because I don't want to believe it.

IN THE MORNING, SOMEONE SHOUTS RILEY'S NAME AND I ROLL over, looking at him, his face slack and pale. I touch his shoulder lightly, listening to the sound of footsteps coming around the side of the house and then the knuckles that tap the half-opened window. Riley startles, his eyes flying open. I notice the grayish pallor of his face, the pink cast to his eyes. He was facedown in the bathroom when I came in last night. At first I was scared, and then I realized he was just passed out. It took me a while to drag him down the hall to the bedroom, and even longer to hoist him onto the bed.

He presses a finger to his lips, pulls the sheet over me. The mattress squeals as he crawls across the bed to the window, pushing it open. "Oh, hey. It's you." His voice is flat, wary.

The voice that answers is amused. "Well, well. Up to the old tricks, I guess. Who's beneath the sheet?"

Riley answers, "None of your business."

"Come on, let me see. I liked that last one you threw away. Liked her so much *I* married her, too." Muffled laughter.

My heart jumps. Riley was married? My breath catches in my throat.

"What do you want?" Riley coughs. He's angry; I can hear it. Sunlight filters through the faded sheet. It's getting hard to breathe with it draped over me. I'm starting to wonder if Riley's embarrassed by me, if he doesn't want his friend to see me.

"Luis Alvarez has pancreatic cancer."

Riley's body stiffens. "Are you fucking with me?" He sucks in his breath. "He let me borrow his car a few weeks ago. He just said he wasn't feeling well that day. That he wasn't going to work."

"Nope, no joke." The speaker's words come out a little softer. "It's too late, man. There's just too much of it.

"But listen, I'm putting together a concert at Congress for his wife and kids. They're gonna need some money. Thought about the Rialto, but I think Congress is better. Won't happen until sometime in the fall, though. All day, all ages, booze with ID, maybe a couple of outdoor stages, too. Probably have to get some local distributors to pony up, but most everyone knows Luis, so it shouldn't be too hard."

"Fuck, that sucks." Riley is silent for a moment. "He's a really good guy."

"Yeah." Pause. "Just give me a little peek, huh?" The sheet wiggles slightly.

"Fuck off. What do you want, anyway?"

"Word of mouth is you're giving nightly concerts for the neighborhood and that the musicianship's not half bad. So I got to thinking: Riley West back in the game? That might sell some tickets. Especially for the inevitable onstage implosion."

"Fuck you."

"Now, now. This is for Luis. He helped us out a lot, back in the day." The other voice is quiet, almost pleading. "You can do this, Riley. I know you can do this."

"Tiger." Riley sighs. "I haven't played out in almost two years."

I make myself as still as possible, careful not to miss a word.

"This is for *Luis*. He's fucking sick, man. Tons of other people have already lined up. I've got the Hold-Outs, Slow Thump, Cat Foley, California Widows, Hitler's Niece, Swing Train, Eight-Men-On, and I'll get more, I promise."

There is a silence. Finally, Riley says yes.

"Good man. Now, have you recorded any of the new shit yet? I've absolutely got to hear what Riley West has been up to."

Riley slides off the bed. I hear him cross the room and pull on a pair of jeans and mumble that he'll be right back.

Slowly, the sheet starts to peel away. Tiger Dean still has black hair, just like on the album covers, but it's no longer whirled elaborately over his forehead. It's short, well combed, and thinning. When I was looking up Riley, and Long Home, on the computer at the library, I found Tiger Dean's website. It said Tiger Dean still makes music with local bands, performs for private parties, and is also available for your graphic design needs. There was a photograph of him behind a desk, one hand on the computer keyboard, the other holding the neck of a cherry-red Stratocaster.

"Hello there." A smile flickers on Tiger Dean's face. I don't trust it. It reminds me of those too-cool guys in high school who always sauntered down the hall nonchalantly slapping the heads of geeks as they passed by. Tiger Dean angles himself a little farther into the window. He's wearing a red corduroy blazer.

I sit up and kick the sheet down my body. I'm dressed in a dirty jersey shirt, still grimy from my shift yesterday, and an old pair of Riley's striped pajama bottoms, rolled way over at the waist. My mouth tastes like cigarette butts. After I lugged Riley into the bed last night, I went back to the bathroom and smoked one of his cigarettes, ashing it in the sink. I finished the fresh beer that he must have just opened before he passed out, too. He'd set it carefully on the side of the tub.

"What are you doing with this little punk girl?" Tiger calls to Riley, leaning in against the window frame. "What are you wasting your time for?"

Last night I sat on the toilet, drinking and smoking, thinking about how I'd just had to drag my boyfriend, who may or may not consider me his girlfriend, into bed, and how I did runs for his drugs, and how I did those things for nothing—for his hand on my cheek when he was sober. And then I finished the beer and went back into the bedroom and walked right up to the side of the bed, testing the floorboards for the creak I'd noticed, and then brought my heel down smack on the floor. A piece of the board popped up, and there it was: Riley's kit, a small square cherrywood box that contained everything he needed. Everything he needed instead of me.

But I'm not going to let Tiger Dean know that.

I look hard at Tiger Dean and slowly, slowly, raise my middle finger.

Surprised, he frowns. "For God's sake." His eyes move to the scars on my arms; I don't try to hide them. "Two peas in a pod," he murmurs. "Playing little fuckery games."

Riley comes through the doorway with a beer, which makes me wince. If he starts this early, it will be a long, uneven day. He tosses the CD through the window to Tiger Dean, who catches it smoothly and tucks it inside his blazer. Riley climbs back onto the bed, nestling the bottle between his knees. He looks from Tiger to me.

"Couldn't resist, huh?"

Tiger casually touches the sunglasses on top of his head; they fall easily over his eyes. "You always had such interesting taste. I just wanted to make sure your work had remained consistent."

"Adios."

"This one seems a little young, though. Little uncouth for my taste."

"Vete a la chingada."

"Oof." Tiger raises his chin to me. "I bet if you knew his real name, you'd be out of here in a goddamn minute. It's—"

Riley starts to close the window on Tiger's fingers. Tiger laughs.

"I'll be in touch. And Riley," he says through the glass, lifting up his sunglasses. "Please, try to delay the inevitable Riley West breakdown until the actual concert. That's what's going to get people in the seats, like the old days."

Riley closes the window. Before he even settles back in the bed, I blurt, "Married?" I wonder if he's going to lie to me. "You were *married*?"

He gazes at me steadily, not blinking. "Yep."

"Like, till death do us part and all that? Ring-on-finger church thing?"

"Happens all the time. Guy finds a girl, they kiss, he buys a ring, they get married by Elvis in Las Vegas on a tour stop. And then, boom. Shit happens, girl leaves guy for lead singer in guy's band. The end." He takes a long pull on his beer.

"What kind of *shit* happened?"

Riley traces the neck of his beer with a finger. His nails are dirty. "Me. I'm the shit. All my shit."

"Do you . . . ever see her?" My heart's thudding. I feel kind of sick. "What was her name?" I don't even know why I want to know, but I do. It's like the puzzle I had assembled for Riley has been kicked apart, and new pieces have been dropped into my hands.

A grin spreads across his face. "Are you jealous, Strange

Girl? Because you don't need to be. No, I never see her. They live in a nice house up in the foothills. Got a baby and everything."

"What was her *name*?"

"Charlie."

"*Tell* me."

"Her name was Marisa."

Marisa. My mind whirs. Ma-ri-sa. A pretty girl's name. Delicate features, I bet. I can see that. I can see Riley falling for someone whose whole body sang *delicate*.

I shut my eyes so he can't see the pricks of tears.

"Aw, no, don't start that." He nudges me with his elbow playfully. "I had a life, Charlie, before I knew you. I'm older than you, girl. I've done all sorts of shit. Even fallen in love and got married. No need to worry about that now."

I push his elbow away, hiccup. "Like change your name?"

He laughs. "Yep. Didn't you know that, though? We all had the same last name for the band: West. Tiger thought it would be cooler that way. He uses his real last name now."

"What about the Riley part?"

"Oh, I've had that forever. Since I was little. I was always fucking shit up in one way or another. My dad used to say, 'Who do you think you are, living the life of Riley or something?' Stupid. But it stuck."

"Well," I say slowly. "What's your real name, then?"

"My real name is Riley West because that's who I am now." He closes his eyes and yawns. "No more questions, okay? Test's over. Put down your pencil and leave your blue book on the table, please."

Frustrated, I say, "I can ask Julie." It's one more puzzle piece.

He finishes his beer, puts the bottle on the floor by the bed.

He wraps his arms around me, burying his face under my shirt. "She won't tell. She'll never tell."

He licks my belly button. "The thing I like about you, Strange Girl, is you don't ask for much. You don't ask for more than you need. You know what a tremendous relief that is, that you just let me be?"

And then he distracts me so much, I forget all about asking Julie his real name, or more about his ex-wife, or even about the box under the floorboards, or about how little I need.

AUGUST GETS MORE AND MORE BRUTAL. EVERY DAY IS OVER A hundred degrees, sometimes hitting one hundred and nine, the heat wrapping me like a fiery blanket. It's insufferable in my room at night and so I've been staying with Riley as much as I can, hoping every night that he'll be home, because he has a swamp cooler. On the nights he isn't there, I drift in and out of a hot sleep, the floor fan pressed right up against my futon.

Riley and I have come to work early this morning. We're sharing quesadillas with over-easy eggs and red chile when the phone rings.

Riley comes back around the corner and pulls me down the dark, greasy-floored hallway to Julie's office. "Linus is sick; she's not coming in," he says, shutting the door behind him. He kisses me deeply, running his hands under my shirt.

"Riley . . ." I feel uncomfortable.

"Shhh. Tanner won't be here until seven-thirty and Julie's in Scottsdale at a retreat. She won't be back until this afternoon." He settles on the couch and reaches up for my overall straps. Our lips sting from chile.

I don't want to do this here, it feels wrong to do this in Julie's office, but he's insistent, and it's over quickly. I rub the cushion of the couch with my hand before we leave the office, to smooth out any wrinkles.

As Riley opens the door, tucking his T-shirt back into his brown pants with his other hand, he stops short; my face mashes into his back.

Tanner is standing awkwardly in the hallway. He has a very

weird look on his face, like he doesn't know what to think, and in that moment, I know he heard us, and my face blazes up with embarrassment.

Tanner squints as though he's been doused in water. He whispers, "I'm so sorry for what's about to happen." He steps to the side.

Behind him, standing by the dishwasher, is Julie.

"The last session of my retreat was canceled. I got home last night." Her voice is cold.

The air around us is heavy and tense. "Sorry, Jules," Riley says calmly, sidling by her as if nothing is wrong. I walk slowly to the dish station, squeezing past her, so scared and embarrassed that I feel sick. I can barely hear myself think, my heart is pounding so much.

Julie looks at Riley, now safely behind the cutting island. She looks at the plate of half-eaten red chile quesadillas, the two forks. She looks over at me and down the hallway to the open office.

"Wash your hands, the both of you, this instant. I can't deal with this right now. Our fucking breakfast rush, if we *have* one, is about to happen. Where's Linus!" she yells.

"Sick," Tanner says..

"Jesus fucking Christ." Julie stomps to the front counter without saying anything else.

Riley soaps his hands next to me at the sink. He arches his head to check the front of the coffeehouse before kissing me quickly on the cheek. He shrugs, which makes me think everything might be okay.

There *is* a breakfast rush and a lunch rush. After, when the café clears out, I help Tanner bus the tables while Julie counts the register. She worked counter all morning while Tanner waited tables, walking back stiffly with her orders and slamming them down for Riley without a word. She wouldn't look at me, which made my heart sink.

When Tanner and I come back into the kitchen with our full bus tubs, Julie's shouting from behind the closed door of the office.

"Oh, shit, this is going to be good." Tanner cracks the refrigerator and takes a can of Riley's PBR. "I mean, not for *you*."

"Shut *up*," I hiss at him, my face draining as Julie's voice gets louder and louder. "It's not funny."

At intervals, we hear: "Why do you *always* make the *worst* decisions?" "How the *fuck* long has this been going on?" "Did you not even *think* about what she said in this office? Is she even eighteen, Riley? Do you have any idea what that means? It means statutory *rape*."

The ugliness of that slaps itself over my skin. I start pinching my thighs through my pockets.

Tanner looks over at me. "*Are* you eighteen?" He has an amused grin.

"Yes," I hiss. "Soon. Eleven days." I'm so embarrassed, I think I'm going to throw up. My stomach is roiling.

"Do you think you can just *fuck* in my *office*?" Julie screams, "And you left a fucking condom in my fucking wastebasket!"

My face drains. Oh my God. I don't know why I didn't wonder what he did with it at the time. Tanner laughs out loud, a barky sound that pierces my heart, which is the last straw for me.

I pull off my apron and shove it onto the dish tray, turning on the machine. The sudden sound of water drowns out the fuzz in my ears. I grab my backpack and leave.

* * *

I walk bleary-eyed through the Goodwill, looking for nothing but not wanting to be outside or at home just yet. I finger odd stacks of electronics that I know nothing about: bold blue plastic boxes of wires and cords and sprockets and springs. I paw through the endless racks of scarred and chewed LPs. I try to keep my eyes open and my breath even. I pinch my forearms. Even if I leave bruises, Riley won't say anything about them, I'm sure of that. Finally, I go back to my room to wait for him.

I forgot to lock the door. When he knocks, I don't answer, and he pushes in anyway, crossing the room to the refrigerator. He opens it, though I don't think he's really looking for anything to eat.

He closes the door and leans against it, looking down at me on the floor. "You really only ever eat at Grit, don't you?"

He's clutching a paper bag and he holds it up to his lips, drinks from it. I watch him and remember the alley behind the Food Conspiracy Co-op those few months ago. He stood the same way, shoulders slumped, paper bag in hand.

I'm between the tub and the wall, where I've been burrowed for the past several hours, waiting. It's true; I only buy food if I have to. Every morning, I'm hopeful that sometime during the day, Riley will make the wrong order and offer it to me: a bagel with hummus instead of cream cheese, an omelet with black olives instead of green peppers. Or I take what he gives me after a run. We never go out to eat. Sometimes I wait until he's asleep and select things carefully from his haphazardly stocked kitchen: an orange, a tortilla slathered in butter, a glass of dubious-smelling milk.

When he's not too far gone, we do incredible things in the dark, on his rumpled bed, but I am afraid to ask him for food and except for the one time on his porch, I've never really talked about living outside and what it means. And he's never asked, which now makes me even sadder than I was before. I'm always asking him things about himself, as much as he'll allow, but he never asks me about me.

I will my voice not to break. "Are we fired now?"

Riley caps his bottle. "Me? She'll never fire me. Though I was little scared there, after she yelled about the condom. I think she's mad about a lot of things, not just us screwing in her office."

Groaning, he settles on the floor next to me, stretching his legs out on the scarred linoleum. "She's royally pissed, Charlie. What you didn't hear, because you took off, is that she knew about us awhile ago. Being the tender lovebirds we are, we walk to and from work together, which she can see from her window above the restaurant, but she decided not to say anything right away. Her apartment is up there. I don't know if you knew that or not. She ignored it. But our relations today, in her office, kind of threw her for a loop."

"And?"

"And ... she's switching you to nights. Actually, what she said was 'I won't hand her to you on a platter.'" He looks amused. "She said, 'She's not a cookie, or a book, or a record on a shelf. You can't just play with her and then put her back.'"

You can't just play with her and put her back. "That was really embarrassing," I say sharply. "Having her find us like that. I didn't even want to do it. You made me."

He gives me a sharp look. His voice gets tight. "I didn't make you do anything, girl. I think you got something out of it."

No, I want to tell him, I *didn't*. But I don't, because wasn't it partly my fault it happened anyway? I didn't want to do it, but I let him anyway.

He lolls his head to the side. Something catches his eye and he leans forward. "Why do you have a suitcase wedged under the tub, Strange Girl?"

Before I can stop him, he slides over and pulls it out. He fixes his glisteny eyes on me, the side of his mouth rising in a smile.

He lowers his voice in a spooky way. "Is this is it? Does the magic suitcase hold the secret to my little stranger?"

He flips the clasps and paws through the shirts until he finds the metal kit. Only, he thinks it's just something neat, because he says, "Cool." But then he unlatches it. His eyes dart over the objects inside, the creams, the tape, the bandages, everything I bought that first day I got here, at the convenience store. My heart's in my throat, watching him.

It's a little mean, a little payback for today, for never asking me about myself. Because it's going to make him scared, and a little sick, being faced with the puzzle pieces of me for a change.

Riley picks up the roll of linen hesitantly and lets it unfurl; pieces of broken glass tumble onto the floor, making their familiar chimelike sound.

He huffs twice, queer sounds, like someone's knocked him in the chest. "What the fuck is this?"

Before I can stop myself, I blurt, "It's me. It's what I do.

What I did, I mean. I'm trying not to do that anymore." I hold my breath, waiting.

It's like he didn't hear me. Angry, he holds out the box, his voice rising. "What is this shit?"

He holds up the pieces of glass one by one, the small plastic container of hydrogen peroxide, the tube of ointment, the roll of gauze.

"It's what I use. To cut myself. Those are my things."

Riley drops them all back in the box as though they've burned his fingers. He kicks the kit violently across the floor and stands up, yanking the hood of his jacket over his head tightly. I close my eyes. The front door slams.

I crawl across the floor and take my kit in my hands, holding it close to my body. I carefully reassemble everything, slotting everything in its place, because it's all precious to me. In my fingers, the glass tinkles, pricks, tiny promises that I have to steel myself to ignore. The linen rests against my palm. I put the kit in the suitcase, push the suitcase under the tub.

The door to my apartment bangs open and shut. He walks straight to the sink, cracking the window above it, and lights a cigarette. "Tell me," he demands. "Like, what is that all about? Why do you have that box? What does it *mean*?"

"Where the fuck did you think my scars came from?" My voice breaks. "Do you think they just ... appeared by themselves?"

He mumbles. "I don't know ... I just ... I kind of kept it abstract." He exhales smoke out the window. "I figured you were all done with that. It didn't occur to me you kept, like, a fucking box of shit *to cut yourself if you fucking felt like it*."

"*You* have a box of shit." It tumbles out of me like water.

Riley's mouth drops open. He didn't know I knew. He didn't think I would look, I bet, or even guess.

"Are *you* the only one in the world who gets to be a fuckup? Am I *spoiled* for you now that you've seen my stuff? Did it make me real? Not a cookie or a cake or a record anymore?" My body is revving up in a dangerous way, my breath coming in gasps.

"Don't." His voice is a warning. "Don't even go there. That's not . . . valid."

"I'm the only one here who's trying not to do the bad thing, who's trying to get better, and you're treating me like shit for it." My palms are flat on the cold, sticky linoleum. I can smell the unwashed floor, the dirt in the cracks by the wall, the whole shitty mess of the building, and Riley, Riley, too: his burnished alcohol stink, the cloud of old cigarette smoke that sticks to his clothes.

I ferried his drugs. I fucked him in his sister's office. I let him see all of me, every bit, and now I'm sitting here on the grungy floor, a dog at his feet. Like a *dog* I wait for him at night. Like a dog, now, stupidly, I only want him to pet me, love me, not leave, and that makes me suddenly, blazingly angry and sad all at once, which feels like fire inside me.

I pound and claw at his legs. He jumps in surprise, his bottle falling, smashing inside the sink. He catches my arms, swearing when I struggle, and for a minute, a flicker of something dark crosses his face, his lip curls; the tension increases in his wrists. His fingers tighten like metal on my skin. He's shouting now, like my mother, *What is wrong with you?* And then one of his hands is in the air, fingers together, palm flat.

My mother and her raised fist flashes in front of my eyes. I shrink away from Riley, shutting myself off, bracing myself.

There is the person people see on the outside and then there is the person on the inside and then, even farther down, is that other, buried person, a naked and silent creature, not used to light. I have it and now, here, I see it: Riley's hidden person.

There's a crackling in my head. My wrists ache.

"Stop making that noise," he says roughly.

I look up; he's dunking a cigarette under the tap. The hot paper sizzles and then silences.

"You were going to hit me." My voice sounds flat, far away.

"Jesus, this is fucked. You're still such a fucking kid. I'm fucking twenty-seven years old. What am I doing? I don't know what the fuck I'm doing." His face is papery with exhaustion as he walks to the door.

When the door closes, I turn off all the lights and curl up in the bathtub in a very tight ball. I imagine myself inside an egg, a metal egg, impenetrable, locked on the outside, anything to keep myself from crawling to my kit, from crawling outside to my bicycle, to wait at the stop sign down his street, to say *I'm sorry*, but for what, for what, for what.

THE NEXT AFTERNOON, BEFORE MY FIRST NIGHT SHIFT, HE'S waiting inside the employee entrance of the coffeehouse, folded into a green plastic chair, reading the *Tucson Weekly*. He stands up, blocking me from walking any farther.

"You okay? We okay?" The last two words he whispers in my ear and I turn my head from his husky breath. "Come on now," he says as if talking to a petulant child.

"You almost hit me," I hiss, sidestepping him. From the doorway, I can see the mounds of dishes stacked in the sinks.

"I'm sorry," he says. "Please, I'm sorry. I would never do that, I promise, I promise, Charlie. Things got a little out of control. I mean, come *on*. Did you think I'd jump for joy when I saw your little box?" He shoves the newspaper into the pocket of his jacket.

He takes my hand, but I yank it away. The Go players look up at us curiously, coffee cups in midair.

"Please, Charlie, I'm sorry." His voice gets softer, worming its way through me. I feel myself giving in. He wasn't expecting to find my kit. Anyone would be upset, I guess. To see something like that. But—

Linus pokes her head out the screen door. "Charlie, Julie's waiting for you in her office, kiddo."

I drop Riley's hand, relieved, and step away from the dangerous warmth of his body. My heart flip-flops the entire time as I walk down the hallway to the office.

Julie looks up at me from her swivel chair, sighing heavily.

"This is hard, okay? I don't want you to think I'm going to like any of this one bit, okay, Charlie?"

She rubs her temples. "Don't think I don't like you, because I do. I just know my brother better than you, you know? Can you understand? I'm not going to . . ." She stops talking and looks away as if she's thinking.

"Hand me to him on a platter?" I finish, looking directly at her. I feel bare today, as though something has been shed from my body. I spent all night in the tub, not sleeping, thinking about the dark that spread across Riley's face, the fight that appeared there just behind his eyes. I looked at my charcoals and papers in the morning and ignored them, going to the library instead. I checked my messages (No Casper; Mikey's in Seattle; Blue says the doctors are rethinking her release); I stole twenty dollars from a woman's purse in the bathroom. The bill was tucked awkwardly in a front pocket. I was washing my hands, wondering about the stupidity of leaving a purse on the shelf above the sink with money hanging out. I didn't really have to think much about it all. Stealing it was a delicious thrill.

Julie turns her mouth down. Her face becomes a little lost. "Riley gets things and he hasn't done the work to get them. He's an addict. He's a liar. He's charming. He's not charming."

She looks right at me. "In the big picture, he's not *old*, but he's had a life and you've had none."

I kind of choke-laugh. "No offense, but you don't know anything about me. Like, at all. You have *no idea* what I've been through and seen."

"Oh, Charlie." Julie puts her chin in her hands and gazes at me for so long, I become uncomfortable. Her sad tone grates at me. I feel for the lapis stone in my pocket, fret a finger over it.

"Never in a million years will a relationship between an alcoholic junkie and a scared young girl work out."

Before I can say anything, she stands up, briskly ponytailing her hair. "We had a terribly violent father, growing up. My brother got the brunt of it. To my dying day, I will protect him, no matter how much money he steals from me and how much he siphons off my soul. But I won't be responsible for collateral damage, do you understand? That, I can control.

"Don't ever have sex in my office with my brother, or *anyone*, ever again. And if you two happen to overlap with schedules and you are here while he is here, I don't want to see anything, *anything*, that even hints at affection between the two of you. Because I will *fire you*."

We stare at each other. I look away first, because, of course, she has me. I need this job, and I need her brother. I nod at the floor.

"Now, go find Temple," she says.

Temple Dancer is a tall girl wrapped in a batik skirt with bells dangling from the waist-tie, a Metallica T-shirt, and dyed blond dreads bundled into a bun on each side of her head. She crosses her arms. "Really? A girl dish? At night?"

"Do you have a problem with that?" I'm angry, Julie's words still stinging my ears.

Temple Dancer's face loosens and she laughs, a deep sound, like owls fluttering from her throat. "Just testing. It's awesome. I'm totally sick of dudes."

Julie appears, changed into drapey pants and a tank top to go to her yoga class. "Girls, play nice. Linus!"

Linus emerges from behind the grill, *Riley's* grill, her face sweaty. "Welcome to nights, Charlie. And I know, I know, I work too much, it's true, even nights. I never leave!"

"Let's try to keep it together tonight, okay, girls? Kibosh on the drinking?" Julie pleads.

"No problem, J." Linus spins a dish towel with her forefinger.

As soon as Julie's gone, two waitgirls burst through the doors to the front, planting themselves right in front of me. Temple Dancer joins them. I've never been in the coffeehouse at night, so I've never met them.

"You're the one that fucked Riley in Julie's office? Oh my God."

"Jesus! You totally fucked Riley in Julie's office. How was it?"

"I thought he was fucking that Darla girl from Swoon? Does she know? Because she will die. She's such a pussy."

"I thought you were with Mike Gustafson. Did you guys break up? You were a totally cute couple. I saw you guys eating fries at Gentle Ben's once."

The comment about Mikey cuts me a little. The comments about Riley horrify me. Darla from Swoon? Did that really happen?

Linus waves the dish towel in the air. "Enough. Officially over, no more questions asked or answered. Temple, do your bit: train Charlie."

One of the other girls says, "I'm Frances. Nights are hell here." She tucks her orange bob behind her ears. "But in a good way," she finishes before taking off to the café floor with her green order pad.

Temple says ominously, "The best and worst thing about nights is when we have live music. It can sucketh or it can giveth. Tonight, our pleasure is . . ." She fishes a sheet of paper from under the counter.

"Modern Wolf. Tonight will sucketh." She jams a finger into her mouth, gagging.

The other girl says, "I'm Randy." She does a little two-step shimmy. She's dressed in a black miniskirt and white T-shirt with a spray-painted red target. Her saddle shoes scuffle against the hardwood floor.

Randy rolls her eyes. Her blond, feathered hair swings against her cheeks. "Modern Wolf sucks ass. This means we'll get mostly bangers and some art types thinking this is prog rock, which it is *not*. It'll be loud and awful and hell getting rid of them at closing."

Temple is spearing receipts on a spindle. "Sucks for you, since you have to clean both shitters and the main floor at the end of the night."

Randy nods. "And we'll all be waiting for you, and stuff, to finish because Julie says we all have to leave at the same time? But we can't help you."

"Because nobody helps the dish." Temple makes a sad-clown face.

"So we'll be getting angrier, while we wait for you," Randy says.

"And angrier," Temple concurs. She frowns. "Jesus, you're going to burn up in that shirt."

Randy cocks her head at me. "We know about you. Julie told us. I have a T-shirt with short sleeves in my bag, if you want it."

Desperately, because their machine-gun conversation has made my head spin, I say, "Do you guys ever shut up?" Behind the grill, Linus laughs.

Temple grins. "Never."

"It's cool with me, you know," Randy tells me, leaning in

280

closer, so that I can see the shine of the piercing in her nose. "Julie hardly ever comes in at night, anyway. My cousin, she was a cutter. She's in law school now. Stuff happens, you just keep on truckin', am I right?"

Move forward. Keep on truckin'. I'm getting tired of everyone thinking it's so easy to live. Because it's not. At all.

Randy gives me a friendly little nudge with her elbow and I try to smile, just to be nice, *Don't be a cold fish,* but I'm starting to feel sick, and heavy inside. I look out the front window at the dark sky. Working at night is going to be a lot different.

Around eight-thirty, Modern Wolf come in drunk and take a long, noisy time setting up; one of them falls off the riser and passes out. Temple empties a pitcher of water over his head. The band has a core of friends who fling themselves into the battered wooden chairs and smoke inside even though they shouldn't and drink enormous amounts of beer they smuggled in stuffed in paper bags. They stomp booted feet on the floor so hard that Linus shakes her head at me and says, "You stupid, stupid children. Why do you think that's music?"

The band reminds me of the ragged kids Mikey and DannyBoy used to take me to see in St. Paul: skinny, loose-jeaned kids, girls and boys, with bad skin and crunchy hair who whaled on instruments in the moldy basements of houses, popping strings and bashing on drums. It was exciting to me, that you could throw yourself into something so much simply because you loved it and it consumed you. It didn't seem to matter if you were good or not. It only mattered that you did it.

Modern Wolf sings, *My heart is a political nightmare / Guantánamo Bay every day / You've searched and seized and strung me up / I'm left with nothing to say / I ain't got nothing to say!*

A girl in a mesh top and hot pants lurches through the

doors to the kitchen area, takes a look at Linus and me, spews fries and beer from her mouth, the dregs caking instantly to her chin, and whispers, "My bad," before Randy shoves her out. I sop up the chunks, holding my breath. They were right, nights are way worse than days. No one ever vomits during the day, except for that time with Riley. I'm exhausted and my head hurts from all the noisy music and there are still two hours until closing, and longer after that to clean. My heart sinks farther and farther.

At closing, Temple brings out a large bottle of Maker's Mark and pours cups for everyone except Linus, who grimaces. Temple raises her cup and shouts, *"Salud!"* I just leave mine by the dishwasher. Even though I've had some drinks at Riley's, mostly when he's sleeping, and that half bottle of wine, I haven't had anything else.

Someone has menstruated in an ugly way on the women's toilet seat and that takes me some time. The men's room is all graffitied walls, piss on the floor, paper towels stuck to the tiled backdrop above the sink. I drop stream after stream of cleanser in the toilet, but it remains a defiantly burnished yellow. My hands burn from the chemicals when I'm done.

While the other girls bustle and laugh behind the counter and in back, I tackle the tables: wiping them down and heaving the chairs on top of them so I can mop. It's a lot more work at night. My face is red from the effort and I'm breaking out in sweat. Modern Wolf is still straggling out, the last of them bleary and unsure of the direction of the doorway. It's Friday; Fourth Avenue will be packed with people going to hear music along the street, to Plush, O'Malley's, the Hut with its enormous, glowering tiki head, all the way down to Hotel Congress with its pretty, old-fashioned awnings. Mikey's probably calling Bunny every night. Maybe buying things for her in truck stops, stupid stuff, like pencils with fuzzy tops.

I wonder what Riley's doing, because we'd be together now, on a good night, maybe listening to records in his living room, something quiet like that that I like. I wonder if he's thinking about me at all.

It's while I'm mopping the sloping hardwood floor, listening to the other girls laughing and drinking and smoking, that I suddenly get really lonely. They're a gaggle of girls, together and happy, normal girls doing normal things. They're all going to go out after, find friends and boys, maybe go to the bars. And I'm mopping shit up and smelling like old food.

The bell tinkles on the front door and happy girl-squawks erupt from the counter: *Hi, Riley, hey, Riley, taking us out for drinks, Riley?* My heart sinks and soars at the same time when he answers, *So sorry, ladies, I've just come to collect my girl,* and then there's an awkward, small silence before Temple says, *Oh, right,* because she, and they, all of them, I know, were really thinking, *But we thought you just* fucked *her.*

He said *My girl.*

My heart leaps, but I don't want him, or them, to see it. I can feel everyone watching me from behind the counter, so I ignore them, pushing through the double doors to the kitchen area. I dump the grimy, slick water in the sink, run my apron through the washer. There are two tiny white cups of untouched Maker's Mark on the counter by the washer. They're called demitasses and they're for single espressos. Linus has been teaching me the names of cups for coffee drinks. I love them because they're perfect and compact and unblemished.

When I finally turn around, the girls are there, giving me

little half-smirks, Riley standing among them, already several drinks down., He wobbles slightly on his feet.

We aren't going to listen to records. He might have said *My girl*, but will he remember that in the morning? I look down at the demitasses. What does it matter if I drink now, too? Would he even notice?

A tiny, tiny part of me whispers: Is there even room for me in what we are? *A cookie, a book, a record on a shelf.*

"I'm almost ready," I say, and turn back to the sink. A wave of resignation washes over me. I down the Maker's Mark and rinse the cups. My throat and stomach burn, but the warmth that spreads through my veins obliterates that. I wipe my mouth and turn around to face them.

"Are you ready?" I ask Riley. "I'm ready to go."

Outside, I have to push through a gauntlet of bodies to get to my yellow bike. I'm fumbling with the lock when someone shouts, "Hey, Riley, man, is that your girlfrien'?" Slurry laughter creeps from the Modern Wolf crowd. In that moment, looking at the sea of drunken, black-shirted boys with greasy, dark hair and boots with dangerous soles, I know that Mikey has heard, or will hear soon, about what I've been doing. And I don't think I care anymore. I feel heavy and numb.

A rumble of *ooohhh*s seeps from the crowd and Riley takes the bicycle from me, puts my backpack over his shoulders, settles on the seat. "Don't be mad," he says quietly in my ear. "I came to take you home. I swear I would never hurt you, Charlie, never. You have to let me show you that."

He angles me on his lap so that I'm facing forward, my hands gripping his thighs, my feet up on the bike's bar.

He tells me to hold on or we'll both die, and we ride to his house.

I THINK THAT *SLOPES* ARE MEANT TO BE *SLIPPERY.* I DON'T know *why.* I don't even know *who* invented the *stupid* notion of them. I don't even know why it *matters.* Who *cares?* Who *cares* about a scarred girl who can't seem to be by herself? Who *cares* about a scarred girl who mops floors and ferries drugs for her boyfriend? The *scarred girl* should care. But she doesn't know *how* and once you let the *Maker's Mark* in, once you let *anything* like that in, like *kissing,* or *sex, alcohol, drugs, anything* that fills up *time* and makes you feel *better,* even if it's just for a little while, well, you're going to be a *goner.* And sometimes, once, maybe *twice,* she starts to say that she's thinking of taking a class with this lady artist, and she *stops,* because a little mouse taps her brain and heart and whispers, *But then you won't get to spend so much time with Riley,* and the words, they turn to stone again, fat in her throat, and she can feel little bits of herself disappearing in the large thing of *Riley and me* and and and . . .

The *slippery slope,* it will never, ever end.

IT'S SO SLY, THE WAY IT HAPPENS. LIKE A THREAD THROUGH A needle: silent and easy, and then just that little knot at the end to stop things up.

Temple is scrolling through her phone, sitting on the stool behind the counter, as I stack coffee mugs and plastic water cups on trays. The band never showed up tonight, and she let Frances and Randy go early, because the place was dead. Linus is in the back, reading a book.

Temple says, "Didn't you date Mike Gustafson? Or something? I know I saw you guys at Gentle Ben's a couple times."

"No," I tell her. "He's just my friend. Why?"

She shakes her head and makes a disappointed, clucking sound. "All the good ones get snapped up, don't they?" She angles her phone. "Check it out. That hot little weasel went and got married in Seattle!"

It feels like moving through mud, making my way to her, bending to look at the image on the phone. Facebook, someone's page I don't know, maybe a band member, and there it is, there *he* is, there *she* is, and they're both smiling insanely, their faces shining. He's wearing a button-down shirt and a red tie with jeans and sneakers. Bunny is wearing a plain and pretty strapless flowered dress, with a crown of tiny, delicate roses in her hair. The roses match Mikey's tie.

All the blood in my body turns cold in an instant. I don't know what sound I'm making until Temple starts shouting to Linus, "I think Charlie's gonna hurl, Linus! Come help!"

I'm heaving, but nothing is coming out. I hold my head over

the trash can, make an excuse: "I think I ate something bad for lunch. I have to go, can I go," and Linus says she'll give me a ride, it's almost closing anyway, but I stumble up and away from her, grab my backpack, leave the coffeehouse in a blur. I forget my bike.

I walk so hard my shins start to burn and then I start to limp. I break into a run at the underpass and don't stop until I'm at his door, pounding.

I'm ashamed that I still feel like I have to ask to go into his house.

He opens the door, pulls me in. *I'm sick,* I tell him, tears coursing down my cheeks. *I'm just sick, so sick.* And then, as though someone pulled a plug in me, everything drains out of me at once, and I fall on the floor.

I can hear Riley swearing and little *Oh, Jesuses, and Oh, honeys,* as he unties my boots, strips off my socks. He picks me up carefully, sliding his hands under me. I'm dizzy. He's a blur.

Riley takes me to his bed.. After a time, his sheets grow damp with my sweat and he peels off my overalls, touches the back of his hand to my forehead. He sets water by the bed, a small bin with a plastic bag inside. I throw up three times and he empties the bag each time. He asks me, *Did you take something?* I tell him no and roll toward the wall. *I lost something, I lost some things,* I tell him. *I keep losing things. I'm tired.*

Riley says, *I'm sorry to hear that, baby.* But he doesn't ask any more questions. He tells me he'll cover my shifts at True Grit. He draws on his cigarette and his eyes are the slick dark of stones underwater. For three days, he works in the morning and he covers my dish shifts at night. He heats bowls of broth. He sets a cool cloth on my forehead. As he sleeps behind me, his breath is a billowy sail against my neck. On the fourth day, I stagger from the bed when there's a knock at the front door. It's Wendy from the drug house, her red-and-yellow hair mashed under the hoodie of her jacket, scratching at her cheek. She says, *I need Riley, where's he at? He around?* Her skin is like the surface of the moon. When I don't answer, she smiles. *Haven't seen him in a while, is all. We get worried.*

You don't look so good, kid, she says. *Tell him Wendy came by.*

All day Wendy appears in my dreams, long-legged and smudge-faced, smoky-voiced and grinning. When Riley comes home late, late, he's not so far gone that I can't press against him in the dark, work at him with my fingers, make him noisy, make him do things to me that he doesn't know hurt me, all to erase Mikey and Bunny, Wendy at the door, erase the gray turning back to black inside my body. We are such a terrible mess now.

I GET UP AND OUT OF RILEY'S BED FOUR DAYS AFTER SEEING
Mikey on Facebook. I walk like a zombie to my own apartment, change my clothes, and walk to the library.

No message from Casper, nothing from Blue.

There are eleven emails from Mikey. I delete all of them,
unread.

Door, shut. World, over.

EVERY SO OFTEN, WHEN I TAKE COFFEE MUGS TO THE SHELF behind the front counter, I sneak looks outside the window at Riley. He's been off shift for a few hours, but he hasn't left yet. He's installed himself at a table by the front window, a thick paperback in his hands. Steam rises from the cup of coffee wedged on the windowsill next to him. He banters with the Go players at the next table. He compliments an old hippie woman on her knit hat as she passes by. We don't speak to each other at the coffeehouse; we follow Julie's rule. So here he is, sitting out front until the open mic starts, when he's allowed to come in and set up the stage for the performers and emcee the show.

This is my first open mic at the coffeehouse. When Riley comes in, he's greeted warmly by everyone at the tables and he walks around like he owns the place, which I guess he sort of does. From behind the counter, I watch him check amps and adjust the mic, things he's done a million times in his life. He looks at home on the ramshackle stage and there's a moment, when he presses his mouth to the microphone and murmurs *Check, check, check,* that my heart starts to stutter at the way his husky voice travels the room. He soft-sings a few lines of Dylan's "Tangled Up in Blue" and everyone in the audience gets very, very quiet. But then he stops and stoops down to the amp to adjust the levels.

Riley introduces the first act, a hip-hop poet who prowls the lopsided stage, waving his arms and slouching his hips. "He's like a fuckin' cheetah on acid," Temple says dryly. He scratches

290

his belly and chest incessantly and drops *bitches* so much that one woman trying to drink her latte and read her paper shouts, "Oh, please stop him already!"

He's followed by a waifish girl with a pixie cut who reads horrible poems about hunger and war in a childish, thin voice. An older woman with hair to her knees and thick ankles peeking from her tie-dyed skirt lugs her bongos onstage; she's actually pretty good. She plays intensely, her grayish hair fanning behind her. The pounding of the drums is so hypnotic, even Linus comes out to the front counter to listen.

Riley sits on a chair just off the stage. He jumps in front of the mic and asks the crowd to give a hearty welcome to a nervous high school trumpet player whose forehead gleams under the bright ceiling lights. Riley dims them, casting the coffeehouse in an amberish light. The trumpet player's hands shake; he plays something sultry that makes me think he and the bongo player should join up. At the break, I collect empty cups and glasses. The tub is almost full when I notice Riley helping a young woman in Docs and a sleeveless black tee adjust the mic. Her black skirt looks like it was cut with scissors; the hem hangs unevenly. Her hair is black and spiky and her face is lit with contempt. She looks like she's my age. Her dark eyes take stock of the room. I haul the tub to the dish area and then go stand by the counter again. Riley's leaning down, whispering something in the girl's ear. She laughs and kind of curls her head away from him. My heart stops. What was *that*?

Temple and Randy catch the look on my face. "Uh-oh," says Randy smoothly. "Somebody's got a jealous streak."

"Don't worry about it, Charlie," Temple tells me, patting my shoulder. She's got henna tattoos on both hands today, swirling designs that wind around her knuckles. The minuscule bells hanging from her ears tinkle as she shakes her head. "There's nothing there. She's been playing here since she was, like, eleven."

Linus comes out from the back, wiping her hands on a dish towel. Her face lights up when she sees the stage. "Oh, man! Awesome. Have you heard Regan yet? She's gonna blow you away. Riley *loves* her."

Temple keeps patting my shoulder. Riley's never said anything about this girl.

"Ladies and germs," he murmurs into the mic. "Please welcome back True Grit's favorite troubadour, our own sad-eyed lady of the lowlands, Regan Connor."

Applause fills the café. There's an eerie wind-down as the room gradually silences and grows attuned to her presence. When the café has stilled, she attacks the golden acoustic guitar with single-minded purpose, her fingers flying. She stands as though she's staring a bulldozer down, her legs planted hard on the stage, one knee bent. Her voice is reedy, scratchy, and divine; she can control it enough to suddenly shift to a whisper or a growly bark.

You can't break me down, she sings. *You can't cut me clear.*

On the sloppy stage in the dim light she looks exuberantly defiant, and her words have rough, girlish hope. The crowd is rapt. Some people have their eyes closed. I look back at her, flooded with envy. She's my age and so confident. She doesn't seem to care what anyone thinks. Her voice is threatening and silky, floating over everyone in the café.

Regan is transporting the room; I watch them, one by one, fall for her.

You can't break my heart, she cries, breathy and furious. *You*

292

can't own my soul. What I have I made, what I have is mine. What I have I made, what I have is mine.

When she's through, the audience roars; even the hip-hop poet shouts, "Dang, dog!" Riley uses two fingers to whistle; his eyes are wild with light. I look from Riley to the girl and then back again, anxiousness *ping*ing inside me.

I'm always losing things.

THE BOXY WAREHOUSE SITS SNUGLY AGAINST THE FAR LIP OF downtown, beyond the shiny buildings that rise and dominate the skyline. Pickup trucks and bicycles clog the wide gravel lot. A hand-painted sign by the double front doors lists artists' studios and three galleries. I look at the ad in the *Tucson Weekly* one more time.

Linus went with me to buy the portfolio, a large, handsome envelope of leather. I used the last of my Ellis money. Linus whistled as I brought out the bills, but I didn't tell her where the money came from.

I didn't tell Riley I was coming here, either. Seeing him happy about that girl at the open mic, the way he talked about her on our walk home and how beautiful her voice was, and thinking of the way I never went to Ariel's class because I didn't want to spend any time away from him, made something wake up inside me, a spiteful, angry thing.

Watching that girl, her confidence. I wanted that. *I* wanted that.

I take a deep breath and enter the building.

The hallway's dusty and cluttered. Some studio doors are open. In one, a small man is swiping yellowy paint repeatedly up and down a blank white canvas. His room is a mess of paint cans, rolled canvases, jars of murky liquid, books. A woman in the room next to his is bent over a tall table, her face pressed close to the paper she's drawing on. Tendrils from spider plants dangle from the tops of her bookshelves. Salsa music drifts from a speaker at her feet. Other doors are closed; behind them

I hear loud thumps, whirs, grinding noises. The air smells mechanical, plastery, and oily all at once.

The gallery at the end of the hall is sprawling and empty, my boots echoing against the shiny wood floor. There are no windows; the walls are bright white and bare. A boy, not much older than me, sits at a long table against one wall. When I walk closer, the table is actually an old door nailed to some two-by-fours. He's typing away at a keyboard. He's dressed like Beaver Cleaver from that old show. "Yes?" he says plainly. Not annoyed, but slightly dismissive.

He glances at my portfolio. "You have work to submit for consideration?"

"Yes."

"Uh-uh. We can't do hard. We wanted digital. You know, like images over email or on a website? Do you have anyone to take photographs for you or can you do it and scan them and send them?" He begins typing again but keeps his face on mine while his fingers dance.

I shake my head. "No, I just kind of thought—"

"No, sorry. You've got to follow the submission instructions." He turns back to the monitor.

I turn to go, disappointed, thinking I'll walk my bicycle back to my room instead of riding. It was hard to ride and hold the portfolio at the same time. My hand got sweaty, holding the portfolio against my bobbing thigh.

"Hey-oh, what do we have here?"

Ariel's friend, the painter, is clutching a sheaf of papers and a gym bag, out of breath. Tony Padilla from the art show.

"I know you. Ariel pointed you out to me at my show. The girl dressed like a farmer. Did you like it?" He smiles expectantly. "My work?"

I swallow, considering. Wisps of dark hair curl from inside his nostrils. "Not really."

He laughs, putting down his papers and bag. "You didn't like it. That's good! We don't always like what we see, do we? We should always say so. Give me a look, yes? I see you're old-school. I miss the days of toting a portfolio around." He slides it from my grasp.

He spreads the portfolio out, kneeling to look at it. Today, he's not dressed in an elegant suit. He's wearing khaki shorts and Birkenstocks with socks and a sweat-stained T-shirt with a rabbit on it. His hair is no longer in a ponytail; it sprays across his shoulders like a black fan streamed with slivers of white.

"You submitting for the show?"

"I was, but that guy . . ."

"That's my intern, Aaron. This is my little gallery. I'd like some new work by younger artists this time around. They tend to be interesting in different ways, you know?" He examines a portrait of Manny. "You have model permissions?"

"What?"

"Release forms. If people are posing for you, they need to sign releases agreeing to have their image shown in public. Aaron, print out some sample release forms. Do you have your résumé?"

I shake my head and he laughs. "I haven't had you in a class, have I? There's a great deal of proficiency here, and something odd, too. But I like them." He peers closer to the drawings, lifting his glasses away from his face. "You're in. Leave them here. I've got hours of videos and films and an installation of a childhood bedroom. And a nudist. But not one drawing. Not one painting. You kids today. If you can't watch it, walk through it, or sit on it, you don't want to make it."

He zips the portfolio gently and hands it off to Aaron, who shoots me a quizzical look as he passes me the release forms. "Antonio Padilla. Tony."

"Charlie." His hand in mine is smooth and hairless, with fine, tapered nails and a single silver bracelet that knocks against his wristbone.

"Your people are ... interesting." Tony Padilla gazes at me curiously.

"They live in my building."

He says, "Is that so," holding his chin in one hand. "Bring one of my cards, too, Aaron?"

Tony sighs. "Well. We have a lot of work ahead of us, putting this show together. One thing I always tell my students, and it always surprises them, God knows why, is that an artist's life is all about work. No one is going to do it *for* you. It doesn't just appear on the page or on a gallery wall. It takes patience, it takes frustration." He looks at the blank walls.

He laughs a little. "It takes spackling, nails, projectors, lights, bullshit, and long days. I expect everyone in the show to pitch in. I hope you're not afraid of hard work, Charlie."

I can feel how big the grin on my face is. It practically busts my cheeks wide open. I haul mop water and bus tubs all night and clean up piss and shit in restrooms and now I'm going to have my work on walls, for people to see. *Me.*

"Nope," I tell him. "I'm not afraid of work at all."

LINUS SAYS, "THAT'S SO GREAT," AND CLAPS HER HANDS. SHE pauses. "I'll bet Riley is psyched."

I busy myself with the mop bucket, wringing out the grimy liquid from the mop. "Yeah, he's super excited." I keep my head down, in case the lie is written all over my face.

"Mmm." Linus gets quiet. She scrapes the grill slowly. "I see. So how much is he up to these days?"

"Excuse me?"

"How much is he drinking?. Some of his prep work has been a little, uh, a little sloppier than usual." She pushes a bucket of scrambled tofu to me and I peek inside. Ashes are dotted along the ridges of the puffy yellow hills. I'm ashamed for him, even though I know I shouldn't be. And I'm ashamed of myself.

He's usually asleep when I get to his house, if he's there, splayed on his velvet couch with a book across his lap, a lit cigarette still drooping in his fingers. The bottles disappear more rapidly from beneath the sink, are replaced just as rapidly. He seems to have stopped preparing for the Luis Alvarez benefit in the summer, the guitar in its case in the corner. The notebook of lyrics and sheet music is shoved under the couch. Sometimes he looks at me as though he can't place me. I've started to come in and watch him and smoke his cigarettes until my own chest feels sooty and clogged. Once, his hand on the screen door as I went off to work, he looked at me and mumbled, "I miss you being here with me at night. Hard without you." And that felt good, but sad, and those things tug-of-war inside me until I want to bury my head in the dirt.

298

I avoid Linus's eyes.

"Charlie, I am an old, sober drunk. I've known Riley now for six years and I know his schedule." She takes a deep breath. "He's in a downward slide and in that slide, we users will take everybody we can down with us. Because if we land in shit, we don't want to be alone in the shit."

I stare at her. Linus, who's always helping people, always cheerful, an alcoholic? I guess that's why Temple never pours her anything to drink at night, now that I think about it. I try to picture her like Riley, but I can't. And what she says kind of pummels me, about him taking me down with him. I tighten my grip on the mop, looking at the dirty water in the bucket, like I can find some answer there.

She says, sadly, "Listen, I don't know much about you, and I don't want to pry, and I also don't want to judge, but staying with him is only going to be hurtful to you. I just have to say it. Can you see that, honey? Like, really see it?"

I jam the mop in the bucket and grab the broom, trying not to cry, because I know she's right, of course she's right, but I try to concentrate on my work, to push the anxiousness away. The band tonight was some sort of polka-punk trio who spewed confetti, and little bits are strewn everywhere. The tables in the seating area have been wobbly for so long, the newspaper underneath the legs is frayed and greasy-black. I should replace it soon.

"He'll be better. I know it." I avoid her eyes, swipe at my own like it's just sweat and not tears. "I can help him. You shouldn't just give up on people."

"Charlie," Linus says glumly, "I've been in recovery for years. If I had a dollar for every time I've heard that, I'd be a rich woman, and not working in some half-ass coffeehouse."

THIS CITY IS DRY AND STIFLING HOT. EVERYONE KEEPS TELL-
ing me I'll get used to it, that I'll grow to love it, that the winter will cool down a little, but the sun is a giant ball of fire
that doesn't quit. Just biking from my apartment to the library
downtown leaves me in a full sweat, with the underarms of my
shirt soaked and my bike seat wet.

There are nine new unread messages from Mikey. It's like
I'm starving him out and I don't know why. I don't have anything from Blue, but I write to her anyway, just one word, *Hey*.
It's like reaching out to get a grip before you fall off a cliff, but
no one is there.

But the last email from Mikey catches my eye. The subject
line says *birthday/a while longer*. I click it open and read it.

> You probably heard by now about me and Bunny.
> It's crazy, I know. We are going to be out on the
> road a little longer now—at least until November.
> I'm taking a leave from school. We're going to do
> that album up in N. California. There's a record
> deal, Charlie. I didn't want to be without Bunny
> any longer, and things just seemed right. When I
> get back, I have something really important to talk
> to you about. And hey, it's okay that you haven't
> written back. I understand. I hope you are okay.
> And, Charlie: happy birthday.

I stare at the word: *birthday*. Then I close down my mail and leave the library.

It takes me a good forty minutes to find the right place on my bicycle. I have to ride deep into South Tucson to find what I want. When I find it, a shabby little *panadería* that smells like sheer heaven, I choose the most cream-filled, icing-topped confection behind the smudged glass of the pastry case. After studying the coffee list, I ask for a *café de olla*. I sit in a sticky chair by the window, the sweetness of the pastry collecting in my mouth, the creamy, caramelly drink warming my hands. I wonder what Mikey wants to tell me that's so important he couldn't just say it on email. Maybe Bunny's pregnant. Maybe Mikey is about to have his perfect life with kids and a wife and a rock band and everything he's ever wanted, while I'm dehydrated and tired and should be drinking water, but I'm not, I'm drinking coffee, spending seven dollars and sixty-eight cents to wish myself a happy fucking eighteenth birthday that I'd forgotten all about.

I RIDE DOWN TO THE GALLERY EVERY MORNING AND HELP Tony and Aaron with the show. The other artists are older than me, in their late twenties and thirties. Tony has them experiment with the placement of pieces while he walks around, rubbing his chin and thinking. He's decided not to frame my drawings, but to mat them simply. Tony was right: there are plenty of installations, including someone's childhood bedroom, right down to a complete set of My Little Pony figurines and her original ballet shoes paired with her adolescent Docs and fishnets. Someone else has spliced found video footage together: on one wall plays an endless loop of people and dogs jumping from diving boards. The colors are washed and dreamy; the jumpers seem to leap through thickets of watery sunshine, pasteled sky. A man with one half of his head shaved and the other in a tall Mohawk has glued eighteen beach balls together in a pyramid and painted crude words on each one. One woman kind of has paintings, but there isn't any actual paint on the canvas. Instead, she's glued squirrel pelts, crow feathers, and chunks of her own hair to the canvas.

A thin, angry-looking woman named Holly plans to lie nude on the floor. "I'm my own exhibit," she explains to me, crunching her black thumbnail between her teeth. "Just having to confront the fact of my presence will be overwhelming for most people."

I don't really understand how the woman's piece will work (what if someone touches her? What if she has to go to the bathroom?), but when I look over at Tony, he winks and whispers to me, after the woman has stomped away, "Holly's thesis defense is going to be spectacular. For all the wrong reasons, but spectacular nonetheless."

They use words and phrases like *theory* and *actualized identity* and *constructed identity* and *core fragmentation*. When Holly saw me with my sleeves pushed up, she said angrily and earnestly, "You need to understand and examine your transgressions against societal norms." She gripped my wrist. "Do you understand the act you've committed against yourself is fucking revolutionary? I'm going to make you a reading list tonight. You have so much to learn."

I memorize what they say as I wander the gallery, following Tony's instructions, moving things this way and that, my hands covered in little white gloves, like Mickey Mouse. I think, no, I *know* that some of them are laughing at my drawings and me. They snicker at Hector and Manny's lumpy faces and bad teeth, Karen's hopeful smile. And when I leave, I go to the library and search for all their terms and words and phrases, working my way through them.

I don't want them to think I'm stupid, but I also don't want to *be* stupid, that's why I take the time to learn their language.

And when I look at my arms, I don't think *revolutionary*. I think *sad,* and *pain,* but not *revolutionary*.

The next time I see Holly, though, I do think *asshole,* and that makes me smile all day.

TEMPLE PASSES ME THE PHONE. "HURRY UP, OKAY?" SHE WHISpers. "We want to make it to the Tap before last call." I look at her enviously; all the girls here go out together at night after work, to bars, to parties; they never ask me to go along. I've been trying to talk more with them, but their group seems tight. I'm too young, anyway, to go to bars. Only Linus seems interested in me, mostly in a motherly way, pushing plates of potatoes and bowls of lentils to me across the grill island. Linus does not go out with the girls. Sometimes she'll tell me she's headed to a meeting after work. "Addiction isn't nine to five," she'll call out cheerfully. "You can feel like shit twenty-four seven. That's partly why I work all these shifts. Have to keep busy, keep the demons at bay."

"Charlie. Sweet Charlie." It's a woman; her voice is throaty, assured.

I twist the phone cord between my fingers. "Who is this?"

"Charlie Davis, soul sister, after all the time we spent together, all that time sharing our blood stories, and you don't recognize my voice?"

My heart drops clear to my feet; my entire body goes up in flame. "Hello, Blue."

THREE

——

A girl is born

ON THE PHONE, BLUE SAID SHE'D BEEN OUT FOR THREE months and living in Madison with her mother. They weren't getting along, she said, so she thought maybe she'd take a trip to Kansas to see Isis until things cooled off. Isis had wandered to Kansas from Minnesota with a man; now she was selling bags of jerky and jack-off magazines at a truck stop. Isis and Blue were sitting in a bar nursing gin and gingers when they thought of me, and the warm place I'd gone to, and my mother. "I called Creeley and talked to Bruce. He gave me her name— very thoughtful, Bruce, and not one for patient confidentiality. I know you two had your moments, but Bruce is a good sort, underneath all his bluster."

Blue called my mother. "She's actually very polite! Thought she'd be some kind of monstertron the way you kept clamped up in Group. Keeps abreast of you through the boyfriend. Or, should I say, not-boyfriend." She paused on the other end of the line and I heard the click of a lighter, the yappy dog-squawk of Isis saying *Oh, you shut your mouth* to someone in the background. "He told her where you worked and, well, I found that number, too. Isn't the Internet wonderful? It's like a big old rock. All sorts of shit crawls out once you kick it over."

She breathed in a long, almost relieved rush. "I miss you." She began to sniff. "It's so hard, Charlie. It's just so *hard*. I need a freaking break."

And now I'm waiting for her at the Greyhound bus station, ignoring leery looks by men with mullets and yellow teeth. I paw the ground with the toe of my boot. Riley wasn't at his house last night when I went over. He wasn't home when I woke up in his bed this morning, either, which made me a little worried. The day is warm, cooler than it has been, but still bright and lovely. It's the beginning of November, and in Minnesota, people are already in winter jackets and boots, huddling against the wind.

I have to be at work in an hour. I buy a Coke from the machine and watch the parade of gray buses pull into the lot. The Coke makes my mouth sticky, too sweet.

She's the last one off, tripping down the final step. She catches herself, blinking in the sunshine, shading her eyes with one hand.

Blue's almost thirty but still looks like a teenager in her tight cargo pants and Lady Gaga T-shirt. It's only up close, like now, that you see her hard life in her face, at the edges of her eyes.

Blue drops the duffel, grabs me in a tight squeeze. "Charlie! My favorite Bloody Cupcake." She steps back, her eyes grazing every inch of me.

"Holy shit, you look good, Silent Sue. Your hair got so long! Tell me his name." She lights a cigarette.

"Your teeth," I say, surprised. "You fixed your teeth."

"The Lumber King of Madison forked over the cash. He felt guilty, I guess, for fucking me all those years. And I can't fucking tell you how fucking goddamn painful it was, either, getting these teeth. Anyway." She digs in her purse again. "Shit. I'm out of cigarettes. Where's your car? Can we stop and get some on the way to your place?"

Blue's teeth used to be blunted little nubs. The meth had scrubbed them down, filmed them, made them as soft as Play-

Doh. Now she has a full, gleaming set of square, white teeth. Her face is no longer blotched and bloated from meds, but smoothed out by facials and foundation and powder. Her hair is a rich gold color.

"I don't have a car, but I don't live very far, just a few blocks away. Here, I'll carry your bag."

Blue stares at me. "Are you serious? No car? In this heat? I'm freaking dying, Charlie." She snaps on large black sunglasses. I shrug.

"Why didn't you fly?" I ask. "I'm sure the Lumber King could afford it."

Blue snorts. "Oh, no. No planes for me. Scared shitless. No way. We don't belong in the air. That's my personal opinion."

She taps carefully alongside me in her heels. I sneak a look down: she still has the rings on her toes. For some reason, this makes me more comfortable. I point out things like Hotel Congress and the tiny movie theater that serves cayenne-and-Parmesan-flecked popcorn and shows black-and-white films featuring people with deep, sorrowful accents.

"So, where's this rock star live? Can I meet him?"

We're at the corner of Twelfth; I point vaguely down the street toward his house. "He's not home now." At least, I don't think he is. Maybe he's back now, sleeping whatever he did off.

"We'll meet up later?"

"Maybe," I answer noncommittally. I'm not sure why I'm uncomfortable with Blue meeting Riley, but I am. I wave wanly to Hector and Leonard on the porch. Hector sits up straight when he sees Blue and brushes at the sweat pool on his chest. He raises his eyebrows at me. Blue says, "I'm just a little nervous, you know? I need something to *drank*," and I point to the liquor store next door, even though the thought of Blue drinking fills me with dread and disappointment. I was hoping she'd be clean. Cleaner than me, anyway.

"Gentlemen," Blue says sweetly. She clicks off to the liquor store.

Leonard's fingers tremble as he packs his pipe, bits of tobacco fluttering to his jeans. Hector helps him.

Leonard rasps, "No trouble, Charlie. Remember? I don't mind your friend, but I don't want any trouble."

Oh, Leonard, I think. *I'm in a heap of trouble.*

BLUE FLIPS THROUGH MY SKETCHBOOKS AND DRAWINGS. "OH my fucking God, Charlie."

She traces her fingers over the faces. "This is amazing. I didn't know you could draw like *this*. Holy moly. And look at your crazy wall."

She glances at the toilet. "There's no door on that."

"I wash *dishes* for a living, Blue. You don't get doors for that. There's a locked toilet down the hall, but the guys use it. Don't forget toilet paper if your modesty gets the best of you."

Blue lights a cigarette and paws through the paper bag from the liquor store, extracting a bottle. She cracks the top, hunts for glasses in the sink, pours three fingers of vodka into each, and hands one to me.

She raises her glass. "You in? This place is fucked up, Charlie. Is everybody here like those guys on the porch?"

I take the glass, easy as pie, and drink it down, not even caring that I have to work in half an hour. It's just that easy now. "I was kind of hoping," I say softly, "that maybe you weren't drinking or anything?"

Blue purses her mouth. "It didn't take long for me to start up again after I got out, you know? Drinking, I mean. Not anything else.." She shrugs but won't meet my eyes.

"Have you been . . . good?" My voice is careful. Blue is kneeling on the floor now, flipping slowly through another sketchbook. Her shirt rides up her back. The skin there is tawny, tender-looking.

Blue winces through a plume of smoke. "I really only ever

311

did the bad shit when I was using, you know. I would lose total control. I'm a real pussy with cutting and burning unless I'm high or something." She looks at me sideways. "You? You cutting again?" Her eyes flick along my sleeves.

"No," I say. "Nothing like that. It's just . . ."

What would she say about the drug runs? I drop my eyes to my lap.

Blue cocks her head. "You okay, Charlie?"

I'm kind of in a mess and I can't get out.

But those words jam in my throat. I swallow hard; they drop back down my throat.

She looks at me for a full, pulsing second. "What about the rock star? He treating you okay? Some guys, *musicians especially,* have a real knack for crapping on women."

I busy myself with cleaning my glass, finding a clean work shirt. "It's good. It's okay. You know."

"He's a little older, huh?"

"Yeah. Twenty-seven."

I turn my back to change into my shirt. I can feel Blue's eyes on me.

"Charlie, have you ever *had* a boyfriend before?"

I slide my shirt down over my face quickly so my mouth is muffled. "Not really. No."

Under her breath, she says something I can't catch.

"What did you just say?" I turn back to her.

"Nothing," she says quickly, getting up and dousing her cigarette in the sink. "No worries."

Then she says brightly, "Well, show me the television and the computer and I think I'll be good to go until you get back."

I pretend to smile, even though I'm wondering what she

said that I couldn't hear. "Oh, Blue," I say. "I have some bad news for you."

All night, the girls at Grit are talking about something called All Souls and the burning of an urn. It's a big parade along Fourth Avenue to honor the dead, with people dressing up and painting their faces like skeletons and lots of weird stuff.

Temple says, "It's the best. We get super busy, no matter what, and everyone who comes in is just stoked to be alive, ready to do some positive energy work. And the costumes! Brilliant as shit."

The café is empty; they have nothing to do. At one point Julie calls to ask how busy we are and when Temple hangs up, Randy nods knowingly and assembles her things and goes home. Tanner's been cut from the day and put on just one night a week and Julie's still washing dishes. The pastry case has been dusty and empty for over two weeks. Bianca got tired of never getting paid.

Temple fiddles with the espresso machine. "Last year, I built wings with Christmas lights and some asshole fell into me and ripped them off. And my friend fell into a fire dancer, so that was crazy."

She tugs at the filter and it suddenly gives, slopping espresso sludge all over her fluttery blue skirt, the one I secretly like because it has tiny bells at the hem. Temple swears. I bend down with a rag to swipe at the dark grounds on her skirt.

Linus comes out from the grill area, wiping her hands on a towel. "It's Day of the Dead, Charlie. *Día de los Muertos*? Fucking twenty thousand people in a human chain walking down-

313

town and burning wishes for the dead. All that shit in the air, you'd think it would do something, right? Community energy and all that jazz. But the world still sucks, doesn't it, Temple?"

"Don't knock it," Temple says. "My parents used to take us to sweats all the time. Positive energy is a powerful force."

"Do you have anything like that back home, Charlie?" Linus asks, gazing at the empty café. Linus always refers to Minnesota as back home when talking to me. *Do you have tortillas back home? You must miss the snow back home. Are you going back home anytime soon, Charlie?*

I glance up at them. "We aren't much for death. Once you're gone, you're gone. We don't like things that interfere with our ice fishing." I say this lightly, because I don't want to think of my dad right now.

They stare at me. "Kidding," I mumble.

Temple airs out the steamer. "It's a real trip, Charlie. You might dig it. It's a giant art party in honor of the human spirit."

I brush the last of the grounds from Temple's skirt, flick one of the little bells so it *tink-tink*s. The human spirit. My dad. Where did his spirit go? Can he see me? What about Ellis, that part of her that disappeared? Is something of her left somewhere? These thoughts scare me.

I think Temple is wrong. I don't think I'd dig that kind of art party at all.

Blue shows up at True Grit at closing time, having changed into shorts and sneakers and a hoodie. Her eyes are fuzzy. I wonder how much of the vodka she drank. I mop the main floor furiously, wondering what she's talking to Linus and Temple about. Blue's arms are covered, but can they see the lines on her calves?

Sweat erupts on my forehead. In gym once, a girl busted the toilet stall door down, catching me in only my bra, my gym shirt in my hands. I changed in the stall, away from the girls, and always wore a long-sleeved shirt under my red-and-white gym shirt. She laughed and then covered her mouth with her hands. After that, everyone inched away from me when I came into the locker bay and drew out my gym clothes. They gave out sharp hisses as I took my things and went back to the toilet stalls. Temple is chatting amiably with Blue. Who was Temple in high school? Was she a hisser or a retreater? Did Linus ever push a girl's head into the toilet, or did she keep her own down, just trying to make it to three o'clock? People have so many secrets. They are never exactly what they seem.

As we walk home, Blue says woozily, "Leonard told me how to get here, so I thought I'd meet you. Hope you're not mad or anything. I don't want to intrude on your space or anything, you know?"

She cranes her neck at the palm trees. "This place is totally weird. All this vegetation is some real Dr. Seuss–looking shit, you know that, don't you?" We walk in silence for a while until she finally asks, "Bar?" She has a hopeful look on her face as she looks up and down Fourth Avenue.

I hold up my hands. "Eighteen. You want a bar, you're on your own."

She reconsiders. "Let's go see if the rock star is home." She gives me a big smile.

I can't avoid it any longer, I guess, so I say okay. I wonder if he's come back since last night. I hope he's come back since last night.

* * *

We can hear him a block away, strumming, voice lifting and falling as he works through a passage. I'm surprised; he hasn't played for several weeks now. A dreamy look passes across Blue's face. "That's him? God, that's fucking awesome."

He's on the porch when we approach, smoke lifting in gentle circles from the ashtray at his feet. "Charlie." He's curiously cheerful. "And Charlie has . . . a friend."

"Blue." She reaches over, takes a drag from his cigarette. That move sparks an ugly wave inside me—immediately, Blue is a million times more comfortable and familiar with Riley than I ever was. I don't understand how she can be that way. What is it about me that *can't*? And is she—flirting?

"*Blue*. Well, that's a beautiful name, Blue. I'm Riley West." He leans the guitar against the porch railing.

Is he flirting back? I can't read his signals.

"Thanks," Blue says. "I mean, it's not my real name, but I like it better."

I look at her in surprise, distracted from my anger. "What? Really? What's your real name, then?"

Blue takes another drag on the cigarette and exhales slowly. "Patsy. Patricia. Do I seem even remotely like a Patsy to you?"

"No," I say, shaking my head and smiling. "You don't seem remotely like a Patsy at all."

Riley laughs heartily. He must be a few down already, because he seems happy. I wish Blue wasn't around. If Riley's going to be happy, I want that all for myself. Lately, it's taking him three or four just to smile. He bows to Blue.

"A refreshment, ladies?" He goes into the house. Blue giggles. "He's cute," she whispers.

She looks out at Riley's neighbors on their porches, drinking wine and rocking in wicker chairs, fanning themselves with newspapers.

"He must like having his own audience. Besides you, I mean." She strums the strings on his guitar lightly. I bat her fingers away, irritated that she's being so friendly with his things. She glares at me.

Riley reappears with icy bottles. Briefly, he nuzzles my cheek, then holds out his beer. Hesitantly, I clink bottles with them.

Blue downs half of hers in two gulps and wipes her mouth, looking from Riley to me and back again. She giggles. "You guys are funny."

"Why?" I take a sip of my beer.

"I don't know. You just are." Her face is shiny. "You guys can kiss or whatever. Don't mind me." I can feel my cheeks heat up.

Riley crosses his legs and offers her a cigarette. "There's a story here somewhere. Something tragic, I'm guessing, in the way you two met?"

Blue snorts and blows out a series of perfect smoke rings. "God, I love unfiltered cigarettes," she breathes. "*Love* them." She takes another large swallow of her drink. "We met at the cutters' clinic. I was there the longest." She sounds almost proud. "Isis came after me, then Jen, and then Charlie. Louisa, though, she was *always* there. Wait. Hey, are you okay, man?"

Riley's face is very still, like he's holding his breath. Blue looks at me. "*Charlie*. Didn't you tell him about Creeley?" She looks at me warily.

Riley clears his throat. "Charlie's been a bit reticent about her history. But it's not a problem. We all have our secrets." His voice is mild. He reaches out and pulls me closer to him. I feel better that he does that. Relieved.

317

Blue nods. "I used to call her Silent Sue, she was so quiet for a while. What did they call it, Charlie?"

I click my teeth together, weighing whether I should answer her.

"See-lective mutism." Blue suddenly remembers, sliding up on the railing, her legs smooth and gleaming. "Like, in certain situations, you just clam up, I guess. I'm a little bit of everything, myself. A mental mutt, if you will."

"Interesting," Riley says. "Hospitals are interesting, aren't they? Everybody you meet is like a little mirror of you. I've done my time, so I know. Very unnerving." The corners of his mouth twitch. I'm beginning to feel panicky, out of step with the way they're talking about me and getting along so easily. I grit my teeth and shoot a look at Blue.

"She was always drawing." Blue stubs out her cigarette. "After she got settled in, they had to practically kick her out of Crafts every day. She was the only one who liked it. I can't make anything artsy for shit."

"She has a lovely eye for line." Riley gazes at me, not smiling. "Have you heard about her little art show?"

Blue continues as though she didn't hear Riley. "God, I hated that place. I couldn't wait to get out. Penned us all in there like cattle, slicing off parts of our brains, right, Charlie?"

"What about you, Charlie?" Riley's finished his drink. "Were you chomping at the bit to get released, too?"

Riley's face is worn and handsome, so familiar to me that a soft ache for him wells up inside me before I tamp it down, watching as he and Blue tease each other with lighters and cigarettes. "No," I say softly. "I fucking loved it. I never wanted to leave."

Blue guffaws. "Well, *yeah*. You were sleeping on a fucking heating grate before you came in. What was not to love?"

Riley squints. "Heating grate?" he says slowly. I look at him. I realize suddenly that he doesn't remember, when were sitting on the porch, all that time ago during the monsoon, that I told him I used to live outside. He doesn't remember. Because he's fucked up all the time. A wave of hard sadness rolls over me.

Blue looks from Riley to me. Her face pales. She smears her cigarette on the railing, mumbles *Sorry*.

Riley murmurs, "Hmm." And then goes in and refreshes our drinks, lights new cigarettes, steers the evening back. They talk about me as though I'm not there, teasing me and laughing when my face gets red. Eventually, the neighbors go in, lights turn off, the street quiets down, but Riley and Blue are still going strong, trading cigarettes back and forth, giggling in the same snorty manner about music and politics.

Finally, I clear away bottles and overflowing ashtrays, fit Riley's guitar back in its case, lift Blue to her feet by her elbow. She whines. "Why can't we stay here? It's still so early! I'm on vacation, for fuck's sake."

But I take her back with me anyway, holding her upright as we navigate the narrow stairs to my room. In my room, I'm suddenly dismayed, looking down at the single futon tucked against the wall. Blue staggers to the toilet, pulling her jean shorts down. "Excuse me," she says. The sound of her pee echoes in the bowl.

She flops on the bed and wiggles her feet. "Somebody take off my shoes, please." I yank off her perilously high wedges and toss them in the corner.

"Turn off the light. That lamp is killing me."

In the dark, I use the toilet and brush my teeth, splash water on my face, slide into boxers and a T-shirt, and stare at her, curled up on my bed, before I drop down next to her. I scoot her over with my hip. I feel a wave of *missing* for Ellis all of a sudden, the way we'd curl together in her bed, whispering, our breath warm on each other's faces. Gently, I rest my hip against Blue's. She's very warm.

Down the hall, a television murmurs.

"What's the rock star say about your scars, Charlie?"

I close my eyes.

"What are you doing here?" Blue asks, drowsy. "Go back to your boyfriend's."

"No."

Blue is quiet for a bit. "You don't have to worry about me, or anything. I mean, I like to flirt, it feels good, but I'm not . . . I wouldn't ever . . . I'm half show, is all I'm saying, okay, Charlie?" She pulls at the blanket and rolls toward the wall.

"And you know," she says, her voice getting sleepier, but with a little edge, "a girlfriend *can* touch her boyfriend's guitar, you know. You were mad at me for playing it and I bet you never even thought you were allowed to pick it up, but you *are*. He's not some god."

That smarts a little, that she's so right, but I don't know what to answer, so I stay quiet. When I think she's fallen asleep, when her breath has become heavy and I've almost fallen into darkness, she suddenly murmurs, "Hey. Don't let me forget. I have something for you. From Louisa."

In the morning, she's white as a sheet but perky, lustily gulping the coffee I bought for her at the café down the street.

She takes a bath in the tiny tub as I wash a few cups in the sink. She's not shy like me; I can see the history of her as she leans back, the water lapping at her breasts. After, she takes her meds, one by one, and then lines the prescription bottles up on the windowsill. I think back to her email, when she said she was on a lot of medication.

"I need grease for this hangover." She pulls on her T-shirt. It's short-sleeved. The burn scars on her arms are neat and deliberate. "And a soda. Like, a giant Coke."

I motion to her shirt, her arms. "You don't ... I mean, if anybody sees?"

She scowls. "What the fuck do I care if they see, Charlie? This is *it*. This is me." She tugs on my long-sleeved tee. "You're gonna live your whole life in the dark this way? It's better to get it out up front. And you know what makes me super mad? If a guy has scars, it's like some heroic shit show or something. But women? We're just creepy freaks."

"Take your boyfriend. I mean, I'm not trying to be mean or anything, I like him, that whole charming rogue thing he's got going on works like butter, but he's got major problems." She mimes drinking. "So, why didn't you tell him about the hospital or that you were on the streets? He can have problems but you can't?" Her words tumble out in an angry rush, surprising me.

I feel the press of tears. She's moving very fast for me. "I don't know." I swallow hard. "I just want to get something to eat, okay? Can we do that?"

I feel in my pocket for my money, but she pushes my hand down. "Don't. It's on me. I'm sorry. I am. It's okay."

She slings her purse over her shoulder. "Let's cruise. If I don't get that soda soon, I'm gonna vomit."

Blue buys us scrambled egg and hash brown burritos with

green chile, and icy sodas. She's ravenous and catty in the diner, whispering about the waitress's wide ass, making dirty jokes about the salt and pepper shakers shaped like saguaro cactuses. She orders an extra soda and a cinnamon bun, the frosting sticking to her upper lip.

We browse in the funky wig shop on Congress. She buys feathery earrings and tries on colorful teased wigs. We walk aimlessly downtown, staring in wonder at the crisp, cakeish façade of St. Augustine Cathedral, the dainty, forlorn Wishing Shrine of El Tiradito, with its cluster of burned-out *veladoras*. Blue spends a long time peering into the divots in the pale, crumbling wall of the shrine, at the wishes and gifts people have left, the sunken candles, the stiff, fading photographs. I touch an empty niche. Should I bring a photo of Ellis here? I run my fingers over the smooth stones.

Blue is very quiet as we walk home. I breathe the early-November air in, look at the wide, endless blue sky. In Minnesota, all the leaves are on the ground by now and the sky is gray, readying for cold and winter. Maybe it's even snowed once or twice. But here, everything is blue sky and endless warmth.

Back in the room, Blue settles on the easy chair with her phone, tapping and scrolling. When I casually ask how long she's staying, her eyes fog over.

"I thought I told you I don't have anywhere to go, Charlie. You're so lucky here. It's so nice. Look at all this fucking sun, even in the winter! It's seventy-three degrees here right now."

She puts her head down. "Do you not want me here, Charlie?"

I do, but I don't, but I do, but I don't.

I change the subject. "What about everybody at Creeley?"

Blue rocks her head from side to side. "I don't really know, I don't keep up. Isis left after you. Louisa's never getting out, that dumb fuck. She's gonna either die or be a lifer, I swear. Oh, shit!"

She scrambles from the chair to her duffel bag, rooting through it until she finds something. She holds out ten black-and-white composition books, tied up in a red ribbon. "Louisa said to give these to you."

They're heavy in my hands. I can picture Louisa, her red-gold hair coiled on her head, smiling when I asked her what she was always writing in those composition books. *The story of my life, Charlie.*

"Aren't you gonna take a look?" Blue asks.

"Maybe later." I slide them into my backpack. It doesn't look like Blue tampered with the ribbon, but still. I don't want to leave them here. Maybe there are things inside that Louisa only meant for me. Maybe I just want her words to myself.

Blue snuggles back in the chair. "Jen S. texted me. Dooley dumped her. She lost out on some basketball scholarship and kinda backslid, but her parents don't know, yet."

"Do you talk to anyone?" I ask Blue. "I mean, go to meetings or anything?"

Blue takes a swig of the beer she bought before we came back to the room. "Nah, I've got nothing left to say. You?"

"I emailed with Casper for a while, but she hasn't answered anything lately."

"You were always like her pet. We all knew it. Big fucking deal." Blue gets up abruptly, begins pulling clothes from her duffel and spreading them on the futon.

I slowly zip my backpack shut. "Casper liked everybody," I

answer evenly, but what Blue says makes me feel guilty. Maybe I *was* a little bit Casper's pet, her special project.

"No, she didn't. She never liked *me*. Do you think she sent me emails when I got out? *No*."

She has her back to me, winding her hair into a bun. There is the swallow, plump and blue on the back of her neck, watching.

To break the tension, I ask what she'll do while I'm at work. Blue shrugs, shuffling to the kitchen.

I want to say *Stop* as I see her slide the bottle from the windowsill, rinse out a glass. But who am I to say? I'm just as lost.

"Oh, you know. I'll be out and about. Maybe go talk to your neighbors." She turns to me and smiles, her new perfect teeth a gleaming wall inside her mouth.

My hand on the door, I say, "Blue, take it easy with that stuff, okay? Maybe we can take another walk tonight, just the two of us. It's nice weather to walk at night." I smile at her, hopeful, but she just gives me the peace sign and scrolls on her phone.

She's not in the apartment when I get home from work. I find her, instead, in Riley's front room. I can hear the sound of laughter down the street as I turn the corner to his house. My stomach curdles with apprehension as I make my way up the porch steps and pause, looking through the screen door at the two of them on the floor, cigarettes in ashtrays, drink glasses everywhere, Blue strumming Riley's Hummingbird as he gently corrects her fingers. He's drawling jokes, she's laughing, her face flushed in the universe of his attention. Just seeing his hands on hers hurts. I know she said she'd never do anything with him, but *still*. And then I feel shitty, because didn't Blue say she was lonely? And here she is, having a good time, with someone paying attention to her.

Her hair is falling against her cheek, a silky fan. Blue—Patsy, *Patricia*—looks really happy and suddenly, just a little, my stomach loosens. After what she said about Casper not liking her like she liked me, shouldn't she be allowed to have this?

She gives me a big grin as I slowly edge in the door, excitedly telling me about Riley treating her to drinks at the Tap Room, dinner at the Grill. He's going to take her on a drive in the morning, she says, see the sights.

My stomach jumps. He's never taken me for a drive. She looks really pleased, her fingers petting the strings of the guitar. I look over at Riley, but he's picking at the label on his beer bottle.

Maybe he's just making promises to her he can't keep, being nice, and he'll just disappoint her. Because: with what car? And where? Is he going to blow off his shift? I start to get a little angry.

I sit down with a thump on the burgundy velvet sofa. Riley looks up, finally noticing me, and leans over, pushing up a leg of my overalls and kissing my knee.

"Oh, hey, yeah, your landlord came by." Blue puffs on her cigarette. "Lonnie?"

"Leonard," I answer dully. She chews her lips, concentrating on the placement of her fingers on the Hummingbird's strings. She has pretty fingernails, white and well filed.

"He wanted to know how long I'm staying, 'cause the room's so small and all, and you know, maybe you'd have to pay some extra money."

My face drains of color. Blue sees this and quickly shakes her head.

"Don't worry, Charlie, I have money and plus, I'm gonna work off the extra rent." She beams. "I'm the new building handyman. I didn't go on all those construction site visits with my dad for nothing, you know. Did you see the stairwell? I fixed it today. We could be roomies forever." She smiles wide, her eyes shiny.

She looks so happy, and expectant, that I kind of melt. It's been sort of nice having her, for a little bit. She's not the same as she was in Creeley.

The girls at True Grit, Temple and Frances and Randy, they talk about their roommates all the time. It might be fun, having a girl to live with. "Yeah," I say, trying to laugh a little. "That might be cool, Blue."

Riley laughs, too, but it has a sharp edge to it. "Hey now, Blue! Don't talk that way. I don't wanna lose my girl to her bestie. She's the only thing keeping me upright. I call dibs." He squeezes my knee a little too hard.

Blue raises her eyebrows. She tries to meet my eyes, but I stand up and offer to get everyone more drinks. I keep getting everyone more drinks, and myself, too, until I stumble just as much as they do.

I let myself get heavier and heavier because I wanted Blue to be different when she came out, I wanted her to be better, so that I could be braver about being better, too.

Maybe this is just the way it's supposed to be.

Later, in his room, the house quiet now that Blue has fallen asleep on the couch, hands snuggled between her knees, Riley exhales against my shoulder. His room is cool; the windows are open.

He's behind me, pressing me against him, his breath against

my cheek. "Your friend, she was just talking shit, right, about rooming with you? I don't know how I feel about that."

I close my whirling eyes. I'm so tired of drinking, and cleaning up after him when he's too high. Dragging him to bed. Getting him up for work. Where am I? What am I doing?

My voice skips, my throat is sore from cigarettes, but I push it out and it comes out angry and I can tell he feels it; his body shrinks back, just a touch.

"You won't even let me have a friend? Like, just one friend?" My words are slurry and I start to panic a little. I don't want to lose it, but the ball is getting bigger, the alcohol is pushing it along greedily.

"Hey, now." Riley's voice is soft. "I didn't—"

"I mean, do you know how hard it is to be around just you all the time? When you're so fucked up?"

Riley is silent.

My voice gets louder. I push his hands away, press myself against the wall, the window open above me. Can the neighbors hear me?

"You never ask me anything about myself. You've never even asked me about my scars. Or about my parents. Blue at least knows, she understands—"

"Hey, listen, everybody's got shit, honey, I just didn't ask because—"

"You didn't ask because I don't think you really care, as long as I'm here when you need me to be." *A cookie or a book or a record on a shelf,* like Julie said.

I roll over. I can barely make out his face because of my spinning head and the darkness of the room. He's so drunk, too, his eyes slopping down his face. Is he even going to remember *this*? "Here's all of it, Riley, here you go. Here's my shit.

"I had a friend and she tried to kill herself, and it was my fault. And I broke my mother's nose and she kicked me out. There was never a heating grate, but here's what there *was:* a loaf of bread can last a week, but you get stopped up." My words are tumbling out, caught in slurry clouds in my throat, but I can't stop.

"When I ask you for change, you'll give it to me because I'm small and I look sad and I'm dirty and you have some secret thoughts about me, because I'm small and sad and dirty. You think maybe you could do things to me, and I would let you, because I need money. And I know this, so when I say we should walk to the park and talk some more, privately, you're happy to come with me, you're excited and nervous."

Riley whispers, "Don't."

He covers his face with his hands.

"I won't look at you in the park when my friends jump you from the bushes. Or when you cry because they're beating you with chains, taking your money, ruining your good suit. I've done my part. Why do you have so much cash in your wallet, anyway? You're so fucking stupid, man, so fucking stupid."

Riley says *Stop,* but I don't, because I want to hurt him, just a little and just a lot, for how he looked at Regan, or whatever might have happened with Wendy, or the way he laughs with Blue and won't let me be her friend, but mostly because I'm so tired.

I'm so tired of *drunk* and *desperate.* I'm tired and angry at *me.* For letting myself get smaller and smaller in the hopes that he would notice me more. But how can someone notice you if you keep getting smaller?

I kick the sheets off, claw my way over him, still talking, even as I jam my overalls up and try to slot the straps. I can't. My hands fumble. I just tie the fucking straps around my waist.

"If you try to make it by yourself, a guy tries to rape you in a tunnel and he's crazy high and strong. He gets his hands all the way down in your pants, his fingers inside you, his shoulder against your mouth so no one can hear you scream. Maybe two guys save you, two nice guys. If you pack up with a group, you better remember the rules of the group, you better remember who runs the group or he will try to hurt you, too."

I lean down close to Riley's face. He shuts his eyes tight. "I lived in a sex house. Someone tried to sell me for money. So I tried to die. There's my story, Riley. When do I get to hear yours?"

I'm panting. He's got both arms crossed over his face.

"Riley," I say, my voice hoarse. "Riley, we have to stop. *You* have to stop. I don't want you to die, Riley. Please, stop. I don't want you to die. Will you stop?"

His voice is stronger than I expected.

"No."

I almost trip, stumbling out of the room. I pull Blue off the couch by her shirt. She wobbles as she finds her footing. "What the fuck, Charlie . . . whaaat?" Her hair is in her face.

I yank her outside, shoving my boots on as she trips across the porch, jamming her feet into her sandals. "What the hell? Did you guys fight or something?"

"I just want to go. Let's go. Please, just hurry up, Blue." I run down the porch steps, taking big gulps of air. I don't know what just happened, I'm confused and drunk, my skin itches. "I need to be somewhere safe. Please. Home."

"Yeah, okay, yeah." Blue buttons up her jeans and trots down the porch. She's still half-asleep, drunk.

I don't want to drink anymore I don't want to drink anymore I don't want to drink anymore I don't want to drink anymore I don't want to be lonely.

I have to hold her up as we walk; her body is loose and jellylike. I say, softly, "Blue, let's stop, let's just stop with all this, okay? You know, messing up."

"Cool," she murmurs. "That's cool, okay, all right."

"Please."

The sky is milky with clouds. I can smell the sweetness of Blue's shampoo buried somewhere under all the alcohol and cigarettes. It's not lost on me, either, that Riley never called out as we left, or ran to the porch. Or anything.

The ball inside me picks that up, too, adds it to the pile.

IN THE MORNING, HOLDING TWO CUPS OF COFFEE FROM THE café down the street, my head splitting open from my hangover, I gaze at the wall in the stairwell. Blue was right; she plastered the holes and cracks, sanded them down. The wall is smooth and fine. Blue looks proud.

The foyer of the building smells clean; Blue was standing by a sopping mop and bucket when I got back with the coffees. She'd done the work on the walls the day before; now she was cleaning the hallway and foyer to get a good look at the hardwood floor, see what sort of sanding work might need to be done. She was remarkably fresh after a long night of drinking.

I don't think she remembers last night. I'm sure Riley doesn't. It took all my strength when I went out for coffee not to go in the opposite direction and turn the corner and walk up his porch steps and—

Sweat glows faintly on her forehead. "What can you do with an English major?" she asks. "Apparently, this." She laughs, making a funny face.

"UW-Madison," she says sharply. "I'm not a total loser, Charlotte."

"I know that, Blue. I think this is pretty cool."

"This is your big day! Are you excited?" She takes one of the coffee cups and sips gratefully. "Fuck, my head."

I nod. "Yeah, I am." I think about it some more, pushing thoughts of Riley away. "I am, I really am excited."

"Cool. You should be. Meet me here later and we'll walk over to the gallery together?"

"Yes, sure thing. I'm gonna go take a nap before work, okay?"

Blue salutes me and I head up to the room. My stomach is in knots, though. I'm still upset about the fight with Riley, and wondering if he'll even be at home, or come to the show later. We feel unfinished somehow, and I don't like it.

I WORK FROM FIVE UNTIL SEVEN AND THEN TEMPLE TELLS ME I can leave for the art show. She's got Tanner working the counter while she works the espresso machine. People are crowded into the café, wearing the craziest costumes, faces dark and deathly. Julie's outside ladling warm cider from a giant tin tub.

Tanner set up the coffee urns on the tops of the pastry cases, with stacks of to-go cups and a box for money. Temple printed a big sign: on yah honah coffee, 1 dollah. Linus is working the grill and Randy's subbing on dishes and running food. "It's cool," Temple says. "We got it. You go rock it, girl."

It's an absolute madhouse on the avenue for All Souls, or *Día de los Muertos*. Belly dancers, kids and adults dressed all in black with their faces painted like skulls; the little kids have flimsy golden wings strapped to their backs. Fire-breathers, stilt-walkers, bagpipers with skirts and skull faces. The noise is amazing, with every sound being undercut by massive taiko drums. People carry giant skeletons on sticks, with top hats dangling off the skulls. One woman is all in black with her face painted like a gold skull and her eyes rimmed in black, like pits. She's carrying a black umbrella with miniature skulls dangling from the edges. A group of people dressed in white, flowing gowns and with faces painted like sugar skulls (something Temple had to show me on her phone: the face is painted white and then overlaid with colorful, flowerlike designs) hold a twenty-foot-long papier-mâché snake above their heads. Cops and cop cars, people in masks, stoned-looking people with all sorts of instruments wandering around. I spot the punks from the Dairy Queen hanging out in front of the Goodwill, smoking cigarettes and scowling at the crowd. They, too, have whitened their faces, drenched their eyes in black. The girl punk latches on to me, flicks her tongue from her purple mouth.

I stick to the sidewalk on the other side of the Avenue, gliding among the people. The sound of the crowd, of the various drums and music, is deafening. The police stay at the edges of the procession, try to keep everyone in the street, but it's hard; people duck in and out, shout and laugh. There are mimes and arts and craft booths everywhere. The fire-eaters drift past me and I gasp as a woman stops right in front of me and eases the flame gently inside her mouth and down her throat. She pulls it out and spits, racing away. I fight my way through the underpass and escape to the other side of the street, breaking from the throng of people and walking to my apartment, All Souls trailing its cries and drums behind me.

Blue isn't in my room. Her clothes are strewn on the futon, though, and the air is dense with cigarette smoke. I swear at the dirty mess she's left behind: full ashtrays, lipsticked drink glasses, crumpled bags from the deli down the street. Shavings of lettuce and tomato are strewn across the carpet. Clouds of toothpaste spit cling to the sides of the sink. I stare for a moment at Blue's fancy phone on the card table; it has a spidery crack down the front, like someone threw it. I get a weird feeling in my stomach. Blue always treats her phone very gently.

Now, looking around the whole apartment, at the whole mess, I realize something is wrong, something's happened. Where's Blue? Maybe she's at Riley's. I take a breath, try to not to feel weird about that, either. Maybe Blue just got bad news or something and threw a tantrum. I'm torn between running to Riley's right away to see if she's there and getting ready. I do some breath balloons. I decide I'm going to get ready. Blue must have just gotten mad about something stupid. I'll get ready, then head to Riley's.

This is the first time I've worn something other than cutoff overalls in months. I found a loose black cotton skirt at the Goodwill and a dark brown peasant blouse. I slip into them, put on the sandals I found in an alleyway, and splash water on my face. In the tiny mirror in the bathroom down the hall, the mirror that only shows a portion of my face at any given time, I smooth my hair down. It's almost over my ears now. I do an experimental tuck, looking at all the empty holes in my ears.

I guess it's kind of nice to see my natural color after so long, after so many years of dying it red, or blue, or black. A deep blond, threaded with dark brown.

I think my face looks better than it did all those months ago; my skin is clearer, there's less color underneath my eyes. I wonder if Riley ever thinks I'm beautiful, or pretty, or even *something*, because he's never said so. Thinking of him makes me feel bad all over again. Last night gives me a little funny knot in my stomach.

No, he said.

I look at myself in the mirror. *No matter what,* I tell myself, *I'm not drinking tonight.*

Back in my room, rooting through Blue's green duffel bag, I find a pinkish tube of lip gloss, run it across my mouth. I pencil my eyes with her eyeliner, smudge the color with my fingers for what I hope is a smoky, owlish look. I just try to do what I watched Ellis do all the time, when she did her makeup.

I wiggle my toes in the sandals, feeling vaguely

uncomfortable. The blouse, the skirt, the gloss; they're all too much *new* all at once. I kick off the sandals, tug on my black socks and my Docs. I'm nervous, and ready, but first I need to find Blue.

Riley's guitar is on his porch, along with his cigarettes and beer. He's blasting ska music inside. The whole street is noisy, with people gathered on porches and in yards, drinking, grilling, and laughing. Crowd noise and drums from All Souls rumble through the sky.

I gather the cigarettes and beer bottles and carry them into the house.

Blue is sitting on the floor in the middle of the living room with her back to me, hunched inside a billow of smoke, album sleeves spread before her. "Blue," I call out, but she doesn't hear me over the music.

I touch her shoulder and she jumps, ashes drifting to her bare knees. She spins around and her eyes are saucer-wide; the pupils jump and skitter.

"Blue?" I wrinkle my nose at the smell of burning plastic and realize it's Blue: *she's* the thing that smells like burning plastic. She wipes her face, pushes the ashes off her knee, and grinds the cigarette into the floor with a balled fist. The whole house smells like it's burning; something chemical that makes my eyes water. It takes me a moment, but I realize what's happening.

Blue's eyes well up. She croaks my name.

"Oh my God." I back away, dizzy, my nostrils burning. I feel sick to my stomach. "What did you fucking do? Why did you do this again, Blue? Your teeth."

It's all I can think: *Your beautiful teeth.*

The pipe is on the floor, by her bare knees. A long cascade of drool is hanging from her chin.

Something flickers in her eyes; a grief suddenly etches itself over her face, drawing down the skin of her cheeks.

She says, *Louisa set herself on fire.*

I start shaking so hard the bottles in my hands clink together.

Blue's fingernails scrape at my boots. She's trying to keep me near her. Her breathing is scratchy and hoarse and her eyes can't stay still in her face. I kick her away, backing off. Louisa? Louisa is gone? My body goes cold, then hot, and then numb.

My ears fill up with ocean and thunder. Louisa. Ellis. This can't be happening again.

I stumble toward the kitchen, calling Riley's name. I'll be okay if I can find Riley. Riley will hold me, keep all my bad things in. He can do that, at least for right now, right? Like he did when I was sick. I can count on him for at least that.

Black dots swim in front of my eyes; my skin is prickling; something claws at the inside of my throat.

Behind me, Blue crying, a thin, reedy whine.

Sorrysorrysorrysorrysorry.

On fire. Louisa *on fire.* I can't breathe.

The first thing I comprehend in the kitchen is the flash of matted red and yellow, Wendy's face smeary over Riley's shoulder, that pointy-toothed grin focused on me. He's pushing at her so violently, her head bobbles, doll-like and loose. They're fucking right there on the kitchen counter, his face pushed into her neck, her bare legs dangling at his hips, jean shorts caught on one of her toes.

Wendy makes a kind of hiccup and winks at me.

In the other room, the record suddenly skids to a stop, a long, terrible rip as Blue drags the needle. Wendy's eyes are popped like swirly lollipops.

The beer bottles slip from my hands and shatter.

She laughs. "Go back to your blades and butts, little girl." Another hiccup.

Riley's head wobbles up. He turns around. I do not recognize the face he is wearing. It is a different face and filled with a fury that makes me so frightened my whole body disappears into numbness. I cannot move.

He jerks at his brown pants, pulling them up to his thighs, advancing on me. I'm frozen. He is shouting at me, but I am leaving myself, I am disassociating, I am floating away from my frozen body. Just like with Fucking Frank. With my mother.

He pushes the girl that is me hard into the wall. The framed *Little Crises Everywhere* album cover behind her falls to the ground. The glass shatters, nicking the backs of her calves, littering the floor around their feet.

He's shouting. *There's nothing here! Don't you see? Don't you get it?* Moisture from his mouth coats the girl's cheek. Somehow, she finds her hands. She beats at his chest.

Fire, fire, everywhere, inside her.

I don't know who you thought I was, but this is it. He mashes the girl's cheek into the wall. *Get out of my house,* he whispers hoarsely to her. *Go back to where you came from.*

Just get out.

The procession has reached its final destination in the middle of downtown. The urn is burning, great plumes of smoke and wishes and prayers for the dead billowing into the air. I have come back to myself in the middle of pandemonium, in the middle of people weeping for the dead, my vision blurry with wetness, black rising inside me. All around me now, the skull faces seem to whisper and clack their teeth. I knock into the heads of children as I run. A woman in black is crying on the ground, her face paint smeared. I think of Louisa as people shove at me, tongues wagging at my face. Louisa who ran out of space, Ellis who went too deep. An image of Louisa comes to me, a nimbus of flame, red-gold hair afire. Chanting washes over me, drums and bagpipes make an ocean in my ears. At the corner by Hotel Congress I see Ellis dancing to the Smiths, and I stop short, my body buffeted and tossed by others. I try to turn away, but there she is again, Ellis bent at her sewing machine, the tip of her tongue at the corner of her mouth. Ellis whispers in my ear late at night in her bed, explaining exactly what a certain boy did to her and how it felt. Ellis punctures my ears with a sterilized pin and hands me wine for the pain. The first time we took acid together at a party we spent hours staring at each other, laughing as we watched each other's faces mutate and swirl into different colors. Listening to Ellis have sex with a boy in a garage, I smelled oil and paint thinner and wondered how much longer it could last. Getting kicked out of school while Ellis stayed behind and falling away from her, the wolf boy and then her parents making her cut me out. Ellis liked to run around, she liked to break rules, but she liked to go home, too, to her downy bed and potato chips and ice cream and a mother who still liked to brush out her hair with her fingers and thought her frequent changes of hair color were the sign of a free spirit. I break through a knot of skeletons, twist around, I've lost my way. Ellis's fat tears as her father, Jerry, sent me away, nowhere to go, I'd lived with them for weeks. The pills on the floor were not mine, they were the boy's, but Ellis kept quiet. Ellis's texts after he'd broken up with her. *2 much. Smthing hrts* Yes, something is wrong. Ellis and Louisa and Riley and Blue and Evan and my father, dead and drowned in the long river, his sadness weighing him down. Is my sadness because of him, or is my sadness because I am of him? Holes. Human holes. I whip my head around the crowd, looking for a hole out of all these human holes, these thousands of faces wishing the spirits to a better place, sorting the souls of the dead. They all have black heads with holes for eyes, holes for mouths, strenuous gaping maws of death. There are too many people in my head. I claw at my body to get them out, to peel out the blackness spreading inside me.

I'm running blind, ghosts swallowing me.

DARK. MY ROOM IS DARK. ALL DARK. I AM ALL DARK.

I fought my way out of All Souls and it was like old days, old times, making myself hidden and smaller on the street, and I found an alley, a Dumpster, and fitted myself between that and the brick wall of a building, darkness everywhere around me.

And now I am back, hollow, and my room has been trashed. The green duffel bag, Blue's purse, her clothes, everything is torn and ripped, stomped on and cut up. A half-empty bottle of whiskey quivers on the card table. Lipstick has been smeared all over my mural wall, the faces bloody slashes. She wrote *Love, Wendy!*

Did they come here together after he chased me away? Did they come here together to ruin my things, laughing, high? Was this another way for them to get off?

The easy chair leaks stuffing, a knife lying innocently on the cushion.

I strip off all my new clothes and stand in the middle of the floor, naked.

You never get better.

I take four swallows of the whiskey. A hundred bees buzz in my ears. The little workers inside me sharpen claws, gather nails. They are singing. I drink some more, get down on my hands and knees, and crawl to Louisa's suitcase in the kitchen, push over the milk crate that held my dishes so they clatter and break on the floor, a thousand white stars, a thousand pieces of salt. I heave at the suitcase, wedged tightly under the tub, until it gives.

A little sound, a cry, escapes from my mouth. My sketchbook is gone. The photographs and my old drawings, shredded. And my kit, my kit, stomped on and dented and emptied out, gauze strewn everywhere in the suitcase, my glass smashed to bits.

Why did I listen to Casper, to Mikey? What was I trying to do, anyway? Thinking things would be any different? Telling me to be quiet. To breathe. To let everything pass. What a load of shit.

I kick the suitcase away and stand up. I close my eyes, drink the last of the bottle, smash it against the wall. I am dark, dark, all dark. I have to cut it out, this thing in me that thought I could be better. I have to remember how stupid I was, how fucking *stupid*—

I stop. Is this how Ellis felt, this moment of certainty? The text messages flicker in front of my eyes.

Smthing hrts. U never sd hurt like this. 2 much. A sparkling lake of bottle glass is beneath my feet. I grind down into it. Let my skin soak up the lake of glass. How powerful am I? How powerful am I. I can grind the glass to my face, erase my eyes, eat glass, and disappear from the inside. There, the window, my hands, that hand, balled and aching. That hand, a fist, give me more, give me more glass, I can drink it all. The glass raining over me from the broken window, it feels like home.

THERE ARE MEN HERE AND I WANT THEM TO FINISH UP AND go. I'm not done. Could you please leave me until I'm done? I need to cut myself away piece by piece until there is nothing left.

I wish the men would stop talking. I wish the men would stop crying. I wonder why the men are crying.

The warmth of a wet washcloth. The smear of ointment. The clean smell and gentle press of medicated gauze, the *zip* of white tape. The men are no longer crying. There is a woman now. She is not my mother.

I wish I could open my eyes.

I don't want to open my eyes.

I hear the sound of crying again and now I recognize that it's me, I am crying.

NOW IT'S A WOMAN'S VOICE AND A MAN'S VOICE AND THE night is moving fast. I'm bobbing up and down on a sea, dark above me, dark all around. Dark inside me.

The woman says, "I'll kill him myself."

The man laughs, but not in a cruel way. "Who couldn't see this coming?"

The woman says, "Not the fucking teenager in the backseat, that's for sure. Dear God, we are going to need junk food. Lots of junk food."

The sea shakes. The voices get farther and farther away and then there is nothing for a long time. Then the sea shakes again and something grabs my leg. I want to yell, but I can't. My mouth is filled with wet stones, like before, the very before. Before Creeley. My mouth stones have come back to me.

The man says, "She's still pretty out of it, but her dressings look good. She's gonna have a shitload of trouble walking for a few days, though."

The woman says, "You asshole, did you eat all the Cheetos?"

The man says, "Did you catch all that about her friend, what was she saying? Like, her friend's a vegetable or something."

The woman's voice is sad. "I had to stop listening."

I stop listening.

* * *

The woman and the man have left again. Rain spatters on the sea. I have to go to the bathroom.

I have to go to the bathroom. No one answers, because I have not said it out loud.

I feel around with my hand and familiar pain shoots up my arm. I'm in the backseat of a car, ridges of the fake leather under my fingernails, a square, unlit light in the drooping fabric of the ceiling. I push myself up and blink. *I have to go to the bathroom.* All I can see from the window is blackness, shadowy trees.

Gingerly, I ease over to the car door, bite my lip to keep from crying out, and push the door open, feeling the stretch and heat of my torn arms and an odd burning on my stomach. I haul my leg out and lean forward to stand up. As my toes hit the ground, lightning cracks through the soles of my feet.

I pitch forward, smashing my mouth and nose into hard dirt. I wail, inhaling dirt, and start to choke.

Hands roll my body over, brush dirt and stones from my eyes and mouth. I blink.

Linus's wrinkled, sun-leathered face. Tanner's shit-eating grin. The matching connect-the-dot freckles on their faces.

I spit dirt from my mouth. *I have to pee.* I move my hands, pat myself so they'll know what I mean.

They burst out laughing. "That's going to be pretty painful." Tanner grins.

Linus pushes the bucket underneath me and spreads my legs. My ass is on part of the backseat. Linus pulls an ugly pair of sweatpants off me. She glances at my thighs and then looks up at me, her face surprised. Of course. How could she know about those scars? She only thought I had them on my arms. "Girl," she says, but nothing else. She sighs.

She apologizes about the pants; they were the first things she grabbed out of her backpack when she and Tanner went to my room, looking for me. She didn't know at first what Hector and Manny and Leonard were doing, she tells me, so she got angry, pulling them away, roughing them up a bit. Linus is a strong woman.

Linus says, "Then I saw they were crying. And drunk, too, but trying to clean you up as best they could with paper towels and handkerchiefs." She tells me they were all dressed up for the opening but came back when I never showed.

My pee spatters into the bucket. Linus waits until I'm finished and then hands me a tissue and empties the bucket by a tree. She tosses the bucket into the trunk of the car.

"Stepping in the glass, that was a nice touch, Charlie. You'll be paying for that for days." She jimmies the sweatpants back up my shivering legs, heaves them up my ass, and pulls them to my waist. She eases me back into the car.

"Your friend Blue said you might be quiet for a while. I have to say, it's a little unnerving."

Her smile is sad and resigned. "We're at a cemetery in Truth or Consequences, New Mexico. Did you know Tanner is my brother? We stopped off for a quick visit with Dad." Farther away, in the blackness, Tanner is kicking a tombstone and spitting on the ground.

"We didn't really get along all that well with old Dad."

She wipes her face, hard, with the palms of both hands and then calls out to Tanner, tells him it's time to go.

* * *

Tanner glances at me in the rearview mirror, the corners of his mouth salty with potato chips. "It looked worse than it really was." He works the salt from his mouth with his tongue. "Remember? I'm studying to be an EMT? I had my practice bag with me. Fixed you right up."

The sky rolls by the window, black dotted with thousands of snow-white stars. I wonder what time it is. My hands drift under the sweatshirt Linus dressed me in, skim over the bandages there.

I am Louisa now. I have no room left.

I feel hollow, but not from hunger. I try to locate something in the hollowness, but I can't. My back aches from lying on the car seat. All of me aches. I sit up, ignoring the sparks of pain tearing across my stomach. Tanner has fallen asleep. His head lolls against the rolled-up window.

Linus clears her throat, glancing at me in the rearview mirror. "Riley's dealer Wendy stole your money and trashed your room. She followed your friend home after you took off. Beat her up pretty good. That skinny guy on your first floor—guy with a lot of books? He's taking care of your friend. Riley and Wendy stole somebody named Luis's car, bought some more drugs who knows where, and started driving out to the casino. After they cleared out the True Grit night deposit, that is. I mean, you know, he's been stealing for months, too, to buy his shit." She tightens her fingers on the steering wheel, keeps her eyes on the dark road.

I think of all the times he gave me money and I went to Wendy's house for him. How Julie was so worried about the register being low on count. I close my eyes. I'm so ashamed.

"He goes on benders, our Riley, though he mixed in a lot of other shit with this one. He's a chipper, but I bet you figured that out, right?"

Riley's cherrywood box. The minuscule crystal-filled bags, the eerie, burning plastic smell.

"They didn't make it to the casino, Charlie." Linus nibbles a Cheez Doodle. "Riley flipped the car. The skank is pretty hurt, but Riley, being Riley, is pretty much okay. He always seems to come out on top, that Riley."

Outside the diner, a pink dinosaur with peeling paint growls, his mouth missing teeth. I've been seeing a lot of kitschy road-side things from the car window as we drive: dinosaurs, robots, rocket ships, bulbous-headed aliens. Is that what New Mexico is? Fake dinosaurs and aliens? Land of the lost.

I watch Tanner and Linus through the car window. They're sitting in a booth. He chews a hamburger and talks on his cell phone. Linus stirs her tea and writes in a notebook. Once, at the coffeehouse, she told me she journals every day, "to keep things straight in my head."

I wonder if they'll bring me something to eat or if Tanner will give me more pain pills. Linus doesn't want him to; I heard them whispering when they thought I was asleep. But I do want them; I want to keep myself formless, adrift. I don't want to land yet.

The sky here is different than in Tucson, a brighter blue, almost candyish. The clouds seem to hang in it so gently, like puffs of smoke. The car is thick with the smell of snack food, sugary soda. A fly creeps slowly across the ceiling. I think of Riley in his kitchen, his terrible stranger's face. The ache rises up in me again, howling and angry. I press my hands hard against my eyes.

Linus is in the passenger-side seat now, sleeping. It's night again. Warm desert air trickles into the car. I wet a finger in my mouth and stick it into the empty potato chip bag, suck on the salt, think of Jen S. that night in Rec, when she sucked salt from the popcorn bowl. That all seems millions of years ago. The clean hospital, a nice doctor, a warm bed. Now I'm back to where I was: drifting, hurt.

When they realized they'd forgotten to feed me, the only place they could find was an Allsup's with dehydrated, suspect burritos. Tanner brought out a bag of potato chips and Gatorade, pretzels and Coke.

Tanner inhales deeply. "God, I love New Mexico. If you thought Tucson was a freak show, you ain't seen nothing yet."

He drums his fingers on the steering wheel. "You feel dizzy? We're going up in elevation. You'll feel better after a few days. Keep drinking the Gatorade."

Whenever I see them in my head, in the kitchen, I try as hard as I can to black them out, but the heat starts up again inside me, the shame, and there they are, pushing at each other, her wet mouth smirking at me and Riley turning around, so drunk, and something else, too, and shouting at me, telling me—

I do cry a lot in the backseat, my face against the window,

Linus and Tanner up front, watching the road. They don't say anything, just let me make noise. I drift in and out of sleep, my face rolling against the vinyl seat, my feet throbbing, the pain cresting and receding like an ocean wave. Murmurs from the front seat reach me slowly, as though through a long tunnel. Words funnel around me: *treatment center. Messages. Mother. Riley.*

Riley. *Riley.* I bury my head in the seat, sobs backing up in my throat.

And, creeping in, like mice after a house has gone to sleep: Ellis. How she felt before she did it. This ocean of hurt and shame. The one she was drowning in.

And I let her drown.

I wake, dimly aware that the car has stopped. Tanner gets out, stretches his legs. Linus unbuckles her seat belt and smiles back at me. "Up, up, kid," she announces cheerfully.

An elderly man in fuzzy slippers waves to us from a wide wooden porch at the top of a dirt-and-gravel driveway. There are dozens of wind chimes hanging from the rafters of the porch, tinkling like glass in the slight breeze. It's much colder here than it was in Tucson. I shiver in the backseat of the car, watching them all.

The man is in a teal bathrobe, drinking a glass of wine. His hair sticks up like white tufts of cotton. Tanner and Linus cross the driveway, hug him deeply, and return to the car for me, the man following slowly behind them. He stoops down a little bit as they extract me, his eyes as curious as a bird's.

"Oh, yes," he murmurs. "Oh, yes, I see. Oh, dear."

The house is warm as Tanner and Linus bring me in, helping me down a hallway to a small room with a single bed and one window. I take in the large, ornate wooden cross on the wall. I think of the cross I stole from Ariel. I'm glad I returned it, even if I never told her it was me.

They arrange me on the bed and drape a blue wool blanket over my body. Tanner presses two pills onto my tongue, holds a glass of water to my mouth.

Through the curtainless window, I can see the sky and its deliriously fat, white stars. I sleep for two days.

On the third day, my feet throb less when I set them on the floor. I hobble, dehydrated and dizzy, down the hallway to find a bathroom. Large framed photographs line the adobe walls, black-and-whites of people, old adobe churches.

In the bathroom, colorful crosses and fragrant bundles of sage have been tacked up. Plump rolls of soft toilet paper are stacked in white towers next to the toilet. There is no shower, only a deep, deep tub. I sit on the toilet, touch the gauze on my arms, my stomach. I think about peeling it off and looking, but I don't. I stay in the bathroom for a long time, listening to the silence, watching a moth flutter on the windowsill. I think this is the most beautiful bathroom I've ever been in. I never thought a bathroom could be this beautiful. That someone would take the time to make it so calming, so pretty.

The old man is at a long pine table in the main room, holding a newspaper very close to his face. There are bowls of plump fruit and nuts on the table, a platter with a baguette and a plate of creamy butter. He looks over his glasses at me.

"Coffee?" He pours me a cup from a French press, nudges a carafe of milk across the table. "The milk is warm, if you take milk. My grandchildren are feeding the horse."

I slather a piece of baguette with butter. I'm hungry now; my stomach makes fierce noises. I bite the baguette; it's so light and crispy, it shatters against my sweatshirt, leaving me showered in crumbs. The old man laughs. "Happens to me all the time. I've never been ashamed of making a mess when eating."

I brush the pale crumbs away. The baguette is pillowy inside, moist. The house is silent except for the sound of my chewing and the occasional rustle of the old man's newspaper. Gradually, I realize it's quiet outside, too. Strangely quiet. No cars, no voices, nothing.

"Did you know Quakers believe silence is a way of letting the divine into your body? Into your heart?" He shakes out the paper and leans in close to me. His eyebrows are like sleeping white caterpillars. "I've never been afraid of the quiet, have you? Some people are, you know. They need tumult and clatter.

"Santa Fe. High desert country. Isn't it beautiful? I've been in this house for forty-two years. This wonderful silence you can hear—what a *funny* thing I have just said—makes it the most divine place on earth. To me."

He reaches over and curls his hand around mine. His skin is dry, dusty.

"It's a pleasure to have you in my divine home, Charlotte."

I feel the press of hot, grateful tears in my eyes.

HIS NAME IS FELIX AND HE'S LINUS AND TANNER'S GRAND-
father. Linus leads me around the house, pointing at paintings
on the walls, sculptures arranged in corners and in the backyard, a huge expanse that looks out over rolling hills and the
horse's stable. She takes me into a cavernous building flooded
with light streaming from the skylights in the ceiling, where
various canvases are hung on the walls and cans of paint, buckets of brushes, and industrial-sized containers of turpentine
abound. Canvases are stacked three deep against some of the
walls. A loftlike space has been constructed at the far end; a
table with an old typewriter and a plain chair sit on the upper
deck. There's a wide stairwell leading up to the loft. Beneath it
are cluttered, top-heavy bookshelves. A young woman works
quietly at a high pine table in the corner of the studio, sorting slides, holding them up to the light and studying them
before placing them in different piles. "That's Devvie," Linus
says. "His assistant. She lives here, too."

I limp around the studio, touching Felix's things gently, the
pencils, the stray pieces of paper, the jars and tubes, the amazing and voluminous detritus: birds' feathers, stones of various
sizes, old animal bones, wrinkled photographs, postcards with
loopy cursive bearing exotic postmarks, a red mask, boxes of
matches, heavy cloth-covered art books, jars and crusted tubes
of paints, so many paints. One table has a series of watercolors
on paper strewn about, slight and gentle washes of purple,
conelike flowers. Another table is just books, heaps of them,
open to different images of paintings and drawings, five or six

Post-it notes pressed to each page with words like *Climate of the palette, Echo/Answer, Don't lie.* The floor is layered with old paint; I trip on a pair of battered clogs.

I look again at the canvases on the walls; I want to say they're sunsets, but they're not so literal. Something deeper, something inside the body, a feeling? *Isn't it beautiful?* Felix said to me. The colors are doing something together, I'm sure of it, I can feel it; playing off each other; some relationship is being described that I can't put into words, but looking at them excites me, fills me up, blunts the ache. I look at Felix's art supplies and wish I could do something right now, make something of my own. I remember what Ariel said at the art opening about Tony Padilla's boat-paint paintings: *Colors by themselves can be a story.* Ariel's paintings were a story beneath a surface of dark and light. I smile shyly at Linus.

"Yummy, yes?" She claps her hands, giddy.

Felix pokes the meat on the grill like it's still alive. Smoke froths his glasses and he rubs them on the edge of his shirt. I look at his gnarled fingers, the thickness of his wrists and knuckles. His skin is flecked with the faintest remnants of paint.

We're gathered around a long wooden table outside. The air is crisp. Tanner has lent me a fleece pullover. Linus is slicing a pungent white cheese and Tanner is carving slices of avocado. Devvie, the assistant, is in the house, fixing drinks and feeding the ancient, limping wolfhound. In the distance, the horse whinnies inside the stable. Strange sounds come from the dark desert beyond us. Whoops and whistles; rustling and bickering.

Felix slaps the glossy meat onto a platter and sets it on

the table, flicking his napkin over his lap. He looks at the sky. "Probably one of the last times we'll be able to be out here like this." He glances over at me. "December is when we get the snow. It's the most beautiful month here."

He looks over his glasses at me and takes a long drink of wine, sighing appreciatively after he swallows.

"This heartbreak," he says, sitting at the table, placing a napkin on his lap. "And I don't mean what happened with that young man, because those things, they come and go, it's one of the painful lessons we learn. I think you are having a different sort of heartbreak. Maybe a kind of heartbreak of being in the world when you don't *know* how to be. If that makes any sense?"

He takes another sip of wine. "Everyone has that moment, I think, the moment when something so . . . *momentous* happens that it rips your very being into small pieces. And then you have to stop. For a long time, you gather your pieces. And it takes such a very long time, not to fit them back together, but to assemble them in a new way, not necessarily a *better* way. More, a way you can live with until you know for certain that this piece should go *there*, and that one *there*."

"That's an awful lot to lay on her, Grandpa," Tanner says. "She's just a kid."

Felix laughs. "Then I'll shut up. Ignore me. I'm just a blathering old fart."

I keep my head down. I don't want to cry at the table in front of these people so I fill my mouth with the salty meat. I slide my fingers under my thighs to keep them from trembling, listen to everyone chatter. I am so empty inside, so ravenous for something that I feel like I could eat for days and not fill myself.

Later, in my single bed in the quiet room, the window cracked open just a little to the luminous sky, the cool air on my face, I do think about *momentous*. Was my father my first momentous? He was there, and then he wasn't, and I wasn't supposed to ask about him or cry, or be anything, really, because my mother was so upset.

Maybe Ellis was a puzzle piece, a big and *momentously* beautiful one that I knocked out of the puzzle box. I'm not sure what Riley was yet. Maybe he was part of the assembling, too? And I'm still not done?

I'm so unwhole. I don't know where all the pieces of me are, how to fit them together, how to make them stick. Or if I even can.

AFTER A WEEK, MY FOG LIFTS A LITTLE BIT. I STILL SLEEP A lot, and I'm so tired, but walking doesn't hurt as much, and it doesn't seem like we're going anywhere soon, so I start investigating Felix's house, which is complicated and rambling. From the front, it appears small and square, but once you're inside, it spreads out in several directions at once, its complex nature hidden by cottonwoods and octopuslike cane chollas. (That's what the tiny book Linus gives me says they are. I take it with me when I walk outside. It distracts me to do simple things, like put a name to a plant.)

There are several bedrooms, all with plain beds and simple wooden dressers. Patterned wool blankets are folded neatly and placed at the foot of each bed. The main room is enormous, with dark, heavy beams crisscrossing the ceiling, like the bones of a skeleton, which Tanner tells me are called *vigas,* and there's an enormous stone fireplace against one wall. Devvie keeps it lit on the cooler nights and it's there that I like to sit, close to its warmth.

Felix has one room for just books, another with only records and a stereo and a slanted, forlorn piano in the center. The kitchen is at the back of the house, off a deck that looks out into the rolling, dark hills. The stable is down the slope, surrounded by coyote fencing.

The studio, Linus tells me, was built with something called genius grant money many years ago. It adjoins the back of the house, rising barnlike over the hills. At night, the coyotes come out, howling, wandering. Felix points out low-flying hawks to me during the day, their forms swooping over the cottonwoods in dark arcs. They cook together, Linus and Tanner and Felix: large, sumptuous meals of fruits and meats, breads and cheeses, papery spinach salads with walnuts and salty feta cheese.

"You know," Felix says to me one morning, spooning blueberries onto my plate at breakfast. "I don't want you to think I'm some old workhorse, slaving away every day at my paints and pictures. Sometimes I don't do any work at all in my studio! I just sit. Listen to music. Page through my books. Maybe write down something I remember. Maybe write a letter."

He pours more coffee into his cup. "Sometimes not working can be work, just more gently. It's important to just be, Charlie, every once in a while."

My feet keep getting better. The cuts and gouges heal up nicely, though they're still tender. Tanner takes off my arm bandages and lets me see the new slashes, the new rivers. I feel hesitantly over the fresh lines on my stomach, but I don't look down.

I didn't go too deep, he says; I didn't need stitches. "Let's think of that as a good thing." He drops the old bandages in the trash, unfurls a fresh roll of gauze.

One night while Felix is opening another bottle of wine, Linus calls me over to a tiny laptop set up on the kitchen table. It's been two weeks now and I've noticed that Linus disappears with the laptop every night after dinner for an hour. Tanner said she was talking to her kids over Skype.

All I could say was "Oh." I didn't even know she had children. Or I guess she must have told me, but I wasn't listening. Ashamed, I realized I had never really asked Linus anything about her life, or her problems with drinking, because I was so consumed with Riley.

Linus points to the screen. I squint. It's a newspaper article, with a photo of artwork on a wall. My artwork. Manny and Karen and Hector and Leonard. It's dated two days after the art show.

Linus raps me on the skull. "Look, dummy. It's a review of the gallery show. Listen." She reads from the review, which sounds nice enough, if a little snarky; the writer uses a lot of words I don't understand; I wonder why they just can't say if they liked anything or not. I catch some of what Linus is saying: ... *seemingly caught adrift amid the digi-heavy and Technicolor nostalgia is a series of charcoal portraits ... revealingly sympathetic ... classical quirk. ...*

"I think they liked your drawings, Charlie!" Linus nudges me in the hip. Her breath is fragrant with honey and green tea. Felix wanders over, waving a finger at Linus. "Click there, click there," he says. Linus clicks; the screen fills with the faces of Hector and Karen, Leonard with his sorrowful eyes and hopeful mouth.

Felix says simply, "Very nice. Very strong line, my dear." He removes his glasses. "But you don't feel it."

I shake my head, surprised. How can he say I didn't feel it? I liked all of them and I worked hard. I wish I could answer out loud, but my words are still buried.

"It's all there, dear. Attention to detail. Beautiful gestural moments." He looks right in my eyes. "But you don't *love* this kind of drawing. Or, at least, have a complicated passion for it. You need one or the other. Ambivalence is not a friend to art."

Felix pats my cheek. "You have your skill, Charlotte. Now

give your skill an *emotion*." He wanders back to the wine bottle. "I have a room you can use," he calls to me. "Devvie will get it ready for you tomorrow."

Linus nods. "We aren't going anywhere for a while. True Grit's closed for God knows how long. Riley stole a hell of a lot of money, you know; people haven't been paid. Might as well enjoy ourselves."

IN MY SMALL, TIDY ROOM, I LIE ON THE BED, HEART THUMP-ing, mind whirring. What did Felix mean, an *emotion*? I worked so hard on those pieces, looked at all the books in the library, did everything the drawing manual said, practiced and prac-ticed. Isn't that what you do as an artist? I think back to Tony's gallery show, when Ariel asked me to come to her drawing workshop. Ariel said I would never get anywhere unless I ex-amined myself. Made myself *my* subject. I choke back a laugh. What does Felix want me to do, draw myself? No one is going to want to see that, a girl with split skin and a sad face.

I press my face against the wall. I can hear them out on the back deck, listening to a soulful singer on the record player, voices mingling with the intermittent cries from the dark des-ert. I have nothing now. Not Riley, not Mikey, not Ellis, not my drawing. I suck in my breath, try to stem a fresh wave of sobs. I'm so tired, again. Tired of *trying*. My nose leaks; my eyes throb with the effort of holding tears back. I curl up, clutch-ing my knees to my chest. I miss Riley so much, even though I know how wrong it is: his smoky, liquidy smell is ingrained in my memory; my fingertips ache when I imagine the velvety slope of his back; my heart catapults in my chest.

I rock back and forth on the bed. My mind fills with the bathroom down the hall with its box of razor blades under the sink. The kitchen with its slinky promise of knives. I uncurl myself, force myself to feel around my body, count off the scars and bandages, the sheer accumulation of my own damage.

There is nothing else I can do to myself.

Louisa comes to me then, an image out of nowhere: on fire, her fine hair rising in flame, skin melting off like butter.

I sit up so fast tape pops on my stomach. I press it back into place, wincing at the pain. My backpack's in the closet. I drop to my knees, digging inside. It's the only thing Wendy didn't destroy.

Louisa's composition books are still tightly bound. I work at the tape with my fingers.

The first page of the first book begins, in small, neat black script: *A girl's life is the worst life in the world. A girl's life is: you are born, you bleed, you burn.*

Louisa's words hurt, but they are true, they ring through me. I read everything that night, each book. I can't stop.

IT'S EARLY MORNING AND I HAVEN'T SLEPT YET, LOUISA'S words still electric inside me. *Cutting is a fence you build upon your own body to keep people out but then you cry to be touched. But the fence is barbed. What then?* When I pull myself out of bed Linus tells me that Felix is letting me work in one of the empty bedrooms, the smallest one. Devvie and Tanner move a tall table, a stool, and boxes of supplies—pads, pencils, inks, pens, and paints—into the room for me. Devvie is an angular girl with a penchant for flannel shirts and track pants. She is something called ABD at New York University.

The room smells musty. Outside, the horse nickers. Tanner takes him out for a ride every morning at this time. I sit on the floor, dirt and dust sticking to the backs of my calves.

Felix said to do something I loved. Or felt complicated passion for. Ariel said to use myself. Louisa gave me the story of her life. *A drunk and a drunk met and they made a mess: me. I was born with a broken heart.*

I trace the scars on my legs, feel up under my shirt at the years of cuts healed and unhealed. It is all I am, now, these lines and burns, the moments behind them. *A girl is born.*

In the musty room, I select a sketchbook with thick, creamy paper, and dark pens. Using a ruler, I begin a frame on one piece of paper, testing the flow of the black pen, its feel in my fingers. It works like water over the paper, no pushing like with charcoal. On another piece of paper, I sketch, lightly, testing myself, testing the images that appear.

A girl is born. I start with myself: a girl with clumpy hair in

363

a yellowy, fuzzy cardigan on the first day of a new school, all her scars hidden under the sweater and her jeans. What a sad girl she is, mouth clamped shut, eyes burning, a force field of anger and fear vibrating inside her. She watches the other kids, how easily they move around each other, laughing, adjusting headphones, whispering. She wants to say *My father is in the river down the street* but she says nothing. She meets a beautiful girl with wild purple hair and white, white skin. The beautiful, momentous girl smells sweet and creamy, like face powder and too much black eyeliner.

The beautiful, momentous girl is *fucking angelic.*

Louisa wrote, *Each aberration of my skin is a song. Press your mouth against me. You will hear so much singing.*

I draw and lose the hours.

As the story progresses, the character of Charlie loses more clothing, piece by piece, her pale young woman's flesh taking on more and more damage as the arc unfolds. I fall asleep on my arms on the table. I wake and resume the story. I am no good at talking, no good at making the right words reel from my brain to my mouth and out, but I'm good at *this,* my pictures and the words I can write. I'm good at *this.*

This is what Felix meant. What you do should fly through your blood, carrying you somewhere.

My fingers begin to cramp, and I need some space, and air. I leave the house quietly. I walk for a long time in the desert, finding a shaded spot under a cottonwood to rest, balancing one of Louisa's books on my knees. It's quiet and empty and full out here, in the desert, all at once. I burrow deep into Tanner's fleece.

Louisa wrote, *People should know about us. Girls who write their pain on their bodies.*

I read and reread her life slowly. It's difficult and it hurts, but she gave me her words and her story, every bloody bit of it.

No one bothers me. No one comes to ask what I'm doing. When I'm hungry, I go to the kitchen and make a sandwich, fill a glass of water, return to the room, and keep drawing the comic.

I think it takes three days, maybe four, I can't tell, I don't know, but at some point, I just have a feeling, something clear and final that says: *Finished. For now, finished.*

I gently gather all my papers and put them in order, place them in a tidy pile on the tall table, clean up the pens, dump the pencil shavings in the basket under the window.

Everything Casper wanted me to say I've drawn instead.

I have a voice. I have a place for my voice.

I look down at the sloppy, too-big sweatpants Linus gave me, the waistband rolled down three times, and the giant NYU T-shirt Devvie loaned me. I think of my overalls back in the wrecked and bloody apartment, my long jersey shirts, the clompy black boots. It's time for different things. It's time for me to speak again.

I strip off the borrowed clothes, shivering in the cool air from the open window. I wrap a gray wool blanket around myself and leave the room, quietly slipping out the back door. I sit on the steps for a long time, in the fresh cold, listening to the desert unfold around me, its chirps and squeaks and howls, listening to the sounds of Felix murmuring inside, Linus and Tanner squabbling over cards.

It sounds like home, all of it.

A FEW DAYS LATER, WHEN IT'S TIME TO LEAVE, FELIX HUGS each of us, even me. I shrink from his touch at first and then, consciously, force myself to relax. He rubs my back with his sturdy hands. He kisses my forehead. Linus and Tanner pack the car; Devvie has made several sandwiches for us, arranged a bag of fruit and cheeses, though I suspect Tanner will want to stop for salty treats.

I adjust the waistband of my skirt. It's army green, cotton, falling just above my knees, four dollars at the Value-Thrift in Santa Fe. I look down at my plain black sneakers, the Santa Fe High School Raiders T-shirt, short-sleeved and light brown, the scars on my legs. What was it Blue said? *Who gives a shit.*

Linus took me shopping and automatically walked us to the denim section of the store and started sifting through hangers of jeans and overalls, thinking that was what I'd like. I left her there and wandered around. When she found me, my arms were full of plain cotton skirts and T-shirts and one pilled black cardigan with shiny silver buttons. I shook my head at her arms full of overalls and said, "Not anymore." She raised her eyebrows, smiled, and took them back to the rack.

Felix says, "Did you know, Charlotte, that there is a whole, interesting history of self-mortification?"

I stare at him, unsure of the word, but then I think I understand.

He nods. "It's true, my dear. Some people used it as a way to get closer to God." He raises his chin to me. "Are you trying to get closer to God, Charlotte?"

I shake my head. "Fuck no," I say. Felix laughs and helps me into the car.

Linus starts the car and we drive, but she stops just where we should turn onto the road, looking in the rearview mirror. I turn around. Felix is lumbering down the gravel, his fuzzy slippers raising rivulets of dust. He bends down by my window, out of breath, motions for me to lean closer.

In my ear, he whispers, "You be *you*, Charlotte. You be you."

IN ALBUQUERQUE, TANNER TAKES THE BACKSEAT, FALLS asleep. Linus shoves the bag of pork rinds in my direction. I pour some into the palm of my hand.

"Linus," I say softly. "Why are you helping me? You don't even know me, and I've been so selfish. Like, I've never even asked you anything about yourself. And I'm sorry. That was shitty." I take a breath. It's what I wanted to say.

Her cheek is fat with food, like a squirrel's. She swallows. "I drank my kids away from me. All those years I spent trying to get sober, they stayed with their dad and they didn't want to see me, and rightly so. I did some truly horrible things that still make me want to puke with shame when I think about them."

She wipes her mouth with the back of her hand. "Life without a mom is pretty shitty. They're mad. They're coming around, but real slow. They're good kids, though, which makes me think they had some kindness along the way, little kick starts of help and love. So that's what I'm doing. That's why I'm helping you. I don't know the story of your mom, but I have to believe she's hoping somebody is looking out for you."

I crush the rinds in my hand, lick the pebbles from my palm. "My mother doesn't think like that."

Linus is quiet for a long time before she answers.

"Yes. She does. Someday? If you decide to have kids, you'll know what I mean. And it'll knock you damn flat on your ass."

IT'S LATE WHEN LINUS DROPS ME OFF IN FRONT OF THE BUILD-ing. The street is quiet, the liquor store closed for the night. I shut my eyes when we passed Twelfth Street. I didn't want to risk looking out and seeing his robin's-egg-blue house.

The foyer light is dim, but the first thing I notice is that the railing and floor have been repainted a light peach color; the entry door is a fresh, crisp white. The hallway smells like lilacs, clean; the walls have been painted a quiet, light blue. I approach the door to my apartment. I can hear music from the room and my heart sinks. Leonard must have already rented the apartment. Did he save any of my things? Maybe he put them in boxes in the basement. But where's Blue? And where am I supposed to go? My heart starts to beat very fast. As I turn to go, the door inches open.

The bruises on Blue's face are fading, but the ring around her eye is still swollen and purple-yellow. There are red lines with small dots left over from the stitches.

Blue breathes in relief. "Charlie. I'm so glad to see you." She opens the door wider. "Are you talking? Are you okay? I thought you might go back to being quiet for a while."

The room is neat as a pin, no more ashtrays, and there is a new, plain wood dresser to hold Blue's clothes. The lino-leum has been ripped up and the wood beneath it sanded and painted a rose color. I realize that the linoleum would have been soiled from my blood; I feel a surge of guilt. Blue bends to run a hand across the wood. "Fir," she says softly. My slashed futon has been replaced with a double bed covered with a fluffy, inviting comforter. Blue has installed plain metal shelves in the kitchen and filled them with stacks of pink dishes and cups, jars of sauces and jams, cans of food, crackers. Another thick shelf sports a microwave. A shower curtain with a map of the world hangs from the ceiling around the tub. A cloth curtain with irises surrounds the toilet.

"I like it here," she says with a shy smile.

Blue has made the apartment more of a home in six weeks than I did in the six months I was here.

On the card table, a painstaking project: Blue has been taping together the contents of my ripped sketchbook and the torn Land Camera photographs of Ellis and me. Some of the pieces are tiny; Wendy was very thorough.

Blue stutters. "It—it was Jen S. She called me after you left for work, about Louisa, and, Jesus, Charlie, I just lost it. I found Riley and we went to that girl's house. I just wanted to get high, you know? I didn't . . . I didn't know it was going to be that stuff, but I couldn't stop myself. Jesus, Charlie, did you know about him?"

The little crystalline bags. The plastic smell the first morning I came to wake him up. I look at Blue and start to cry. Her eyes widen in alarm. "Charlie, *what?*"

I tell her I'm sorry, I'm so sorry, but that I lied, that I bought drugs for Riley, that everything was horrible, and that I was drowning, and that I don't want to be underwater anymore.

Blue shakes her head violently. "I'm out, Charlie. I'm really done. I'm not gonna do that stuff anymore. I promise. I *like* it here. It's fucking *nice,* this town. My God, the *sun.*"

I press my forehead against the wall, suddenly exhausted all over again, emptied, now that I'm back.

She says, "That person I was at Creeley, that wasn't really

me. Sometimes with people, you just become something, like, your role happens *to* you, instead of you choosing it. I let that happen when I got here. I let it slip over me, even though I didn't want to. I don't ... I'm not that, Charlie. I want to be friends. I think we could help each other. I like you so *much*."

Her hand on my back is warm through my shirt.

"I don't want to be Louisa," she whispers. "I don't want to die. I don't want to be that, ever. Help me not be that and I'll help you."

I believe her. She says my name. She says Louisa's, over and over. We cry like that, for hours, together, me against the wall, Blue pressed to my back. Holding each other, like you're supposed to.

THE GREEN SCREEN DOOR SLAMS SHUT BEHIND ME. EVERYONE turns around; everyone's face closes up. I hang my backpack on the wall peg, walk to the dishwasher, tie on my apron, jerk out the dish rack, and start to unload plates and cups. When I turn around with a clean dish tray, they're staring at me: Randy in her saddle shoes, Temple busying herself with the coffee urns, silvery ankle bracelets tinkling.

Randy dumps an armload of cups into the soapy water, splashing my apron. She knocks me in the shoulder lightly.

"It's about fucking time," she says. "We've been reopened for three days already and wondering where our favorite disher was."

My second night back at work, Julie pulls me into the office. I don't look at the couch. I try not to look at anything except my water-pruned hands as Julie tells me what I already mostly know. That Riley and Wendy totaled Luis's car; Wendy broke three ribs, cracked her collarbone, and punctured her intestine. That Wendy attacked Blue at the apartment when Blue tried to get her to stop destroying my things.

Julie twists the rings on her fingers, her voice wavering. "Riley came out with bruises, a DUI, driving without a license, a possible robbery charge for stealing the night deposit, and the theft of an automobile." She lays a hand on the bowl of lapis lazuli.

"He was in jail. Now he's up north at a men-only rehab. It's not his first time in rehab, but you probably guessed that." She clacks the stones together. Her eyes well up. "I've been doing a lot of thinking, you know? Maybe some of this is my fault, always helping him when he fucks up. He can't come back here, ever, to work. He can't. And legally, holy hell. If he wants to stay out of jail, he has to complete a yearlong work-rehab program and stay clean. And am I supposed to press charges about stealing my money?" Tears run down her cheeks. "The world is so fucking awful sometimes and then you have to really start thinking, what's my role in this awfulness? Did I make some of this awful?"

There's a heavy weight inside me. I have to get rid of it.

"Julie," I say. "I knew, I mean, I think I knew, but I didn't want to *know*, that he was stealing from the register. And . . . I helped him. I . . . bought stuff for him. And I'm sorry. And I understand if you want to fire me."

Julie shakes her head, wiping her eyes. "You bought stuff for him?"

I nod, my face burning with shame. I wanted him to love me.

I say it aloud, but very quietly.

Julie reaches out and takes my hand. "Love is a real shit show, Charlie, but it's not that. It's not buying drugs for someone. You don't deserve that, honey. You just don't."

I try to let her words just sit in me, rather than rejecting them. It's hard, but I do it.

I keep going, my words spilling out fast. "Linus said Grit is in real trouble. We talked about it on the way back from New Mexico and I've been thinking, well, Linus and I have been thinking, and talking, and we have some ideas about how to get Grit on track, if you want to listen."

Julie blinks, snuffling. She finds a pen and opens a notebook.

"I'm listening," she says. "Fire away, because I'm dying here."

I LIKE LIVING WITH BLUE. I LIKE HAVING A FRIEND, A *GIRL* friend, again. Ellis is still inside me, and she always will be, but Blue is good in her way, and kind.

Sometimes, when I get home from my shifts at Grit, we take the bus to the midnight movie and buy salty yellow popcorn and chilly, overly iced sodas. I'm pleasantly surprised by Blue's endless supply of money. She shrugs whenever I ask; *My father feels guilty,* she says. *Money is his salve.* "It's weird," she says, her face assuming a complicated texture of pain and grief. "I don't want to talk about it. Maybe we can talk about it someday. Can we get extra butter on the popcorn this time?"

I can't sit at the card table weeping or in the tub staring at the ceiling, thinking of ways I could have done better, could have helped Riley more or gotten out sooner, saved Ellis, made myself better, because all those things are wrong, I realize; they solve nothing, wondering what could have been done; I know that now.

I have to wait my bad feelings out and that means staying busy, means working at Grit, means spending time working on my comic, rereading Louisa's composition books, thinking about who might want to read her story and mine.

It means going with Blue to meetings. It means sitting in the brightly lit basement of a run-down church on hard chairs that scrape the cement floor, drinking muddy coffee and listening to people stutter out their stories. It means really *listening* to them, and thinking about them, and thinking about myself.

Blue and I look around for a group like us, cutters and burners, the self-harmers, but we can't find one. Blue says, "Heh, I guess we'll just have to keep talking to each other, then, huh? Who would have thought it'd be us, eh, Silent Sue?"

I miss Casper, but I understand now why she had to let go. Maybe I was, in the end, just one more hurting girl for her, but she was kind to me, and she has to be kind to others, too, because even that small kindness, even for such a brief time—it was something.

It was something.

One night Blue comes home with a shiny new laptop. Once she gets it set up, she makes me get a Facebook account. Laughing, she says, "Social media is perfect for you. It's totally for people who don't like in-person interaction. But Twitter isn't you, because it's chatty, so don't go there."

I don't do much on it, mostly just scroll around the news or look at Blue's page. But one night I see I have a friend request.

It's Evan.

I don't feel scared that he's contacted me, or nervous. I feel fucking grateful, in fact, that I can press Accept with all my heart, because he's *alive*, and I thought for sure that he'd be dead.

The first thing he messages me is a newspaper story. The story is a few months old, but it has a photo that stops my heart.

Evan writes, *EVIL HAS BEEN CAPTURED.*

The house, Seed House, was shut down, Fucking Frank arrested for selling underage girls for sex, providing drugs and alcohol to minors, and so much, much more. In the photo, his face is gaunt, no longer full and angry. He looks frightened.

And then Evan says: *In other news, this is day 92 of sobriety for me. How the hell are YOU, Charlotte?*

I can't stop smiling as I write back.

THE *PANADERÍA* PASTRIES SELL OUT EVERY DAY. LINUS AND I had the idea to get them for a discount before they threw the leftovers in the Dumpster. Julie lets Linus work on a new lunch menu with more healthy items, less reliance on potatoes, grease, and cheese. She agrees to a punch card for coffees. One day as I'm clearing dishes and lugging my tub from table to table, I look up and see a new splotch of real, vulgar graffiti on the fake brick walls of the coffeehouse. I stand, looking at the walls for a long time, turning, taking in the whole space, the amount of light from the windows high on the walls, thinking about how we can fix this.

Blue comes in one night to help paint the walls and the bathrooms, arriving with cans and rollers and brushes from the shed at Leonard's. Temple helps me haul out ladders from Julie's office and push the tables and chairs into the center of the room. Randy and Tanner work on the tops of the tables, painting them different colors, adding different patterns to some, sanding and gluing old postcards to others. Blue and Julie and I paint for hours, a soft wheat color that glows in the morning and looks ethereal at night. "But now there's nothing on the walls," Julie says. "They look so empty."

"Not for long," I answer.

I'm working the counter on Temple's smoke break one evening when Ariel comes in, tentatively, as though unsure if she's in the right place. Her mouth opens in pleasure when she sees me. "You! What a lovely surprise. I was at your show, but I didn't see you."

I take a deep breath. "I stole your cross. It was me. And I'm sorry."

Ariel dips her head. "I know. I understand. Thank you for returning it." She reaches out. "May I?" she asks. I nod.

She lays her hand carefully over mine. "I lost my son, so I know what it is like to be . . . empty, but full, with hell. I know you know what that means. That's all I want to say about that. But I want you to know that I am glad you are okay. I am so, so glad."

I nod, trying not to cry. She pats my hand, asks me for a double espresso. I'm relieved to be able to turn away and do something so she can't see the tears falling. She walks around while I work the machine.

"I haven't been in here in years," she shouts over the noise of the machine. "It had gotten so grungy. My friend told me to stop by." She peers at the walls. They're hung with brilliant, intricately woven landscapes: women working in fields; complicated cityscapes; a tawny mountain with a sun hovering just above.

"My goodness," she says breathily, moving closer to the walls. "These are rather exquisite. Who did them?" Her voice rings out in the new, clean café.

"The cook," I answer proudly, swiping my face dry and turning around with her demitasse. "Linus Sebold."

LINUS ASKS TO ME TO FIND A NEW BOX OF ORDER PADS FOR the waitstaff in Julie's office. It's a busy evening; we've been packed with a different, older crowd since we made changes. The art kids still come, but we've lost some of the rockers. I miss them, but Julie needs this thing to run, so Grit needs people who buy food and drinks, not throw up on the floor.

As I'm puttering behind Julie's desk, searching through boxes, it appears before me, tucked plain as day underneath the corner of her office phone.

A piece of paper, a phone number, his name, scribbled doodles and circles and stars.

One moment I'm looking at the paper and the next I'm saying, "May I please speak to Riley West?", feeling myself high above, floating near the ceiling, watching my hands shake as I press the phone to my ear. On the other end, there's the sound of slow feet, a heavy sigh.

"Yeah?"

Can he hear my thudding heart through my body? Does he know it's me by my silence? The words clog in my throat. Is that why I hear him sigh again, why he says, "Sweetheart"?

"Riley."

"You can't call me here, okay? Listen, you can't—" His voice is measured, careful, soft. He's trying not to attract attention, I bet. I feel a flush of anger and try to bat it down, but before I can, it's up and swinging. It's out before I can stop it.

"Do you even remember being with me, Riley? Did you even care, at all, like, *ever*?"

Adrenaline forces me along. "I mean, was I just a freak show for you? Was I?" I feel scared, I feel loose and lost, but each word that comes out feels powerful.

A sterile, automated voice cuts into the line. *This phone call will reach its limit in four minutes.* That's right. I remember that; at Creeley, the community phone shut out after ten minutes.

"Charlie." He's crying, a childish whine, like something a person does when they don't want other people to hear. The sound of his crying sneaks into me, scratches at my heart. He says my name again. I scrape at my wet face with the back of my hand.

"I *loved* you, Riley." It hurts, saying it out loud, letting it balloon up and away from me.

"Please," he cries, *"baby—"*

The line goes dead.

I open the drawer in Julie's desk: a stapler; heavy, gleaming scissors; thumbtacks. Roll call of easy elixirs.

On the drive back from Santa Fe, Linus said to me, "My life is like a series of ten-minute intervals sometimes. Sometimes I want to give myself a fucking medal for making it through an hour without a drink, but that's the way it has to be. Waiting it out."

I slam the drawer shut. I have to make myself wait it out, this thundering inside me, wait it out in ten-minute intervals, five-minute intervals, whatever it takes, always, now, and forever.

I gather the order pads in my arms and walk out the door, shutting it firmly behind me.

TEMPLE IS EMCEEING ANOTHER OPEN MIC, THIS TIME WITH fewer rockers and more poets, when Linus hands me the counter phone. I have to bend down to the floor to hear the voice on the other end. I notice the dust motes and coffee grounds lingering beneath the lip of the counter and make a mental note to clean more carefully later.

"Oh, my dear Charlotte." An old man's voice, soft and crackly. "How would you like to come and work for me for a while?"

Felix Arneson says, "I'm in New York and Devvie—you remember my assistant, Devvie—has finished her dissertation. She's leaving me. I'm bereft, but I'll survive."

"I don't ... what?" I lean closer to the phone, unsure if I heard correctly. "You want me to work for you? Me?"

Felix chuckles. "I need someone who doesn't mind the desert, the isolation. It's fairly boring out there, you know. I mean, there's a wonderful city nearby, but out where I am, well, you know. You were there! You'd sort my slides, put my files in order. Lots of things, really. Answering the phone, email. Ordering my supplies. It's room and board and just a little money. What do you say? I think you rather liked it out there."

I don't think about it all that long. It hurts here, I'm okay, but it hurts here, and I want to be somewhere quiet, where the ghost of Riley isn't everywhere.

There was such a stillness in the land around Felix's house.

"Yes," I say. "Yes, I do want to work for you."

He'll arrange a ticket for me to New York, where I'll meet

him at his hotel. He promises to take me around when he's not in the gallery, to museums, to bookstores. Then we'll fly back together. "I'm afraid to fly," he whispers. "Isn't that funny, at my age? I am going to die, after all, but I'm afraid of a little hop across the sky. I'm willing to fly you all the way out here just so I don't have to fly back by myself."

I admit that I have never flown in an airplane.

"My goodness, then," he says. "What a pair we'll make. And you'll have that little room, too, to do your own work. Linus tells me you're working on a kind of book. I can't wait to hear about it."

JULIE AND LINUS STAND BEFORE ME, RESOLUTE. I TELL THEM no again. "I leave in four days," I insist. "I don't want to go with you."

Linus says, "I know it seems horrible, Charlie, but he's worked really hard for this moment and I think it's important to support him in his recovery. Even assholes need help sometimes."

Julie takes my hands. "He's making his amends, Charlie. This is one of his steps. Honestly, I've never seen him like this."

They're letting Riley out for Luis Alvarez's benefit concert. He'll be accompanied by an aide; he'll wear an ankle monitor. Performing is the only way Luis's wife won't press charges against Riley for stealing Luis's car. He'll still have to do the yearlong work-rehab program. He wants me to go to the concert.

Blue sets her cup of coffee on the counter at True Grit; she's been listening to the conversation quietly. She makes the tiniest of motions with her chin, a shadowy *Don't let anyone make you do anything*. I've come to know all of Blue's new looks, the chin dips, the eye wideners, the disapproving scowl. In Creeley, she had only two looks: anger and misery. It's as though being here has opened Blue up in ways that haven't happened for me.

I squeegee the mop out, the handle wavering in my hand. Is it the grease on my fingers or something else?

"Okay," I say finally. "Okay."

BLUE LOOKS AT MY BACKPACK, THE NEW PINK SUITCASE SHE bought me at Goodwill. Everything is packed. Her mouth turns down a little.

"I can't believe you're going," she says quietly.

"I know."

"I mean, I think it's good. It'll be good. But I'll miss you."

"I'll miss you." I take her hand.

"Felix has a computer?"

"Yes."

"You'll Skype me? Once a week?" Her eyes are intent, pleading.

"Yes, definitely."

"What about a phone? Will you get a cell?"

"I can't afford that. He has a phone, I can use that."

"You'll call me all the time, you'll call me and give me his number, right? And I'll come visit. That'll be fun. Like once a month, okay?" She's breathless.

Her fingers tighten around mine. "Yes, Blue."

"You'll find meetings? I'm going to start going with Linus."

"Yes, I promise."

"Okay," she says at last. Her eyes start to brim.

"Okay," I say.

"We have to hold on to each other, Charlie. We can't let go." Tears splash down her face.

"No," I answer, my throat tight.

"We aren't like other people."

"No."

"You're my family now. I'm yours. Do you understand?"

This last part she says into my hair, because now she's hugging me, tightly, and I don't want her to stop, ever.

Yes, I tell her. *Yes.*

THE LUIS ALVAREZ FAMILY BENEFIT IS PACKED. PEOPLE ARE strewn all over Congress Street outside Hotel Congress in downtown Tucson. Separate stages have been set up for pre-show bands and the road is blocked to cars. A mariachi band strolls through the crowd. Luis's photograph is on placards placed outside the hotel doors. He died shortly after Riley stole his car. Tiger Dean chats with a television crew, his hair pomped and his sunglasses perched on his head.

I catch sight of Mikey with Bunny, holding hands; he's no longer in dreadlocks; his hair is a short golden cap around his head. I haven't seen him since I got back.

Mikey turns and sees me. My stomach lurches as he smiles and walks over, Bunny staying behind to chat with someone. I can't help but notice the glint of plain gold on his finger. Blue stays by my side, quiet.

"Hi," he says shyly.

"Hi."

"Charlie," he says. "I'm really happy you're here. I'm really happy to see you."

I motion to his finger. "So, things are pretty different for you now."

Mikey nods. "You could say that." He laughs.

I take a deep breath. "I'm sorry for the way I acted, Mikey. *Michael*. I'm sorry. I should have answered your emails."

He sighs. "I figured you probably deleted them. I was going to come see you soon, anyway, at Grit. Our tour got extended for a couple of months and we did end up making that record. Things are going to happen, it looks like."

He takes a deep breath. "I have something for you. Charlie. I was going to bring it by Grit if I didn't see you here."

He reaches into the pocket of his jeans and pulls out a folded piece of paper.

"This is really difficult for me, Charlie, so let me just say it." He closes his eyes and when he opens them, he looks right at me, hard, but smiling.

My heart flips a little, nervous about what it could be. "What? What is it?" I start to unfold the paper.

"I saw her, Charlie. We had a stop in Sandpoint. Where she is, in Idaho. And I saw her."

Beside me, Blue grips my elbow tightly, takes the paper from my shaking hand. I can barely see for all the water in my eyes. I can barely breathe. *Her.* Her.

Ellis. My hands shake; the paper rattles.

"Oh my God, Charlie. She's okay. I mean, she's not *okay-okay*, but she isn't totally gone. She's *there.* You have to sit with her for a while and ask her really, really, specific things, but she's *there,* and when I said your name, I swear to *God,* her whole face lit up."

Mikey is crying a little, breathing heavily. I look down at the address on the paper, her name. My body is on fire, but in a good way, an excited way.

Like, bursting-with-love fire.

Ellis, my Ellis.

"Fucking outstanding," Blue murmurs. "Outstanding."

"Thank you, Mikey," I whisper. "Thank you so, so much."

TIGER DEAN GAVE JULIE COMP TICKETS AND BACKSTAGE passes. Julie, Blue, Linus, and I stand backstage, marveling at the production, the crew hustling back and forth, the energy pouring from the audience. The punk bands come out first, too loud and sweaty and writhing, but the younger kids love it, screaming and moshing. The weather is perfect, comfortable and cool, the sky cooperating by being endlessly blue and beautiful. Tiger Dean does a set with a band of young guys dressed in identical gray suits and bolo ties. The crowd loves him because he's Tiger Dean, but as Riley always said, his lyrics suck.

Regan, the singer from Grit's open mic, emerges from the opposite wing of the stage, dressed in the same raggedy black skirt she wore back then, the same beat-up Docs. She mumbles her name into the microphone and then lurches into her set. People in the crowd weave back and forth, totally into Regan. Far down at the lip of the stage, there are several men on cell phones, watching her intently and holding up second phones to record her. Julie whispers to Linus, "Scouts. Riley told me he sent his old manager her demo."

Tiger Dean walks onstage as Regan finishes singing, clasps her shoulder in a half-hug. She tromps off the stage. Tiger clears his throat.

"We have a very special guest here tonight, folks. One of my oldest and dearest friends and a fine musician I'm sure you've missed for the past couple of years." Tiger pulls out a paisley handkerchief and mops his forehead. "Now, he's been going through a real rough patch for a while now and I think he's on the mend. At least, I hope he's on the mend.

"Because I need him to write me some fucking songs," he finishes, mock-whispering. The audience laughs.

Julie leans close to me. "They only let him out to do this show. He has to go right back after. He's got an alcohol monitor on his ankle. The monitor measures your alcohol consumption through your sweat, so if he even has a tiny sip of something alcoholic, it can detect it."

Tiger leans into the microphone. "Riley West."

The audience erupts in applause, calls, and whistles. People rise to their feet, stomp the ground. My heart stammers in my chest. Blue slips her hand into mine.

And then he's there.

He appears across from us, in the opposite wing, in a simple short-sleeved button-up blue-and-white cowboy shirt with tan piping across the chest. He's wearing his old brown pants and black sneakers. I wonder where his favorite brown boots are, but then I notice the silver gleam of the alcohol monitor peeking out from the cuff of one pant leg; it wouldn't fit inside a lean boot. He's cut his messy brown hair; now you can see his whole face, which looks cleaner, less puffy. Looking at him, I realize with a pang how terrible he really looked all those months, and how I didn't see it, or how I didn't *want* to see it. There isn't any bulge in his breast pocket. "He's quit smoking," Julie whispers. "Cold turkey."

He's scared as hell. I can tell because he hesitates just slightly before walking out, slipping his guitar across his shoulder as he walks. His hand wavers as he raises it to the audience and then I notice something I've never seen on Riley West's face.

A furiously red blush.

He licks his lips at the microphone, adjusts it, and sips from the glass on the stool beside him. He does a double take. "This drink tastes like water. That's not like me."

The crowd laughs. Someone yells, "Riley, you look great, man!"

Riley shades his eyes and looks out over the audience. "Yeah? You want to date me? 'Cause nobody else sure will, at this point." Laughter. He takes another sip of water. "This is the first time I've ever sung in public with just water in my glass."

"Do it, Riley."

"You can do it, Riley."

Riley takes a deep breath, settles the guitar against his body, stretches his neck, and looks directly into our wing. His eyes lock onto mine.

His face slackens for an instant. I turn my head away, heart thudding. When I glance back, he's facing the audience, smiling his huge, crooked grin, the grin he gave me the first time I saw him outside True Grit, with Van Morrison drifting in the air, the men playing Go, the punks eating ice cream at the Dairy Queen.

He clears his throat. "You know, I met this girl recently and she was real cute and everything but a little bit sad, you know how girls can get, right? But I thought, *Hey, Riley, maybe you need a sad girl, kind of balance you out, maybe if you put your problems with all her sadness, you two can't help but be happy.* Right?"

I freeze. He's talking about *me*.

The audience says *Ri-ight.*

"It worked for a while. But you know me, I screwed that one up. I forgot that we need to, you know, talk about *stuff.* Or that maybe I should, you know, sober the fuck *up.*"

Laughter.

"Luckily, I've now got a lot of free time to consider the error of my ways, courtesy of the State of Arizona's excellent correctional and rehabilitation services. And here's a song about that girl."

He begins to strum, his body relaxing with each movement, each minute. Once he said to me, "I do this because it makes me feel rich. Not rich like money in my damn pocket. Rich like a sweet kind of heaviness in me."

The song is a slow one, a real foot-dragger, as he liked to call those types of ballads. The kinds of songs, he told me, that shuffle along sadly and that most anyone can memorize easily and sing along to.

I'm fixated on him, the ease of his fingers on the strings, the difference in his face, the unraveling that's happening in my own body. The feeling of utter, inescapable sadness that I feel, watching and listening to him sing about *me*. His voice is different without cigarettes and alcohol. It's leaner, more interesting. The song is called "Who Knew I'd Make Her So Blue." Gradually, I realize it's a song about the night he found my kit and we fought in the kitchen; it's a song about both of us.

I didn't talk to Riley. I never told him how I felt until it was too late. I just let him lead me, because I was so grateful to be noticed. And he didn't talk to me, either, because he was drunk all the time, or felt he needed to be, and I never said *Stop*.

This song is his talking, just like my comic, just like Louisa's composition books, are our ways of talking.

This song is his *sorrysorrysorrysorrysorry*. To me.

When it's over, Julie has her fist in her mouth and Linus is dabbing at her eyes. Blue squeezes my hand so tight the bones hurt. The audience stands up, roaring. Riley takes another drink of water. He says, "Wait just one moment," and walks off the stage, in our direction.

The closer he gets to me, the more the world tilts, warps, silences, like clouds are moving in my ears, but I stand steady. Julie says, *Oh*. Linus says, *Riley*. Blue lets go of my hand and steps away.

He has a new smell now, clean and burly, oatmeal soap and a little aftershave. No deep smell of tobacco and sweat and alcohol. When I raise my eyes to his, they are full of water.

He opens his mouth to say something and then thinks better of it. He lifts my hand, closes something inside my fingers.

And there it is again: that little zing of electricity, a hot wire from him to me, from me to him.

When I open my eyes, he's back onstage.

He sings John Prine's "Christmas in Prison," two Dylan songs from *Nashville Skyline,* and then he pauses.

"You know, these kids today—"

Laughter.

"I'm just a short-order cook, really, and I used to work with all these damn hipsters all the time and they're always pecking away at their little phones and having funny little conversations like, hey, what if Coldplay did a Madonna cover, or what if Jay-Z did Joan Baez. You know, that kind of shit."

"Have my baby, Riley!" A woman, cackling.

Riley answers, "Did you not listen to that first song, lady?" The audience laughs.

"Anyway," he says, clearing his throat. "There was one person, she's here right now, as a matter of fact, and I wrote that first song for her, if you must know—"

People in the audience start craning their heads in every direction. I step behind Blue.

"That great girl, she had a great idea. It's gonna knock your socks off."

He tilts his head back dramatically and then lets it fall forward. Just before his chin should smash into his chest, he jerks his head back and up and begins furiously picking at the strings. *"I got chills,"* he growls.

It takes a moment, but then the crowd howls in recognition, probably picturing Sandy and Danny juking along the teeter-totter boat in the fun house at the end of the movie, Sandy's hair all frizzed out, Danny going apeshit for her leather pants.

Ellis loved everything about *Grease* and we watched it all the time and every time, she'd say, "But totally? I'd do Kenickie, not Danny," and every time, I'd pretend she'd never said that before, because that's what friends do.

Riley is giving me her song.

Julie and Linus laugh. Blue raises her eyebrows. The audience claps in time, begins to sing along.

Out from the wing comes Tiger Dean carrying a bass guitar, and a very heavy, jowly young dude dressed in tiny Captain America underwear and nothing else, strapped into a marching snare drum and banging away.

They sing in unison with Riley, the three of them marching in a circle around the stage, turning the song from a lazy, sexy countryish cover to a rousing, mean-tempered thing.

Ellis was right, I think without sadness. She would have loved this song, sung this way.

All of the people outside Congress at the main stage are on their feet. Phones are held aloft, flashes percolate in the crowd. Other bands leak onto the stage, join the fray, add voices. Regan Connor appears, slightly embarrassed at the antics, but she's game, stomping her boots and singing, too. Julie and Linus jump up and down, singing along. Blue stands apart. She's the only one who notices as I turn and walk away, out of the wings. She takes my hand again.

I look back at the stage. Riley's with his people, in his place.

Blue leans close to my ear. "What is the cereal doing, Charlie?"

"The cereal is *not* eating me." I repeat it until she says I can stop.

"Let's go," I say. We leave the backstage area and make our way through the hangers-on, the crew, leaving Riley West behind.

We take the long way home.

ON THE AIRPLANE, I TRY HARD NOT TO DIG MY FINGERS INTO my thighs or cry, though my blood is thundering. The young woman next to me struggles with her seat belt.

"Oh, hey," the girl says. "It's okay. First time? Gum. You need gum. Me, I fortify with Xanax. You want some gum?" She digs through an enormous chocolate-brown leather purse.

I shake my head at the square of gum she offers. She kicks off her sandals and wiggles her toes, pulls her hair back into an elastic, and sighs. "Talking helps. Gets your mind off things. Where you headed?"

"New York." Casper said to talk, so I will talk. "I've never been there before."

"Oh, you'll love it! It's totally cool. What are you doing there?"

I swallow. She has an open, hopeful face, full of freckles. "I'm going to work for an artist. As his assistant. I'm an artist, too." It doesn't sound so bad, saying that last part out loud.

Her eyes widen. "For reals? Sweet. I was out visiting my dad for a few days." She makes a choking motion at her throat. "Gah. Parents. They're so lame, right?"

Her fingers are slim, with colorful rings. Her dress is filmy and clingy and the straps slide down her creamy shoulders. The tangles of earbuds wrap around her neck and on her lap is a shiny-looking phone that buzzes and jingles and flashes. She's well fed. She's well loved. She can say her parents are lame because they are not. Wherever she goes, she will always be able to return to them.

Maybe in New York, I'll buy a postcard for my mother. Maybe I'll manage to write something on it, something short. Maybe I'll buy a stamp. Maybe I'll even send an email to Casper, only this time I'll call her Bethany. We'll see.

I don't have a tender kit anymore. I'm walking into life unprepared for the first time in a long time.

A fleshy boy across the aisle leans toward the girl, tilting his phone. "Check it, Shelley. Look at all these hits."

She laughs, angling the screen to me. "We went to this really great show last night. Check out this dude."

There he is on YouTube, surrounded by Tiger Dean and all the Tucson bands, whacking his guitar, that big grin on his face, wailing away at "You're the One That I Want." "Oh my God, he's so hot," Shelley breathes. "That was the funnest song." She turns to the fleshy boy. "Nick, what was that other song, that super-sad one? I totally cried, didn't you?"

Nick stops fiddling with his laptop. "'You Were Blue,' or something like that," he says. The lyrics *ping* through my head, just like they did last night as Blue and I walked home: *We were lost in a storm / The clouds gathered ahead / You were crying to me / All the pain in your heart / I tried to give you / Sad girl / All the love I had left / But when push comes to shove / I'm as empty as the rest.*

I clamp my hands together because they're trembling. The call comes out over the speaker. Shelley and Nick begin shutting down phones, computers, sliding them away.

Tears form behind my eyes as the plane begins to move down the runway, faster, faster. I reach down into my backpack, straining against the seat belt.

Hands shaking, I take out two pieces of paper. One is the note Riley pressed into my hand at the concert. I unfold it slowly.

Charlotte—I do remember, and I did. I do. Take
care of yourself.

He has signed his name.

Irwin David Baxter

I'm laughing and crying at the same time. The plane is tilted
backward, my head forced against the seat. We're seated far in
the back and the sound is deafening; our part of the plane wobbles and bucks. Heads have turned in my direction. I don't care.
I'm not *sorrysorrysorrysorrysorry*.
Shelley is looking at the note and back at my face. She folds
the paper back up and presses it into one of my hands, takes
the other in two of hers. She holds that hand very tight. Briefly,
I feel Shelley suck in her breath, and then the light rub of her
finger over my bare arm.
"I had a friend in high school who did this stuff," she whispers. She lowers her head conspiratorially.
"Just breathe," she whispers. "It's only scary for a minute.
Then we'll be up in the air and everything will be fine. Once
we're up, we're up, and there ain't nothing we can do, you know?
You gotta give in. The hardest part is getting there."
I think of Louisa and her notebooks, her skin, all her stories,
my skin, Blue, Ellis, all of us. I am layers upon layers of story
and memory. Shelley is still whispering, her words soft in my
ear. In my other hand is the other note, the one Mikey gave me
at the concert, the one that says:
*Eleanor Vanderhaar, 209 Ridge Creek Drive, Amethyst House,
Sandpoint, Idaho.*

Blue said we have to choose who we want to be, not let the situation choose us.

Momentous, Felix said.

I'm choosing my next momentous.

I close my eyes and begin the letter that I know I will write on my first night not in Paris, or London, or Iceland, but in New York, surrounded by lights and noise and life and the unknown.

Dear Ellis, I have something really fucking angelic to tell you.

AUTHOR'S NOTE

When Charlie Davis watches her roommate Louisa slip off her blouse, she is stunned: *I'd just never seen a girl with skin like mine.*

Years ago, I did not want to write this story.

Years ago, on the city bus, making notes for another story I was writing, I glanced up when I felt someone slide into the seat next to me. I planned to give her only the most perfunctory of glances and go back to my notes, but then my breath caught in my throat.

She had skin like mine. Feeling my eyes on her, she hastily slid down her sleeve, cloaking her thin, fresh red scars from view.

I can't tell you how much I wanted to pull up my own sleeves and say, "I'm just like you! Look! You are not alone."

But I didn't. Frankly, I was unnerved by her. After years of wearing long shirts, hiding what I had done to myself, in the hopes that I could "have a life," I found myself reeling back to when I was at the very depths of myself, more alone than I have ever been in my life.

Years ago, I didn't want to write the story of my scars, or the story of being a girl with scars, because it is hard enough being a girl in the world, but try being a girl *with scars on your skin* in the world.

I let that girl get off the bus without saying a word. And I shouldn't have. I should have let her know that even mired in the very depths of herself, she wasn't alone.

Because she's not.

It's estimated that one in every two hundred girls between the ages of thirteen and nineteen self-harms. Over 70 percent of those are cutters. It's important to remember, though, that these statistics only come from what's reported, and they don't account for the increasing percentage of boys who self-harm. It's my guess that you know someone, right now, who self-harms.

Self-harming is the deliberate act of cutting, burning, poking, or otherwise marring your skin as a way to cope with emotional turmoil. It can be the result of many things, such as sexual, physical, verbal, or emotional abuse. Bullying. Helplessness. Sadness. Addiction.

Self-harm is not a grab for attention. It doesn't mean you are suicidal. It means you are struggling to get out of a very dangerous mess in your mind and heart and this is your coping mechanism. It means that you occupy a small space in the very real and very large canyon of people who suffer from depression or mental illness.

You are not alone. Charlie Davis's story is the story of over two million young women in the United States. And those young women will grow up, like I did, bearing the truth of our past on our bodies.

I wrote the story of Charlie Davis for the cutters and the burners and the kids on the street who have nowhere safe to sleep. I wrote the story of Charlie Davis for their mothers and fathers and for their friends.

Charlie Davis finds her voice, and her solace, in drawing. I find mine in writing. What's your solace? Do you know? Find it and don't stop doing it, ever. Find your people (because you need to talk), your tribe, your reason to be, and I swear to you, the other side will emerge, slowly but surely. It's not always sunshine and roses over here, and sometimes the dark can get pretty dark, but it's filled with people who understand, and just enough laughter to soften the edges and get you through to the next day. So: go.

Go be absolutely, positively, fucking angelic.

ACKNOWLEDGMENTS

It took nine years and fourteen drafts for this book to reach you. It may be true that in the beginning, it's just one writer, a pad of paper, a pencil or a pen (or a computer, or a tablet, or dictation into an iWhatever), but in the end, it took a whole lot of people to shape a story into the story you have just finished reading.

This book wouldn't exist if Julie Stevenson hadn't taken a chance on me (and Charlie). Thank you from all the corners of my heart for making my writerly dreams come true. And for understanding when my daughter stole my cell phone and hid it in her baby carriage.

Speaking of writerly dreams: how lucky am I to have the editorial wizardry of Krista Marino? You opened up *Girl in Pieces* in ways I didn't think possible. Thank you for believing in Charlie, and for always pushing me *that much* further.

To the team at Random House Children's Books—Beverly Horowitz, Monica Jean, Barbara Marcus, Stephanie O'Cain, Kim Lauber, Dominique Cimina, Felicia Frazier, Casey Ward, and Alison Impey (Alison—thank you for finding Jennifer Heuer, who dreamed up the gorgeous, heartbreaking, and kick-ass cover!)—thank you for welcoming me to the fold and for your tireless support and enthusiasm.

Thanks to the Minnesota State Arts Board for helping artists and writers in the state of Minnesota achieve their dreams. *Girl in Pieces* was written with the help of several MSAB grants, over several years, in several different places: in a small office over the Trend Bar in Saint Paul, Minnesota, and in the libraries at Hamline University and the University of Minnesota.

Thanks also to the Creative Writing Program at the University of Minnesota for nurturing me as a writer during my time in the MFA Program, and as a desk-jockey as coordinator of the program. I received constant warm encouragement from Julie Schumacher, Charles Baxter, Patricia Hampl, and M. J. Fitzgerald.

Drs. Justin Cetas and Alivia Cetas provided sound medical advice and funny late-night texts as I revised the book. Elizabeth Noll, Tom Haley, and Holly Vanderhaar cheered me on and listened to me ramble and cry. My workshop mates at the Taos Summer Writers' Conference were kick-ass and funny, offering sage advice and spot-on critiques; thanks especially to workshop mastermind Summer Woods, who continued to encourage me long after our time in the desert was done.

Thanks also to Marshall Yarbrough, Diana Rempe, Caitlin Reid, Nick Seeberger, Diane Natrop, Isabelle Natrop, Kira Natrop, Mikayla Natrop, Swati Avasthi, Amanda Coplin, Lygia Day Penaflor, Laura Tisdel, Joy Biles, John Muñoz, and Chris Wagganer, and to all my fellow writers at the Sweet Sixteens, especially Jeff Giles and Janet McNally for talking me off a ledge.

And finally, thank you to Nikolai and Saskia, for drenching me every day in love; and to Chris, for twenty years of patience, laughter, and undone dishes.

ABOUT THE AUTHOR

Girl in Pieces is Kathleen Glasgow's debut novel. She lives and writes in Tucson, Arizona. To learn out more about Kathleen and her writing, go to her website kathleenglasgowbooks.com and follow her on Twitter at @kathglasgow and on Instagram at @Kathglasgow.